Bard FICTION PRIZE

Bard College invites submissions for its annual Fiction Prize for young writers.

The Bard Fiction Prize is awarded annually to a promising, emerging writer who is a United States citizen aged 39 years or younger at the time of application. In addition to a monetary award of $30,000, the winner receives an appointment as writer-in-residence at Bard College for one semester without the expectation that he or she teach traditional courses. The recipient will give at least one public lecture and will meet informally with students.

To apply, candidates should write a cover letter describing the project they plan to work on while at Bard and submit a C.V., along with three copies of the published book they feel best represents their work. No manuscripts will be accepted.

Applications for the 2014 prize must be received by July 15, 2013. For further information about the Bard Fiction Prize, call 845-758-7087, or visit www.bard.edu/bfp. Applicants may also request information by writing to the Bard Fiction Prize, Bard College, Annandale-on-Hudson, NY 12504-5000.

Bard College PO Box 5000, Annandale-on-Hudson, NY 12504-5000

COMING UP IN THE FALL

Conjunctions:61
A MENAGERIE

Edited by Benjamin Hale and Bradford Morrow

From Adam naming the animals in Genesis to Ovid's *Metamorphoses*, from Melville's *Moby-Dick* to Stevens's "Thirteen Ways of Looking at a Blackbird," writers, philosophers, and scientists have been fascinated by our interplay with the rest of the animal kingdom. Our relationship with our fellow creatures is complex, difficult, contradictory—we pamper them as pets, fear them as predators, use them as beasts of burden, slaughter them as livestock, eat them. Aristotle devoted three books to them. Descartes deliberated about whether animals have souls, and decided they didn't. Linnaeus cataloged them. Darwin connected us to them.

Paul Celan wrote, "there are / still songs to sing beyond / humankind." *Conjunctions:61, A Menagerie,* is a gathering of those songs. Edited by Benjamin Hale and Bradford Morrow, this issue embraces the world of beasts through new writing about the nonhuman creatures with whom we share the world. It includes new work from animal behaviorists, fiction writers, and poets such as Temple Grandin, Jonathan Ames, Vint Virga, Dale Peterson, Sallie Tisdale, T. Geronimo Johnson, Luis Alberto Urrea, Barbara J. King, Susan Daitch, Martine Bellen, and many others.

One-year subscriptions to *Conjunctions* are only $18 (two years for $32) for more than seven hundred pages per year of contemporary literature and art. Subscribe or renew online at conjunctions.com, or mail your check to *Conjunctions*, Bard College, Annandale-on-Hudson, NY 12504. For questions or to request an invoice, e-mail conjunctions@bard.edu or call (845) 758-7054.

CONJUNCTIONS

Bi-Annual Volumes of New Writing

Edited by
Bradford Morrow

Contributing Editors
John Ashbery
Martine Bellen
Mei-mei Berssenbrugge
Mary Caponegro
Brian Evenson
William H. Gass
Peter Gizzi
Robert Kelly
Ann Lauterbach
Norman Manea
Rick Moody
Howard Norman
Joan Retallack
Joanna Scott
David Shields
Peter Straub
John Edgar Wideman

published by Bard College

EDITOR: Bradford Morrow
MANAGING EDITOR: Micaela Morrissette
SENIOR EDITORS: Robert Antoni, Peter Constantine, J. W. McCormack,
   Edie Meidav, Pat Sims, Alan Tinkler
COPY EDITOR: Pat Sims
ASSOCIATE EDITORS: Jedediah Berry, Andrew Durbin, Nicole Nyhan, Eric Olson
PUBLICITY: Mark R. Primoff, Darren O'Sullivan
EDITORIAL ASSISTANTS: Emma Horwitz, Cassandra Seltman,
   Soli Shin, Emma Smith-Stevens

CONJUNCTIONS is published in the Spring and Fall of each year by Bard College, Annandale-on-Hudson, NY 12504. This issue is made possible in part with the generous funding of the National Endowment for the Arts.

NATIONAL ENDOWMENT FOR THE ARTS
A great nation deserves great art.

SUBSCRIPTIONS: Use our secure online ordering system at www.conjunctions.com, or send subscription orders to CONJUNCTIONS, Bard College, Annandale-on-Hudson, NY 12504. Single year (two volumes): $18.00 for individuals; $40.00 for institutions and overseas. Two years (four volumes): $32.00 for individuals; $80.00 for institutions and overseas. For information about subscriptions, back issues, and advertising, contact us at (845) 758-7054 or conjunctions@bard.edu.

Editorial communications should be sent to Bradford Morrow, *Conjunctions*, 21 East 10th Street, 3E, New York, NY 10003. Unsolicited manuscripts cannot be returned unless accompanied by a stamped, self-addressed envelope. Electronic and simultaneous submissions will not be considered. If you are submitting from outside the United States, contact conjunctions@bard.edu for instructions (please do not send International Response Coupons as postage).

Conjunctions is listed and indexed in Humanities International Complete and included in EBSCO*host*.

Visit the *Conjunctions* website at www.conjunctions.com and follow us on Facebook and Twitter.

Cover design by Jerry Kelly, New York. Cover art by Chad Wys. Front cover: *Nocturne 93*, 2011. C-print, 30 x 20 in. © 2011 Chad Wys. Back cover: *Nocturne 113*, 2011. C-print, 30 x 23.1 in. © 2011 Chad Wys.

Available through D.A.P./Distributed Art Publishers, Inc., 155 Sixth Avenue, New York, NY 10013. Telephone: (212) 627-1999. Fax: (212) 627-9484.

Printers: Edwards Brothers Malloy

Typesetter: Bill White, Typeworks

ISSN 0278-2324

ISBN 978-0-941964-76-0

Manufactured in the United States of America.

TABLE OF CONTENTS

IN ABSENTIA

Edited by Bradford Morrow

IN MEMORIAM

Chinua Achebe

November 16, 1930–March 21, 2013

*Distinguished author
Wise humanist
Beloved colleague*

EDITOR'S NOTE

THINGS GONE MISSING. People vanished or changed beyond recognition. A once-bedrock belief now so alien as not to seem believable anymore. A woman's threat of suicide. A man's phantom limb. Another who comes home from prison only to find that home is no longer what it was, friends no longer who they were. Love gained, love lost. A promise forgotten. A couple gone off the grid into the woods and ghost-plagued madness. An exceptionally ill-timed death.

These are among the many scenarios explored in the pages of *In Absentia*. What we have assembled here is a literary compendium about the presence of absence. From Joyce Carol Oates's story of a young protagonist whose devotion to working with bonobos at a zoo leads him on a journey far beyond the normal districts of primatology to Karen Hays's essay on a wide spectrum of subjects—not the least of which is the metaphysics of the fourth dimension—these works attempt to observe the unobservable, to see what isn't quite there.

We are honored also to include three previously untranslated "dramolets" by Robert Walser as a special feature. Walser, who personally knew more than most about loss and absence, is seen here in a fresh light thanks to Daniele Pantano and James Reidel's deft translations. I want to thank Dr. Petra Hardt of Suhrkamp Verlag for her generosity in granting us permission to publish these historically important pieces. I believe that readers who already admire Walser's vision and achievement will find his remarkable plays a cause for celebration.

—Bradford Morrow
April 2013
New York City

Betrayal
Joyce Carol Oates

THE FIRST CLEAR SYMPTOMS were at Thanksgiving, last year. Our son arrived hours late. It has long been our family custom to gather at our house at 4:00 p.m. and to sit down to eat at about 5:30 p.m. and yet it was nearly 6:00 p.m. when Rickie arrived—after having assured us he would arrive at about 1:00 p.m. We were so grateful to see him that no one, even Father, had a harsh word to say to him, though we noted how defensive Rickie was, saying he'd been driving six hours, stuck in traffic on the damned freeway, and wasn't in a mood to be criticized now.

Outside it was deeply dark, windswept, and wintry. And wet. When Rickie entered the house, a gust of wind accompanied him and struck at the crackling fire in the fireplace, which Father had been tending with a poker. And there came with him a smell of rain so sharp it seemed metallic, odors of earth and leaves and something rank as an animal's wetted hide that pinched at our nostrils.

We were already sitting at dinner. Rickie's place awaited him. He mumbled an excuse and disappeared upstairs for ten minutes presumably washing up, changing his rumpled clothes, but when he appeared again downstairs we saw that he'd done little more than run a comb through his matted hair, which hadn't been washed in a while, and he was wearing a long-sleeved T-shirt and jeans, not freshly laundered, and running shoes. He'd left off his Sigma Nu hoodie at least, upstairs.

Some of us were offended, frankly, that Rickie should sit down at Thanksgiving dinner looking so disheveled. His jaws were unshaven, his eyes were edgy and glittering. His laughter was high pitched, a nervous sort of laughter, that faded abruptly like a switch shut off. Rickie's younger nephews and nieces and cousins were hurt that he paid virtually no attention to them, as he usually did.

Practically the first thing Rickie said when he took his place among us, as warm platters were being passed in his direction, was that he would "forgo" turkey this year, thanks!

Forgo turkey, we protested, how can you *forgo turkey* when

8

turkey is the point of Thanksgiving, we pointed out to the unshaven boy in the soiled San Diego Zoo T-shirt, but, Rickie said with a smirk, Not for the poor turkey it ain't.

Ain't is not a word we use in our family. Not a word that Rickie, with a *cum laude* BA degree from Stanford and whose SAT scores were in the highest five percentile, would use. *Ain't* was a jab in the ribs meant to offend and annoy and so *ain't* did offend and annoy us, particularly Father, who stared at Rickie, speechless. Mother, who'd been preparing for Thanksgiving dinner for two days and who'd purchased an "organic" twenty-two-pound turkey for the occasion, blinked and stared at Rickie as if he'd slapped her.

We asked, are you a *vegetarian* and Rickie said, yes, that was right. A *vegetarian*! Since when?

But Rickie just shrugged. He appeared to be starved, spooning large portions of Mother's bread-crumb stuffing, mashed sweet potatoes, candied carrots, and broccoli-with-almonds onto his plate. We recalled his legendary appetite for any kind of meat including pizza-with-sausage and cheeseburgers, when he'd been a teenager in our household.

Mother said, trying to smile, "Well! At least I hope you are not one of those *vegans.* . . ."

In Mother's mouth *vegan* was uncertainly enunciated. Rickie laughed and said, "No, Mom: not yet."

Mother's bread-crumb stuffing was particularly delicious this year, made with apples, prunes, chestnuts, thyme, tarragon, fine-cut onions, and celery. In the lush salad of many gourmet greens were tiny sections of clementines, dried cranberries, chopped escarole, cherry tomatoes from Mexico. The mashed sweet potatoes were (secretly) laced with marshmallow—one of Mother's prized family recipes. All of these foods, plus chunks of thick raisin bread, Rickie ate as if he were famished. (It was curious to see how Rickie avoided even looking at the turkey carcass on the sideboard, which looked as if ravenous hyenas had attacked it. And even the harmless gravy boat, with its rich, oily turkey gravy.) When we asked him about his closest friends from college, he replied in distracted grunts. Mother dared to ask him about Holly Cryer, a prep-school girlfriend whom Rickie often saw when they were both home from college, but Rickie only frowned and shrugged. Instead he spoke excitedly of Mitzie, Claus, Herc (for Hercules), Kindle, Stalker, Big Joe, and Juno. We said, "Oh, but Rickie, those are *animals.* That is your *work.*"

Rickie was currently an intern at the San Diego Zoo, at the bonobo exhibit. That day it seemed that, in our company, listening to our conversation, Rickie had been frequently elsewhere, and listening intently to another conversation that drew him more powerfully. Almost dreamily now he paused in his rapid chewing to gaze at us one by one, around the table. As if he were counting us, or hoping to discover, in our familiar faces, something he recognized. We could see a fringe of dark-matted chest hair just visible at the stretched neckline of his zoo-issue T-shirt.

"Oh, hey, Mom, Dad—all you guys: I've been trying to tell you. My *work* is my *life*."

Certainly it was good news, that Rickie was employed now, if only as an unpaid intern. (For an unpaid internship might lead to paid employment someday—that was the belief among the families of recent college graduates like ours.) And it was good news that Rickie seemed to be devoted to this work.

But since his employment was only temporary, at the San Diego Zoo, and not the employment for which he'd been preparing himself for four years at Stanford, this was possibly not so very good news.

It had been his parents' dream that Rickie would go to medical school. Or, failing that, Rickie might go into high-level medical research—at a pharmaceutical company, for instance. (Father, a quite successful corporate lawyer at Helix Pharmaceuticals in Vista Flats, California, whose long-ago dream for himself had been scientific research, had contacts in several prominent pharmaceutical companies.)

Yet, Rickie seemed happy. Rickie seemed *defiantly happy*.

Just after graduation, when he'd returned home to Saddle Creek, from his Stanford frat house, Rickie had seemed very unhappy. It would not be an exaggeration to say that Rickie had been seriously depressed. That spring he'd been interviewed for a number of promising entry-level positions with California employers but—so far as we knew—no offers had followed. He'd planned to backpack in Zion Park with some frat brothers but that too had fallen through, or Rickie himself had canceled. And there had been a girl, or girls— Wendy, Lisa, Scotia, Dane—whom he never mentioned any longer and did not wish to be asked about. We'd been worried about Rickie staying out late with his high-school friends in Saddle Creek—who were as depressed as he was, having also failed to get jobs following graduation from UCLA, Pomona College, USC, and UC Berkeley— and then sleeping late, collapsed on top of his bed clothed; or, awake at last at about midday, on his cell phone, speaking in a lowered, urgent voice to an unknown party for long periods of time interrupted by peals of hysterical laughter. Rickie had also, following Father's encouragement, applied to a miscellany of West Coast universities to enter a PhD program in biology, but even where he'd been accepted as a graduate student, he hadn't been offered a fellowship. And so, he'd been inert with disappointment, lying on his bed or sprawled on our family-room sofa stretched out like a rubber band that has lost its elasticity.

Son, don't do this, we pleaded with him. Don't *give in.*

Particularly Father was repelled at the thought of *giving in.*

Rickie was unshaven then. Bristly whiskers marring his boyish face. And his eyes glazed with boredom, or something worse.

He wasn't *giving in,* he protested. He was *exploring, within.*

Anyway he couldn't help it. His generation was the Walking Wounded, devastated by graduating from college and being expelled into the world that didn't give a shit for them, BA honors from Stanford or whatever.

Sure, some of his college friends had definite *plans.* Not his closest frat-brother friends but others who'd gotten into med school, or law school, even if not first-rate schools—still the contrast with Rickie's own life, narrow and circumscribed as his bed or the family-room sofa—no wonder he was feeling *down.*

Had to take solace from the fact that there were plenty of others in his generation who frankly had *no plans,* not even *prospects for plans.*

At Saddle Creek Academy, which was in the highest percentile of California private schools, Rickie had taken nearly every science course offered, most of them AP courses. And he'd had other AP courses. Usually high grades and the praise of his teachers. And the SATs—we hired tutors for him, reasoning that, as other parents hired tutors for their children, we would be disadvantaging our son by not hiring tutors; and the expenditure, which had been considerable, had paid off. With Father's encouragement Rickie had looked ahead to medical school at San Francisco, Yale, Harvard, as well as Stanford—the very best.

One of his closest Sigma Nu brothers had died only a few weeks after graduation, in his parents' basement TV room in La Jolla. A lethal combination of (prescription) Prozac and Oxycodone the twenty-one-year-old had bought from a fourteen-year-old dealer in the parking lot of Saddle Creek High.

There were signs we might have noted that Rickie might not get into his first-choice med school. For though he'd been an A student in high school, in his first year at Stanford he'd run into a solid-concrete wall, as he described it, with organic chemistry, physics, and calculus, got messed up at midterms, and never quite recovered his self-confidence; without informing his parents he shifted to a less demanding major—some sort of science-culture studies, "environmental biology." Why'd he want to spend his life analyzing chemicals in a lab, examining the molecular underpinnings of animals without any notion of what the original animal looked like, or *was*; sure, it was exciting that the genetic code was being broken, through such exacting experiments, but Rickie found abstractions *bor-ing*!

He'd always liked animals—some animals. Like horses, giraffes. He'd loved our mixed-breed shepherd Strongheart, who'd pined for Rickie when Rickie left home for Berkeley, though, when he'd lived in our household, Rickie had had a decreasing amount of time to devote to the eager dog whose care and tending naturally fell to Mother. (Not that Mother complained!—Mother was never one to complain.)

Yet, Rickie's luck turned when he received a summer internship at the San Diego Zoo. We hadn't had any idea that Rickie had applied for such a position, at such a place, until, as Rickie proudly announced to us, it was a *fate accomplished*.

Father had said, speaking carefully as if fearing he might be misunderstood, "An internship is—unpaid?"

But Rickie's good spirits could not be dashed, now that they'd been fired up like gasoline sprinkled onto a dying fire. He told Father that working at the San Diego Zoo was known to be so cool for kids his age, everybody said they'd pay the zoo for the chance.

Mother said, "It sounds just wonderful! Rickie can try again applying to medical schools, or to graduate schools, and with this internship in his résumé, he'll be a—shoo-in."

Shoo-in was gaily uttered by Mother, in an outburst of optimism. *Shoo-in* was not an expression ever heard on Mother's lips before this moment.

Two weeks after Rickie's first day as an intern at the zoo, we flew south to San Diego to visit with him. In his infrequent calls and e-mails home he'd told us how "great" his colleagues were and how "special" bonobos are—not just "great apes" but unique among these, genetically the closest of all primates to *Homo sapiens*.

Even before we saw Rickie in his zoo uniform assisting an older staff member at the bonobo enclosure, even before we saw Rickie grinning and "signing" to one of the friendly bonobos through the immense glass window protecting the bonobos from zoo visitors, we felt unease, that our son whom we knew so well was being seduced by this new milieu, which was so exotic and so strange to us.

We'd arranged with Rickie that we would meet him in front of the bonobo enclosure at about noon, and would take him to lunch; but when we arrived, breathless and just slightly intimidated—for the San Diego Zoo is an enormous place!—there was Rickie standing at the side of a tall, broad-shouldered woman with ash-colored hair addressing a gathering of about a dozen visitors. Seeing us, Rickie just smiled, nodded, and waved, without speaking to us. You could see—that is, we could see—that our twenty-one-year-old son greatly admired this woman, as he'd admired a few of his Stanford professors; so intently did he listen to her words, observing the bonobos in the enclosure as she spoke of them, it was as if Rickie were memorizing the experience and didn't want to be distracted from it.

But how happy Rickie appeared! This was something of a surprise, for we hadn't seen Rickie so boyishly enthusiastic since his small triumphs in high-school athletics years before. And how very different he seemed, in his smart red San Diego Zoo cap, red sweatshirt, and fresh-laundered denims, from the melancholy boy laid low by lethargy, depression, and irony in his boyhood room at Saddle Creek.

Mother whispered to Father, "Oh! Is that *our son*? He looks so . . ."

"He does," Father said. "Thank God!"

Unobtrusively we drew near, to listen to the ashy-haired woman talk about the bonobos and answer visitors' questions. Truly, the woman, whose name tag identified her as *Hilary Krydy*, was impressive. She was tall and fit and her face was both plain and powerfully attractive, with an energy and purposefulness that exuded from within. She might have been Mother's age but looked much more robust and youthful. We were directed to look closely at the bonobos, as Hilary spoke. An exhibit in a zoo at which we might simply have glanced—registering some kind of large, antic "monkey"—now took on dramatic significance. In the enclosure, which looked like an actual wilderness landscape with rocks and boulders, small exotic trees, a pond, the coarse-furred little apes were wonderfully lively and alert as if showing off for their human audience. They rose from all fours with a sort of gawky grace to their hind legs and "walked"— very like human beings. (Mother said, "Oh—are they imitating *us*?" Father chuckled, saying, "Certainly not. Their species precedes *us*.") We could understand that Rickie would be drawn to the bonobos as crudely inferior types of himself.

Father observed, in the gravely creased face of an older bonobo, who held himself apart from the cavortings of the younger bonobos, an expression of—recognition? *Identity?* For a moment it seemed almost that their eyes locked: Each was an *elder,* and had reason to be exasperated with his young offspring. Then, to Father's surprise and disappointment, the seemingly dignified patriarch leapt onto a boulder, glared, and grinned at Father with bared yellow teeth and, with rubberlike, prehensile fingers, grabbed and shook his large fruitlike genitals in an unmistakable gesture of antagonism. Father winced—such vulgarity! Of course, the creature was just an animal. Father was grateful that Mother didn't seem to have seen this obscene display as other visitors pretended not to have seen it.

Younger bonobos, very lively, charmingly childlike, jumped about onto rocks and off rocks; set up a high-pitched chatter of merriment that must have carried for some distance in the zoo; winked, grinned, spat, and "signed" at observers, who waved and called to them in return. Mother was most taken with the comely female bonobos nursing their hairy young, or hugging the young to their droopy, enlarged teats, which did resemble the breasts of a nursing *Homo sapiens* female, to a degree; she saw, too, the uncanny flat-faced beauty of certain of the females, and the adorable gamin faces of the very young. Rickie glowed with pride as if the bonobos were in some way *his*—a gift of his, for us.

It was thrilling to Rickie, we could see, when the ashy-haired Hilary turned to him, suggesting that he answer a visitor's question—which Rickie managed to do, quite intelligently. (We thought!)

Only when Hilary's mini lecture ended and the visitors moved on to the next enclosure did Rickie hurry to greet us, with a hug for Mother and a handshake for Father; he was eager to introduce us to Hilary, a senior staff member. Impulsively Rickie invited Hilary to join us for lunch but she declined; she could see, as our heedless son could not, that we were not enthusiastic about the invitation, wanting to spend some time alone with our son.

At lunch, in a restaurant inside the zoo, Rickie chattered happily about his internship, his fellow interns, and older colleagues; he'd become, within a remarkably short period of time, something of an expert on bonobos, it seemed, and spoke to us in an excited, disjointed way about the exotic species of "ape" as if we'd made the long drive to San Diego not to see him, but to see and hear about his newest favorite animal.

Some of what Rickie recounted to us was an echo of the guide's talk. In his boyish voice, it did sound fascinating to us, initially.

"Bonobos, often called 'pygmy chimps,' should not be confused with the more common, more widely distributed, and far more aggressive chimpanzees. That's an insult to us. I mean—to them." Rickie paused, as if to let this sink in. "Bonobos are much more attractive than chimpanzees, as you probably noticed—smaller, more slender, with heads that more resemble human heads, as well as other humanlike features." (In fact, we had not so much as glanced into any of the other ape enclosures in our haste to get to the bonobo enclosure.) "Genetically, bonobos are our closest primate relatives. Bonobos 'laugh' as we laugh—virtually. Bonobos walk upright as we walk upright—almost. Wouldn't you know," Rickie's voice lowered to a mournful growl, "of the great apes it's the bonobos who are the most endangered species. Go figure!"

"That is so sad!" Mother said.

"Shit, Mom, it's *tragic.*"

Rickie seemed annoyed by Mother's innocent remark, as Father was annoyed by Rickie's profanity in Mother's presence.

"But not surprising," Rickie added quickly, seeing the disapproval in Father's face, "since bonobos are the most peace loving and the least aggressive of apes. *Not* like *Homo sapiens.*"

"Do chimps kill 'em and eat 'em?"—Father had to ask a facetious question.

Rickie winced. This was a topic he didn't like to consider.

"Well—maybe. . . . Chimps are definitely 'opportunistic' carnivores, and bonobos, at least bonobo babies, would be vulnerable to them. But I don't know for sure. I'll ask Hilary."

Rickie went on to say that bonobos are found today in the wild only in a small area of the Democratic Republic of the Congo while common chimps are found in western to central Africa. Bonobos are famous for "making love not war." Bonobos are *sexy.* Bonobos are feminists. Bonobo males are feminists too. Bonobos love their babies. A bonobo mother has a baby only every five or six years. A bonobo mother bonds with her baby as much as, or more than, a human mother bonds with her baby. Bonobos are—

Father interrupted to suggest to Rickie that they change the subject? We'd come to San Diego to talk about *him.*

"Sure, Dad. Cool."

Slowly then the radiance began to fade from Rickie's face.

Rickie was clean shaven and well groomed. His wavy fawn-colored hair was neatly cut and his zoo uniform T-shirt and jeans were clean; his running shoes didn't look nearly so bad as Rickie's running

15

shoes usually looked. Mother had to resist an almost overwhelming impulse to touch Rickie's smooth forehead with her fingertips as he and Father talked of more serious matters. The boy didn't look a day over seventeen!

Father was pointing out that the internship was just for the summer and Rickie had "no future" in the San Diego Zoo or in any other zoo without a PhD in—zoology? environmental zoology? Seeing a sulky look on Rickie's face, Father said, with the air of a surgeon cutting into flesh just a little more emphatically than required, "It's a tragic time for *us*. I mean—*Americans*. We are reaching a saturation point of highly and expensively educated young men and women— like you—who have BA degrees from outstanding universities, even honors degrees. There are just too many of you—that's the fundamental, Malthusian problem. But you are not unified, you don't form a distinct cluster. You're likely to be scattered, living with your parents. Not at all the way the world was when your mother and I graduated from college, in the late 1960s and early 1970s—everyone couldn't wait to get away from home. . . ."

But this struck a wrong note, a hostile note Father hadn't meant to strike. And at the moment, Rickie wasn't living at home but was renting an apartment near the zoo with another recent Stanford graduate whom we had yet to meet.

Father said, "Well—you're lucky to have part-time employment in this marketplace. Of course, you aren't exactly *employed*—you are *volunteering* your time. Some of your prep-school friends who graduated last year or earlier seem to have given up seriously looking for jobs. There's a rush to graduate schools too. In most fields, if you are second-best, forget it. Manual labor like lawn work and service jobs at Wendy's, Taco Bell, KFC is for illegal immigrants or the dumbest high-school kids. No one wants an overqualified Stanford graduate. No one wants *adolescent irony*."

Rickie's boyish tanned face darkened with the blood of adolescent humiliation.

Mother tried to soften Father's harsh words by speaking warmly of Hilary, whom she'd scarcely met, and the "pygmy chimps"—"So very *lively*."

There were exhibits at the zoo, Mother said, where the animals are just so boring, they don't move and don't look at you, because they don't have the brains to see you; and sometimes, like with the great snakes, or some kind of dwarf "tapir," you couldn't be sure that there was anything in an enclosure at all.

"Animal life *is* boredom," Father said. It was like Father, in times of crisis, to speak in such terse, brittle remarks you were led to think that they were aphorisms of Montaigne you should have known, or clever, cutting jokes of Oscar Wilde.

Rickie had been eating haphazardly, pushing food around on his plate. We'd scarcely noticed then—we would recall only in retrospect—that Rickie hadn't ordered a cheeseburger, chicken nuggets, or a pizza slice with pepperoni sausage but a large Waldorf salad containing no meat. With the sudden and surprising belligerence of the patriarch bonobo who'd so offended Father, he said, "Nooo, Dad. Don't think so. The fact is, *animals* are not different from us: *We are them.*"

"But," Mother said, flustered, seeing the anger in Father's face, "we are not *really*—are we? We can talk, and we—we wear clothing; we can add up numbers in our heads, and we can—well, make tools—cook food—*grow food*. Not many animals can do such things, can they?"

Rickie shrugged as if Mother's question was so foolish, he wasn't required to answer. Father said stiffly, "Well. We are *mammals*, I suppose—but not ordinary *animals*. I draw the line at that."

From that point onward, relations with Rickie became increasingly difficult.

We were expecting Rickie to return home in early September, when his summer internship ended, but in late August he called home excitedly to inform us that, though his applications for graduate programs had been rejected at sixteen California universities ranging from Stanford and Berkeley to San José State and UC Eureka, his internship had been extended for another six months!

"Oh no," Father said.

In a stricken voice Rickie said, "What d'you mean, Dad—*no?*"

Father said, "I can't continue to support you in a—hobby kind of job. In a summer-vacation kind of job."

Rickie protested, "Working with bonobos is *humanitarian work.* It isn't just some trivial pastime. Everyone I know at the zoo would inform you you are *so mistaken.*"

"Rickie, it's *unpaid labor.* The zoo pays its staff; you can be sure it pays its administrators generous salaries. Why should you, an intelligent young man, with a BA *cum laude* from Stanford, volunteer for *unpaid labor?*"

As Father spoke, Mother was listening to the conversation on a cordless phone. Quickly she said, hoping to deflect the conflict, "Rickie, what good news!"

"Mom, thanks. I'm glad that someone is on my side."

"Another internship will give you all the time you need to send out more applications, to different universities, or to look for a job. And your father can help you—he has contacts. It's a *godsend*."

Godsend was a buoyant word we'd never heard on Mother's lips before.

Later, when Rickie reluctantly came home for a weekend, Father tried to reason with him, in private.

"You do understand, son, that you should be making a serious effort to support yourself at the age of—is it twenty-one?—twenty-two? You are welcome to stay with us while you're looking for employment or applying to graduate school, and we are willing to support you as an intern for a little while longer, but, you must know—the idea is to be *self-supporting*. If there is any lesson of evolution it is that each generation must become independent of the preceding generation—that is a law of nature! You will want to marry, Rickie, won't you?—you will want to have children?"

Rickie said, with a hoarse, deep-throated laugh, "I will? Who says?"

"But—it's *normal*. It's what is—*expected*."

The family has not wanted to acknowledge that, on both sides, there have been instances of disastrous marriages and divorces; there were examples of younger people, like Rickie's sister, Amber, who'd tried and failed at a sequence of highly promising jobs in the entertainment industry, as she'd tried and failed at marriage. There were joint-custody children flying between households and there were children "in therapy." And there were long, stoic marriages that, in their intricate difficulties, and in the compromises made on both sides, were not perhaps exemplary in the eyes of a restless young man like Rickie.

It was then that Rickie said, frowning severely as he scratched at his armpit, "Well—I look into the future, I guess, and it's like I'm looking into a mirror in which there's no reflection."

What a strange utterance! We had no idea what it meant at the time, nor would we have ever.

Rickie had to be cajoled into coming home for Christmas, which had always been his favorite holiday; another time he arrived late for dinner; another time he insisted upon "forgoing" meat—in this case, a delicious Virginia ham Mother had prepared with cloves, fresh pine-apple, and brown sugar. Of course Rickie ate—in fact, stuffed him-self—with everything else on the table including several desserts. We noted that his table manners had disintegrated—often, he ate with his fingers. His untouched napkin fell to the floor at his feet. Cagily, Rickie didn't allow himself to be drawn out on the sensitive subject of the bonobos or what his future employment might be but simu-lated an intense interest in our conversation about—whatever it was our Christmas-table conversations were about. (It's impossible to remember even our most intense dinner-table conversations even a few hours later. Politics? Football? Illnesses, surgeries, therapies? Christmas presents, to be returned the next day for credit?) Near the end of the lengthy meal, when Rickie was finishing a second piece of chocolate-cream pie, Father leaned toward him and said, as if reluc-tantly, "Rickie, we should discuss—you know. What you might be doing when the internship runs out."

Rickie's expression froze. But he spoke politely enough, saying, "Sure, Dad. Cool."

"You have to understand, those—*bonobos*"—Father pronounced the word with fastidious disdain—"are not a serious future for you. You would have to return to school and get a PhD, at the very least. You'd have to be trained in—some kind of bonobo zoology. There is no future at the San Diego Zoo, Rickie. Please understand. We are not being—controlling. We are only concerned for your future happiness."

"Good! The bonobo work is my happiness."

"But—those are *animals*. They are not your *family*."

"We've been through this, Dad. They are my *family*."

Mother left the table, upset. Father tried not to raise his voice. The other guests—Father's brother and sister-in-law; Mother's sister and brother-in-law; Rickie's sister, Amber; and his younger brother, Tod; cousins; Grand-daddy and Grand-mom, among others—sat hushed, embarrassed. Father said, "You are saying reckless things, son, which you can't possibly mean. Who is it who supports you, for instance? And who loves you?"

The words *supports you* had an immediate sobering effect. Rickie said OK, he was sorry. Just that he felt strongly about his work, as other interns at the zoo did. It wasn't a job but a *vocation*. Mitzie; Stalker; Bei-Bei; Claus; Kindle; Herc; Big Joe; Juno; Juno's new baby, Astrid—they were *so real* to him, there was nothing else like them in his life. The other day he'd been allowed to assist a vet who was examining Big Joe—Big Joe was the patriarch of the clan, whom the younger bonobos liked to tease. Big Joe had screwed up his face as if he'd been about to kiss Rickie but had spat at him instead. (Was this funny? No one except Rickie seemed to think so.) Big Joe was the alpha male, with a real sense of humor! Rickie smiled, recalling a private, precious memory.

Dryly, Father said, "Good. I'm glad that someone sees humor in this pathos."

There followed weeks of unanswered phone calls. Unanswered e-mails.

A steady stream of attempts from Rickie's family to contact him, ignored.

In late February Father left a phone message for Rickie, straining to keep his voice steady: "Son! I've calculated, we have spent more than two hundred thousand dollars on your education and what do we—or you—have to show for it?"

And: "Is this how you repay us, son? Going over to the *animals*?"

At last in March we returned to San Diego. We had little hope of confronting Rickie otherwise.

At the zoo, at the bonobo enclosure, we didn't see Rickie anywhere. A crowd of appreciative visitors watched the bonobos cavort and play—exactly as they'd done on our previous visit. In the animal world, time did not budge.

We inquired at an administration building but were told that Rickie was "no longer an intern" at the zoo. His internship had expired at the end of December.

No longer an intern! How was this possible? We'd been told that Rickie's internship had been extended for another six months. . . .

We asked to speak with "Hilary Krydy" but were informed— somewhat rudely, we thought—that the senior staffer was traveling in Africa right now and was not accessible by e-mail.

We had a street address for Rickie, in a haven of close-clustered stucco buildings a few miles from the zoo; the neighborhood was what Mother worriedly called "mixed ethnic"—a predominance of Hispanics, Asians, and very black blacks. When we rang the doorbell at 1104 Buena Vida a bearded and shaggy-haired man with bloodshot eyes answered the door to tell us sourly that "Rickie Asshole" no longer lived there. We were stunned by this crude remark and when we tried to identify ourselves, the bearded man said, smirking, "That asshole's your son? You can pay me then. He owes me fucking $646 in back rent."

The bearded man was barefoot, bare chested, in filthy jeans. He might have been in his midthirties—much older than Rickie. The apartment seemed to be primarily one large room in which blinds were drawn on the windows to cut out the bright-winter March sunshine. Furniture was mismatched and clutter lay everywhere. A rank animal odor of unwashed laundry and male sweat prevailed beneath a smell of incense and ripened fruit. The bearded man complained of Rickie Asshole "cutting out on him"—"reneging." In a kitchen corner of the room he was preparing a complicated drink in a blender: protein whey, bee pollen, fresh-ground flax—"It has to be eaten within ten minutes of grinding, or forget it"—oil of flax, unpasteurized goat milk, unpasteurized yogurt, and slightly rotted bananas, strawberries, and raspberries. Mother thought to placate the ruffled man by asking him about the concoction he was blending and he said with a grim smile, "It's to prolong life. The doorway to longevity is through proper diet."

The bearded man had no idea where Rickie was and told us we'd be better off checking the zoo. He'd lost his internship, but continued to hang out there, so far as anyone knew.

We returned to the zoo. Where is our son? we demanded. Our son seems to have disappeared off the face of the earth.

Again, the administrators spoke to us cautiously. We thought, evasively.

If only we'd recorded these conversations!

Desperate, we returned to the bonobo enclosure. Strangely, each bonobo in sight appeared to be female at that moment. The slender creatures were exceptionally affectionate, grooming, caressing, hugging, and kissing one another amid much excited chatter. (They were sexually adventuresome with one another, and even with the youngsters, but we tried not to notice.)

Then, as if they'd just been released from another part of the enclosure, a swarm of males came in—the younger, playful bonobos and at the rear the patriarch who had to be Big Joe, who'd insulted Father previously. Big Joe moved with a stiff sort of arthritic dignity, the hair of his large head seemingly parted in the middle, like a gentleman banker of the 1950s. Rudely, the younger bonobos rushed past him, jostling him and taking no notice of the furious glares he cast at their sleek backs. The younger bonobos were fueled by an infectious sort of energy—leaping, swinging, wrestling with the females and one another. (We tried not to stare.)

"Oh, look!" Mother cried. "Behind that rock—do you see?"

There crouched a lanky male bonobo with narrow shoulders and a small head; his face was a childish gamin's face but his eyes were hooded and covert.

"Do you see? It's him—Rickie! Oh God."

Mother began frantically crying, "Rickie! Rickie!" while Father tried to restrain her. Zoo visitors were astonished to see a well-dressed middle-aged woman making a gesture to climb over the railing, to press herself against the glass wall, arms outspread. "Rickie! Come back, Rickie! You know us—don't you? Rickie!"—so Mother pleaded. The female bonobos gazed at her with sympathy welling in their dark-brown eyes. Big Joe was glaring, grinning, stomping his feet, scratching his belly and genitals in an effort to direct attention to himself. The lanky bonobo at whom Mother was calling had quickly retreated to the rear of the enclosure, hiding his eyes behind his hands.

Mother clutched at Father's arm to keep from fainting.

"You saw him, didn't you? Oh—you saw—didn't you?"

"Y-Yes. I think—yes. I saw our—son. . . ."

We must have caused a commotion since security officers arrived, to escort us from the San Diego Zoo. Mother was so agitated she had to be driven in a motorized cart with Father seated despondently beside her.

"Oh, what have they done to him, those terrible apes," Mother lamented. "How have we failed him, our son. . . ."

Grimly, Father said, "It's our son who has betrayed us. He has *gone over to the animals.*"

The San Diego Zoo has refused to cooperate. No one in authority will take our allegations seriously or even speak with us any longer. Through an attorney the zoo has issued a statement that our claims (of "abduction," "seduction," "coercion" of our son) are *totally unsubstantiated.*

The head of the great apes department has insisted to us, on the phone and through his attorney, that it is impossible that our son has in some way "disappeared" into the bonobo clan. There are just thirty-seven bonobos at the zoo, including newborns, and each is, of course, documented; approximately one-half of the bonobos were born in Africa and the rest had been born in the zoo. Certainly there was no possible "human male" who had hidden among the bonobos and dwelled with them—this was the height of absurdity.

Father agreed that what Rickie had done was absurd. That would be between Rickie and his family, someday soon. For the time being, we are convinced that Rickie is living in the San Diego Zoo bonobo enclosure in his new, bonobo form; he has, as Father charges, *gone over to the animals.*

This document is a preliminary draft of our prospective lawyer's brief. It is not intended as a legal paper and it is not (yet) in a state to be submitted to the San Diego County Courthouse.

Each Sunday we return to see Rickie. Clean shaven now, our son has become lighter on his feet; his arms have grown longer, in proportion to his torso and legs. His toes are large and distinct and appear to be prehensile. His face is boyish yet wizened and quizzical, as with an ancient sort of wisdom; like his lively bonobo brothers he is shameless in his sexual proclivities with both young males and females of all ages. At our most recent visit last Sunday for the first time Mother said, with a sharp sigh of despair, "Oh maybe—it isn't our son. Maybe what we are looking at is—just an animal."

We gripped each other's hands, staring into the enclosure. Mother was quietly weeping and Father stood tall, brave, and dry-eyed. We were gazing into what might have been a wilderness setting—somewhere in the depths of Africa—where, amid a pack of bonobos, across a hilly distance of about thirty feet, the lanky-limbed bonobo with a curious ring of hair at the nape of his neck like the remnants of a collar observed us with an inscrutable expression—regret, exasperation, embarrassment, defiance? We saw as he turned away a just-perceptible wave of his furry hand as he trotted off with his brothers and sisters into a shadowy cave at the rear of the enclosure.

Orange Roses
Lucy Ives

In a kind of fantasy in which I frequently indulge, I discover a way to become so interested in work that I no longer speculate in the negative about the emotional lives of others. In other words, I give up paranoia in favor of business. To actually accomplish this, by which I mean, *in life*, would mean becoming the most American poet of all time.

In order not to despair, I have to first imagine the day then execute.

Jacques says, "Philosophy is comparing different kinds of philosophy."

I dream about an elevated walkway. A converted ruin. I keep wondering, is it relatively harder to live in the United States now than it has been at other times, and on what grounds could I even make this assessment.

I was trying to remember the numerals "5 3" because I needed to keep a code in mind while I went between screens on the "Droid Eris." I realized I could not think of a single discrete event that occurred in 1953.

Transparent philosophers; it's a sentence about their activity.

I lend Zachary my copy of *The Basketball Article*, by Anne Waldman and Bernadette Mayer. I don't expect it back, but he returns it within a month.

It is sometimes like there are two possible descriptions of the social event, generally speaking: one in which the individual despairs; one in which the individual, as such, is obviated.

I write a poem:

> I just let the flowers die
> I was a terrible person but I didn't care
> Being a person is a specific kind of art
> If you knew me you would know why I am
> Telling you
> I am in the greatest actual comfort
> When I shift my pleasant game
> To the interior
> Where it is right now
> THWACK is the sound a racket
> Makes in a shittier poem
> But we're not indoors
> This is just a voice
> Which makes it sound like we are indoors
> And there are far fewer
> Natural noises now
> It's truer than if
> We were anywhere else

Lucy Ives

This feels like what Dara means about the fascination of "real life," or what is "based on a true story." In this sense, all my desperation (flailing) and plans, the attempt *not to do nothing*, are also an invention—and therefore not the necessary precursor to some real act.

If I want to do something new or progress, I have to travel farther into a style I have already established. I may at this point add detail. In this sense, the work becomes a fiction of perspective.

I would like to write a story about a person who is continually transformed, who is a woman and becomes a donkey, a cat, a plant, a pencil, a mote, an old woman, etc.

An interest in what seems to be the case precludes my accession to a purely fictional form.

Current technology: IF a representation of reading, THEN legible. IF a legible representation of reading, THEN a caricature?

He spoke to his wife. He told her not to hit herself in the face. He said that she should not be hopeless, that she could not be hopeless. She had too much to live for. If she were a great writer she would never have had these thoughts. She said that she did not know what she should do. He said that it was easy, that there was a choice, that she was no longer five years old. She silently wished to herself that she were five years old. She silently felt as if she were five years old, and all the world were still ahead of her, every literate thought and act.

For me conceptualism could be something like, "Write a twelve hundred–page novel set in 1872, detailing the travels and observations of a French novelist in the North American countryside."

List of various details:
a. A click
b. A wooden peg
c. Black saliva
d. Dizzying shine

I notice the poverty of my own writing during a reading and feel intense regret. Do I become like those I parody in my prose to Sam? I am "just" like them?

A memory from a wedding: I congratulate the bridegroom on a "beautiful ceremony," and he grimaces, plastic face thinly muscled over.

Rousseau: *"J'ai vu de ces gens qu'on appelle vrais dans le monde."*

Lucy Ives

The scene in Buñuel's *The Phantom of Liberty* in which a sniper is sentenced to death and then released by officials from his handcuffs: He shakes hands with his lawyer and lights a cigarette, descends an elaborate staircase to sign autographs in the courthouse lobby.

One student has written that he does not understand why he was not permitted to bring his "philosophical ideas" to bear in his paper.

Something we talk about yesterday evening: If one is a witch, it is because (i.e., it would be because) one can (*could*) turn people to stone.

Quality of time. One wishes to assign qualities to it, but then these are the qualities assigned; planned and not discovered. Why should the unexpected be of such value, when we are trying to sense not it but rather that in or against which it occurs?

The human could in fact only be transfigured through imitation?

I meet with Julia, who remembers me as "Canadian," or "Kim Deal."

In a dream Peter is in front of an ocean. I am transformed into a bunch of daisies bound with orange string.

I make a list of numbers and cross them off as I finish pages. The numbers do not correspond to an actual projected page limit, but act rather as a prop to make venturing into prose bearable. I tell myself, "You will not have to keep doing this forever," which, of course, I won't.

1928 letter from Williams to Zukofsky: ". . . virtue exists like a small flower on a loose piece of earth above a precipice."

I find a stanza from a poem I wrote when I was twenty-three:

Yellow-red

Roses at a blue gate

Boys brush aside sand

Orange roses
        White,
        Red

Lucy Ives

Why on television is it always clear which is the "right" person with whom to share one's affections?

I remember almost a decade ago Rob talking to me on the phone about stories he was writing about his father. Rob said writing made him want to shop. Could this show how some illogical behavior is more meaningful than others.

Those whom no one loves, live, and perhaps are happy.

I can see that someone cannot quite explain, but she covers her confusion with a weird smile, under which she hides her lack of authority. Now I am smiling.

List from observation:
a. Naturalism
b. chapping in eighteenth-century pastel
c. treatise on hems, bows
d. symbolical coat
e. mask, or *loup*
f. shade, tambourine
g. figured damask coat, or banyan
h. *Praktische Anweisung zur Pastellmalerei*
i. 1792

I go to the gym and spend fifty minutes on the treadmill and elliptical machine. I watch television. Wanda Sykes tells Ellen about her grapefruit-sized tumor (she is forty-seven). I do some sit-ups. At the supermarket the checkout girl tells me about the time she wore "really heavy pants" and a white T-shirt in the rain.

Reason is a language. In this sense it is no more or less perfect than other languages.

I walk uptown to Thirty-sixth for an opening. Ben's painting (of the Italian flag with a bucket over it) has already sold. Later on the train he tells me he spoke to someone our age who has no hand but only a thumb at the end of one of his arms: "I shook his thumb." If I also had such a thumb this is what others would say of me.

Maybe I have a boring way of treating life. I watch a man across the street throw cardboard boxes at a second-story window.

Language, since inorganic, is not suffused by time and does not "die," despite the expression. And yet without the depth of time, the possibility of sequence, there could be no meaning.

Have lunch alone with Sam because Christian doesn't show (cannot get out of bed). For some reason Sam humors me. I say something about how useless is the term "fiction."

31

Lucy Ives

List of events:
a. They discover a beetle in milk.
b. Flaubert critiques the pious death of a child.
c. A drunk slips her phone into a toilet.
d. Someone paints a roof to look like snow.
e. A fuchsia bud.

The present is whatever must be alleviated by a message.

At a lecture I make no effort to take notes but rather withstand my boredom by consuming it, avidly even, as if it were a broth. I find that later when I am outside on the street I have begun to dread the possibility that I allow a sort of lust for passivity to overtake my life.

In a dream I ride to a village built in what I privately term "the Austrian style." I die and walk along a sunny highway.

It's not simply that you become "depressed"; that is far too inexact. You can forget how to do a thing, how to make the gesture that accomplishes your desire. You forget to try to reach whatever this or that may be, because you generalize. You only reason with yourself, you make no attempt. There is in fact no way to justify this sort of behavior.

In a dream I am with someone I love. I enter a café made of unvarnished wood; diners sit single file on enclosed balconies with rugged plastic windows.

<u>Plot:</u>
1. A white scratch.
2. Emma pauses near a smudge.
3. Orange roses wrapped in hair.

I find a fragment, partially highlighted:

This is the sense in which people speak of art as "doing," which is to say, confusedly. Anyhow, sometimes one has hunted successfully in the wreckage that constitutes her fear.

<u>I imagine it as a point in time that is also a view, smeared laterally and with no regard for the artificiality of the gesture, and here one might "feel" (apprehend) the affections of the artist.</u>

I think about how in the end it is true, something that we see in other people, or what frightens us, is death, possibly our own, or just a sign of it, like, *in* another personality. This is at any rate what threatens me and makes me fear, rather than love, others, if I do. What is curious is that these sensations or affections never happen in a single moment, which is to say, never take the form of an event. That they forever manifest themselves in this strange otherwise, a present that isn't "happening," is what seems to make it impossible not to agree to go along with (i.e., *feel*) them.

1994. Six dresses by Rei Kawakubo. Bias-cut silk skirt, paisley, tie-dye, attaches to T-shirt. Cold skin of the model. In verdant shade effected by topiary. Laceless work boots in glossy black calf, fawn interior, tongues in grass.

Lucy Ives

I seek the approval of others often, and less often others, or some others, recognize I do so.

In a dream I enter a store selling lamps from the 1950s. Porcelain. Californian cream/white.

I have humiliated myself so much and am not even famous. Or: the humiliation of the nonfamous is basically unreal.

In a children's-book illustration a female figure rides on the back of a bearded monkey and cats scatter in her path.

Why is it writers are so much less good than they once were? Is it possible that it is more difficult than it once was to speak of life, which is to say, *a* life, as a whole? Obviously we understand that there is living and death, but there is a very little idea of a formal (which is to say, cultural) relation to either one of these states. This is very American. People are like their parents only on account of obsessions, since there is no way of living, only "lifestyle." A given period has no symbolic value.

I read somewhere that Keats's statement about beauty is about ambition.

I sometimes look younger than I am and sometimes older. There is no sure way to look one's age. To look one's age, one would have to know what one's age looks like, and this no one really knows. I suddenly remember a day in Berkeley when I was on a residential street and a man walking the other way turned and slapped my ass as I passed him. And I went to work in lush abundance.

During a time of waiting, a lot of things won't be apparent.

I spend several weeks trying to write a summary of a famous novel and end up with a single sentence that has nothing to do with it:

Somewhere it's possible a statue sails through a thin floor or the limb of a tree is mistaken for a fist of marble; intervening leaves shake as if with delight, a rancid jelly.

Ben is sick and has been reading Louis L'Amour. What is the first example of the "American aesthetic" as purveyed by Europeans; could one locate this in certain objects, texts. What would such an argument look like. The political cartoon of the segmented snake, for example.

I have never known how to write poetry. It is not a question of relating language to a person one is but rather of relating it to the exact person one is not.

Lucy Ives

<u>A stanza:</u>

~~It's not that this is a feeling opposed to~~
~~Or distinct from others~~
~~This, Lucy, is feeling~~
~~This is the knowledge of feeling~~
~~You are smart~~
~~You are slightly intelligent~~
~~It is like a mastery of self~~
~~An art~~
~~That you will die in~~

Torpor

Brian Evenson

WHEN THEY SLEPT she had gotten into the habit of resting both her hands on his arm. Now that his arm was gone, what was she to do?

Before, they had had a good arrangement, or had come to have one once she had sorted through matters. She had begun with splints, using them first for just one hand and then for both. They kept her from waking in the middle of the night with stabbing pains. But still, even with the splints, her hands would eventually start to throb, and that was enough to awake her. More than enough. She tried drugs, but they did nothing but make her groggy. *What you need*, a friend told her, *is better drugs*. The doctor she approached for a prescription told her instead that it was simple; she just had to keep her hands elevated. So she had tried to keep her arms bent at the elbow and the elbow planted on the bed, to sleep with her hands waving in the air on the stalks of her forearms. Either they fell down as soon as she fell asleep or she awoke with her arms locked and sore. She stacked pillows next to her and splayed her hands onto them, but it didn't elevate them enough. Nothing worked, nothing at all. But then one night, his back had been turned to her and he was sleeping with his arm hemmed to his side and she had simply reached out and placed her hands on his arm and he, sleeping, had let her, and then she had slept the sleep of the dead all the way through to morning.

It had gone on like that for many nights in a row: she lying awake, restless, until he rolled over and pressed his arm along his side and then she could wriggle her way toward him and lay her hands upon his arm. Then sleep. She had grown not only to like it but to need it, and the few times he had been gone at night and not in the bed, she had not been able to sleep at all. Those nights, the stabbing pains had been worse than ever.

37

*

For better or for worse, she had promised. She knew that was what she had promised, but how was she to have known that worse meant that there would one day suddenly be less of him? It had been like that: One day he was whole and complete and the next day his arm was three-quarters gone. When he first came home, with it wrapped in gauze, she had of course understood that she couldn't touch it, that it would hurt him to do so. She had respected that, kept her distance. But then the wound had annealed, the scar tissue had thickened and then hardened, and the stump became just that: a stump. By that time, it felt like she hadn't slept for a year. It hadn't, of course, been that long, but that was what it *felt* like, and that was what she meant when she'd said it to him. But, touchy, he'd misunderstood. *The tragedy here,* he'd claimed, *is not whether* you *can sleep. This,* he said, shaking the stump in her face, *is the tragedy. Stump,* he claimed, *trumps stabbing hand pain.*

But did it? Were they really playing at some game that had trumps? A game in which only the person with the missing arm, the three-quarters missing arm, was allowed to feel pain? She hadn't thought so. And indeed, with a little time, a little patience, as his own pain lessened and he learned not to try to pick up, say, a glass with his missing hand, he went from feeling offended to saying—quite sensibly, he believed—*But I still have a good bit of my arm left: Use that.*

But no, it wasn't the same. When he turned now, as he always did, to sleep on his side, and she scooted across the sheet and closer and rested her hands on him, she could, true, fit both hands on what remained of the arm. But one hand always slipped off the stump to fall lower, against his ribs. And if she scooted higher in the bed so that that hand wouldn't slip off, it was the other hand that did so, spilling off the shoulder and down against his neck. Either made it too low. Admittedly that meant that she was throbbing in just one hand instead of two, but she still couldn't sleep. *Can't he just wear his prosthetic through the night?* she found herself sometimes wondering at two or three or four in the morning. But this, she knew, would be asking too much. If he wore his prosthetic during the night, the doctor had told him, had told *them,* he wouldn't be able to wear it through the whole day without having aches and strain and even, potentially, shooting pains of his own. No, despite their closeness she just could not ask—and even if she did ask, she felt, he would almost certainly say no.

So, for months she was sleepless. She placed one hand on her husband and then held the other there in the air, over the place where the arm used to be. She held it up as long as she could, or placed it on a pillow balanced on her husband if he was asleep enough that she could get away with it. But it was not the same. The best she could manage was a kind of grumpy torpor. And it was not, she became more and more convinced, enough.

And so, late at night, listening to her husband breathing beside her, one arm already tingling, sleep refusing to come, she found herself imagining what it would be like to be in bed with a man who had not one arm, but two.

From this, everything else followed, inexorably. It was a simple thing to take a lover. Not because she was sex starved, or to find passion, or for anything of that sort—for indeed, so she told me as she again pulled the sheet high enough to cover her breasts, she loved her husband passionately and desired him and always would.

No, she did it for afterward. For the moment when, both of them spent, her lover would roll away.

As he perhaps dozed a little, she would stealthily slip on her splints and then, carefully, place both her hands on him. And then, finally, if all was just right, if he stayed there on his side, if he didn't move, if he didn't mind having her there pressing on him, then she, at last, would once again be able to sleep.

By the Time You Read This
Yannick Murphy

"DEAR PAUL, BY THE TIME you read this, I will be dead. If you don't stop seeing that other woman, I will come back to haunt you. I will be the face in the mirror when you shave. I will be the wind you hear at night. I will be the creak in the stairs and the loud shudder of the settling roof beams that wakes us up from our sleep."

"Dear Cleo, I hope you never understand why your mother did this. If you ever find yourself close to understanding I want you to call and get help right away. Please promise me that. There are plenty of numbers to call in case of emergency on the fridge. (You might even consider calling Irving Propane; their staff has always been helpful and ready to come out to the house at a moment's notice if we think we hear even the slightest hissing sound of gas leaking from our pipes.)"

"Dear Paul, have you ever noticed the birthmark on my labia? If not, you should look now. I'd hate to go to my grave thinking that I was married to a man all these years who didn't even notice such an intimate detail about me."

"Dear Paul, I'm doing this because I want you to respect my last wish, and that last wish is that you stop seeing that woman because I don't want Cleo to know the woman you left me for, even if she might be some amazing person you think Cleo should get to know, a choreographer, or symphony musician, or nuclear physicist. All that she'll ever be to me is a slut."

"Dear second-grade teacher Miss Debbie, thank you for always letting me come to class early so I could help you set up the classroom. Even though you were hugely overweight, I liked the way you looked and smiled at me. I liked the candy you would give us when we behaved well, and I am sorry that I told you that I thought you were bribing us. That was just something my father said, and I was repeating it. At times he takes things very seriously, and once, while watching election results, he threw our television out the window when a certain president was elected that he didn't like."

"Dear Cleo, I want you to throw away what you don't want, and keep what you want, of all that I owned. I think my pearl ring would look good on you, so don't throw that away, and don't throw away my mother's sorority pin, as there are little diamonds embedded in it, and it might be worth something someday. Also, even though the brown Creuset baking dish in the pantry looks old, it's French and very good for roasting new potatoes, and wipes clean easily, so I would say don't throw that away either. Don't throw away the hand-held eggbeater, those are quite rare, ever since whisks became the rage, and you can't even buy one on eBay these days. Remember not to put the colored Pyrex bowls with the white interiors into the dish-washer, as their colors on the outside will fade. Definitely throw away all the boxes and boxes of colored slides your father's parents took on their trip to Alaska. They are just pictures of icebergs and flowers without any people in them."

"Dear Mom, I hope I did this right. My biggest fear is that I wake up in a hospital room and you are staring at me with fear in your eyes. The same fear you had when we were in that car accident and I hit my head on the windshield and there was so much blood you had to take off your shirt to stop the blood from flowing, and I was so embarrassed when the police came because you were wearing a white bra that looked dirty, like you had just come out from under the wheels of our car."

"Dear Dad, I hope I do this right, and really cleanly, because I want you to shake your head and say what you always used to say, which was, 'That girl can do anything once she puts her mind to it.' I want you to tell Mom that crying won't make me come back. I'm never coming back (well, if I do come back, it will just be to haunt Paul if he's still with that slut, so don't worry, I won't be coming back to where you and Mom are). Tell Mom something like the load of life was too hard for me to take, and now it's her job to hold it for me, just like when I was a girl and we would walk along the road back from school, and my backpack was too heavy and I would ask her to carry it. Make it sound like she still has a purpose in life."

"Dear Paul, tell me that you'll be so bent out of shape after my death that you'll fall into my grave after I'm lowered into it. Tell me you'll take out all of my pictures and put them on display on the dresser. Tell me you'll sleep with a pile of my clothes you pushed together to make look like a body and that's the only way you can fall asleep at night. Tell me you'll take Cleo to every place we've ever been together so you can say, And this is where we held hands, and this is where we kissed, and this is where I told her I loved her. Tell me you will remember that love more strongly than when I was alive so that it almost hurts, but not too much, of course, I still want you strong enough to take care of Cleo. Tell me you'll remember she has an appointment with the orthodontist in two weeks, it should take over an hour, so tell her to bring a good book to the office, and not one of those trashy YA books with the airbrushed covers. Tell me you'll bring her something good to read. She's almost ready for *The Lord of the Rings*; maybe they have redone the cover, and there's a trashy-looking YA cover with a swarthy, shirtless Frodo on it and you will have better luck getting her to read it than that old edition we have with its spine breaking off and thread hanging from where it was bound."

"Dear UPS man, thank you for all the years when you saw my car parked in town and decided to open the hatch of my unlocked car and put my package into it so that you could save time and gas by not having to drive all the way up the hill to my house. Thank you for always waving at me on any country road I ever saw you on, which was sometimes towns away from our town. (You certainly put in a lot of miles.) Thank you for always handing my dog a biscuit when she climbed into your truck, and thank you for not yelling at our chickens that also climbed into your truck and pecked the corrugated metal steps, and instead you just said, 'Shoo, shoo' in almost a whisper. I think we will see each other again someday. I really do. Don't forget to wave like usual. Maybe then I will find out your name."

"Dear Cleo, when you get your period, start off with tampons right away. Those pads can be uncomfortable, and with all of your swimming you'll want the tampons anyway. But of course, you probably know this, and you are probably saying, 'Geez, Mom' right now. Don't let your father get his panties in a wad about you dating boys. You've got good sense, and tell him you'll use it. He might bring out a baseball bat and sit on the front porch the first time a boy comes calling on you, but kiss him on the cheek before you leave on the date and tell him you studied a self-defense book at the library and you know how to rip the guy a new asshole if he tries anything on you."

"Dear sixth-grade English teacher Mr. Sun. Despite all of your grand teachings (I will never forget the meaning of 'hyperbole,' one of your vocabulary words, for example), I have not retained the knowledge of when to use 'lay' or 'lie.' They say 'lay' takes an object, but I still don't understand that. And the title of that book *As I Lay Dying* has screwed me up for years. Then there was that billboard when I was a kid, 'Winston tastes good like a cigarette should.' What was the matter with that grammar? I'd like to know. Anyway, I do thank you for a great sixth-grade class. I loved that short story called 'The Ledge' about the man and his son and his nephew who lose their skiff on a hunting trip to a small island and when the tide comes in, the father has to hold the boys aloft for as long as he can before they all drown from the freezing water that encroaches upon them from all sides. You might have known then that I would grow up to be the type of woman who would do this act now, which is what I will have done by the time you read this, since I loved those morose stories so much. (Was that just a run-on? I apologize if so.) You might have said then that I was a dead ringer for this kind of act I'm about to commit now."

"Dear Paul, I'm sorry I did this, in a way, I mean maybe all men are going to cheat on their wives eventually. You're certainly not the first. Maybe I'm just sorry I'm the type of woman who got upset enough about it to take her own life. I'm sorry you didn't marry the type of woman who just said, 'Fine, you want to fuck someone else, then I'll fuck someone else too.' I guess I should have gone out and found myself some other man, and then let it subside, and let us be together again. I couldn't do that, though; I couldn't stand to think about you with someone else. I think I did what was best. Don't you? Stupid how after all these years, I still want your approval. I should have been the type of woman who could just leave you, and wish you well, and feel sorry for you, and maybe, from time to time even stomach you and meet you for lunch and notice you were still wearing your hair in a ponytail after all these years, and recognize the sweater you were wearing as one I once gave you but that you've now forgotten where it came from. Listen, I'm going to throw that sweater out right now before I finish this note because, damn it, I don't want you wearing it in the presence of that slut. I've been thinking about that other lover I should have taken, instead of taking my own life. I mean, I don't know who I would have taken anyhow. There are all those fathers of the girls on Cleo's swim team. They're all smart and in shape, or at least they care about being in shape. I think I like one of the head lifeguards at the pool. He is younger than the rest of the fathers of the swim-team girls, but I have noticed him noticing me. I think you know him. He's the one with the big sparkling-blue eyes. He's tall. He's got a chest broader than yours, and he's got more muscle than you do. (Oh, did I just write 'got'? Yikes, I meant to say, 'He has more muscle than you do.')"

"Dear whatever your name is, of course, in my eyes, you are Dear

Yannick Murphy

Slut, but I should really take the 'dear' out anyway because 'dear' and 'slut' are probably too incongruous to appear one right after the other and there is probably some rule my sixth-grade English teacher, Mr. Sun, could tell me about placing two incongruous words right next to each other. So, Slut, I am writing this to let you know that even though I have never met you, I feel I should let you know that it's probably your fault I have taken all these pills because I know Paul and, really, I don't think he would have let himself go this far with you if you hadn't probably pushed yourself on him in some way. I wondered for a while what you looked like, but now I really don't want to know. I'm sure you're beautiful and thin, and have something unusual about you that Paul found irresistible. Maybe you have a lisp. Maybe you even have a limp, or one hand that is missing a finger. Has Paul taken you to the restaurant that's a house with the famous shepherd's pie and the jazz band whose drummer in the warmer months has to fit himself inside the massive fireplace because there is no other room for him, what with all the tables they try and fit in to accommodate the crowd?

"Has he held you the way he held me from behind at night where he is able to whisper in your ear? Has he told you about that dog he had when he was younger that followed him everywhere and then got killed by a tree his father felled and how his father chainsawed the tree into pieces to move the log off the dog, but it was too late, the dog was not going to make it, and a gun had to be used? Does he hold your hand when you walk to hurry you along the way he does me? Has he told you his favorite time of year is winter? Has he made you take long walks in the snow and pointed out the tracks of snowshoe rabbits and families of deer? Has he told you about Cleo? How beautiful she is and how when she was first born he suddenly became more frightened than he had ever been in his life because he realized he now had something he could lose and afterward he would never be the same? Has he told you how she inhales books and is really witty in a dry way you would not expect a girl her age to be? Has he told you she looks like me? She does. Our baby pictures are almost identical. Do you know Paul eats his chicken with two forks? I could never understand that, but the next time you see him eat chicken, notice how he will ask for an extra fork and not a knife. That is, if you really decide you are going to keep seeing him after I have killed myself and after he has grieved and realized I was his only true love. Are you really still going to want to be with him after all of that? I would think not. He might be somewhat of a basket case for a while.

44

We've traveled all over the world together, and I know things about him that he hasn't told anyone else. He knows almost everything about me, except there are things, private things I am not going to discuss with you, that I think he has overlooked, but in the scheme of things, they are not so important after all. They are just minor blemishes, in a manner of speaking.

"Once we traveled to Spain and I fell off a moped that I was trying to start and I gave it too much gas and the moped reared and I fell on the ground, which was littered with big rocks, and I cut my knee terribly. He said he thought I was trying to show off when I did it. We didn't have disinfectant but we did have Grappa di Julia, a liquor that bubbled when it came into contact with my deep cut. He might tell you, after he finds me, how I was unstable anyway, and that it was not finding out that the two of you were seeing each other that made me kill myself. He might tell you how I hitchhiked while I was six months pregnant on the French island of Réunion and that I could have been kidnapped, but he would not be telling you the whole story because he does not know the whole story. The whole story is that I did not hitchhike anywhere, I just told him I did to make him feel bad that he had left me for the day to go to the caldera of a volcano. (I wasn't supposed to travel to high altitudes, being pregnant, so he went without me. I was jealous that he got to go see the active volcano and I didn't.) I came back to the house we were staying in with two very long baguettes I bought on my long journey home that did not involve my thumbs for hitching a ride, but only involved my legs with the swollen ankles from carrying a child curled like a pill bug inside of myself. So you see we cannot believe everything people tell us because sometimes they do not know for sure themselves."

"Dear Mom, you will probably react in the worst way to my death, and you are the one person I least feel like writing to. I bet you might have some advice for me now if you saw how I was thinking about killing myself. In this circumstance, you might have quoted some religious line you heard in *The Sound of Music*. If you were here with me you would say, 'Whenever God shuts a door, he opens a window.' And I would look around the room and say, 'The windows are already open, they've been open a while, and there are no more to open.'"

"Dear UPS man, Cleo is ordering a goose egg that she bought. She has an incubator for it. Please put the package inside the door. I would hate for the egg to become overheated and for the poor little chick to die before it has even had a chance to break free. I hope she has enough time to let the goose, when it hatches, imprint on her. She has little time these days since she is on the swim team, such a far drive away, and they practice so often and they go to so many meets. She is getting quite good, and just bought one of those Fastskin suits that are so tight I almost need a crowbar to get it on her. I wonder who will help her into the suit when I'm gone."

"Slut, if you are still with Paul after I've hung myself, do me this one favor, and make sure he compliments Cleo a lot. I believe there is nothing more valuable to a girl than a father who is able to tell his daughter how smart and beautiful she is. I think sometimes he doesn't want to tell her how beautiful she is because he doesn't want her to become full of herself and conceited. But I don't think there is a chance of that. If you haven't met her already somehow, you will realize when you do meet her (and of course I'm hoping you don't meet her and that Paul, in his grief over losing me, breaks up with you) that she is unassuming and forthright, and also very beautiful. She is one of those girls whose eyebrows you wish you had because they taper so nicely. She is tall and slender and can make you laugh easily. I guess I would be wrong to say I will miss her since I will no longer 'be' but I miss her right now, and she is just in the next room reading, only a plasterboard's thickness away. It is inconceivable to think that I won't miss her when I am dead, that's how much I love her. Do you have children? Probably not, since I have decided you are most likely young. I was kind of hoping that you did have children, or at least one child, and when trying to convince Paul to stay with you after I killed myself, you would have the monumental task of trying to sell not only yourself to Paul, but your child. Maybe he is a son, and has been having a hard time of it in school. Maybe he is a 'different kind of learner' and needs aides to go with him from class to class and take notes for him and give him the first lines of essays to get him started. Maybe someone holds the pencil for him and does the computation for math homework while he watches, wondering about what will be on the lunch menu that day. Maybe you don't tell Paul any of this, and what you tell Paul is that your son has the uncanny ability to tell who it is when you hear the phone ring. You make it seem like your son has some kind of powers the average child does not have. He can tell the minute he sees the color of a license plate what state it's from. I suppose you are questioning why, if I love Cleo so much, am I willing to leave her. I think maybe I have raised her too well. Let me explain. She can bake. Cream puffs and biscotti are in her repertoire at the tender age of twelve. She can sew, not just mend. A quilt she made that she tells me is the flying-geese

46

pattern lays/lies on her bed. She quotes Shakespeare verbatim after just reading lines of him in one sitting. She can scoop up her pet goose in her arms and walk with it in the field and stroke its head and imitate the goose when it hisses. She is armed for the world, you see, and hardly needs me anymore, except of course for getting that racing suit on."

"Dear Paul, by the time you read this note, I will have asphyxiated myself in the garage, but I did want you to know that I was thinking beforehand of the time we traveled to Madrid and you tried your hand at the Spanish tongue and kept asking the bank teller, 'Do I have a pen?' instead of correctly asking, 'Do you have a pen?' and I remember how I could not stop laughing, and when you realized your mistake, how you started laughing also, and the people on the line behind us were getting angry and started saying things we could not understand and throwing their hands up in the air, which we thought was very Spanish and made us laugh harder. I remember the time in Scotland when we were worried about waking up in time to catch our train back to London and the proprietor of the bed-and-breakfast said not to worry, he would come knock us up in the morning. Do you remember how hard we wanted to laugh then? We had to run up to our room while we covered our mouths to make sure we didn't laugh in front of him, and then after we made it to the room and slammed the door behind ourselves we fell onto the bed laughing, with tears streaming down our faces, and behind us a window with a breathtaking view of the Edinburgh Castle and black clouds sailing in the Scottish sky. Paul, I killed myself because I couldn't imagine those memories living alongside the more recent memories of you cheating on me."

"Dear coach of the swim team, I shot myself because my husband and I were having some marital infidelity problems, nothing more than that. I don't believe I'm insane, or that some kind of insanity or psychological neurosis runs in the family. I'm telling you this because I want you to treat Cleo as fairly as possible. Understand that she's no different from all of those other kids. She's not suddenly going to get so upset at not winning an event that she's been training for months for that you feel you have to put her on a suicide watch. (By the way, she has been telling me lately that she would like to improve her butterfly. I think she thinks she comes out of the water too high when she takes her breath, so maybe if you have time sometime you could work with her on her body profile.)"

"Slut, I slit my wrists because, well you know why. I don't want you to be a mother to Cleo, but maybe, once in a while, you could tell Cleo things a mother might tell her daughter. Things like, after changing into your swimsuit, don't forget to reach inside and to, one at a time, lift each breast up higher so it looks fuller and doesn't look like your breasts are silver-dollar pancakes."

"Dear UPS man, I ran in front of your truck because I got tired of waiting for a package that was never delivered. What I mean to say is that I was hoping my husband would fall back in love with me after having a torrid romance with a younger woman, and he never did. Did you ever have that package in the back of the truck and maybe it was undelivered? Maybe it is sitting in some holding facility in Maine where outside blueberries grow this time of year and seagulls alight on the rooftops. (Maybe you have seen Paul with his slut on your rounds, and you are shaking your head reading this, saying you could have told me all along that he would never leave the little hottie and that I was history long before the Christmas rush began last year.)"

"Dear Paul, I walked off into the woods alone one winter's night because you were the one who always told me that dying from the cold was probably the nicest way to go, that even right before I died I would not feel cold at all any longer and I would see everything around me more clearly than I ever had before. It was very Native American of me to do it this way. By the time you read this letter, you will have to imagine me leaning up against some maple tree having died feeling very alive, every leaf blowing past me sounding like a roar."

"Dear Mom, by the time you read this I will have jumped off the bridge over the falls. Please keep an eye on Paul in the future. After all, the women he dates will leave an impression on Cleo. Feel free to let Cleo know your opinion of these women. I won't be there to teach her the meaning of 'slut,' 'whore,' 'wanton,' 'cradle robber,' etc."

"Dear Mr. Sun, do you happen to know of any other expressions or words for women who would try to land a man at any cost? I would look those words up in a thesaurus or dictionary myself, the way you taught us to in sixth grade, but I am a little caught up right now, and it is more time-consuming than I thought. When you get them, would you please write them on a list and send them to my daughter Cleo at the following address:"

"Dear Cleo, I did this because I love you."
"Dear Paul, I did this because I hate you."

"Dear Mom and Dad, I wish there was a way you would never have to learn I did this."

"Slut, it's none of your business why I did this."

"Dear Mr. Sun, I did this to myself. I have done this to myself. I will have done this to myself. I shan't have done this to myself. I had to do this to myself. I have had to do this to myself. I will have had to have done this to myself. I myself have done this. I done did this."

"Dear Paul, just one last thing, I'm putting a roast in the oven, so by the time you read this letter, it will probably be done. I wanted to leave Cleo one last good meal. Don't make her eat that cube steak again, even if it is on sale; it was way too tough and bits of it got caught in her braces and every time she flosses she pops a spring and has to make a new appointment."

"Dear Death, here I come. Be forgiving, be swift, be the answer."

"Dear Death, you will have to take a rain check. I don't really want an answer. I can't really remember the big question anyway. All of my questions are small. Where is the hydrogen peroxide? I need to use some on Cleo because she has come down with swimmer's ear. Who has fiddled with the water heater, and why am I stuck in a luke-warm shower? If lightning, when it hits the air, is hotter than the sun, then why doesn't everything around the lightning bolt melt? Why aren't the nearby trees reduced to just puddles of sap? Can I pass a school bus on the road if it's stopped to drop off kids but the stop sign hasn't been extended by the driver? Besides, there are too many things going on here for me to want to kill myself right now. There is a goose egg coming that we will have to turn around in the incubator every morning and night. There is a storm coming, and I love how the lightning lights up the sky and the gray barn looks almost white. Also, there is a new barred owl in the tree by our window and I'd like to hear his call again tonight, as it is peaceful right to the bone. Also, the dog needs her second dosage of heartworm medication, and I better be around to give that to her. And one more thing, I am too tired right now to tie a noose/slit my wrists/pop pills/run the engine in the closed garage/jump off a bridge/pull a trigger/freeze to death/ get run over. I think I just might lie/lay down for a while and close my eyes and when I wake up I can decide what's the best thing to do, but right now, I am so tired and the bed looks so comforting and the sheets, just off the line, smell like flowers and sunshine."

Six Poems
G. C. *Waldrep*

YEW BODY

lathed, the wild gantries of the eye
feast of simian circuitry, the hawthorn
expressed as milk in the moth's
supersaturated trajectory, the grave-
cloths light is mending in its cruel
belvedere, wrung like violent calends
—world tree vs. anaphylactic
and the glistening proteins blot
enucleated, the eye quells the muscled
androgynies the lymph collects
as debt—to expurgation—remove
the catchments from the purities
of fiction, the green-on-gold of law's
not uncurious javelin zinc-clad
around, as edge, this stone coping's
barrowsleep &, thespian, lief
mass in the deepest basins, *I see it*
feelingly through the madonna car
park—your extravagant rhabdomancy
in the rectangular ash-petal, brine-
serrate, slender, the dead go on
thin & drinking, (emptied) bag-o-scars

G. C. Waldrep

PROFILE OF NACRE, HABIT OF WOAD

lost lines & lilypress,
what rough sphere
collects towards
autumn's bell-ransom

the soul's habit
is exclamatory, run
swiftly in this psalm-
marathon (arbor
of my newest-blood)

a third nation
emerges, at dusk
ghost-émigrés
blent in trouble's spire

if I tell you
a temple spoke to me
in aching-plenitude
of the sweetgum's
choir-depth, may

a dream flex its
one perfect muscle—

I want to be there
fatherless, unfathering
brother-in-sight
(warm enough, pain-

without-weeping, pine
is like a pail
of jewel-blood's
absence-in-memory)

G. C. Waldrep

HARRISVILLE
i.m. Gennady Aygi

address history
honor's rose-in-foil
theft-of-throne

my friend, (my
only ever-friend-)

it is now a late
season, myth
has abandoned us

someone or some-
thing in the night
ravaged
the indian pipes
I'd been eye-
nurturing, -saving

I press
their milkynight
stalks & bells
into this tine-page

the season
genuflects, sharply

my friend, (my
only ever-friend-)

address/history
as egg-mission-bud
my heart-('s
companion)-(loss))

G. C. Waldrep

SHAKER FARM
Jaffrey, NH

mercy's
ghost-trombone

folds itself
into a single
specimen-
rose

mercy's
trysting-lobe

debrided
(as by surgeon)

moat me,
a velvet brass
whets
its gift-drawing

each stroke
of music's knife

a throat
a sweet wind

brushes, un-
petaling
hive-planet

's blush-sonata

we pass
through, (over)

SYZYGY

solace implicates:
agent: upon agent:

comfort strokes
the pleats from its

velvet gown:
away from the fire:

it is more clever:

than blood, dumb
circulation's

circuit: syzygy:

the fire eats away
at the vestibule,
do not linger here

call the falcons:

to their young:
the art of hunger

is a neolithic crypt
set into light:

tourists visit: we
walk among them,

glad for the cover,
all these bodies

rapt: gyreward:

watching all these
other bodies:

graphite: organdy:

a *physical* agent,
I meant, not this
rapid oxidation:

angle of insight:

wax pericope:

little love notes
light keeps sending,

really it is unfair
to call them scars:

ATTAR-PRESENCE
i.m. Gennady Aygi

or if hidden in flesh
ecliptic
a purchase agent
voids the mainspring

man's beetling prose
buries the body,
always   paragraph-
sepulture-knot

lift & filter
this perduring life,
sleep-as-
range-of-motion
for the soul's joint

(a liquid pain
solitude assuages)

G. C. *Waldrep*

dig deep into debt's
waking body, my

semblance-hyphen

unrepeatable (
temple-of-first-love)

AWOL
Robert Olen Butler

THE NIGHT MY MOTHER DIED, I was sleepless in a hotel room in Miami. From what Stan—Dr. Sparkman—tells me, from what the nurses told him, I figure I was awake at the moment she passed. I wasn't there but I was awake. Before I left her, Stan assured me she could live on as she was for a long, indefinite period. If it was at all important I should go ahead to Miami. So I came down to say good-bye to the stockholders, and they stood up and applauded in thanks and regret at my passing. At my retirement. He built all this for us from nothing, they said. What a guy.

She was demented.

Not at first.

She broke her hip in assisted living in a nice place in Buckhead, where my dad had died a few years earlier. She was standing in the center of her living-room floor and she was ninety-two years old and she was talking to a nurse, trying to explain Bach to her, which was filling the room at the time and which the nurse had asked her about, and my mother up and fell. Just like that. And her hip was broken. Stan says the breaking of the hip likely preceded the fall. But there it is.

When her surgeon the next morning warned me that one person out of two over eighty years old who breaks a hip dies within six months, I thought my mother would beat those odds if anyone could.

She didn't. She broke her wrist as well. She couldn't rehab the hip. So she spent the rest of her life flat on her back in a nursing home. Another nice place up in Buckhead, with me just twenty minutes away, mostly downtown in the Georgia-Pacific Tower, helping the oil fields and construction sites of the world manage their risks.

She moved from hospital to nursing home with a clear mind.

"I went into a swoon over an adagio is what happened," she said, her very first words when I sat down beside her bed, her never having thought to explain in the hospital. She was buttoned up to the throat in her flannel pajamas, the institutional blanket smoothed over her and the bed cranked up so she could read. We'd brought the stand-up wrought-iron lamp that had stood by her reading chair for as long as I could remember. "From the Brandenburg Concerto Number One," she said.

I said, "Dad always thought Johann would do you wrong."

She extracted her right hand from beneath the covers to slap me lightly on the wrist. "Your father and I had an understanding about me and Herr Bach."

I caught her hand before she could take it away and I held it. She turned her face away from me.

"Do I smell of piss?" she said.

"A little bit," I said.

"I'm in diapers," she said, her face coming back to me. "But they better not talk to me as if I were a child."

"I think they realize that," I said. "The nurse said she liked your spirit."

"They ain't seen nothin' yet," she said.

I squeezed her hand, gently.

She took it away.

The gentleness felt patronizing to her. She didn't say so. But she looked me hard in the eyes for a moment. Then she softened. "You got your drive from me, you know," she said.

Not from Dad. From her. She was right.

"I know," I said. "And I'm grateful." I didn't take up her hand again, though I had the urge.

She was fine. She was who she was when she first moved from the hospital to the nursing home.

She taught me to drive myself. I learned things elsewhere, as well. I just wish I'd been smarter about applying them.

The dementia was beginning by the next time I saw her, less than a week later. I didn't recognize it. In my first visit I'd hung a framed print on the wall beyond the foot of her bed. She wanted to see it always. Van Gogh's *Starry Night*. Bach's adagio spoke to what she always hoped for in herself but I doubt ever really found. The painting was what she lived with always. Even a quiet night of church spire and olive tree, of rooftops and mountains, of clouds and moon and stars: Even these were roiling, ever roiling, caught up in a ceaseless vortex of anxiety.

She nodded to the painting. "Your father went out there last night and he hasn't come back," she said.

I laughed softly.

"I don't care," she said. "He needs to walk more."

I took it all as an imaginative little riff on her disaffection with my father, a common theme ever since he'd died in hospice care in their assisted-living apartment shortly after their sixty-fifth anniversary.

But in fact she meant it literally.

As this thing in her brain began to spin more rapidly, she would often begin our visit by pointing him out to me. There he was, beside the olive tree. Or on the mountain slope. Or at the church door. I had to see him wandering out there before she would go on.

And then she'd swirl on to me. How I was about to ruin her life and mine by letting myself go off to war.

She was convinced; she was unremitting; I could never figure out how simply to stay quiet or deflect her. It would follow much the same script each time.

She says, "Please don't go."

I say, "It's all over. I'm back."

"We should leave the Vietnamese alone," she says.

"That all ended decades ago."

"You can still run away."

"There's no need anymore," I say.

"You can go to Canada. Your father and I can visit you."

"Ma," I say, using the softest name for her but the sharpest tone she'll tolerate. "The Vietnam War is over. I'm back and I'm safe."

"Don't leave me," she says. "I can't bear it."

"I'm here."

"A year would feel like a lifetime," she says.

"Ma," I say.

"You'll die over there," she says. "You'll die alone."

And sometimes she got stuck on the part about *her* being left alone. At least that would shift her sense of time back to the present, but the big problem with her being left alone in the nursing home was that there was so much for her to do in the middle of the night. The nurses needed her help and she tried and tried but she didn't know how.

I heard this last theme for weeks before it made sense.

How stupid I'd become.

I was an intelligence lieutenant in Vietnam. For the first few months I ran a little all-purpose shop out of Plantation, about thirty klicks up Highway 1 from Saigon. When we interrogated suspects I always had my boys play it by the book. But it was 1971. Units were standing down. Five months into my tour, our unit went home and I got reassigned up-country into I Corps. The First Cav had just stood down up there and everyone was very nervous, butt to butt, as they were, with the North. I ended up working under a captain who had long ago stopped playing it by the book.

We were in a field office within smelling distance of the Gulf of Tonkin and the thing that finally came back to me in the nursing home was a night during that summer of '71. A young Charlie in black pj's was caught with wire cutters and a couple of grenades on our perimeter. They took him to be a sapper. He might have been an unfriendly, but from how easy they grabbed him and from his measly arsenal, he was no proper sapper.

It didn't make any difference in those days. He was locked in the back, in our interrogation room, which was bare except for a cot and a piss pot and a chair, and I pulled the midnight-to-dawn shift, sitting at the captain's desk in the front of the shop, reading cast-off paperbacks and sending in an MI sergeant to wake our Charlie every hour. Just wake him up thoroughly. This went on around the clock. It was as simple as that, the method. Never let him finish a dream. You had to grill him good in the first twenty-four hours because by the second day he was utterly disoriented and by the third day he was hallucinating pretty much all the time. As it was, we never got three coherent sentences in a row out of this guy, much less useful intelligence. But the captain sure was one hell of a tough-guy interrogator.

So one afternoon near the end of the third month of my mother's failing mind, she was explaining to me how she really needed some help in the middle of the upcoming night, either from me or my dad—hadn't she always been there for us when we needed her?—because she was going to have to do the work of ten nurses and they didn't even give her a sponge and a bucket. And abruptly I knew.

I went out of the room and down to the nurses' station and I asked what the procedure was in the night. What did they do to take care of her?

She was the peroxided, ready-to-retire head nurse with a serious groove between her eyebrows that instantly furrowed deeper. "Is something wrong?" she said.

I remembered enough about interrogation from forty years ago to hear that tone of voice and let *her* tell *me* what was wrong. "What do you think?" I said.

"She was clear last night," she said.

"Are you sure?"

"Diaper rash can come on quick," she said. "We love your mother. We're vigilant, I assure you."

I nodded. Diaper rash. I could well imagine. For the state inspections of nursing homes, this must be an obvious objective measure. And I bet the lawyers of litiginous family members love a slide show of diaper rash for the judge.

"And what do you do to prevent it?" I said.

The head nurse straightened in her chair and relaxed her brow and announced, "We check her diaper every two hours, day and night."

"Day and night," I said.

"Yes, sir," she said.

"You go in every two hours through the night and wake her to check her diaper."

"She goes right back to sleep."

Stan, who doesn't do nursing-home rounds but took my mother on as a favor to me, was appalled at the procedure and leaned on the home management to put her on a bedtime-and-rising diaper routine. She lasted another three months and not once got the rash, but her mind was so fucked over by then, she never recovered.

I awoke thinking it was something in the room. Then it was something outside. Some sound. But there was only silence. I knew at once where I was. No confusion. No flashbacks. The hotel sat on Brickell Key and my balcony looked across a river-sized slice of Biscayne Bay at the south downtown Miami skyline. Nothing out there would make a sound at this hour.

I sat up, pulled the covers back, put my feet on the floor. Where was I going? Nowhere. Just to a sitting position with my feet on the floor. Back to Atlanta in a few hours. I'd been gone barely thirty-six.

The last time I saw my mother alive she was sleeping hard at noon, even though I was beside her. Not a coma. She'd wake up. But only enough to turn her eyes to me. She'd stopped talking.

The last time she spoke to me, two days before, she lifted her hand for mine as I was about to go back to the office and she held on tight and she said, "Kenny."

And my name struck me as if for the first time. As if she'd only just then named me.

She said no more.

She let go.

I went out.

But sitting on the side of the bed in the hotel room in Miami, I knew what she wanted to say next. Don't go.

61

Up the Hill
Miranda Mellis

1.

I HAD READ THE STORY again to the child, who lay expressionless like a rag doll in the small bed. The three dogs circled. They growled up the hill but I saw nothing. I tried to ignore them but they made so much noise I couldn't fall asleep next to the child as I sometimes did, so I left to go down the hill to my own sleeping area. But halfway down, one of the dogs ran after me and, jumping up, he took my sleeve between his teeth as if to drag me back. Was he trying to warn me about something? Was there something down there, where I usually slept, that would endanger me? It was hard to see through the dusky gray half night of the always-lit city. There was a noise repeating; a flat, echoing sound like an enormous lid closing, or reverberating blows and shots from above. I turned on my phone, worried that something really *had* happened. But there were no messages and no one called. I watched the phone expectantly and then tried to go to sleep with the child, as the dog would not allow me down the hill. But I couldn't get back to sleep for the sense of warning and danger, never letting me sleep or perform any other task.

2.

Before I had commenced reading to the child, the several older daughters had come down on their way to a bright house overlooking the sea, where they planned to vacation. They took the healthy children and the little baby with them, and left the rag-doll child for me. I read to her, as always, but those dogs were so restless and impossible, pacing around and staring down the hill. If there was something there, why didn't they go get it? And why wouldn't they let me go down to my mat either? The one who dragged me back up before, I thought at first had forgotten who I was, that he had grown suddenly senile and mistaken me for someone he couldn't accept. But when I felt his gentle though intractable jaws around my neck as I lay reading to the child, it occurred to me that he meant me no harm. On the contrary, he was protecting me. I longed for the return of the sun even as I dreaded the weariness I would feel then.

3.

The following night I slept on my own mat at last and then I re- turned up the hillside. The child played quietly on her swollen little mattress in the grass. The dogs slept around her. The hillside was scrubby, patches of dirt here and there, and the house up the hill showed its true skeletal paucity under the light of the sun: burned out long ago, abandoned. Down the hill I saw my own mat, looking slept in, sprawling messily sideways, the blankets mussed up, though I thought for sure I'd left it neat. Accusing myself of forgetfulness, I went down, straightened out my mat again, neatened up the blankets, and then went back up. One of the dogs awoke during these plain ministrations and happily trotted over, licking my hand and wagging his tail. Suddenly he ran down the hill. My eyes followed him and with a little shock I made out a figure standing over my sleeping mat, looking down on it, kicking the blankets with his foot. I looked back at the dog but he had closed his eyes. His snout reposed on his crossed wrists. The child was staring down at the figure as well. I decided it would be best to go down and see who this person was, mussing up my bed. Perhaps this was what the dog had been warn- ing me of the night before, though at the moment the canine showed no concern.

As I made my way down the hill, the figure turned to leave; I could see in his movements the haste of fear. I called out softly and would have run if he had. He turned to look, though, and paused willingly. But the farther down I went, the farther he appeared to be until it seemed like time alone would never shorten the gap between us, when suddenly we stood face-to-face. Whoever he was, he had a wor- ried face, an uneasy half smile, as if hiding something. The whole thing seemed to bode badly. But then his aspect changed: The sun- light caught in his hair, the tight muscles around his mouth and eyes smoothed out. That was when I realized he was also only trying to overcome some difficulty. He had been looking for a lost cat in my blankets but had not found her. He nodded as if we understood one another and went on his way.

I heard the dogs barking. Not wishing to linger with this comrade in any case, I made my way back up the hillside to the child on whose behalf the dogs and I were there, after all, and who had a right to her story.

Halfway up, one of the dogs ran toward me as if to escort me the rest of the way. There was that noise repeating, large, and regular like a planetary clock, or reverberating blows, or shots from above. I sat down, read the child to sleep, watched the phone expectantly, and then thought I'd go to sleep but I already was asleep.

After I woke up I went to the drugstore and a cashier said, "Pretty windy?" "Yes," I said, "a bitter wind." "*Well*," he replied, "not if you're flying a kite." I was very surprised to hear him say that. No one flies kites here!

Back up the hill the dogs were again restless and impossible, pacing around and staring up at the grass around the burned-out house on the hill. In fact the windblown grass, flattened and undulating, resembled the fur of a dog. But if there was something up there, why didn't the dogs go after it?

I looked up and there was the man again, searching around, presumably for his cat. I called out and he turned as if startled. Recognizing me, he gave a half wave and continued with his searching. "If there is a cat around here, the dogs will know," I called. But the man shook his head and cupped his ear in the universal pantomime *Can't hear you.*

4.

My replacement's overdue; it's time I got back to my own life. No-body's called in a long time, and that's worrisome. I can't leave before my replacement arrives, though; of course I can't leave the mite alone on this hill. The dogs protect her but they can't read to her, can they? They can't feed her, can they? My replacement is already overdue, and it is hard to know how to be patient, when all I can think about is getting back home. The child notices because I read distractedly now, looking up all the time to see if my replacement's arrived yet, or if somebody's called, or I rush through things and I don't pay atten-tion to the details and the timbres, the right way to perform the story, to inhabit the stories' various characters. For instance, you are always supposed to use a booming voice for the part of thunder, which will then make the child sit up wide-eyed, but, being dis-tracted as I am due to my ever-more tardy replacement, I mistakenly read that part in my regular voice and the child put her hand on the book to stop me going any further, such a violation it was. Indeed, the more distracted I am from my duties, from the child—which I naturally am distracted from because I am not even supposed to be here anymore—the more undistracted the child is from *me*. She never used to pay much attention to me. Now that I am counting the seconds before I am relieved, she keeps her eyes glued to me at all times.

5.

When it comes down to it, this child is not my problem. The dogs will watch over her and protect her, and my replacement will surely come, but I have a life of my own, don't I? *And I have a right to a life of my own*, don't I? I never signed away my life when I con-tracted for this job; I am a temp and that stands for temporary. I am being taken advantage of as well; my pay stopped the day my replace-ment was supposed to arrive. I am being disrespected here, and I am not going to take it much longer.

Miranda Mellis

6.

I need to leave this place and go back to my own life. The question is, do I take her with me? I don't think people back home would appreciate *that*! As it is I've been gone far longer than I said I would be, and I'll be coming home with a lot less money than I originally thought since I am living on my savings while we wait for my replacement.

I do not bother to read to the child anymore, who is more listless with each passing day. The dogs don't scamper around the way they used to; they surround her protectively and even snarl at me occasionally.

I saw the man looking for his cat again the other day. I ran down the hill to try to speak with him. In the back of my mind, I wondered if he would replace me. But when he saw me coming (I must have *radiated* desperation), he ran as fast as a cheetah.

7.

Today I am leaving: I can no longer put my life on hold. The child takes no notice of me and seems to spend most of her time curled up in a ball with the dogs all around her. If the reader's duties are that important to her survival, I don't know why they didn't do more to make sure my replacement would arrive.

It is possible that she is dead.

8.

As I was leaving, my replacement arrived! It's Murphy's Law: I should have packed up a long time ago. My replacement has shiny red hair down to her knees and a basket of apples. She is full of energy; why not? It's only her first day. I had nothing pleasant to say to her so I chose not to say anything at all. I pointed to the book and the child and she rushed, all concerned, to get to work.

I walked downhill to gather all of my things. When I looked back, the child was sitting up, listening to the reader, vaguely talking to herself, while the dogs patrolled the area a little wildly as they used to do, acting as though the abandoned house up the hill was haunted, unnerving the reader just as they had unnerved me, just as if it didn't matter at all who did the reading.

Pach'
Robert Coover

ON A SLIGHT RISE ON THE WAY into what he knew when a boy as the Presbyterian No-Name Wilderness church camp, within view of the artificial bump of land their little movement grandly called the "Mount of Redemption," Pach' Palmers stops to take a leak beside the panel truck that is his present home. It's his first time to see that goddamned mine hill since the day he got arrested on it five years ago. When he came back to West Condon after his release a couple of years ago, looking in vain for Elaine, he was able to pick up the old *Chronicle* van, and once he got it running, he headed out here to the Mount, but he turned back at the edge of town. He was starting up a new life, it seemed like bad karma, as Sissy would say. What a crazy time, what a crazy day. Life does throw up some fucking doozies. That one cost him a stretch in the slammer. Pach' lifts his cock and aims his stream toward the Mount, wishing he could piss away that awful day, the worst day of his life.

What was he really thinking that day? Did he think the end of the world was coming? That Jesus was going to come flying down out of the storm, superhero cape flapping, and whisk them all off to paradise? He was so hot for Elaine's body, he didn't know what he was thinking. He was holding on to her hand, hoping to find someplace they could at least kiss, last chance and all that, but they were on a barren hillside with one sick, rickety tree, surrounded by freaked-out Jesus worshippers, the whole world watching, and nowhere to go. And anyway there was no budging her. Elaine was completely lost to the moment and stubbornly stood there in the rain, her tunic pasted to her skinny body, rain and tears streaming down her face, looking out on the crowds or else up into the sky. Down at the foot of the hill, those they called the powers of darkness were massing up, including all the reporters and photographers and state cops, and overhead: the mind-rattling yak yak yak of police helicopters. All their own people, showing off all they had in their wet, flimsy tunics, were praying, singing, crying, and flinging themselves about in holy fits, their tunics turning black and brown in the mud. It was pretty arousing. He had

68

a massive hard-on impossible to hide under his soaked tunic, which not even fear of the impending apocalypse could shrink. He was able to bend his underwear elastic band down over the head, and belt it in somewhat with the rope they all wore at the waist, but it kept slipping and when it did it stuck out a mile. He thought: Well, Jesus, here I am, take me, sins and all. Then the town newspaper editor showed up. Mr. Miller. The guy who'd pretended to be a friend and fellow believer, but who'd turned on them like Judas. Exposed them. Made them look like dumb-ass jerks. Everybody said he was why Bruno's sister went crazy, why in the end she'd died. So he was a killer, too. They were all charging down on him. The Antichrist. Or anyway the Antichrist of the moment. He let go of Elaine's hand and joined them. It was like something he had to do. He remembered pummeling the guy there in the pouring rain, hitting him over and over, wishing he could kill him, the girl's corpse somehow bouncing around in the middle of it all, pointing her blue finger at everybody. The guy's clothes got torn off and in the end Pach' was pounding a lifeless, naked body dressed in mud and blood. People were jumping on it. Somebody had an ax. Pach' thought they *had* killed him. Only sometime later did he learn the poor sonuvabitch had somehow survived. Elaine's mother had had something to do with it. He was grateful for that. He was sorry about what he'd done. Doubly sorry, because when he went looking for Elaine again, he found Junior Baxter whipping her with a switch, and he piled into the spongy tub of shit, second time that spring, throwing him into the mud and punching him with both fists—only to have Elaine start clawing him and scratching him and throwing her nearly naked body down on Junior to shield him and screaming at Carl Dean to go away, go away, and with that, he lost it. He turned and pitched himself like a howling maniac at the advancing state troopers, taking down a couple of them before they all piled onto him. He was sent up to detention for six months for that, though he doesn't remember anything after seeing Elaine's little body on top of fat Junior with blood all over his stupid face.

All that happened five years ago last Sunday. The nineteenth of April. He might have made it here for the anniversary had it not been for a leaky radiator. Just as well not. They were probably all over on that hill again and he would only have repeated the whole mess or made it worse. So long ago. Seems like a different lifetime—fuck, it *was* a different lifetime. Pach'—he wasn't called Pach' then—was an ignorant young dickhead with a susceptibility for big total answers. He was president of the Baptist Youth Group and full of furious opinions (how easy it was to speak of God and Jesus then, they were like pals on the track team, he was elbow to elbow with them, slapping butts) when his high-school reading and writing teacher Mrs. Norton drew him and his friend Colin into her goofball Seventh Aspect fantasies, and then, after the coal-mine disaster, they followed her when she got mixed up with the lone survivor, Giovanni Bruno, a weird lunatic like all so-called prophets, one thing following another with a kind of mad, irresistible logic. Religion's appeal, no matter how nutty, to the down and out. He knows all about that, having been there all his life. The need for divine intervention to serve up just desserts, give the loveless something to love, cure the incurable, take revenge upon the wicked. Focused God-sanctioned hatred. Oh yes, he felt all that, sometimes still does. He has an explosive nature, he knows that. He has learned to keep things in check, but as a kid he was just so damned angry all the time. He might have killed somebody, and often wanted to. It was what made him let go of Elaine's hand. He let go of everything when he let go of that hand. Everything. A complete fucking idiot. He hated Miller at the time. Now he thinks of him as pretty much the smartest guy he ever knew. Sure dumb of him to turn up out there, though, after all he'd done. Must have been Bruno's sister who dragged him out. It was her body he was trying to reach when he got set upon. Pach' can understand that. Same with Elaine now. Why he's here. Except Elaine's still kicking.

Trying to track Elaine Collins down is mostly what he's done ever since they uncaged him. The six months' rap became a year for mouthing off and throwing his food on the floor and getting into fights with the other punks in detention, and they gave him another five in the state pen after he blew up and punched a sado guard. Laid the sick asshole out cold, sorry only he hadn't broken his neck. They might not have let him go anyway. His fucked-up parents had split and left the cheap development at the edge of town and he had no idea where they were, nor wanted to know, so as a juvenile there was no one he could be sent home to. No other relatives wanted him, he was too ugly. After a row or two in the pen, he settled down into his old camp-counselor ways and they finally let him go after a couple of years. He was supposed to keep in touch with a parole officer, but he never did. He boarded a bus and came back here. He couldn't have afforded the train, were it still running, but it wasn't. The closing of the coal mines had also meant the closing of the rail links. West Condon itself was like it had always been, only more run-down, needing a fresh coat of paint. His old home town. Shitsville. He wasn't shopping, he was looking for Elaine, but she and her mother had left town along with most everyone else he knew, and, except for vague rumors of Brunist doings around the country, there was not much local news about them, so what he got out of the trip instead was his panel truck. He had wanted to apologize to Miller, tell him he was fucking right, they *were* all dumb-ass jerks, right on, man; but the *Chronicle* was closed, Miller had flown the coop, nothing left on the newspaper premises but a print shop run by an old schoolteacher and track coach he once had, who said Miller was working for network TV, something Pach' never saw except sometimes in bars. Where no one was looking at the news. The paper's rural delivery van sat out in the parking lot, its tires flat, battery dead, lights busted out, muffler falling off, hoses and fan belt shot, no shocks at all, but the body was not too rust eaten and the engine looked repairable. The coach let him have it for a token dollar. A tall, sour ex–coal miner named Lem Filbert had a garage at the edge of town and he hired himself out to him in exchange for a tow, some used parts, a set of retreads, a meal a day, and Lem's mechanical know-how, serving as night watchman on the side for he was already sleeping in the thing, Lem's widowed sister-in-law providing him some old bedding. A part-time nurse of some kind who had plucked eyebrows and was so religious she dressed like women in Bible pictures. She joined their group around Bruno at the end, but he didn't remember seeing her out on the hill that day. Maybe she didn't want to get her clothes wet. She was the one who told him Elaine's mother, Mrs. Collins, was now married to the singer Ben Wosznik and was doing missionary work somewhere over near the Carolinas, or else maybe Florida, and yes, far as she knew, her daughter was still with them, so when he had the van rolling again, he headed east. Lem worked hard and demanded hard work, but he was good to him in the end, filling his tank and stuffing a few bucks into his pocket Pach' knew he could not afford.

The Brunists, he discovered when chasing around after them, had gone big-time while he'd been locked up. They had churches all through that part of the country, radio and television programs, billboards and piles of pamphlet handouts, songs on the hillbilly stations, tent meetings said to draw thousands. Hundreds certainly: He saw them, looking for Elaine. The end of the world? Still on. Sometime. Soon. Patience, jackass, patience: that old church-camp skit. Back in West Condon, nobody had seemed to know much about any of this. So much happens in this country that no one ever hears about. Around here, on their home turf, except maybe for Lem's sister-in-law, the Brunists were a joke. They'd all made fools of themselves, dancing around half naked in the rain, waiting for a Rapture, as they called it, that never happened. It was embarrassing. They should have disappeared into jokes the next day, but instead they're a big religion. Hard to figure. Of course, Jesus Christ: same story. People are weird. Key apparently has been Elaine's mother. Old Lady Collins is a powerhouse and an organizational genius and a saint, everybody says so. He remembers her as a big, horsey lady, nearly six feet tall, with raw, red hands, dressed in print dresses and wide, white pumps. She had a way of belting out battle cries like some kind of general or football coach and was at the same time given to throwing herself around and bawling like a stuck pig and talking to her dead husband like he was in the same room with her. Pach' was always afraid of her and knew she didn't like him very much.

The search for Elaine was mostly fruitless, but he didn't work all that hard at it either, even obsessed as he was. Something in him kept holding him back. Afraid of what he might say or do maybe. Especially if she didn't want to see him, and why should she? So he took odd jobs, slinging hash, working on the roads, making deliveries, and wandered about, following their trail, but seemed to fall into a funk and back off whenever it looked like he might be getting close. Go to a country bar instead. Get sloshed. Man of constant sorrow. He hadn't forgotten Elaine's Day of Redemption betrayal, how could he after what it cost him, but his sweeter memories of her and his hopes of winning her back were what had gotten him through these bad years, so he has kept chasing her even while shying away, fantasizing some kind of future with her and whacking off to the memory of her little body, just as he'd done all through his prison days, just as he is doing now, standing at the edge of a gravel road under the warm April sun, his fist pumping.

He especially liked to think back on that night on the way home from the mine hill with a carload of chicken feathers when he kissed her and grabbed her leg and more besides—and she wasn't mad after. It was Easter Sunday, a week before the day when the world was supposed to end, though it felt more like the world was just beginning. Wasn't that the point of Easter? He has had a good feeling about that day ever since, in spite of the stupid Jesus story that goes with it. Colin Meredith was along that night, and they parked on a side street and, by agreement, Colin got out to take a walk. They were coming from a service on the Mount and dressed only in their Brunist tunics and white underwear, and the feel of her flesh through the thin tunic is what he remembers, first her shoulder and armpit (the knotty edge of her little bra), then her leg, then her whole body as he pulled her hard against him, grabbing her tight little bottom through the tunic and cotton panties, her tummy against his, everything twisting and leaping and shivering, the gearshift somewhere in the middle of it all like an extra dick. He scared her, and he was scared too, as she began to bawl and get hysterical, and he backed off, apologizing, starting to cry himself and cursing himself for his rough ways. He kissed her cheek softly, whispering his sorries to her, and blinked the lights for Colin to come back, and then, later, as they were walking from the car toward Giovanni Bruno's house, he told her he loved her, really loved her, and she smiled a trembly little smile—there was a chicken feather in her hair like a pale flower petal—and his heart lifted. The next day at school, Elaine, tears running down her face, told him Junior Baxter had called her a whore, and he dragged Junior out of history class and thrashed him right there in the hallway in front of everyone and the principal threw him out of school, but Elaine took his hand and said if he had to go, then she was going too, and they walked out of there together, achingly in love, the only time he'd ever felt so loved or loved so hard in all his life.

Well, love. He doesn't know what it is, only what it isn't, and what it sometimes feels like. Back then, he was just trying to get into her pants, because he thought that was what guys were supposed to do. Now he knows that's the least important thing. Everyone and everything fucks. Can't help it, really. But love: That's the rare thing. The hard thing. And not God love, which is just a fake way of loving yourself. Human love. For someone else. Like he loves Elaine, without knowing what it is, or even needing to know. Only kind of redemption he knows now, all he can hope for. He pulls over again, gets out, stretches, combs his fingers through his beard, climbs back in, touches his "Elaine" tattoo through his T-shirt for luck, turns on the radio, tunes in the local country-music station. Why all these highfalutin thoughts? Because he is closing in on her once more and all the old anxieties are back. The urge to stop, turn around, and forget it. All along, he knows, it has been like the going was more important than getting there, with the where of the "there" being uncertain enough to give him an excuse always to change direction. Kidding himself. But not this time. For once he knows exactly where she is and knows she's staying put. He has seen the fresh new signs pointing the way: "International Brunist Headquarters and Wilderness

Robert Coover

Camp Meeting Ground." He either goes there now or throws his life
away again. "No Trespassing": that sign too. Well, forgive us our
trespasses, goddamn it to hell. He tosses his leather jacket in the
back, takes down the plastic naked woman touching her toes, dangling from his rearview mirror, and stows it in the glove compartment, starts up the truck again. Sniffs his armpits: fuck it, have to
do; pops some minty chewing gum in his mouth, which is mostly his
way of brushing his teeth. The song on the scratchy old car radio is
a religious one, sung by a bunch of young people. Sounds like a live
recording not made in a studio. "Wings of a Dove." He thought he
heard the radio announcer, old Will Henry (that dumb rube still
there, some things never change), say something about the Brunists,
but he may not have heard right through the static.

It's Easter when Elaine is always most on his mind, and it was
Easter morning about a month ago (he would have blamed the coin-
cidence on God if he still believed in God; instead he attributed it to
luck and the way wanting something badly keeps you tuned in to the
world) that his trek back here began. He had picked up a job working
in the kitchen of a fancy eatery just off the Blue Ridge Parkway in
southern Virginia, the trail having gone cold somewhere east of the
Smokies, and at work on Easter morning he'd spun the dial looking
for some good music. Maybe something about heartbreak and rough
traveling, for he'd awakened feeling melancholic, adrift in an indifferent world, going nowhere. Nothing on the radio but fucking church
services, one after the other. It was that part of the country. He was
about to turn it off when he heard a congregation singing Ben Wosznik's old tune "The White Bird of Glory," the one that starts with the
mine disaster. It was a live broadcast coming from a Brunist church
in Lynchburg, and when the song was over, the preacher sent around
the collection plate, asking for contributions to what he called the
new Brunist Wilderness Camp and Headquarters, and giving their
local church address for mailed-in contributions. "We shall gather at
the Mount of Redemption to meet our dear Lord there face-to-face!"
he declared, quoting the lines of the song, and apparently that was
exactly what they meant to do. On the nineteenth of April. Buses
were being chartered. Pach' took off his apron and quit his job on the
spot, thoroughly pissing off his employers, who were gearing up for
their annual Easter buffet brunch, and headed to Lynchburg, that
radio station tuned in the whole way, intent on getting there before
the service was over so he could talk to the preacher. In spite of having to ask directions five or six times from people in their Sunday

74

best, offended by him and his ratty vehicle, he made it in time to see a handful of fresh converts in Brunist tunics getting baptized by light, and was able to corner the preacher after, but it wasn't easy to get anything out of him. He was one of those smug, greasy fucks with peroxide-blond hair and a smarmy style, and Pach' couldn't hide his loathing of him. His own beardy, unkempt appearance also put the preacher off, he could tell by the way the man's eyes narrowed when he took Pach' in, probably didn't even smell all that good. It might have speeded things up to let it out that he was one of those twelve First Followers the preacher had blathered about in his sermon, but it would have taken too long to explain and he didn't want to risk having Elaine alerted. Luckily, he had a few bucks in his pocket, so he took them out and said he'd heard what the preacher had said about the Brunist camp and he wanted to contribute to it, and that softened Blondie up enough to get what he wanted out of him. He'd have made it here sooner, but he had to earn gas money along the way and he had a lot of breakdowns. And, well, maybe, also, sure, the usual cold feet.

Not cured yet. At the turnoff into the camp, he nearly drives right on by. As if distracted. Thinking about tomorrow. Feeling hungry. Needing to clean up first. Wash the van. Whatever. But he brakes (some tents over there in a field, beat-up cars, a camper or two) and makes the turn. The gravel access road dips down slightly into a green, leafy space, fresh smelling. The camp is located in a wet bottomland fed by the No-Name Creek that gave the camp its original name. They sometimes had problems in wet summers. The Baptists rented this campground from the Presbyterians each summer for four weeks in August, and he was always a regular, rising eventually to camp counselor by the time he was a high-school junior. The best four weeks he had each year. He was somebody then. Ugliness was good. It was strong and knew the ropes. He was good with the younger kids, took them on hikes, showed them how to do things. He could probably still walk the whole camp blindfolded. There are wildflowers along the side of the road, patches of daffodils, bluebells deeper in. It's a rich, beautiful day, one of those days that makes you feel like you're going to live forever. A T-shirt day. He has rarely seen the camp this time of year, though they used to hold the Easter sunrise services out here on Inspiration Point when all the churches joined in, and he turned up at a few, mainly to check out the girls of the other denominations.

He is stopped at the gate by some burly guy with a gun. Didn't have those in his day. Didn't have those barbed-wire fences with the "Keep Out" signs either. All along, he's been afraid of being rejected. Or maybe hoped to be. Now here it comes. In bib overalls, plaid shirt, and muddy boots. The guy wants to know his business and he knows he should say he is a believer and has made a kind of pilgrimage here, but he can't get it out. Feels too phony. Instead, figuring Ben Wosznik would probably be the most friendly, he asks for him.

"Yeah? Who should I say . . . ?"

"Tell him the name's Palmers."

"Palmers? Hey. Not Carl Dean Palmers?"

"That's right."

"I'll be durned!" The guy rests his shotgun on its stock and a grin breaks across his weathered face. "Well, praise God, brother, welcome home. We been praying for you. This is some surprise. C'mon, I'll take you to Ben."

He leaves the van by the gate, follows overalls into the camp on foot. There are other changes. Telephone poles and electric street lamps. Phone box in front of the old stone lodge. Which looks spiffed up. The weeds have been beaten back. There's a flower garden or two, bird feeders. The cedar cabins are under various stages of reconstruction. Some are missing, including the one he used to stay in as a camp counselor. Just the little cement support blocks left standing like miniature tombstones. Crowds of people milling about, busy with one thing or another. Lots of kids running around. Almost like a small town. They stare at him curiously, and his guide shouts out who he is and some smile and wave or come over to shake his hand, others frown or look confused or mutter amongst themselves. No one familiar, though five years is a long time, people change; he has. Elaine? He'd know her, no matter what, but no one like her in sight. Ben is working with a crew on one of the cabins. At first Ben doesn't recognize him (Ben's changed too: thick, gray beard now, fulltime spectacles, more of an old man's shape), and then he does, and he gives him a warm, firm handshake. "Mighty glad to see you, Carl Dean. We thought you was still in the penitentiary."

"Been out for awhile. Heard you were back here and decided to stop by, say hello."

"Well, I'm glad you did, son. Can you stay?"

"Got no special plans for right now. Could you use a hand there?"

"You bet. First, lemme take you to Clara."

Pach' finds himself, while walking alongside Ben toward the lodge, feeling like a kid again. Almost like he ought to take Ben's hand.

Something about the old man. A kind of inner power. Certainty. Good guy to have at your side when trouble strikes. Serve time with. He can call you "son" and you don't feel offended. The sort of dad, in fact, he wishes he'd had.

The old lodge and dining hall has been done up on the inside too. Still smells of fresh varnish. Used to have dangling yellow bulbs powered by a generator at the back; now it has proper lighting, but also gas lanterns hanging from the beams. There's a new coal stove at the back where some cots are stacked, piles of bedding. What most catches the eye, though, is a blown-up photograph hanging by the fireplace. It's of Giovanni Bruno himself, standing out on the Mount in the rain, holding a mine pick like a mean cross, doing his ancient-prophet act. Gives Pach' a chill. Next to it is Ely Collins's framed death note, the one that started it all. The trigger. Rocketed Pach' straight into the fucking pen. Pach' used to build the log fires in that big fireplace for their Baptist camp-revival meetings, set out the folding chairs and put them back, clean up in the kitchen. Which, he can see at a glance, has also been modernized. Women are working in there. Large folding tables are being laid out for a meal. Ben explains that it's a luncheon for the workers and Pach' is invited to join them. Pach' tucks his ball cap in his back pocket, combs his fingers through his tangled hair.

Elaine's mother seems less happy to see him. "We thought you was still in prison in solitary confinement, Carl Dean." They are standing in a room off the main hall that has been fitted out with filing cabinets, desk, chairs, wire baskets full of paper, a lot of equipment, even a patterned red carpet. There are two young guys in there helping out. They seem excited he's turned up. "It's what Colin said."

"Colin likes to make things up, Mrs. Collins. I've been out for over two years."

"Do tell." Clara Collins seems hardly to have changed at all. A little bonier maybe, hair shorter and grayer, more businesslike. Pants and sneakers instead of dress and heels. She casts a searching gaze over him, peering over her spectacles at his rags, his beard, his thinning but unruly hair. "Are you still a Christian, Carl Dean?"

"Well, I don't know what else to call myself, ma'am. But I don't have the same feeling anymore. It's one reason I came back here."

"What other reasons did you have?"

He knows he is turning red. He's afraid if he opens his mouth, he'll just stammer something stupid. Finally, he says, "I wanted to see everybody again. I was lonely."

That softens her up enough to bring a faint smile to her face and she pushes her glasses up on her nose and says, "Looks like you could use a good cleanup."

"Yes, ma'am."

"I'm afraid we don't have room here at the camp to put you up."

"That's OK. I sleep in my panel truck."

"He's just passing through," Ben says. Maybe he also winks. "I figgered he could park down at the ball field with us for a week or so while he thinks about staying on. Remember the parable of the hunderd sheep, Clara. It's a honor to have the boy back with us."

Mrs. Collins hesitates. Pach' can read her mind: That's too close to Elaine. But she sighs and nods. "Meanwhile, Darren and Billy Don here can show him about. . . ."

Later, Pach' is alone up on Inspiration Point, having managed to ditch Clara's two helpers. Needed some thinking time on his own, he said, and they seemed to appreciate that, being heavy thinkers themselves. Bible-school dropouts named Darren Rector and Billy Don-something. Or maybe they were thrown out; their story is ambiguous. They want to interview him for the Brunist church history they're assembling, a history they seem to think is going to unravel the mysteries of the universe. Something he hopes to avoid, he'd have to tell them what he really thinks and blow what little cover he has, but it seems important to them, so he said maybe, after he's been here a little while. This is his one shot at Elaine and he doesn't want to ruin it with his big mouth, but if he can get her to leave with him, maybe he'll let Darren and Billy Don have it just before they take off.

The first thing they did was move his panel truck down to the trailer parking lot. The old softball field. He was sorry to see it being used like that, but didn't say so. He asked who else was parked there, learned a few new names. Mobile homes with coming-of-light bumper stickers. When he remarked on the size of Mrs. Collins's house trailer, they said that was because while they were on the road it was also the church office. He wondered if Elaine was in it, but tried not to stare at it. Does she know he is here? Probably. Scuttlebutt gets around quickly in shut-up places like this. A lot like a prison, he has been thinking since he was led in through that barbedwire fence. Maybe she's hiding from him. Well, he can wait. He learned from the two boys that she and Junior Baxter still have something

going, though they have only just got together again for the first time
this past week when the whole Baxter clan turned up for the anniversary celebrations over on the mine hill. Elaine is a very private person, they said. She and Young Abner, as he's called now, are often
seen together, but they never hold hands or even talk to each other.
It's more like a religious thing. One of the Baxter girls was pointed
out to him as they passed the cabin. Cute. She was staring at him
and, when he glanced back a couple of minutes later, beginning the
climb up here, he saw she was still staring at him.

On the walk up, the boys filled him in on the years of the Perse-
cution, the international following they now have, Mrs. Collins's
plans for a tabernacle temple to be built on the Mount of Redemption. There was a lot of money being spent here, much of it apparently coming from a local rich guy named Suggs. But they were able
to acquire the camp in the first place, they said, thanks to the
Presbyterian minister's wife, Mrs. Edwards, who arranged for the sale
and then joined their church. This was unexpected news. Reverend
Edwards was the guy who helped kidnap his friend Colin Meredith
and keep him away from the Mount on the Day of Redemption.
Pach' remembers him as a klutz in a porkpie. With a nervous smirk.
All day on the hill, Pach' kept worrying that Colin would miss the
Rapture. He learned later that Colin tried to kill himself in their
house. "Mrs. Edwards is one of our most important converts," the
boys said. "She's now the camp director." He remembers Mrs.
Edwards very well. Nature girl. Fantasy stuff. When he asked, they
told him she was probably working down at her vegetable garden
with Colin. So Colin's here too: also news. They offered to walk him
over there, but he told them he knew the way.

He remembers the Point as higher than this. Back in his days as a
camp counselor, it seemed to him that you could see the whole universe from up here, and then he felt like part of it, it part of him.
Now the universe makes him feel like a spot of bird shit. Far across
the way, he can see the Deepwater coal mine tipple and hoist, poking into the blue sky like a fairground ride, the water tower glinting
in the sun. Also the Mount of Redemption, off to one side of it. He
doesn't recall ever seeing that hill from up here but it must have been
there. Goes to show that you see only what you're ready to see. Or
want to see. It's the trouble with religious people. They see everything through a peculiar lens and can't see anything past it, even if
you point it out to them. Only way is to break the lens. He once tried
to kiss a girl up here when he was about ten, but she didn't like it

and didn't kiss him back and told the camp counselor. Which ended his summer camp that year.

He hasn't had a lot of luck with kissing. Elaine was always more a hugger than a kisser, being self-conscious about her bad teeth. But she's a good hugger. Probably the best hug he ever got was over there on the mine road at the foot of the hill the night before the supposed end of the world, the night Marcella Bruno was killed. He'd got turned on watching people in front of the bonfires they'd built to sing and pray around, the way their bodies were silhouetted inside the thin, fluttery tunics when they passed in front of the flames. He was jealous of Elaine and hated it when she walked in front of the fires so others could see, but it excited him too. Of course, those were sinful thoughts, and on the very eve of what might well be the Last Judgment, so he tried not to look, but he couldn't stop himself. Not until Elaine's mother stood in front of the flames and he found himself staring at something he knew he shouldn't see. He turned away, feeling hot and confused, as if his acne were erupting all over his body. Then the lights on the mine road, the rush to the cars, the awful thing that happened. He stood at the lip of the ditch, hugging Elaine, watching that poor girl die. Her smallness, her lips slightly parted, eyes closed, her fragile, broken, worried look. How many had hit her? Had he? Wrecked cars everywhere, lights pointed in all directions, some straight up into the sky as if trying to get someone's attention up there, his own car ditched somewhere behind him. Where it stayed until the county hauled it out weeks later and sent him a towing bill up in detention. Elaine was sobbing in his arms, her back to the ditch, and while he was staring down at Marcella over her shoulder, the girl's eyes suddenly opened and a red bubble ballooned out of her mouth, popped, dribbled down her chin. And that was it and his knees began to shake. Her brother stooped to kiss her lips and rose up with blood on his mouth, that's what he remembers, though his vision was pretty blurry, his head may have been playing tricks on him. Elaine wrapped her arms around him tight and held him close, close, dressed in almost nothing as they were, and whispered in his ear that she wanted to be in heaven with him forever. Brought tears to his eyes as he, chastely, except for the club pressed against her tummy, couldn't do anything about that, hugged her back. Forever turned out to be less than a day.

He turns his back on all that shitty history and takes the back route down to where he supposes Mrs. Edwards's vegetable garden to be, a trail somewhat overgrown, evidently not much used, in spite of the heavy traffic in the camp. When he was a kid, he saw his first rubber along this trail. Didn't know what it was and pointed it out to the wife of the Baptist preacher, who was taking them on a nature walk to witness God's bounty. Probably he had a stupid grin on his face because she slapped it. It's still a beautiful walk, maybe even more beautiful than it was then. Flowers, birds, trees, all kinds of sedges and grasses. Some of them pink now, this time of year. They all have names; he'll never learn them. Though, if he stays here, maybe he'll try. Mrs. Edwards had a thing for nature, as he recalls, birds especially, maybe she could teach him. He can work with her in the garden. She was a frequent visitor to the camp when the Baptists rented it. Came to see if they were taking proper care of it, he supposed, but always in a nice way. She was slim and pretty and dressed casually and he had fantasies about her, wishing for a mother like her, and sometimes he followed her around. One day, down in the wild place on the other side of the creek, she took her shirt off to sun her tits. He scrunched down in the weeds, stunned by the amazing sight, waiting and praying (yes, he was praying) for her to take the rest off. She never did, though over the years he saw other things. He used to wonder: What if he made himself known? Couldn't be done. She was from another world. It was like trying to step into a movie. There was only the watching.

The vegetable garden is amazing. A little farm. Mrs. Edwards is seeding a newly hoed patch when he arrives and introduces himself. She's older now, of course, has a baggier look and a double chin, is wearing glasses halfway down her nose, but there's still something fresh and girlish about her. She seems glad to see him, lights up with a cheerful smile. "Colin! Look who's here!" she calls out. Colin comes over from where he has been setting out stakes for tomato plants. Colin was always a bit odd looking, but now he's weirder than ever. Sickly pale and skinny, a wispy Chinaman's beard, buggy eyes and granny glasses, wearing a floppy, white sun hat and rose-colored shorts, his silvery-blond hair fluttering about his shoulders like a mad woman's. The way he moves reminds him of Sissy. Of course. Why hadn't he realized that before? Didn't understand any of this back then. A complete green-ass. "It's Carl Dean, Colin!" Colin stops dead in his tracks, his eyes popping, his face twisting up like he's about to have a fit. "*No! It isn't!*" he cries and then runs away, screaming wildly for help. Mrs. Edwards throws down her garden gloves and starts after him, turning back just for a moment to cast Pach' a dark scowl. "Who *are* you really?" she demands, then returns to the chase. Well. There went his gardening career.

81

*

His building career shows more promise. With a little help from Ben and the others, all strangers to him, Pach' has been able to step right in with the crew this afternoon and work beside them. The cabin they are working on, which used to house eight kids in bunk beds, is being remodeled for use as a two-bed sick bay plus a separate treatment room for burns and cuts and other minor emergencies. They are adding storm windows, electric radiators, and insulation, covering the drafty floor with some old hotel carpet, same stuff as in the lodge office, putting a partition up between the two beds in case of different sexes, and installing the camp's first flush toilet, plumbed to the new septic tank and cesspool, and even unskilled as he is, there's a lot Pach' can do. The cabin has already been wired up for electricity and Wayne Shawcross, the overalled guy who let him in here, is showing him how to put in wall plugs and overhead light fixtures, and Ben has also taken him on as a kind of apprentice carpenter. He's strong and that's appreciated too. He's enjoying it, more than any other work he's done since he got out, and in spite of the luncheon blowup, he can already feel the urge to want to stay and work with all these guys, whom he's quickly come to like, and get the job done. Be part of something bigger than himself. How much of religion, he wonders, is about this feeling?

At the luncheon earlier of baloney sandwiches and potato salad, they made a big fuss over him, treating him as a kind of returning hero. Given his intentions, it was embarrassing and he only wanted out of there. Clara made a welcoming introduction and led them in prayer, thanking God for his safe return, and then prayed for all the things they wanted. Darren Rector, reciting a little church history, praised him for his brave attack on the powers of darkness, which he said helped many others to escape arrest and carry on with their evangelical work (he didn't know that), and expressed everyone's sympathy for his suffering on behalf of them all. Which he compared to the ordeals of Daniel and Samson and Paul. Not at all how it was, of course. He supposed Rector was just buttering him up for the interview. Elaine wasn't there, still avoiding him evidently, but just as well, he was glad she didn't have to listen to all that horseshit. Mrs. Edwards wasn't there either, nor Colin. The word about what had happened in the garden had evidently gotten around; the hero worship was not unanimous. There were surly mutterings here and there, and Junior Baxter's glare was so fierce it would have cut through steel plate, his short-cropped red head looking like it was on fire from inner rage. He's younger than Pach' but he's already getting an old man's soft heaviness in the jowls and belly and he now wears a little red tuft on his upper lip. Which was pulled back in a snarl. On the other hand, his kid sister gave Pach' a sweet, lingering smile. Somewhat vague. It just sort of stayed on her face. Her food had to be cut for her. Not all there.

Then an old fart in a wheelchair rolled away from the Baxter table and in a loud voice wanted to know if he really was Carl Dean Palmers like he said he was. His friend had not only not recognized him, he'd screamed like he'd seen the devil, scaring the whole camp. They'd all seen pictures. He didn't look like the pictures. So who was he really? Ben said of course he was Carl Dean. They'd had a long conversation, talking about the last time they were together, couldn't be anyone else. "The devil is a great dissembler, Brother Ben! What I'm asking is can he prove it?" Pach' tossed his driver's license out on the table and the cripple said that didn't prove anything, and then everyone started shouting, accusing the geezer of spoiling Carl Dean's homecoming and trying to sow discord in the camp. On the one hand, Pach' agreed with the old fossil, he sure as hell wasn't Carl Dean Palmers anymore, hadn't been for a long time. On the other, if the sour, cantankerous sonuvabitch hadn't been in a wheelchair, he'd have popped him. He got up to leave, but Ben put a hand on his shoulder and reminded everyone of their Christian obligations to one another and then put his guitar around his neck and led them all in singing "Shall We Gather at the River?" After a moment, Abner Baxter stood up and joined in, and then so too, reluctantly, did the others at his table. All except the guy in the wheelchair, who spun it around, turning his crooked back on them.

Now, while Pach' works with Ben on the new sick bay, Baxter and his pals across the way are trying to hang a front door on their cabin and neither crew is talking much to the other. He doesn't think he's the cause. Deeper than that. People aren't getting along, just like before, and trouble is brewing. Ben sees him watching them with a frown on his face and says, "Let them be, Carl Dean. They ain't much good to us anyhow, so we at least get some work out of them for the time being. But that cabin has got other purposes. They ain't staying there."

Could he, he wonders? Stay here? Stay in this camp where he's always felt most at home, here with all these friends, more like family than his own family? Could he go all the way, put a tunic on again, win Elaine, help defend Ben and Mrs. Collins from the abominable Baxters and the local establishment, build something that will last? While he's asking himself that, Clara Collins comes rushing out of the lodge all excited with what is apparently big news: The mine owners have accepted their offer for the Mount of Redemption. Papers are being drawn up. There are whoops and cheers and Wayne throws his painter's cap in the air. Time to bring out the beers! But, no, not here. Mrs. Collins falls to her knees there in the wood chips and closes her eyes and lifts her hands and launches into her full-throated God howl and all the others drop to their knees too, and join in, praying to beat the band. An old coal miner from out east declares it's a miracle and that is noisily amenned. Nothing Pach' can do but follow suit, get down on his knees, take off his ball cap, and tuck his chin in, anything else would be an insult to these people, but he's feeling awkward as hell, a total hypocrite, the devilish reprobate they have taken him to be. Fuck. He could never do this.

When Pach' reaches the flowering dogwood tree a little before sundown for Saturday-evening prayers, she is already there. Standing beside her mother. Five years gone past, mostly thinking about her, and suddenly here she is. He'd thought, after so much buildup, he'd probably be disappointed, and he'd arrived, hands in pockets, talking to others, trying not to look her way, staying cool. That lasted about a minute. The sight of Elaine Collins again in her cotton tunic has liquefied his sinews. He knows his heart is doing that stupid pounding, romance thing but he can't do anything about it. She has grown up some. Taller now than he is. Gangly, but not like her big-boned mother. She's staring at him in a forthright way he has not seen before. He doesn't know what that stare means but it cheers him to see her there beside her mother, and not by Junior Baxter. He nods to her as though in recognition and, when she doesn't nod back, looks away.

"Looks like you brung us luck, Pach'," Wayne Shawcross says with a grin, passing by with his wife, Ludie Belle, and Pach' grins back, feeling a kind of twitch in his cheek (the grin's too wide, it's not something he does often), and says, "I can give it to others but I never keep none for myself." Ben and Clara still introduce him as Carl Dean, but he introduces himself to people as Pach', which is his name for his new life. "You mean like what you got there on the knees of your jeans?" Wayne asked this afternoon when told his name.

84

"No. Like Apache." "You part Injun?" "That's what they told me."
"I think my granmaw was probly half Choctaw, but she wouldn't
never admit it. It was like having nigger blood back then." He'd got
the new handle in prison. He'd lied and told them he had Indian
blood, partly just to set himself off from the others, partly to shuck
off the old life, be someone other than the self he'd come to hate.
And who knows, given his old lady's careless habits, maybe it was
true—didn't she like to claim when she was drunk that she'd got
pregnant with him off a toilet seat? He was the only virgin in the
men's prison, where rape was part of the new-boys break-in rituals,
and he meant to stay that way (didn't quite), but he had to fight for
it. Five guys, including a couple of trusties, grabbed him and ripped
his pants down, and the biggest of them said, "Bend over, Tonto, I'm
gonna stick it to your holy huntin' ground." He was able to tear himself free and laid into the lot of them, starting with the fat asshole
who called him Tonto, leaving him with less teeth in his mouth than
he had before, and he was still holding his own against all five, even
with his pants around his ankles, when the bulls finally showed up
and broke it up with chains and truncheons. Lost him any hope for
parole that year, but it earned him the nickname of the Crazy
Apache, which over time got shortened to Pach', which of course
most people hear as Patch. Whatever. Just so it's not Carl Dean. Or
Ugly.

She's still staring at him. He tries a smile this time. Same result.
He has showered and laundered his rags in the new camp laundry,
trimmed his beard, put on a T-shirt with only a couple of holes and
a denim vest, combed his hair. Ben dropped a Brunist tunic by for
him, but he decided not to wear it. There are others without tunics,
so apparently it's OK. Two of those are a country singer and his
woman who are introduced to him as famous singers from Nashville, though he hasn't heard of them. They're first on the program
because they have a gig after. At the bar in the old Blue Moon Motel
at the edge of town. Can't be too famous. But a place to escape to
maybe for a beer. What he misses most this time of day. They seem
cool, the guy anyway. The woman is mixed up with the fortune-
teller Mrs. Hall and her flock of gossipy widows, came to the prayer
meeting in their company. She's said to be in touch with the dead.

The days are lengthening and the sun is probably still shining on
Inspiration Point above them, but twilight has already settled on this
little grove down here in the valley behind the lodge, oddly making
the dogwood flowers seem to glow, and Elaine, standing under them,

seems to glow as well. How beautiful she is in this strange, pale light. Now he's the one staring and she's the one to look away. He can feel Junior Baxter's seething fury off to one side, but it means nothing to him. She's here and he's here, that's all that matters. On his way from lunch to the work site, Ben saw him craning about and said, "I spose you're looking for Elaine. She ain't feeling all that sociable today. Be careful, son. I think your coming here has give her a fright. She'll be at the prayer meeting tonight. You'll see her there." All afternoon he has been plotting out what he'd say to her when they finally met, how he loves her, needs her, or else how he just wants to be friends again, have someone to talk to, whatever seems most likely to work, but all that has vanished from his head, and he knows it will all happen without a word or it won't happen at all.

There is apparently something sacred about the little tree, which is why they are meeting here. The two country singers do a song about it. "All who see it will think of Me, / Nailed to a cross from a dogwood tree. . . ." They're pretty good, especially the guy. Duke something. The woman, Patti Jo, has a sweet voice, not very big. The easy, familiar singing mellows Pach' out (it was right to come here), and when they follow that with a singalong version of "In the Garden," he joins in. Old campfire standby. *And the joy we share as we tarry there* (he is watching Elaine; she is not singing, her head is down; she looks thin and fragile and he longs to gather her into his arms and take care of her), *none other has ever known. . . .*

"Now, my son, the Lord be with thee, and prosper thou, and build the house of the Lord thy God, as he hath said of thee." This is Wayne Shawcross reading from the Old Testament, somewhat laboriously, his finger tracing the lines in the dim light, about somebody building a church. Could be referring to building the camp, but, after the news today, it's the tabernacle idea that has them buzzing. "Moreover there are workmen with thee in abundance, hewers and workers of stone and timber, and all manner of cunning men for ever manner of work." Sure. Cunning. Count me in. Wayne plows on in his wooden monotone: "Arise therefore, and build ye the sanctuary of the Lord God, to bring the ark of the covenant of the Lord, and the holy vessels of God, into the house that is to be built to the name of the Lord." There are a lot of amens and praise Gods now, people are getting excited, even though they probably don't know what arks and vessels Wayne is talking about. Elaine's head is up, a kind of startled expression on her face, but she is not joining in. "The Lord hath chosen thee to build a house for the sanctuary: Be strong, *and do it!*"

As Wayne looks up from his reading, pocketing his spectacles, the amens raining down, Elaine's mother steps into the holy ruckus and in her sharp, clear voice starts to spell out what she calls the glad tidings about acquiring the Deepwater mining property and what that means to them. The two singers take it as a cue to lead everyone in singing "The Sons of Light Are Marching," the song they sang on the march out to the hill that terrible morning. Pach' led the parade, walking backward, bellowing at the top of his lungs so they could hear him all the way to the back. Hammering the ruts and gravel of the mine road with his bare feet as though to say good-bye to both road and feet. Must have hurt. Doesn't remember. Remembers Elaine marching right there at the front, watching him, almost desperately, singing with him in her timid little voice, the dead body they were carrying in the folded lawn chair rocking along above and behind her like a kind of canopy, helicopters rattling in the sky overhead, photographers and newsguys and the curious trailing along beside them, the whole mad procession watched by state troopers in black uniforms and white visored helmets. "O the sons of light are marching since the coming of the dawn! We shall look upon God's Glory after all the world is gone!" Their own battle hymn. "So come and march with us to Glory! For the end of time has come!"

When the song is over, Duke and his woman wave their good-byes. "Peace!" Duke says. Pach' wants to leave with them, needs a beer, relief from all this shit, but he can't, wouldn't look right, and he still has hopes of connecting with Elaine. Before Mrs. Collins can pick up where she left off, Abner Baxter unleashes a few Bible quotes of his own, like he's been threatening to do all along, quotes that seem to equate the temple idea with idol worship. That's how Pach' reads them anyway, and the look on Clara's face suggests it's how she reads them too. Elaine watches her mother with some alarm, her hand at her mouth, her shoulders hunched, while Baxter rails against pride and vanity and speaks up for the poor. "For the poor shall never cease outta the land, and therefore I command you, saying, saith the Lord, thou shalt open thine hand wide unto thy brother, to thy poor, and to thy needy, in thy land!" He is getting a lot of shouted amens and some people start clapping in rhythm to all his "thys." This probably has something to do with how their money is to be spent. It came up at lunch too. People who want a place to stay, not another church. Pach' can only watch. He's on the other side of the world from these people now. He only wishes he could go take Elaine's hand and lead her out of here.

*

Elaine puts her arms around him and hugs him close. She tells him tearfully how much she loves him, how she's missed him. Don't ever leave me again, Carl Dean. She calls him Carl Dean? Probably. Pach' doesn't seem right. She's such a tender, fragile person, she can't even imagine savage Indians. When he slides his hand down to hold her little bottom, she doesn't complain, she just presses closer to him and releases a little gasp, a kind of sob. He can feel her tummy pushing against him. "I love you, Elaine," he whispers, and she trembles and grips him tightly as the sweet night closes down around them. He tugs gently at her bottom to rub her tummy against his hard-on. He desperately wants her to take it in her mouth. But would she, could she? No, but Sissy does, lapping lovingly at it with his little puppy tongue. Pach' is somewhat alarmed by this, and he pauses to worry about it. He spent a lot of time and spunk jerking off in prison, but otherwise he stayed clean. Except for little Sissy, as they called him. Her. Sissy was more girl than guy and the men called him "she" and "her," and eventually Pach' did too, but never in ridicule. Sissy had a little dick and it got hard like a pencil stub when he was excited, but he was curvy and cuddly with innocent blue eyes and puckery lips and a snow-white bottom, soft and round as a little girl's. "Sissy" was for "Sister," both as in family and in nun: He liked to dress up like one, using prison blankets. Even the screws thought this was funny, and several of them were probably serviced by Sissy in that costume. He was in for drugs and as an accessory to murder, a murder committed by his boyfriend whom he then tried to hide. His boyfriend died in a drug-crazed shoot-out with the cops, and Sissy was taken in. And one sad and lonely night when Pach' could not stop thinking about Elaine, Sissy took him in his mouth and he let him do that. Sissy said he'd never seen one that big and it almost frightened him. Eventually he had Sissy in other ways too, but always while thinking about Elaine. And now, lying in the back of his van only yards away from her (he has been unable to take his gaze away from the lighted windows of their trailer, even though the blinds are pulled) and humping his pillow while fantasizing about her, it is Sissy who has taken *her* place. That's weird and he doesn't think he likes it. Sissy eventually got a tattoo of a little heart with a large Indian arrow through it and the words CRAZY APACHE—not over his heart, but on his little white left cheek, otherwise without a blemish. Sissy cried when Pach' left prison and Pach' felt bad too.

Poor little Sissy. Oh, what the hell. Out of affection, Pach' lets him finish up.

The first time he blew his wad it was like an accident and he didn't know what was happening. He thought he'd been visited by angels. His old lady, who was not otherwise very religious, had a thing about angels and other supernatural creatures and he was still pretty susceptible to all that. He sometimes thought he heard angels in his room, flying around like bats. Maybe they were bats. When he started getting serious about Christianity at the Baptist Church, it felt like growing up, and he looked down on his superstitious mother after that, though actually all he'd done was stop believing in Rudolph while sticking with Santa Claus. Then along came Mrs. Norton who introduced him to Santa's big daddy Domiron off in some other dimension, and made him feel like some kind of highbrow. He finally got rid of all that shit in prison. Reading the Bible helped. One of the few books you could have in stir. He decided to plow straight through it, beginning to end. He read first with a certain awe (this has been *the* book for twenty centuries!), then with increasing irritation (who wrote this stupid thing?), finally with disgust and anger. A total swindle. Blaming God for writing it is fucking sacrilegious. Got interested in troublemakers instead. Which was just about anybody who got anything done. Jesus, for example, the wild-ass bastard. Before checking out, he got a pep talk in his cell from the prison chaplain, who interrupted him while he was saying good-bye to Sissy, and he let the bastard have it. "Jesus was all right," he said, "but Christ sucks." When the chaplain left, shaking his head, Sissy started giggling and bawling hysterically at the same time and told him he was completely crazy. His Crazy Apache.

Should he open another beer? He shouldn't. Only half a six-pack left and no easy way to get more. Not much money for buying it even if he should break out of this place for a time, and as long as he helps out here with the building, no way to earn more. He has at least been well fed. Wayne Shawcross's wife, Ludie Belle, invited him to stop by their house trailer after the prayer meeting for something extra to eat. She's in charge of the camp kitchen, so has a well-stocked fridge. She probably keeps a bottle somewhere too, but he didn't want to ask. Not yet. Same with telling them about Elaine. They are good people and he wanted to talk with them straight out about his feelings—they'd seen what he did after the prayer meeting—and he even thought he might show them his tattoo, but when they asked him what he was doing here, he told them what he'd told Elaine's mother.

Which is also true. He *has* been lonely. And both of them seem like pretty serious believers, so he has to be careful.

The lights have gone out in the Collins trailer, which looms imperiously over him, aglow in the light of the full moon. In his imagination she sleeps in her Brunist tunic. The one she was wearing on Easter night all those years ago. When he thinks of her, that cotton fabric is what his fingers feel. Tonight, when the prayer meeting ended, he got up his nerve and walked over to her, his hands in his pockets, to say hello. It was an awkward moment with everyone watching and he knew his acne was flaring up. When he was actually in front of her, he couldn't think of what to say. He found it difficult to look into her eyes, but when he dropped his eyes, there was her body draped in the thin tunic, and that confused him all the more. Finally he just nodded and said, "Hi, it's me." She only stared at him as if he'd just threatened to kill her and, without saying a word, left immediately with her mother. Well, he thought, at least she didn't tell him to go away. It's only his first day. He can be patient. Meanwhile, he has opened another beer, it's Easter night, the moon's filling up the sky, and they're in his car again. She's trembling, but she has been through this before, and is ready now. "Stay the fuck out of this," he says to Sissy. "Go take a walk and don't come back until I blink the lights."

Six Poems
Justin Wymer

[AN ABSENCE NEEDS VERY FEW ATTENDANTS]

An absence needs very few attendants
and shatters into babel if attention cuts into it
because no one can outstare loss.
Yet constricting hands still blush.
Provided that you keep these nude disclosures of
sunlight folded in the hollows of your joints
if she touched me she touched me in choirless
swarms aware that at each vesper slushing past
the footbridge we are at stakes with ourselves.
And love is routine questioning. . . .
Preening were the wiry thistlings of clouds
yet surrounding us they crepitated
they were taproots the yellow kept wrenching out
of our skinsuits our holes as sure and frank
as a Madonna picking a golden hair out of
a scab in her baby's cheek. Injuries are
always complete. Likewise heady
our July evening had resembled a sweet rind—
so that when I closed the shutters
in the small of my back and huffed
a trapped mosquito's simmering green disinterest
so that I could mend, she knew enough
about steam to resemble stagnant water.
This revealed in the light lines of
a dime-colored script scribbled above her lip.
I can honestly say I know what it feels like
to have lain claim to but smothered a seraph
that lay crouching inside me before it leapt out into
a shining coil of syllables. And that affection must be
synthesized. It needs only the smallest of bodies.

91

Justin Wymer

BEING PRESENT

In an effort to begin I trace a halo with an ember
through the nostril of the deer skull floating past
the power line. That isn't
right. In an effort to be
in a trance, like bone in the clenched cheek of
a rapt child, I imagine a morning waterfront
in Nerja where the just-opening jewelry stores eye
the dented marl for likenesses of sheen and timbre. Then
there is the coast to contend with—
but I have only handfuls of dusky foam
to plump me buoyant. To think
that a boy I know stepped out of the dahlia
shower, recounting how Vikings dipped their helmets in
whales' blood to make the reflections of stars more
lively so the sea more navigable. Looking hard is
a private slap—a form of many-fractaled torture. In temptation
to fill my hands with smells other than hand
I dip my hand in the river before ice stops it
from redoubling the limbs of dilute maroon-
yellow honey mead hanging from above the bank. It is just starting
to get chill. Nothing waits longer than its body permits.
To retreat, I think in blinks. Every aspect of a wild rabbit
telegraphs semblance to
an orphan's particular type of terror. I once caused
a violet to bud twice in winter. That isn't enough.
When I glance behind my shoulder
looking for a single sturdy leaf I am bludgeoned
by the carcinogenic scent of teased-out gardenia
petals, and I turn back, and I curl downward. Once,
I felt a pride. It was rivulet riddled
as the rank wallpaper of yellow breath that sears
the roof of the mouth of a woman with shingles.
To find tenement amidst empty
clouds, among the vaulted atrium of
abundance . . . *Moment*: the drafty chink in the skin of
time, where every convergence of need with
thought seems perfectly clear. So the want of stillness is a clear
mistake, a kind of inoperable task, like picking

spines from a watery beachfront when the sun melds
those remnants of life into sand.
Which is the only property living can own?
When I utter anything, nothing settles down.
Here and now
it is cloudy.

A HAWTHORN, ROOTED CLOSE TO OTHER GUESTS

This is not
nature—the way
pain interrupts
its answers, ashen

awl-tipped
limbs waving
and brushing them-
selves, chill crushes

carried across
the ravine; and
a wing of
their broken flutter,

that desiccated
battle din, is
hooked by a frosty
steam, and it balds.

Though the awls are
hollow point—the un-
graspable locusts
having left

behind veins of shadowy
larvae inside them.
And the hollowed-out
scent of cold rain. And

suddenly—a corridor
of ropy light
twines round
the stems and

fills those absent
bodies with steamy
voices they cannot
share, cannot

reveal, retaining
a skin that shields
unerringly—And so
the sudden remains

only as an answer
the stilled silk
flowers
prod up to reach

on this dog's grave
(what symmetry
can gather itself
entire, in the

open air?)—a calm
tended to by
the wrinkled spines of
shucked chestnuts.

I would invoke
the radiance of the mirror
uncovering itself
inside the glistering

jetsam-spread of leaves, or
the receding waves of
these flowers, fathering
the dusk into them.

Justin Wymer

PRAYER AT EVENTIDE

Against the ailing sky
I come to you, anxious in this mottled
meadow's palisade that, shaken by your tatty ethering
breath, appears to wave round me
drunken tentacles, woven into
the tardy wind—just now—and shaken into
sluggish palsies, which are unrest, upright. The past in me is
a cluster of branches eaten down to dank lace
by potato bugs, under the flat
magazine clippings of stars—glossy branches
through which, on better days, the leaves above
welcome me, vitreous, finicky
as a foul-played gambit, brandishing a current of
sure hands, piled over one another quickly,
in competition. Though honestly,
what belief am I made to enter into
each day, by the necessity of turning

a key . . . And though the wind carries guesses and the fragrance of
losses alongside gains, over the far-off crumbling
estuaries—collecting the particled crystal glaze one seeks in
forgiveness—the desire to see
a needle glinting up through
the patchwork of one's accomplished, minted
life—tenable, at least—warmth in one's hands and
things, at least—I come to you as
a pale sapped sallow, as
a green mist, with a retinue of punctual pod music
pressing into my shoulder, as the inexplicable necessary mis-
imagination which could be
a spider on your ear—or even something smaller
which hopes to wake you, to make you
extend the charged shoots of
your hair into every nerve
that has ever felt

lightness, or that one gift found when the day opens its
reliquary and squanders its feast of

golds upon my bed. So understand that when I enter
gladness, even the smell of alms in the quick
blue draft sniffed in the wake of rabbits'
hurry—even at this remove from
you—even the brush of
an eloping wind can make me beautiful again

PHILOMELA

I center on the bird, hear nothing but
shuttered silence, shifty
and caged as if it has just been broken up
and stitched together by one white
dull listless tawe, pressed whole and unfrayed
again by two thumbs, strengthened by folding
sluicing threads of wind into a garment elms hold—
Till the birds scratch through the blanket, gasped
scratches—like thin sticks of graphite
smoothed from overuse till the points are
flattened horizontal. Birdbreaths
push through beaks barely opened, as if
they had expected something once but now are
pecking their own sinews for they have been
overworked and have received
nothing. The scratch
is graphite being rubbed quickly. Quickly
and constantly over an armrest of wicker.
Furniture whose rough outer skin has been
picked smooth by cold, dry wind.
The silence that follows is nude, ground
glass on white muslin, and cannot be
sensed when there are walls—it must continually be
handled, nakedly, absentmindedly.
These quick calligraphic
gasps are not replies and do not seek
replies. The porous
silence that follows is a tepid
extinguishing elmglint, and
gives no room for any softnesses but came from

soft throats. I do not hear it again
until the sirens are beheaded by faceless wind—sharp
skeins of timothy twining round and purpling their own
heads in gusts—yes, they are faceless—and this one
crinkling into the crease of my knuckle
waits for smoky gauzy birdsong (not
song) but the scratches, too, have been picked
away. I still do not hear the bird
again, but I had wanted that particular
word, splitting out and spreading over and
over, that single word, tripping never on itself
but chained to so many twins of itself—
as if, in moving close to it, I might come to

CHAIR

The steel keep of its black iron arms curve round it—an embrace
viewed as such from behind, in the fur-mist. And
the sculpted arms an oval keep of
the drizzle. And the spokes in the chair's
patrician-postured rectangular back: no shoulders, just
an empty space where a horsefly-blue voice tonight settles—
though not unfamiliar to me, not this wind this time—in the keep
an absent body through which I can view the severed vertical
        stripes
whose luster is interrupted where the moon discards
its protean doilies. In that keep, ten feet
from the newel of my thoracic pillar—and down
the funneling stairs of thought—trundles the oval
echo of a particular obsession—the fright of
anonymity in multiplicity, the minty
driblets of light on the chair, the intractable
beadwork that extends into the absence—neither
a wave nor a wildness—nor the timbering wind
that has arrived and heaped in an O in the chair and
disheveled the little pits of dew. The emptiness of
the chair is a permeated throne for risky thought. And I, on
the verge of warm and simple sleep, close to
the cliff of the courtyard's tallest hillock, and the untethering

quickness that assembles in me—as when one notices a very still
    object
aged and bent toward a gradient of light—
plead, *Let me past the rail—just for a moment.* But who is there
    to ask. Who is there
to pay. No ferryman, no angels, no hungry flicker of familiar
    clocks—Who but
the ambulance that foams florid across the distant milky city sky—
granting my body an ermine frock, as it lifts and settles its burden
down again.

Seven Poems
Ann Lauterbach

A READING

1.

Mutable stipend

saturated in the bright room

with a thin blue rug.

The pivot has some mystery

as in the dream: huge

white birds flowering down.

The morning was brilliant

but then junk

broke loose to scatter sky.

Was I meant to consult

this tissue of meaningless harbingers?

2.

Make no mistake: behind

the curtain, a continuum.

Blink, sun.

Behind the curtain,

old dark thrown across space.

I have an inky drawing of a hairy

stick pressing the wind.

Lovely, now, the milky shade.

Behind the curtain, junk

orbits and a serenade to those

who keep watch while the ditch

fills with lost things. The distant river

flirts with light. The water is alight.

3.

In the dark of a former moon,

an abridgement.

If this were prose, little

agreements would obtain,

and you could turn toward

the missed like an angel on a fence.

I mean a bird, a bird

in prose. The spun ordeal

arises as a missing object

its body enclosed so to be

a convenient newsy thing,

the missing soldier's spouse.

What exactly is intended

to be kept in this regressive frame?

Some figure? Some petty marker?

She will trade her mother's

ring for passage. Let her come aboard.

Veet! Veet! The blue jay's yell

is hollow the way that light blinds.

UNTITLED (PORTRAIT)

Up here in the ancient gold trim   the news not yet visual

so that he or she or we are invisible to the naked eye

whereas the gold trim on her gown is etched

falling down along and over to the hem

like an evening sky.

             Or like nothing yet announced

so the missing and the present are singular in their dress

as we await the address and the black

river of reading aloud over the phone

George Eliot's intervention between the walls

so that we walk through them as if turning a page

we agreed again you and I as we have agreed before

you are not going to be with me on the other side of the wall

despite George Eliot and despite the man

in his pink house with the book

whose cover image is reiterated on the wall

the picture of the beautiful woman in black

who had to decide whether to be her portrait

or to be someone else

someone not like the mother or the sister

not like the man in the hotel room in his bathrobe

with his whore and his

unspeakable

so that the only thing to be said

is *you cannot do that with me in the room*

the walls of the room and the long view across the river

where there are others in their rooms

and the house from the other side of the river

looks immense

as the life within is immense.

CLASSICAL AUGURY

City of words

rotunda and desert wanderer

climb the absence

follow this simple curve into the footprint

Ann Lauterbach

or find indifference   a shelter

as if lost within a cave

confounded

within the merry leafy compost

city of words

ideal translation and misfortune

to hesitate at the sequel to traipse backward onto the

path

stunted underfoot to wait until the sugar dissolves

until the rat's nose upends a leaf

seeing as the windows are shut

the heads are mounted on rose hips and thorns

prayer is spoken into the dark

city of words

bring the ruin to its proper place among nouns

open its mouth   peer into the rosy throat

surely not a new day

her name is common

she walks along the fibrous tissues and sticks

recalls the fictive cause to save to go back   to align

to dwell among first attributes of space

but what are these?

Hasty dim angels.

Are they above, below?

Beautiful plural sloping toward duration.

Ann Lauterbach

LANDSCAPE WITHOUT VIEW

These intensities their wake the jar

fret the word

snow on dry leaves *fret fret*

the jar dark inside within in the dark

body o body not that anyone is here

the thick stiff night's

curled domain

am as of now how it is spoken

the slide between

the mere passage

fret

and surely the blind spot

the occasion

emphatic   these intensities

not sheltered not yet drawn

by the most implicated

106

what it looks like

to halt   crassly halt

and the new digital figure

axiomatic grace

semblance ushered from sequence

avenue or image

sucking at the animate

these contagious exceptions

fugitive incursions

even so the turbines hum

licking at stone

the contagion of stone

peevish annunciation

melded onto a screen

as if intimate

invisible constraint

as if tempered

as if conditions prevailed.

TO THE GIVEN

Dear instructor,
tonight I am

word poor and so   unchained
and the world seated

could be
sensed partially

your back to it, my looking away,
trace of a cry in the air

accumulating from afar
a clarity of means

because
entrenched in beloved

semblance

to climb into the given as

music or the simplest conduct—

touching the threshold

migrating

serene as matter or

untouched

traveling—the wind—

made only for space

perceived

as elegy's long flight.

And so

darkening chanced over the neck

the shoulder's ache

not referral to the outside

having not yet aspired

darkening yet

the test or turn savored

the instance   leaning forward

to hear

a part song of some duration

shelter of what is not said

chanced, here and there, over, darkening—

splendid matter erased.

Could look through to the voice—

could look to find where the voice—

have you a word

dear instructor, for this?

UNDER THE SIGN

Having dreamed of my dead sister
raging with urgent

need, she
conducting us through intolerable

passages, now forgotten, I
have burned my right hand

after sunset
small dark clouds above

the river I cannot see
while listening to

a scratched CD of a Haydn
piano sonata so that

Ann Lauterbach

certain passages

rapidly repeat

and having spent some moments

thinking of the vision

that accommodates

all that is unforeseen

as the world now

becomes without sequence.

UNTITLED (AGAINST PERFECTION)

All that left aside   left awkwardly on that side done away with

in immediate neighborhoods of chivalry. Wait. Under the

cleft sign to read will be continuance, a kept event because there was a

delivery of sorts. Because it had come to pass near?

Wait. Old tingaling sat down sweaty

thought the portrait was of Mick, thought she had long hair

then, then stopped. Wait. And wanted these not to die

not to pass on. Wait.

112

The lad's charm charmed by the lad his demeanor *thank you* so young

among the crowded the high bed lifted charmed

while the gaze without therapy   without the car.

Wait. She has this she has the left hand a paper

she has the kiss long afterwards they had passed

had kissed in the smallest room had found the ring of fear

                    and still things happened, kept happening, went on

although the mode shifted in degree and measure. Wait.

Had these come withered now under such guise as the planet's remembered

cycles, their friction carried out against clouds, anxieties, waste, then what

was planted or planned would approach through the center of conviction—

yay or nay—buttressed into abstraction, possibly scented with lemony

highlights in our visual age. Okay, I too have had it, the tale, the tremors, the

incidents so enjambed that only the edgy molecule catches on, breathes its

minuscule agenda onto skin like that of a peel.

The peel of evening across high bricks.
The peel of an orchid's deadly grip on perfection.

The Tower
Frederic Tuten

SOMETIMES HIS URINE was cloudy. Sometimes gritty with what he called "gravel." Sometimes his piss flowed bloody and frightening. No matter how disturbing, Montaigne recorded his condition in his travel journal as coolly he did the daily weather. He was always in various degrees of pain, and he noted that too, but dispassionately, like a scientist in a white lab coat.

Even before he suffered from kidney stones and the burning pain that came with them, Montaigne had long thought about death, and not only his own. He had thought about how to meet it and if doing so gracefully would change the encounter. His closest friend, the man he had loved more than anyone in the world, was to love more than anyone in the world, had died with calm dignity. In his last minutes, in his last words, his dear friend did not begrudge life or beg for more time or express regrets over what was left undone or make apologies to those he might have or had offended or injured. Montaigne thought that when death approached, he would neither wave him away nor welcome him, but say to death's shadow on the wall, "Finally, no more pain."

I put my book aside when she walked in.

"I'm leaving you," she said. She had a red handbag on her arm.

"For how long?"

"For always."

"And what about Pascal, will you take him?"

"He's always favored you." I was very glad. I could see Pascal sitting in the dining-room doorway, pretending not to listen.

"Yes, that's true."

"Don't you care to know why I'm leaving?" she asked, petulantly, I thought.

"I suppose you'll tell me."

"I will, but maybe another time." She stared at me as if wondering who I was. Then she started to speak but was interrupted by a car-horn blast. I looked out the window and saw a taxi with a man behind the wheel.

"May I help you with your bags?" I asked.

"I'll send for them later, if you don't mind."

"Who will you send?"

"The person who comes." She stared at me another moment and then left.

I heard a motor start up, then the swerve of the car leaving the curb. Pascal took his time walking over to me and then, with a faint cry, he jumped into my lap, curling himself on my open book. I stroked his head until he made that little motor purr that all cats make when they pretend to love you.

One day Montaigne went all the way from his home in Bordeaux to Italy for its famous physicians and for a change in diet, for that country's warm climate and healing sky. He went to soak himself in the mineral baths, which sometimes gave him relief—also noted in his journal. He recorded but never whined about the biting stones in his kidneys or the bedbugs in the mattress in a Florence hostel or complained about that city's summer heat, so great that he slept on a table pressed against an open window.

He traveled alone. Once, in Rome, Montaigne hired a translator, a fellow Frenchman, who, without notice or reason, left him without a good-bye. So, armed with maps and charts and curiosity, he went about the city with himself for company and guide. In that ancient city he witnessed horrific public executions of criminals, men drawn and quartered while still alive. He visited the libraries of cardinals and nobles, returning to his hostel to note in the same disinterested voice the books and the tortures he had seen and the hard stone that had that day passed through his urine.

I knew there was no hope in lifting Pascal up and dropping him on the carpet so that he would leave me alone to read. I knew he would just bound up again and sit on my book again and that he would do the same one hundred and one times before I gave up and left the room or left the house or left the city. So I took the string with a little ball attached to it that I kept tucked under the pillow and let it drop on the floor. He leapt off my lap and began pawing the rubber ball. I pulled it away and he followed with a one-two punch. Montaigne had once asked himself: Is it I who plays with the cat or is it he who plays with me?

The house seemed full now that she had gone, the rooms packed with me. I wandered about savoring the quiet, the solitude, the way my books, sleeping on their shelves, seemed to glow as I passed by— old friends who no longer need share me with another. I thought I would spend the rest of the day without a plan and do as I wished. Maybe I would sit all day and read. Maybe I would go out with my gun and empty the streets of all the noise. I would then at last have a silent, empty house surrounded by a tranquil, soundless zone. That was just a thought. I have no gun.

After his beloved friend died, Montaigne went into seclusion, keeping himself in a turreted stone tower at the edge of his estate. It was cold in winter and hot in summer and not well lit, the windows being small. He had had a very full life up to the point of his withdrawal, if fullness means social activity and a role in governing. He was a courtier in the royal court and the mayor of Bordeaux and was always out day and night doing things. But now in that tower Montaigne was determined to write, which he did, essays, which some think were addressed to his dead friend. His mind traveled everywhere, his prose keeping apace with all the distances and places his mind traveled. He wrote about cannibals. He wrote about friendship. What is friendship, he asked, and answered: When it is true, it is greater than any bond of blood. Brothers have in common the same port from whence they were issued but may be separated forever by jealousy and rivalry in matters of inheritance and property. Brothers may hate each other, kill each other, as the Old Testament so vividly illustrates. But friends choose each other and their intercourse deepens in trust, esteem, and affection; their intellectual exchange strikes flames.

He stayed in his tower for ten years, his world winnowed down to a stone room of books and a wooden table. Crows sat on his window ledge and studied him, imperturbable in their presence. His wife visited and in his place saw a triangle. Sometimes he would look at his friend's portrait on the table, a miniature in a plain silver frame, and say, "We've worked enough for now, let's go to lunch. What do you think?" Sometimes he just stayed in place until the evening, when he dined on cold mutton and lentils and read in the wintry candlelight. Once, as he climbed the stair to his bedchamber, he noticed his bent shadow trailing him on the wall. Just some years ago his shadow had bounded ahead of him, waiting for him to catch up. Now he grew tired easily; writing a page took hours and he was always in pain. He pissed rich blood. He howled. But he sat and wrote until he finished his book. Then he went on his extensive travels.

I went into the kitchen and made a dish of pears and Stilton and broke out the water biscuits; I opened the best wine I had ever bought, one so expensive that I had hid it from her, waiting for the right occasion to spring it. I sat at the kitchen table. Pascal leaped up to join me. I opened a can of boneless sardines, drained the oil, slid the fish onto a large, white plate, and set it beside me so that Pascal and I could lunch together. He was suspicious, sniffed, then retreated, and then returned to the same olfactory investigation until he finally decided to leave the novelty to rest. The bouquet rose from the wine bottle like a genie and filled the room with sparkling sunshine and the aromatic, medieval soil of Bordeaux. It pleased me to think that Montaigne might have drunk wine from the same vineyard, from the same offspring of grapes.

I went up to her bedroom and opened the closets. So many clothes, dresses, shoes, scarves, belts, hats. The drawers were stuffed with garter belts and black bikini panties that I had never been privy to seeing her wear. Soon the closet would be empty and I would leave it that way. Or leave it that way until I decided what to do with the house, too small for two, too large for one and a cat. She had left the bed unmade, the blankets and sheets twisted and tangled, as if they had been wrestling until they had given up, exhausted. I sniffed her pillow, which was heavy with perfume and dreams. Pascal came in and danced on the bed, where he had never been allowed. I left him there stretched out on her pillow and went down to my study.

It welcomed me as never before. My desk with its teetering piles of books and loose sheets of notes and a printer and computer and a Chinese lamp, little pots full of outdated stamps and rubber bands, an instant-coffee jar crammed with red pencils, green paper clips heaped in a chipped, blue teacup, a stapler, an old rotary phone, framed prints of Goya's *Puppet* and Poussin's *Echo and Narcissus*, Cézanne's *Bathers*, and Van Gogh's *Wheat Field in Rain* greeted and accepted me without any conditions. I could sit at my desk all day and night and never again be presented with the obligation to clear or clean an inch of the disorder. Now, if I wished, I could even sweep away every single thing on the desk and leave it bare and hungry. Or I could chop up and burn the desk in the fireplace. I would wait for a cold night. There was plenty of time now to make decisions.

I went back to the living room and turned on the TV and madly switched channels, finding I liked everything that flashed across the screen, especially the Military Channel, where I watched a history of tank battles and decided I would rather have been in the Navy if it had come to that. Montaigne, surprisingly, detested the sea, from where much contemplation springs. All the same, perhaps the swell of a wave and a splash of the brine might have made him a more

117

dreamy man of the sky than the solid man of the earth, where he was so perfectly at home. Later, watching another channel, I bought four Roman coins, authentic reproductions of Emperor Hadrian's young lover, Antinous, whose death he grieved until his last imperial breath. On another channel, I ordered a device that sucked wax from the ears. It was guaranteed that my hearing would improve within days. But then, after it was too late to change my mind, I realized I did not need or want to improve my hearing. Except for the music I love, I thought I don't care to hear well at all. Most of what is said is better left unsaid and left unheard. It is the voices from the silent world of the self that matter, like the ones that Montaigne heard and wrote down in his tower room. I thought I might demolish the house now and build that tower in its place and live in the comfort of its invisible voices, and sit there and transcribe the voices as they came.

I grew bored with TV and realized that I missed reading my book of Montaigne's travels, that I missed him. Montaigne was someone I was sure that I could travel with, because he was someone whom I could leave or accompany whenever I chose. And there would be no recriminations, no arguments, no pulling this way and that about where to eat and how much to cool down or heat up the hotel room—or any room anywhere. I went back to my chair and opened Montaigne's book, sure that Pascal would soon arrive and jump up. But a half hour passed and he still had not come. I missed him and the game we played. So, after several more minutes, I went to find him. He was nowhere to be found. But the window to my wife's bedroom was open and I surmised he had left through it and to a world of his own making.

I was about to settle back to my reading when there was a strong knock at the door. I opened it to a man in a blue suit.

"Is she here?"

"Not presently," I said.

"Will she return presently?"

"Who knows?" I said.

"Well, I looked for her everywhere and thought she might have returned here," he said, peering in the doorway.

"Not here," I said, slowly closing the door.

"Do you mind if I come in a minute? Just to rest my feet."

"Have you been searching for her on foot?"

"Not at all," he said, nodding over to the cab standing before the house. "But I'm exhausted from looking for her."

"Come in," I said, not too graciously.

He went immediately to my favorite chair but before he could plunk himself down, I said, "That one's broken."

He sat down on the couch and gave me a sheepish grin. "Thanks, buddy."

I pretended to be reading my book but I was sizing him up, slyly, I thought. I did not find him remarkable in any way.

"Is she a reliable woman?" he asked.

"Absolutely. And punctual too."

He looked about the room and folded his hands the way boys are told to do in a classroom. "Does she read all these books?"

"Some, but not all at once."

"That's very funny," he said, with a little sarcastic smile. Then, changing to a more agreeable one, he asked, "Got something to drink? Worked up a thirst running around town looking for her."

"I just opened a bottle of wine you may like."

"Is it from California?"

"No."

"From France?"

"No, from New Zealand."

"I'll pass then. How about a glass of water, no ice." I didn't answer. He stared at me a long time but I waited him out. I noticed he wore burgundy moccasins with tassels and was without socks. That he had an orange suntan that glowed.

"She has me drop her off at the mall and says to come back and get her in a an hour or two. But she never shows up."

"Was your meter running?"

"My Jag's in the shop. The cab's from my fleet."

"By the way, have you seen a cat out there in the street?"

"A salt-and-pepper one with a drooping ear?"

"Yes."

"No, I haven't." Then, in a shot, he added, "Is she your wife?"

"We're married," I said.

"She told me you were roommates."

"We do share rooms, though not all of them."

He stood up, pulled down his jacket, which seemed on the tight side, and came up close to me. "You're better off without her, pal. With all due respect, she's a flake but the kind that fits me."

He went to the door and I followed, my book in hand, like a pistol. "Would you still like that water?" I asked, in a most agreeable way.

"Don't tell her you saw me," he said.

"Cross my heart and hope to die," I said.

119

He gave me a long look, half friendly, half bewildered, half menacing. "You're not so bad for a dope."

He sped off in his cab—Apex. Twenty-four Hours a Day. We Go Everywhere. The street was empty. The sidewalk was empty. The houses and their lawns across the road were empty. The sky was empty. The clouds too. I shut the door and returned to my favorite chair and went back to my book.

Montaigne wrote brief notes to his wife, describing his adventures with bedbugs and the summer heat, never referring to his urinary condition or to his pains, which worsened with each day. He noted that the Italians painted their bedpans with scenes from classical mythology, favoring those of Leda and her admiring swan. They were comforting, those bedpans, so unlike the severe white porcelain ones in France that never thought to combine art with excrement.

I was near the end of the book and that left me in a vacuum for the remainder of the day. I thought that now that I was at large, I would need to plan for the evening and the night ahead. I would leave tomorrow to itself for now. But then the door swung wide open and she appeared, fancy shopping bags in hand.

"Well, aren't you going to help me?" I relieved her of two of the larger bags and settled them on the sofa. "There's another one on the porch," she said, as if I had been malingering. I retrieved it and another one at the doorstep, a large, round, pink box.

She sat on the sofa and kicked off her shoes. She looked about as if in an unfamiliar place. "What have you done?"

"To what?" I asked.

"To the room! It looks different. Did you change anything?"

"Nothing."

She looked at me suspiciously then said, "Something's different."

"It knows you've left. Rooms always know when someone has left."

She pretended to yawn. "Sure."

"And they shift themselves to the new situation," I added. "Like when a person dies in a bedroom and the walls go gray and cold. Or when a child is born and the room goes rosy and roomier."

"Has anyone been here since I left? I can smell that someone has."

"Now that you mention it, yes."

"Was he wearing a blue suit?"

"I didn't notice."

"Let me show you something," she said, removing her dress. She fussed about the shopping bags and pulled out a red skirt and red

120

jacket with large buttons. "Whataya think?" she asked, fastening her last fat button.

"You look like a ripe tomato."

"It matches my handbag," she said, waving it before me. "I realized after I left this morning that my bag needs something to go with it."

"Everything matches and matches your hair too."

"You've always had a good eye," she said.

"For you," I said, in a kind of flirty way that I wasn't sure I meant.

"If you don't mind, I'm going upstairs to pack some things."

"Let me know if you see Pascal up there, please."

"That's another thing. I cringed every time you explained to a guest that Pascal was named after some French philosopher," she said, turning from me.

"If you had ever seen Pascal stare up at the night sky and give a little shiver, you'd understand," I said.

She was already halfway up the stairs and I wasn't sure she had heard me. But then she shouted down, "Did he say when he'll come back?"

I pretended not to have heard her. She came down the stairs again and said, "Well?"

"He didn't say. But his Jag is in the shop."

"I don't care about the books. You can keep them all," she said. "They prefer you anyway, like the cat."

"I named him Pascal, after his namesake, who asked for the patience to sit. I named him Pascal because he sits quietly in the window box and I can see in his eyes that he is training himself against his nature to learn to sit."

She gathered up the red dress suit and the handbag and, without a word, went back up the stairs. I returned to my book but my heart was not in it. Montaigne was on his way back to Bordeaux to his wife and his old life of solitude and voices. To his old known comforts. For all its vaunted claims, travel is a deterioration, taking minutes off one's life with every passing mile. So, for all his bravery, his condition worsened with each jolt of the carriage, with each bug bite and bad meal. By the time he finally arrived home, the blood in his urine had grown darker, the pain stronger, the loneliness greater.

I returned to the kitchen and to the remains of my lunch, still scattered on the table like the flotsam of a minor wreck. I sipped a glass of wine. It tasted of damp nails forgotten in a dank cellar. I sat there as the dusk filtered through the kitchen window, softening the edges of the table and the chairs and the hulk of the fridge. My hand looked like a mitten. Montaigne should never have left his tower, I thought, and gave voice to it in the shadows, " You should have stayed home," I said, advice given too late to an old friend.

Then I went to the door, thinking that Pascal might be there sitting on the step, waiting for me to let him in after his adventures in the wide world. Or maybe he would be just sitting and waiting for the night and the chill of its distant stars.

—*For Edmund White*

Three Stories
Joanna Ruocco

BATTLE FATIGUE

AT THE END OF THE SCHOOL DAY, we felt so tired and our school bus driver felt so tired, and the school bus driver, driving past the farms on the dirt roads with the cows near the fences, near the roads, eating silage, and driving also past the farms with tractor attachments grazing in pastures, very quiet and steady, unattached to the tractors, in the pastures and all around the barns, and driving also past eggs for sale and dogs running with us but falling back because the school bus was heavy downhill and fast around the hairpins blasted from rock, and driving slowly over the river on the single-lane bridge just exactly as wide as the axle plus the width of the tires, and driving slower still, because he was so tired, he would shut his eyes and sleep and steer the school bus between the weedy borders of the road in his sleep, and sometimes his feet would drift up with the pedals and the school bus would stop, and I don't know how long we would stay where we stopped; no children got off at those stops because we slept too, in the rows of green seats, our heads against the windows. Once I woke up on the school bus. We were driving through the side of a house and through the house, and the old ladies were hiding from the bus in their rooms putting their faces against the cats in their arms, but then we drove through the other side of the house and into the river, and we bounced on rock after rock in the river that follows the road through the village and we came to my house through the fields from the river, and my mother was digging a hole in the field. It was too small for the school bus. The school bus stopped by my mother. So many years had gone by that the farm animals had died, and my mother wanted everyone out of the bus, to see the geese in the hole and the pigs and the ram and the horse and the cows and our gray-bearded dog and my father sleeping in the hole on the cloves of garlic we planted. The other day I reminded my mother of that time by the hole, the bus in the field, the geese and the pigs, my father on the sprouted cloves, and how no one stirred in the bus but me. I got

123

off; it was my stop. The bus stayed in the field all night. My mother did not remember. She said I had been taught to call too many things sleep.

FRIENDLY FIRE

Humans have drives. There is the sex drive. There is a drive for food, the food drive. The food drive might have a more basic name, the eat drive. "Eat" doesn't sound more basic than "food." They have the same kind of strong, basic sound, but eat is more basic than food. There are all kinds of foods but only one way to eat. You have to put the food in your mouth. You have to put some solid nutrimental thing inside your mouth and do something with your mouth, even if you don't masticate, even if all you do is push the thing down whole with the muscles of your tongue and throat.

They took out part of her friend's colon and stomach, and her uterus, but for a while food still got into her stomach from her mouth, and traveled through her intestines and came out in the regular way; the food didn't taste like anything, but she put it in her mouth; she ate the food. It was eating. It's strange when food doesn't taste like anything. It's still eating, but you feel strange. You put the food in your mouth and it's good normal food but there's something wrong with your mouth. Your mouth doesn't make any saliva or the saliva drips out through your lips before you can stop it. Your cheek is between your molars when you move your molars on the food. Her friend didn't like this eating, but she did it. What else could she do? Humans need to eat. The time may come when you can't put any-thing in your mouth at all, and then you know there has been a change, a deep change in what you are. Something dead is changed from what it used to be when it was alive, and you are changed in that way. You aren't dead but you are beginning to be dead. You feel strange, as though you are wearing yourself like a suit of smelly clothes. After you are dead, you are a corpse; before you are dead, you have a corpse; you're wearing it. It feels stranger and stranger.

They told her friend that the time had come when the food couldn't go down her throat. There was nowhere for the food to go; part of her stomach was still inside her but it was filled with other things; if they removed the things no stomach would remain. They said six of one, half a dozen of the other, and her friend agreed that, if it was all the same, doing something and doing nothing, it was better to do nothing because nothing is less invasive. Her friend sat at the table with her family members and talked to her family members while her family members ate food but her friend did not eat food, would never eat any food again, her mouth no longer served that function. Her mouth was part of the corpse she was wearing.

She had not been invited to eat at her friend's house since her friend stopped eating, so she did not know exactly what her friend did at the table. She did not know if her friend set herself a place at the table or if she sat in her chair at the table with nothing in front of her. If she set a place for herself at the table, did she put food on the plate and a fork on the napkin, or did she leave the plate empty or did she perhaps put some nonfood item on the plate, like a thumb-sized cactus in a plastic pot? She thought putting food on the plate would be torture, because the smell of food makes you hungry, and her friend must be hungry all the time, except maybe the hunger had become inseparable from the nauseated feeling, and so hunger didn't make her want food in the way it made other people want food, it just made her sick. In that case sitting upright at the table would be torture even if there was no food on her plate, and besides she could smell the food from the plates of her family members, if she could still smell, which was far from certain. She might forget, if there was food on her plate, that she could not eat the food, even though she felt sick, even though her mouth was a corpse's mouth and her throat was cracking with the dryness, and with disuse; she would pick up the fork and put food in her mouth and then remember and have to spit out the food. Would something go wrong if she swallowed the food, even a little food? Would it lodge somewhere in her, sit on top of the things in her stomach and rot so the rottenness gassed inside her and the gas came up to her mouth and her nose and burned and stank until she went to see them and they snaked the food out of her? It would be difficult not to put anything in your mouth after so many years of putting food in your mouth, all kinds of food, whether you were hungry or not.

In newspapers, people are always writing about Americans eating without paying any attention, Americans eating mindlessly. You could, as an experiment, give an American a bowl of soup with a trick bottom and fill the bowl endlessly from soup buckets under the table and the American would not stop eating the soup. This experiment was described in the newspaper. Her friend was suddenly less American. She was more dead and less American. When you're dead you're not American anymore; this is one of the changes. You don't have drives, you're not a woman or a man or white or black or American or Korean or a mother or a son. But her friend was not dead and it must be difficult to behave as though you're dead, to put nothing in your mouth, to stop being American before you're totally dead, to stop being a woman or a mother before you're totally dead, to get emptied of the drives that make you what you are before you're entirely absolutely totally dead.

She wondered what she would talk about with her friend if her friend invited her to dinner. She would bring her friend something, a plant, not a cactus, for her plate, in case her friend sat there with the empty plate in front of her. You can't fiddle with a cactus, and her friend might appreciate having something to do with her hands while not eating at the table. She might want to fidget because she wasn't dead and she couldn't be comfortable; she was in pain; she felt sick all the time. She might need to fidget, to distract herself from the pain, and Americans distract themselves by eating, but not her friend anymore. She was past that. All of those things—being American or being a woman, being an American woman—those are temporary things, states you pass through on your way to something else. Phrasing it like that made it sound like a journey, a spiritual journey, and she would phrase it like that to her friend if it came up at dinner; she would focus on the journey, not on the something else you get to, because the journey is an archetype, everyone believes in the journey, but people can't agree about the something else. Beliefs about the something else are personal and she didn't want to pry. Of course, she wondered what her friend thought, and it did seem natural to try and get her to talk about it. It did seem like it would be the natural topic. After all, her friend was an eyewitness. Her friend was so close to it; she was beyond almost everything that had made her who she was. It wasn't prying because, really, at this point, what could her friend expect to hold on to, to keep to herself? She could still speak; her mouth still served that function; and so she should speak. What she said would not be personal. What she said would just be witnessing, not her pain and fear, but the pain and fear of it, the something else, the thing she was filled with.

Joanna Ruocco

TWILIGHT

What is the quickest way to become a good person? This is an important question. There are many causes competing for our time and money and most of the causes are not administered efficiently; a large fraction of your time and money goes not to the cause but to other things, things that do not make you a good person, like web maintenance. A pit latrine might make you a good person, but how much time and money would you have to give to a cause before it equaled one pit latrine? You could go somewhere and build a pit latrine yourself, with your own two hands, in the dust, in the sun, but first you should remember that you do not shit in pit latrines. You have a flush toilet. Even if you've never thought about liking the flush toilet you will probably admit it's better than a pit latrine. Why are you building a pit latrine instead of bathrooms with flush toilets? This is the problem with causes. They are wrongheaded. You will misstep. You will not have done the right thing. Are you a good person if you do bad things? All of this thinking is not quick. Listen, this is quick. Go and donate one pint of blood. This will take an hour. Go and donate another pint of blood. Go and donate another pint of blood. Do it twelve times. Even traveling from blood drive to blood drive you can get it all done in one day. Maybe you're a small person and you only have ten pints of blood to give. That's OK! Every person can only give as much blood as he or she has, six pints, eight pints, ten pints, twelve pints of blood. If your iron is low, that's OK, you can give anyway, and if you have tattoos or sex partners or you have spent time in sub-Saharan Africa, or if you are sub-Saharan African, or if you have a blood-borne pathogen or weigh ninety pounds or just turned eleven or were alive in the seventies, it's OK, no one will say anything, the needle goes in and the blood goes out along the tube into pint sack after pint sack after pint sack, no questions asked, and soon all of the blood will be out of your body, and if you give as much blood as you have, and you bring a friend, and your friend gives as much blood as she has, and your friend brings a friend, or two friends, and those friends bring friends, before very long all of the people will have given all of their blood, all of the blood will be outside all of the people, all of the blood nonviolently removed from all of the people everywhere on the planet. Listen, because this is how to be good, this giving of blood, this giving of pint after pint of your blood; this is the best, quickest, most wonderful thing you can do. It is better than founding an international orphanage for peace. It is better than sheltering rescue dogs or transforming vacant lots into gardens or getting appointed UN ambassador or researching anti-cancer vaccines. It is better than moving into the forest, living off the grid alone in the forest, even if you wash beneath a cold-water pump, even if you only eat ferns, even if you plant six trees for every one you cut down. Listen, right at this minute there are eighty billion pints of blood inside people on the planet. That's ten billion gallons! There are ten million in-ground swimming pools in the United States of America. On average, one in-ground swimming pool con-tains twenty-two thousand gallons of water. Every pint of blood inside every person on the planet could still not fill all the swimming pools in the United States of America, but that's OK! Enough swim-ming pools could be filled with blood to make a stunning visual impression, from up close, but from the air especially. You would see the suburbs inset with jewel-bright kidney beans, and darker beans too, and ovals and squares; the suburbs would tessellate darkly and ripple with shining black layers of flies, and every pint of blood from inside every person on the planet would dry at last into fragrant dust, garnet dust, and every pint of blood from inside every person on the planet would lift into the wind and snow down like shattering a nitrogen rose. We would all be a part of it. We would all be together a part of it, all of us, the explosion of the same human rose. The beau-tiful must not be confused with the good—I read that somewhere, something like it, carved in a rock. But listen, don't you want, deep down, to be a beautiful person? Isn't that the thing you really want? Don't you want to become good just so that you can finally be beau-tiful? Well, now you know how. The only trick is to keep your heart beating, to keep your heart pushing the blood through the tube, not to give up the whole while, to push and to push, until the valve sucks air.

The Cubes
Karen Hays

Cube No. 1: iron

{001} May

AT SEVEN YEARS OLD, you're deaf to the courtship racket. You don't hear the life-or-death urgency in it. You don't reflect on the long winter or wonder about or grieve for those that didn't make it. Spring has not yet keened in you. This is what you would hear if you followed your dad and the two neighbors out into the street on that warm May evening and then slunk off to find a place where you imagined you might anguish the old man by spending the night alone and undiscovered: nothing. Just some waiting-around sounds. Strands of birdsong

{100} scaffold

so loosely interwoven you could slip whole daydreams through them. Some unseen bugs, stridulating. The silly calls of frogs recently risen from pond bottoms and toads freshly sprung from their hibernacula. The solicitations of all the would-be father creatures falling on your ears damp and warm—a lullaby song. At seven, you're just your father's whisker. The work you do is automatic, compulsory, reflexive. You wag in his gaiety and when he is inattentive, droop or slink off to filch a candy. When something is wrong with him, you go silent like a worried cricket. This is what you'd hear

{010} nerves

if he allowed you to tag along but told you to

129

Karen Hays

keep quiet, and so you crept off unnoticed and had just begun to doze under a tree feeling hot and hypnogogic, a garland of limp dandelions dripping milk from their knotted straws onto your skin, drawing dirt to that glue from faraway places—the rust and soot, the filigreed pollens and foliated silicates, all mired in dandelion latex, with troubles akin to yours, stuck and imponderably small: nothing, and then the Morse code of your father's footfalls. His slick-soled dots and dashes. Your dad taking a short step with

{010} soles

one foot, quick scooting the other foot over to meet it, stepping again in the same or maybe the opposite direction, hopping or gliding the other foot over to join it, and then coming to a measured stop once more somewhere in the middle of the stone-clad street. His feet tapping out the lexicon of a Perfect Moment. Wise men know when. Anyone can chart the magic by which a pollywog becomes a frog, but how the frog survives the long winter is a secret buried in the finery of his cells. Freezing isn't something that just happens to him.

{001} hand

No, the frog orchestrates the whole process. That way he can go slow and earlier than the weather would have it. He can go early and on his own terms. From the inside out instead of the opposite. Like this: Some bacteria seed clouds then ride the fallout like pollen rides wind. The geometry of their membranes makes a framework for ice to grow in. It's irresistibly regular, repetitive. The frog inoculates himself by eating them. Some think that life began with random carbon molecules sticking to electrostatic particles of iron-bearing clay and then, because clay aligns itself in long

130

{100} augury

chains, becoming concatenated into slinky strands of RNA. By this theory, the first organic molecules were replicated at the mineral's mercy until the molecules took over the job and became self-replicating. Like a suggested mental illness. With frozen frogs, it's the opposite. Some ancestral life form provides the template for the mineral—ice, in this case—to grow in. In order for the ice to do no harm to the frog's cellular architecture, it must grow around but never within his cells. It only takes thirty seconds of contact with the frozen ground to set the whole thing in motion.

Cube No. 2: augury

{100} iron

Here is what you would see if you opened your eyes on that day in May 1895 and instead of young Margaret at the tree's foot, you were among the compass-eyed songbirds high in the branches above her: three men standing in a triangle formation, their backs to the sunset and their faces to the sky. It's the apogee of thunderstorm season—the peak time of day, peak time of year—but right now the sky is clear, the shadows long and sharp-edged, and none of the men needs to visor his brow nor squint his eyes to see what

{001} caper

hovers in the sky overhead. Two of the vertices hold fixed and still, but the hawk's-billed man at the apex seems to be practicing some kind of dance step. Margaret's dad shuffles to and fro in slow, halting fashion, shifting the triangle from equilateral to obtuse and back again. He's not do-si-doing with his own shadow as someone with eyes trained to the ground might think, but with

131

the airborne flock of diamonds the two neighbors are holding steady for him—the three kites and the one kite skeleton, a black cube tacked to the latter's wooden sternum. He's waiting

{010} oscillating

for the right moment to yank the line he's just paid out from the spool in his hand. That is when, with the help of the two men he begged out into the street with him, William Abner Eddy will snap the Western Hemisphere's first aerial kite photographs. Photons will stream through his airborne camera's open shutter, exciting the electrons on his film's silver surface and bringing them to a short but lovely state of conductance. Once developed, the pictures will offer a low-flying bird's-eye view of their neighborhood in rural Bayonne, New Jersey. Though their hometown has recently been

{001} lexicon

dubbed the Peninsula of Industry, the street they live on is situated in a relatively undeveloped portion, and there will be little in Eddy's pictures to hint at the nickname's origin. Audible in no way will be the iron-on-iron screech of trains as they make their cross-continental exchange—crates of Newark Bay oysters for boxcars of coal and barrels of Minneapolis flour—or the buffeting toots of the barges as they ferry the coal from Constable Hook to the only city whose vertical ambitions seem to rival those of Margaret's kite enthusiast father. Across the harbor, New York rises by

{100} void
{010} survey

stories, grids, guy-wires, and pigeons. Her father promises his kites will soar higher than all of those, but how high can they? High enough to photograph Perth Amboy

132

down the shore or Niagara Falls beyond the highlands? To the southwest, workers can't pull clay out of the ground fast enough to satisfy the masons charged with stacking Manhattan, and to the northwest, Tesla's alternating current power plant is in its final phase of testing. By autumn even electricity will course over long distances. No, today there will only be this suggestion of unnatural geometry along one of the photos' horizons:

Cube No. 3: survey

{010} augury

Past a mirroring strip of watery foreground and the thick brow of grass perched atop it, beyond a distant mansion's boxy silhouette and just to the right of the captured line of Eddy's kite apparatus, the needles of Rockefeller's oil refinery will ascend. More prominent will be the shadows of tree trunks slanting off unbroken, the dapples, and the canopy at the photos' edges. They will simply say *to everything a rhythm* and *some of what has been will always* and *a picture in no way predicts or suffices*. There will be no people, birds, frogs, ghosts revived or prefigured.

{100} void
{001} genesis

In 1888, Margaret Eddy is born in New York City. KC Bolt and Nut, the steel manufacturing plant where my grandfather will work, opens in Missouri's Blue River Valley. *The Father of Biochemistry*, Emil Fischer, marries the future mother of his three sons in Germany. And a series of exercises devised by mathematician Charles Howard Hinton is published in London. If practiced hard and often enough, Hinton's exercises are supposed to illuminate a path—

albeit dimly—to the fourth dimension. One publication targeted for a mainstream readership is advertised in ladies' magazines under the grossly apocryphal title *Ghosts Revealed*.

{010} void
{001} aboutface

Einstein isn't even ten years old when Hinton's exercises are published; the theory of relativity isn't even a photon in Albert's eye yet. Forget about space-time. In the beginning, the fourth dimension is just a geometric axis at right angles to the x, y, and z our brains are hardwired to comprehend. This direction is *w*, and it runs perpendicular to every line that could ever be drawn in space. Hinton believes that to comprehend this dimension would be to see the world for how and what it truly is, objectively at last, and to finally know his life's purpose.

{100} nerves

And so the mathematician undertakes geometric pilgrimages. The route is dark, but the turns can be memorized and the ingress eventually navigated without the benefit of eyes or even hands. Picture the path winding like the corridors that concealed the beasts and gladiators beneath the floor of the Coliseum, spring-loading them for madness, but without the hypogeum's stone walls for travelers to scuff palms along or bump muzzles against. Hinton and his followers will have to find their way without the benefit of their senses. To escort them home, there will only be the knotted threads of their own attention.

Cube No. 4: nerves

{100} survey

Soon afterward, her dad's newspaper, *The New York Herald*, prints pen and ink

134

renderings of the Bayonne photographs. Margaret doesn't make much of them. She has ridden the circular elevator to the top of the Pulitzer on Newspaper Row and stood on the observation deck crowning its cuprous dome; at 309 feet, the fully electrified structure is not only the world's tallest building and an innovative brick-iron hybrid, but also a lightning rod to shield what's being heralded as the *Technological Revolution.* Her father says the growing number of electrical appliances these days puts everyone at an increased risk of

{001} conductivity

incalculable accidents,[i] like fires and electrocutions. (Tesla's Manhattan lab burned to the ground just two months previous.) After a long time standing among the carriages and manure-pecking pigeons, of staring upward and somewhat losing herself in the facade's arches and the weight-bearing caryatids and the vertiginously small crowning lantern, of craning her neck and feeling herself sickeningly minusculed, Margaret had finally consented to enter the Pulitzer on her father's hand. In a subsequent fever dream her brain conflated the experience with images she'd seen in books of the Sistine Chapel's frescoed ceiling. In the dream, her dad had disappeared when

{010} iron

the Pulitzer building transmogrified into Adam's lifted finger. Inside, she had risen like a nerve between its cast-iron tendons and its fired-mud flesh. The brick skin was nine feet thick at street level but only two at the high gilded thimble. She awoke before God stung her like a pranking schoolboy with the terrifying arc of static from his finger. The day she stood with her dad on the

135

observation deck, she had seen farther in all directions than she ever had before and it had stirred some previously unnamed thing within her. An urge to wing-test? An unsettling clairvoyance?

{001} forewarning

Predicting the weather is what the business with the kites had been about to begin with. When Eddy made the meteorological scene, weathermen were using kite trains to convey their thermometers, anemometers, and electrometers thousands of feet into the atmosphere. To finally forecast, to know the future. No height was too high. By bowing the diamond kite's crossbar, opening a lozenge-shaped hole just so at the two sticks' intersection, eliminating the tail, and connecting the kites in parallel instead of series, Eddy was able to attain unprecedented lift and forgo the tangling that had bungled so many other weather experiments.

{010} void
{100} vista

The best tandem system is not to fasten one kite to the back of another, he says, *but to give each kite its individual string and allow it to branch upward from a main line.*[ii] He tells Margaret that in the broad, flat plains and prairies to the west and south of them, a person must travel hundreds of miles to obtain a vista. And since enmity in the form of men and weather requires time to cover distance, a *view from aloft*[iii] is more than just a look ahead; in times of war and storms, it's a tactical advantage.

Cube No. 5: vista

{100} nerves

Since right turns have a knack for angling a man back to his starting place, Hinton

136

chooses the cube to accompany him on his pilgrimages. He writes: *I have found that whenever I took any other unit I got wrong, puzzled, and lost my way.*[iv] Using a set of painted children's blocks, Hinton assembles, razes, and reassembles poly-unit cubes. Each time he stacks the blocks in a different configuration and each time he creates a mental map of their concealed inner faces. The hidden superficies make an empty grid of color-on-color panes. His mind roves over each block in turn,

{001} sugar

securing every square before moving on to the next. The route to the fourth dimension winds in the x-y and is vertically notched in the z, stepped like the pyramid at Chichen Itza. The ascent is made perilous by darkness and the kind of havoc wrought by tropical heat on rock previously employed as seashells. In the Yucatán, there are a dozen sacrificial sinkholes for every venerated temple, the limestone overeager to weave its chalky way home, the bedrock melting underfoot, rust-stained and soluble. To get you there, the route must be profoundly disorienting. It must also span a

{100} void
{010} void
{001} seizure

vacuum, a terrain where gravity is nil and *down* and *up* are meaningless. Anyone who dared traverse that road would have to cling to something—to what?—to keep from slipping and plummeting off. I don't know how many of Hinton's followers were jolted from their exercises, startled awake while falling with cartwheeling limbs into that mental abyss, hypnic jerks causing them to fling out their insensate arms and legs. I don't know if any of them ever came close to

{010} scaffold

swimming through a wormhole, or getting dissolved by antimatter, or facing countless spectral versions of themselves filigreed in a

web of alternate universes—all things that Hinton's fourth dimension prefigured. I do know that if you slice a cube along its four diagonals, you'll wind up with six pyramids whose tips point to a tiny starburst-shaped hole in the cube's middle. I know that if you reverse the roles of voids and solids then, you'll get a molecular model where planes are electron seas holding everything together. To make ferrite, place iron atoms at each block's heart and vertices. Expose that lattice to your thoughts and it'll create a tintype like a family portrait. What does it hide, foretell?

Cube No. 6: scaffold

{010} vista

Margaret was born on the fiftieth anniversary of the first public demonstration of the telegraph. On January 11, 1838, Vail and Morse wound two miles of cotton-wrapped millinery wire within the Speedwell Ironworks, using nails to tack the line to the red barn's interior. The local paper declared *time and distance annihilated.*[v] When transcontinental telegraph lines opened shortly afterward, it became possible to warn towns of approaching weather. In 1895, the Signal Corps for whom Eddy reports still frowns on forecasting and strictly forbids the utterance of *tornado*. To the west, plains- and prairie-dwellers heed the behavior of animals instead.

{001} instinct

The balking and the bawling. They hearken to the eerie speechlessness of birds and frogs, are alert to a preternatural verdure in the

138

sky above, a deadly calm in the air, a burden on the breast, a dot-dash percussion in the bones that begs *what hath God wrought.*[vi] Wise men know when. When it's time for the frog to go, his cells release their water and replace it with glucose—antifreeze his liver synthesizes from his diet of snails and crickets. Glucose is just a little less sweet than table sugar and has a much lower freezing temperature than water.

{100} void
{001} blood

Minneapolis, 2012. I check out a library book that says diabetes endures in my gene pool because high blood sugar conferred frost-protection on my Ice Age ancestors. It says diagnoses spike every winter. A diabetic may be in real trouble if her blood sugar doubles, but during torpor, the wood frog's glucose level rises by one hundred fold. The ice-nucleating bacteria make a lattice for the crystals to cling to before it's cold enough for them to grow on their own. The frog's heart beats while the ice cobwebs its way between his muscles and skin and gradually filigrees his

{100} iron

organs. It beats as the lenses of his eyes grow opaque and his blood begins to thicken. It beats until his blood turns to a slush of golden plasma and deoxygenated black hemoglobin. Eventually his heart, lungs, and brain all slow to a complete standstill. His cells are candied and suspended in their mineral fretwork. Picture it beautiful. A father like a frost phoenix. He thaws in the reverse order that he freezes: heart, brain, then legs to hop away with. Out on the street, Eddy's shoes say *a patient waiter is no loser;*[vii] his footwork omits most of the

{010} analogous

letters. Meanwhile, across the cold Atlantic, Emil Fischer has just wrapped up a decade of research on the carbohydrates, becoming the first to diagram the molecular configuration of every sugar ever known or imagined. Previously there was no making sense of them. How could substances with the exact same chemical formulae have such disparate properties? Like Hinton, Fischer believes the answer is arrangement. Carbon is a tetravalent atom. Just as a square must have four edges, a carbon atom must bond with four other molecules or elements. If all four are different, the carbon atom is deemed *handed* and *asymmetric*.

Cube No. 7: analogous

{010} scaffold

According to *Ghosts Revealed*, the thing to do is get twenty-seven differently colored wooden blocks and assemble them into one big 3x3x3 cube. Because adjoining faces touch each other regardless of the viewer's orientation, contact—touching—is every arrangement's one inarguable truism. Next you need to learn to nullify the cubes' solidity in your mind, to see through each mass to the colors of its neighboring faces, to somehow envision all squares simultaneously. The slivers of breath between blocks symbolize the intangible fourth dimension, are whiffs of the abyss an incautious practitioner could slip into. If you get lost at

{100} void
{001} sanatorium

any point in the exercises, there is an analogy like this one to bring you back: You are to a four-dimensional being what a square is to a cube. Think of it. To get forward, go back. Fancy you're a sheet of paper having a chance encounter with a

140

block. Imagine how your flatness edits your perception. When you're confined to a plane like a person on heavy duty antidepressants, the most you apprehend of solids is their planar dimensions, the outlines of the faces you're in contact with. Are they sugary-handed reflections or merely old photographs? Your interface with

{010} void
{001} o/missive

the cube will lead you to conclude that it is a close relation of yours. A square. Flat. Since you have no awareness of the third dimension, when the cube is taken away, you can't trace its path. It just disappears. *Why don't you write, you rascals?*[viii] Think of the pattern a block rolled across your skin would create. It would pulse like an electric current or your memory of visitors soon after that *incalculable accident.*[ix] The third dimension grows out of the second one multiplicatively. Generationally, in fact. We are, all of us, composed of innumerable planes, stacked up.

{100} soles

How many sheets of paper tall are you? And in how many different languages, with how many different words, can you signal for help on those planes of pressed pulp? Words are to pictures what axes are to dimensions. In what other incomprehensible direction might you extend without even knowing? Since 3-D objects are bounded by planes, 4-D objects must be bounded by solids. When you're solid, the most you can apprehend of other objects is their solid aspects. Four-dimensional objects appear to us like solids, but have the magic abilities to suddenly vanish, reappear, and pass right through

Karen Hays

Cube No. 8: soles

{100} analogous

us. It's a Saturday evening toward the end of summer in Bayonne, 1897. See up close and over-large the two scuffed soles of a man's shoes, side by side, the toes pointed heavenward. See beyond these a pair of long, trouser-covered legs, foreshortened. In spite of the heat, a jacketed torso. Travel up from the soles until you reach the intersection of the arm and spine axes. See the right arm raised and folded like a wing overhead. Trace the forearm from the bent elbow down to the hand, which holds a monocular eye glass. See swimming in its lens

{010} iron

an eye—tremulous and flecked. See in the eye a pool of brown tannins and green vitriol crystallites and, in the center, the well of iron gall ink their mixture synthesizes— black from electronic loss and the iron's change of valence. Even the sky is iron avid, stripping its electrons. Now turn around and face skyward. Follow the glass and the gaze in a direction parallel to the pointing shoes and the other arm that is outstretched. In the upheld arm's hand there is a black disk and in the black disk, a little white wormhole. The eye and the

{001} essay

opera glass are trained on this. The white hole is the iron gall ink's equal-but-opposite. It's the ghost writing etched by the black pupil onto the page that faces it—acid and ferrous. That's how tightly the man's eye is locked onto it. Speed up as you approach. Speed up at a rate inversely proportional to your distance from it. Race through the aperture in the disk and come out a minute before you went into it. Float slowly upward now. On the ground below, the prior you

142

contemplates the pattern of scuffs on a stranger's pair of slick-soled shoes.

{010} void
{001} loneliness

They belong to a man who has been dead for over a century. Their etchings are the flight patterns of every departed father so the worm's-eye you scrutinizes them for anything that heralds the future you or your future circumstances, uses them to take the auspices. Meanwhile it's August and there's a bank of clouds to the southwest obscuring the sun as it makes its slow, liquid-edged descent. Keep rising until you reach an altitude of 150 feet where you find alas not your own dad, but William Abner Eddy floating flat on his back, his expression dreamy. He's just

{100} oscillating

risen above the nuisance dapples and is hovering in a cloud of dark, color-stripped foliage, enveloped in a soft, granular whiteness. The overall effect, he will later pen, is like *the shadow of trees cast by the moonlight.*[x] He will remain thus for less than a minute, flitting in and out as his alignment of disk and opera glass and the apparatus's reflector permits, contemplating sugary cupolas and canopies a mile and a half distant—his hard earned bird's eye view. Meanwhile, below you, Margaret's dad has already put soles to gravel and taken the reel from his friend's hands.

Cube No. 9: oscillating

{100} soles

Let the analogies accrue like cells around a budding organism; in this way, gain dimensions: Just as Carl Sagan believed that our romance with carbon-based life forms limits our ability to conceive of extraterrestrial versions based on other tetravalent atoms, Hinton argued that our solidity renders us blind to the immaterial fourth dimension. How weird that our senses should conspire to limit our perception, but how intuitively obvious. Think of the sightless woman who can hear you blinking, the unhearing man whose skin is as sensitive to sound waves as the membrane of your ear drum reverberating, whose mind converts

{010} kin

the vibrato of your blink into a hummable tune. Hinton believed that in order to be open to the fourth dimension, one must first dial down her sense of solidity, to eliminate certain insidious *self-elements*.[xi] The only way to eliminate a 3-D bias, he said, is to divorce oneself from locative prepositions, to get rid of *above* and *below* and *beside* and all of their subjective self-referential brethren. He called this first step *the casting out of the self*.[xii] Since prepositions are off limits, you'll have to think only in terms of the remembered colors of concealed adjacent square faces.

{010} augury

In time, the cubes will begin to course through your mind all on their own, like a live thing, like a daydream or a bit of genetic code, like a program defragmenting the compartments of your narcissistic brain, editing it down to something cleaner and more objective, burnishing it of self-referential rust. God help you, you will think you are doing the cubes, but the cubes will be doing you. The process will be pleasurable in a self-obliterating kind of way, but the goal of gleaning some overarching truth will recede and the cube song will become the predominant thing.

144

{100} void
{010} void
{001} tidings

It will hum and twirl and capably dip you and after all of the excruciatingly horrid mind-expanding visualization, a kind of nirvanic vista will open up. The squares will become facets of a disco ball, throwing little planktonic bodies of light in a whirling gyre onto the six walls of your dark cubic room. This won't be the fourth dimension. It will be another form of your brain's obfuscation. It will be compulsion, dizziness, delusion. It will be *autohypnosis*,[xiii] toxic iron buildup, electroshock treatment. One woman described her terminally ill husband's habit like this: *Just as a would-be athlete twists*

Second Story

Cube No. 10: tidings

{001} oscillating

and turns on the parallel bars, using time and energy to develop his muscles and gain strength which can be used later in any direction which he may desire, so Francis assumed that this power gained by practice in visualization, seeing mentally the block of cubes on all sides simultaneously, could also be used in any sphere and on any subject; in fact, it was ability to see through anything, and must eventually lead to clairvoyance.[xiv] One recovered practitioner implored anyone thinking of dabbling with Hinton's cubes to *please believe me when I say that they are completely mind destroying.*[xv]

{100} void
{010} void
{001} void
{100} essay

145

It's hard to say if non-identity is the goal or only a prerequisite of the passage. Have any who made the journey returned or at least sent back their reportage? Argentine poet Jorge Luis Borges opined that the introduction to Hinton's most popular book on the fourth dimension reads a bit like a suicide note. Borges suggested that the book was *perhaps an artifice to evade an unfortunate fate* and wondered *why not suppose the same of all creations?*[xvi] Indeed. For Hinton did attempt to duplicate himself, at least for a little while, in his 3-D life, landing himself in

{010} lexicon

quite a bit of trouble in the years preceding the book's publication. In 1886, Hinton surrendered himself to the police for crimes of bigamy. His first wife was four months pregnant with their fourth child, Sebastian. Hinton secretly married a second woman in order to legitimize the twin boys she had borne him. Friends and family worried that the scandal would induce the backstairs couple to kill themselves. Instead, Hinton was sentenced to three days in jail. The following winter he handed his manuscripts to his editor and fled with his first family for a brief teaching gig in Japan.

Cube No. 11: lexicon

{010} tidings

A Saturday evening toward the end of summer in 1897. The Hintons are settling into Minneapolis, where they have just relocated subsequent to Hinton's dismissal from Princeton. Sebastian is ten, and back in New Jersey, Margaret Doubleday Eddy, a girl who Sebastian will only meet on the superficies of these cubes, is nine. A sudden gust has just shorn the black paper from her dad's airborne camera obscura, ruining the Vistascope's view by letting too much light into its hollow chamber. Down come the three diamond Eddy kites and the one Hargrave box kite and, below them, the gaily swaying

{001} augury

paper cube. Eddy imagines a *skylight room* where an occupant could *fresco* one of four orthogonal scenes onto the *ground-glass ceiling* by tugging one of four curtain cords attached to the Vistascope's mirrors.[xvii] Strong winds and clear skies typically co-occur just before sunset. It's the best time for tornadoes and taking kite photographs. Last May a tornado outbreak killed five hundred people, but the weather bureau still refuses to heed Eddy's urgings and adopt a permanent warning system. Trial forecasts were conducted until *tornado* was deemed more dangerous than the violence it names and the chief signal officer rendered the word

{100} void
{001} void
{100} May

taboo. Tornado-related research skidded to a halt then, raising a plume of cloud-seeding dust to hover over the field for half a century until 1938, when the ban was finally lifted. Named or not, more tornadoes occur in May than any other month. In May, the sky is alive with pollen, lightning, photons, music. Lengthening daylight triggers testosterone production in all of the male songbirds, catalyzing the growth of their brains. Their vocal centers burgeon with new neurons. It's not just the fledglings packing on brain cells, but also the fathers from whom the young birds learn their songs.

{010} genesis

Fathers shed the previous year's notes during

147

the summer molt and grow new ones while sprouting their breeding plumage. Each spring fresh syllables are added and old ones omitted. Like his change of feathers, the replacement song seems the same and is only subtly different. In the Northern Hemisphere, May is when the lower atmosphere begins to take its slow annual breath, drawing down the CO_2 that accumulates all winter long from the decay of dead plankton and plants. The carbon wheel spins it into new sugars and arias. In the Northern Hemisphere, May is when most suicides are committed.

Cube No. 12: genesis

{010} lexicon

Suicide is partly heritable, vocabulary totally learned. Brain scans show songbird chicks practice their fathers' notes in their sleep. Likewise, toddlers require naps to master new verbiage. During the forecasting trial, more deaths were blamed on the dankness of root cellars and storm shelters than on tornadoes themselves. According to one article, *newspapers and residents of the plains acknowledged that they had occasional twisters, cyclones, whirlers, hailstorms, or hurricanes, but never tornadoes.*[xviii] Warnings began in 1884, when the first tornado was photographed, and ended in 1886, when the Hintons embarked for Japan. There Hinton built bamboo climbing frames for his

{001} void
{001} void
{001} void
{001} survey

children to climb through; he called out x-y-z coordinates and they raced to find the named intersections. Re electricity, somehow

148

Hinton intuited that lightning is matter twisting through the fourth dimension. He felt that our own 4-D proportions must be *infinitely minute or else we should be conscious of them,* operating at the scale of our *ultimate particles,* or atoms.[xix] Hinton's granddaughter grew up to become a Manhattan Project physicist. After America bombed Hiroshima, Joan Hinton moved to China and began working in an iron factory converting spent grenades and plane wings into desperately needed cook pots and farm machines.

{100} forewarning

The year before Joan Hinton was born, her father, Sebastian, patented the world's first jungle gym. He modeled the rectilinear iron lattice after the bamboo climbing frame his father had constructed to rid Sebastian and his siblings of their prepositions and obfuscating *self elements.*[xx] On a Tuesday at the end of April, when Joan herself was just a baby, Sebastian Hinton hanged himself in a clinic in Stockbridge, Massachusetts. Sebastian's widow told their children that their father died from smoking, though it seems that in her mind laziness was the primary culprit. The strongest permissible weather warning then was still:

Cube No. 13: forewarning

{100} genesis

Conditions are favorable for destructive local storms.[xxi] The Kansas twister in 1884 sounded like a locomotive, but moved so slowly its photographer had thirty minutes to set up his box camera. *Railroad cars just arrived, 345 passengers.*[xxii] The cyclone hit rainless, its funnel as skinny as the tail of a trick roper's lariat. Thirty-two years to the day later, Sebastian got married. He hanged

149

himself two days shy of his seventh wedding anniversary. My grandfather was a seven-year-old in KC then. A refrain I would hear again and again mirrors Hinton's widow's indictment of inactivity as the root of depression.

{001} nerves

Time is to the essay what contact, touching, is to the cubes: objective at least. True and vocable. Sometimes the best you can do is put up the temporal vertices. Dates are points stretching into timelines, becoming dot-dash easements on the plats of history. Orthogonally placed, plats make a house of cards for your personal mythology to dwell unnamed within. Dear reader, if you are exasperated by this shoebox of flood-ruined photographs and 4-D trading cards, I am quadruply. What if I told you that I recently overheard arguments, that suicide was threatened, that from my high window I saw

{010} void
{001} void
{010} May

two identically dressed stick-limbed seven-year-old boys standing in the yard with their hands on their hips and elbows sparred against each other, with their spines crescentic and diamond sternums lifted, and I needed more than anything to know the name of the kite their frames mimicked, as if my knowing might somehow anchor them, and that Joan Hinton had died the Tuesday previous, and that later that week the largest outbreak of tornados in Minnesota history began birling my curiosity for tabooed words of warning and thwarted prediction methods, that meanwhile in my son's bedroom, a clutch of baby finches

{100} sugar

hadn't learned to sing yet, but loudly

150

cheeped for sustenance. What if I told you that when Eddy was nine and still a midwesterner, his European brethren, Fischer, Hinton, and Tesla, were seven, six, and three respectively, and that Tesla, dwelling among the Dinaric Alps' limestone escarpments and karstic pits, induced a crackling electrostatic display on his beloved pet. *Is nature a gigantic cat,* he wondered. *If so, who strokes its back?* The previous day had been so cold that Nikola had seen a snowball explode in *a flare of light like a loaf of sugar cut by a knife.*[xxiii]

Cube No. 14: sugar

{100} forewarning

Hinton is working as an examiner of chemical patents in DC when, the day after Sebastian's eighteenth birthday, his office gives the stamp of acceptance to sugar expert Emil Fischer's barbiturate. Bayer markets the sleep aid as Veronal. Sebastian is twenty the spring his father, asked to give a toast to women philosophers, stands and dramatically dies of a cerebral hemorrhage. A year and a day later, on the eve of April Fool's, 1908, several quarts of ice cream meant for Margaret's party go missing from the Eddy family's back porch, inducing Eddy to try his hand at forensic science.

{001} vista

To catch the thieves, Eddy attaches three cameras to a kite train and sends the assembly soaring. Outside, he passes the reel to a mittened Margaret so he can tug the strings that will set the airborne shutters winking. Inside the cameras, photons energize the molecules of film where the light strikes the silver gelatin. Like kids let loose for a short spree on a modern playground, the electrons circulate at

151

lightning speed around the film's crystalline surface. A game of freeze tag breaks out at the jungle gym and it's pluses versus minuses; negatively charged electrons flow like free

{010} void
{100} void
{001} void
{010} blood

radicals until they are trapped in the holes of the film's hexagonal lattice. (All cubes are hexagons when looked at edge-on in overhead perspective.) Hungry ions of silver—the pluses—wait in the interstices to nab and not let go of the conducting minuses. Once the metal has locked onto all of the electrons, the jig is up and the pairs are frozen. They're now sensitivity specks, the nuclei of latent images. Like the fourth dimension, the specks can't be seen, but exist nonetheless. They're sugar cells preserved in icy fortresses, genes for an illness so far unexpressed, unqueried relatives.

Cube No. 15: blood

{010} sugar

In 1908, no one knows how things hold together yet. If every atom is surrounded by a cloud of mutually repellent electrons, how do elements ever get close enough to enter into bonds? With what magic? Before you can understand how a molecule with asymmetric carbon operates, first you have to know how its four different bonds are oriented. There are only two ways that four molecules or atoms can array themselves about organic carbon. Because of this, the axes of sugars are either left- or right-handed. Like the offset of our internal organs—our hearts, livers, and insulin-regulating pancreases.

152

{100} May

Maybe genes divide us into those who succumb to winter and those for whom spring is more dangerous. Like DNA and newborn babies' hair whorls, sugars are not superimposable on their reflections. A clue, thought Fischer, to the *highly esteemed vis vitalis.*[xxiv] When viewed under a polarizing microscope, natural sugars like RNA's ribose and blood's glucose rotate the light in a clockwise direction, spinning it like a Northern Hemispheric tornado. Synthetic versions twist it counterclockwise like a Southern Hemispheric tornado. Above the equator, more suicides are committed in May, but below it, the month to watch out for is September.

{001} void
{100} void
{001} scaffold

And, yes, sugar tastes sweet to us not because of the specific atoms it is made of, but because of the way those atoms are arranged along its molecular axis, because of organic carbon's handedness. Alcohol groups angle just so off the carbon chain, making them the perfect keys to unlock our tongues' sense of sweetness. Evolution is the ultimate tool-and-die maker. Tireless. This winter I read that in order for heritable illnesses like diabetes and hemochromatosis to endure in the gene pool, they need only see us through child-bearing age. After that, they can kill us however they want.

{010} o/missive

Sugar produces lightning when smashed hard and fast enough for its pluses to cleave from its minuses. Sparks fly when charges reunite, as charges always must. Dear reader, it's getting harder and harder to cast myself out of the essay. I'm wound like a right-handed protein, en route to excess sugar in the blood and iron in the brain. I'm wondering about electrical conductivity and whether blood sugar and body iron ought to be considered when selecting the voltages electroshock patients receive. That's all I'm going to say about that. In this arrangement, *blood* and *seizures* don't share a vertex.

Cube No. 16: o/missive

{010} blood

I can't think right is how my grandfather described it afterward. If I'm correct and he was suffering from undiagnosed hemochromatosis, a condition in which iron is continually absorbed and stored in the organs, resulting in a range of symptoms including peculiarly dark skin, diabetes, impotence, heart arrhythmia, joint problems, and mental illness, his difficulty tracking and focusing may have existed prior to, and only been exacerbated by, his three ECT treatments. Anyway, it's too late for me to ask him. I hearken to my own eerie speechlessness instead, the crepitus in my too young limbs, my blood's dot-dash susurrus.

{001} analogous

My grandfather, his three brothers, and their father before them: dates and names are most of all there is. So I study men whom history has favored and pray my ghosts will whisper through their hybrid house of cards instead. They are men who share particulars with my own kin, who lived when my grandfather's grandfathers did. There are preppers, birdmen, tinkerers, and inventors. Liars, writers, heartbroken, and sick men. Men of thought and action. There are men who shot themselves. Who poisoned

154

themselves. Who dangled. Dear reader, there are nooses and scaffolds. There are shoe soles swaying pendulously overhead.

{010} void
{100} void
{001} void
{100} essay

Because *beginning* is a soothing myth to believe in. Because origins betoken explanations. And stories seduce forgiveness. There's always a predecessor and a preceding condition. How many wood frogs do you think froze to death before evolution nailed cryogenics? Sure, I know undiagnosed illnesses and gag orders aren't synonymous. And yes, maybe my grandfather's disorientation is what this exercise, without my knowing it at first, was all along meant to simulate and protect against. I'm not sure if I inherited an actual disease or if I'm just conditioned to fear my inheritance. Doctors query blood but so too do essayists.

Cube No. 17: essay

{100} o/missive

Dear child, you look hauntingly like my late grandfather, but I'm the only one in our family who will concede to the likeness. Do I see something that isn't there or do similarities go unacknowledged by those for whom the resemblance is ominous? You gave the mutant blue chick your great-grandfather's name without knowing it; you two never met and we seldom speak of him. Then you changed your mind and named the finch Prix instead. Pay the price for his weird genes, he did. My obsession with the sickly songbird evolved into a curiosity about the origin of blueness itself

{001} soles

155

which in turn led me to iron's role in blue pigments, to its electron structure and the life-or-death consequences of its changing valence, to iron's role in nearly every biological process. Iron is the most limiting nutrient for most life forms, but is so reactive with oxygen that the biological reactions in which it partakes must proceed stepwise and be carefully mediated by less volatile elements. When life first evolved, the atmosphere didn't contain oxygen. Last May, Georgia Tech scientists published research suggesting ancient RNA used iron to more deftly accomplish the folding, binding, and catalysis that magnesium manages today.

{010} void
{001} void
{100} tidings

I found the name of the kite I was looking for. I found space-time and seven-year-olds aplenty. Ridiculously. I found an old Xerox of a family tree whose boughs and fruits were named but unfamiliar to me. I espied the name of my great-grandmother, Lena May, born the year Eddy took the first aerial kite photograph. When I discovered Hinton's exercises, I scored a form to file my obsessions in at last. The siderophilia needed no explanation until it evolved into a posthumous diagnosis for my grandfather and the chain of male kin who died by their own hands.

{010} May

Now even the sky is iron avid. Give it an atom of ferrous iron and it will instantly strip it of an outer electron, oxidizing it and changing its valence. I'm thinking of rust and built-in obsolescence. Evolve or die. Some of the Earth's earliest organisms were photosynthetic bacteria. They cranked out oxygen for a billion years before the waste gas began building in the atmosphere, toxifying the air and precipitating the planet's first mass extinction. Before that, the oxygen glommed onto the tons of ferrous iron dissolved in the ocean, forming vast stores of minable iron here in Minnesota.

Cube No. 18: May

{010} essay

My grandfather was a crane operator for Armco Steel, formerly KC Nut and Bolt, from his late teens until emphysema from inhaled particulates forced him to go on permanent disability in his fifties. The May he died idle, I was off studying geology in Massachusetts, fawning over meteorites—the magnetotactic bacteria some seemed to harbor, and others' migraine-mimicking crystalline structure. Also there was a man, a steel sculptor and Minnesota native. Does some weird psychical siderophilia accompany the body's ravening for iron, or does the theme recur simply because of iron's ubiquity? Which I'm only just now beginning to appreciate?

{100} lexicon

Many suicidologists feel the greatest insight into the self-extinguishing mind can be found not through anatomical or pathological queries but by analyzing the troves of notes people who kill themselves leave behind. When text analysis programs tally the types of words used in suicide missives, they find first-person singular pronouns are prominent, whereas *we* and *us* are rarely written. Common features of fake suicide notes, abstract terms like *love, loneliness,* and *understanding*, are conspicuously absent. More prevalent are concrete nouns— physical objects and recurring chores,

157

Karen Hays

{001} void
{100} blood

{010} forewarning

{001} iron

casually mentioned. That's because *idle mental labor*[xxv] is as anesthetizing as doing the cubes is.

Are we like those rats parasitized by toxoplasmosis? The ones that are almost erotically drawn to the scent of their predator's urine and by proxy their own deaths? The rodents who go out actively looking for cats? Are we like the zombie snails whose translucent eyestalks have been pirated by brown-banded broodsacs, the parasitic flatworms that physically resemble maggots and drive their host snails to seek high branches where songbirds, the creatures in which the broodsacs reproduce, mistake their eyestalks for maggots, gobble the snails, and then shit out baby broodsacs for more birdshit eating snails to ingest? Dear god.

Looking over my notes just now, I realize that my son's bird, Prix, to whom I desperately and futilely administered parasite medication, fledged on the twelfth anniversary of my grandfather's death. Jesus. On a May afternoon, Prix and his sister hopped out of their nest and perched for a little bit. A few weeks later, a new record for the most tornadoes in a single day in Minnesota was set. The prior record was twenty-seven, but I still lived in Kansas City then. When I was a kid we never went into the basement when the sirens began to spin.

Here's what you would see if you opened your eyes on that day in May, and instead of a woman at her high window you were a pigeon in the eaves above me: zones, perhaps, of lightness and darkness. Maybe a

158

compass rose. For a long time scientists thought the iron-rich cells in bird beaks were magnetic neurons, but last spring an article in *Nature* reported that they're really only macrophages—iron-bearing white blood cells. Hemochromatosis is all about macrophages, but bird navigation may spring from photosensitive eye pigments. Light brings eyes like camera film to secret states of conductance.

Ground Level

Cube No. 1: iron

{001} May

At seven years old, you're deaf to the courtship racket. You don't hear the life-or-death urgency in it. One day spring will keen in you, but for now you don't reflect on the long winter or wonder about or grieve for those that didn't make it. This is what you'd hear if you followed your dad and the two neighbors out into the street that spring evening and then slunk off to find a place where you imagined you might anguish the old man by spending the night alone and undiscovered: nothing. Just some waiting-around sounds. Strands of birdsong

Basement

Cube No. 19: hand

{001} iron

so tightly braided an old man could hang himself with them. *I were better to be eaten to death with a rust than to be scoured to nothing by perpetual motion,* scribbled Shakespeare's iron gall ink and goose quill pen.[xxvi] Not I. Is idleness the root of depression? Self-sacrifice is unique to humans and highly social insects. For busy

159

bees and their kin, suicide is tied to sex and parasite infections, not to idleness. Men with *poor reproductive prospects*[xxvii]—gay men, incarcerated men, men suffering from illnesses that diminish sexual function— are more likely than other men to kill themselves.

{010} conductivity

Now the ice cream's been stolen. The party carries on inside without them. Eddy takes the line back from mittened Margaret so he can ensure the cameras are safely reeled in. Cradling the cocoons of evidence to his chest, he hurries inside, racing past electrostatic balloons and excited, ice cream-less party guests. There is seasonal muck on his shoes that puddles wherever he treads. He heads noisily down the wooden stairs that lead to the red-lit darkroom, where, with his sets of tubs and chemical elixirs, his stacks of receptive papers, he develops the film as fast as he can.

{100} instinct

Upstairs, debutantes and balloons wheel and titter in his wake. Four atoms of metallic silver are all you need for an image to nucleate. Four per sensitivity speck. The developer does the rest. The man does. A latent image doesn't care one whit if it's ever made visible to a man, but a man seeks proof of himself again and again. A child, a photo, a word, a book of words, a patent. Because it takes time to cover ground, intuition converts a bird's eye view into temporal distance, gratis. What height must one obtain to surveil a distance of

{010} loneliness

years with his cameras? To forecast the future or be in two places at once, to bridge the imponderable distances or espy the end of the mark that he'll make? See a seated

Eddy poring over the images, his eye trailing
his index finger, and, after some scrutiny,
finally fixing on what he's after. His pointer
stops its dowser's roving and taps on a gray
pair of figures. Two young men appear to be
eating something in the shade of a tree not
far from here. Because the photos were
clicked at a height of several hundred feet,
Eddy can't

{001} void
{100} caper

resolve the features of the culprits' faces, but
his suspicion tells him they belong to some of
his daughter's acquaintances, spurned boys
who, because they didn't receive invitations
from Margaret, must've decided to prank
them. See Eddy, his hawk's bill down, his
eyes staring so hard the whole thing
maddeningly dissolves, becomes something
akin to a landscape by one of those modern
French pointillist painters, a palimpsest of
translated Morse nonsense, a relic's ink
mingling with its mirror opposite. Iron, egg
shell, and wasp gall tannin. Eddy hears the
hard soled shoes and high pitched voices
through the wood overhead.

Cube No. 20: caper

{100} hand

He thumps the two men's miniatures with
one hand while stroking his mustache with
the other, inducing it to shed a bristle onto
the pungent paper. See him under the tree
next, at the terminus of his short and
calculated walk to Newark Bay. See the
chop on the water, Eddy's hands on his hips,
his diamond silhouette like the sunset-
stretched shadow of the kite he patented.
The giddiness of the chase gave way to
chagrin at first but is developing now into
something slightly more complicated as,

161

{001} augury

looking down, Eddy takes in the sight of the several empty froth-coated

ice cream cartons. With his kite-borne camera, he had been in two places at once, had doubled himself, and in so doing, had duped time more than he had space or matter. But he hadn't predicted or prevented the burglary from being committed. Meanwhile, across the cold Atlantic, Werner Heisenberg is six. In a couple of decades, Heisenberg will take sick with May allergies and retreat to a North Sea island. Admiring the vista from his high window, he will concur with quantum physicist Niels Bohr that indeed *infinity seems to lie within the grasp of those who look across*

{010} kin

the sea.[xxviii] Perched thus, Heisenberg will experience a bolt from the blue. It's like Hinton said. Sometimes you have to give up your physical frame of reference. A change of scenery may buy you a spot of clairvoyance. Prepositions off limits. Heisenberg will formulate the trickery of electrons in a way that seems to apply to ice cream thieves and elusive relatives: information gained re exact whereabouts is information lost re trajectory. One's a dot; the other, a dash. Waves and matter collude in secret. Only photos hold still. Here's what was happening in the invisible finery of the cells:

{100} void
{001} void
{010} aboutface

One said: *to everything a rhythm*. And another replied: *some of what has been will always*. They played telephone and passed it down the line until the final cell declared: *A picture in no way predicts or suffices.* You fool. Hinton said that the worst thing about a self element is that you don't know how it hampers your vision until it is finally gotten rid of. I apologize if the dots got the dashes wrong. The whole thing is shot through with uncertainty. I am not so naive as to think an essay could save a life after all.

Cube No. 21: aboutface

{010} caper

Now I see it's the opposite. As Hinton strove for an objective glimpse through geometry, I hoped to obtain a vista by stacking planes of verbiage. Hinton chose disorientation through the cubes, where I took iron's folds, catalysis, and scaffolds. Our planes were ever plumb, but our routes dizzyingly helical. The way is handed and heady—the bad, not good kind of sweet. To go up, spin clockwise. To get down, kick the chair out. As oxygen began polluting the Earth's early atmosphere, some organisms evolved mechanisms to avoid it. They concatenated their iron into cubic chains; they became magnetic.

{001} survey

Each magnetic bacterium has a single strand of iron-bearing beads within it. The beads are uniform in shape; their crystalline lattice, cubic. The iron aligns the microorganism like a compass needle, constraining it in the x-y direction, but allowing it vertical freedom of movement. With its whip-like flagella, the bacterium can propel itself up or down the water column it lives in. Because oxygen levels fluctuate with time and depth, the bacterium must be able to ascend and descend. In the Northern Hemisphere, the microorganisms' flagella propel them clockwise upward and

163

Karen Hays

counterclockwise downward. In the
Southern Hemisphere, it's the opposite.

{100} void
{010} void
{001} void
{100} conductivity

The motility of magnetic bacteria mimics the
quantum spins of electrons themselves. At
the Earth's surface where pressures are low,
at least by comparison with its solid inner
core, iron's outer electrons keep their
distance from one another. They spread out
and live alone. When there's plenty of room,
coupling isn't worth it. In order to dwell
peacefully together, paired electrons have to
assume opposite orientations—one spins
down, the other up. Electrons living singly
align themselves parallel to the Earth's
magnetic field, all spinning upward.
(Divorce and suicide show a close correlation.
Marriage has a strongly protective effect.)

Cube No. 22: conductivity

{100} aboutface

A psychical and physical delicious mad
almost erotic inherited ravening for iron, I
seem to have. When I wasn't quite seven,
Borges edited an anthology of literature
named after his story, *The Library of Babel*.
In his introduction to Hinton's *Scientific
Romances*, Borges poses the idea of art as
foil to ill fate. The fictional Library of Babel
is a hollow honeycomb—its hexagonal walls
lined with shelves, its shelves lined with
texts—containing every possible book that
the combination of twenty-two lowercase letters, commas, periods, and spaces permits,
including countless tombs of nonsense,
obscenely recursive manuals, the heavily
sought

164

{001} nerves

Vindications,[xxix] the true story of your own death and—the best one in the narrator's jurisdiction—*Combed Thunder.*[xxx] The winter Margaret was born, electric, telegraph, and telephone lines formed a dense cross hachure over New York City. Like interlocking plumage barbs or a collage of groomed thunderclaps. The cables were oriented at so many angles they made a complicated harp-works for the wind to strum and whistle-winged pigeons to perch within. Then, when Margaret was two months old, they collapsed in the unforecast spring blizzard that dumped forty inches in almost as many hours. After that, the city buried its

{010} hand

infrastructure, but kept of course its vista-seeking pigeons. When Tesla's white-winged muse alighted on the sill of his window for the final time, her eyes shone brighter than any light *ever produced by the most powerful lamps in my laboratory,*[xxxi] auguring, Tesla felt, the deaths of both the bird and his scientific ingenuity. He loved her, he said, as a man does a woman. Oh heavens. They say pigeon wings only whinny when the birds ascend in a panicked hurry, activating the whole flock's nervous energy. In the essay's first arrangement, *forewarning* is stacked on *nerves* is stacked on *conductivity,*

{001} void
{010} void
{100} seizures

but in the next iteration, some of the faces that touch the void now will be brought into the cube's interior and I'll be able to tell you what happened to Eddy's wife the year Tesla's pigeon died, when my grandfather was seven, shortly before Sebastian did himself in. I'll be able to tell you about Fischer and sons' ill fates and the significance of age seven. Half of the faces are turned away in every arrangement. Can you see how the essay is winding down and I'm completely terrified that I haven't told you enough yet? I'm so sorry.

Cube No. 23: seizures

{100} conductivity

Symptoms of the disease mirror side effects of electroshock treatment. Take *anomic aphasia*, a profound difficulty recalling the specific names of things. Meanings decouple from the shapes and sounds of their labels. Like titles on the book spines in the Library of Babel, words don't even hint at what's between the covers. Words would rather rhyme than be conductive. Letters align in parallel as if rhyme were a kind of magnetism, as if it were energetically conservative for syllables to point the same direction. Our first clue that there was something wrong with Prix came when he began having seizures.

{001} vista

His lights would suddenly blink off and he'd fall with a *fwump* to the floor from his perch. That's when I developed this dumbass idea about the lack of UV incident to the mutant's feathers. Where his siblings were rainbow-hued, Prix was moth-wing gray with hints of blueprint blue at his feathers' tips. He always looked unfinished. There are no foods that impart blueness, no true blue roses. There are only two routes to blue that I know of: the scattering of light and iron's changing valence. Turns out, blue feathers are just brown keratin shot through with vermiform tunnels.

{010} void

166

{100} void
{001} void
{010} instinct

So too is the brain labyrinthine and foamy. In one study, it was estimated that twenty percent of brain volume is extracellular space. Interconnected channels twist around globs of glia-wrapped neurons, providing a medium where chemical and electrical signaling can take place. The fluid in the channels acts as a conductive liaison between blood vessels and brain cells, conveying glucose, neurotransmitters, and other electroactive compounds across membranes. Substances move through the channels via diffusion, taking random walks and making progress through collisions, ricochets, bombardments. Like light through blue feathers, the progress of salts between neurons is random; the structure itself isn't.

Cube No. 24: instinct

{010} seizures

I'm reminded of Hinton's attention slinking between block faces. I've woven my way round a family yen for suicide, have tried to atomize the underlying story to see all of the objective superficies simultaneously. Did I say or censor too much? The rate of diffusion is always controlled by the volume of pore space and the path's tortuosity. It winds, dear reader. Dies or evolves. If you were to shine a light on this weird wasp's nest, would its pockets scatter the wavelength bluely? Like the sky above or a mutant bird's first feathers, like the veins in a wrist?

{001} scaffold

Some geophysicists think the iron in the Earth's core is under so much pressure its atoms are packed into a *Crimson Hexagon*[xxxii] rather than a loose cubic lattice.

Karen Hays

Instead of flowing at ease around an orthogonal structure, keeping their distance from one another and maintaining parallel spin-up orientations, valence electrons would pair up, polarize, and flow with absolutely no resistance, making the core's iron unlike any at its surface, making it superconductive. Superconductors emit magnetic fields and can even levitate magnets. In one study, scientists theorized that the Earth's inner core was one solid iron crystal. Some hemochromatotics set off

{100} hand

airport metal detectors. Just imagine hovering instead of dropping the instant you kicked the chair out. Imagine riding a magnetic plume instead of crashing to the ground like the winged Prix did. The average adult's blood bears about a hummingbird's heft of iron, but a hemochromatotic man may have ten times as much stored in his skin, brain, liver, joints, pancreas, and pituitary gland. Roughly the weight of our whole clutch of baby finches. Rather than the prophetic light of bird eyes, The Library of Babel is illumined by too dim fruit lamps. Suicide and pulmonary ills cull a great

{001} void
{100} void
{010} sanatorium

portion of the library's custodians. In its *Crimson Hexagon*, texts are *smaller than natural [. . .] omnipotent, illustrated, and magical.*[xxxiii] I tried coloring the diagrammed essay with twenty-seven shades ranging from arterial red to venous purple, but found the hues of bruises and bloodletting—the rust and spectrum of meaty valences, the meteorites' scintillating scotomas—to be more disorienting than simply assigning themes

168

and crystallographic indices to each of its faces. Both ways, it was harder than DNA to read. If you want clairvoyance, I guess you should get a fucking DNA test. Here are the blueprints for a heritable disease:

Cube No. 25: sanatorium

{010} instinct

A slavish insatiable mad ravening for iron, have almost all bacteria and I. Our parasites hunt us for our ferrous iron. Picture this: A bacterium cracks open a molecule of your blood's hemoglobin, frees the four iron atoms whose job it is to shuttle your oxygen around and systematically strips each one of a valence electron. This is the M.O. of bubonic plague. Holy holy. When our immune systems detect infection, they send out macrophages (the kind of iron-bearing white blood cells long mistaken for magnets in the beaks of pigeons) to ensconce the invaders and escort them back to

{001} analogous

home base, aka the lymph nodes. In his book *Survival of the Sickest,* hemochromatotic Dr. Sharon Moalem says macrophages are like the Trojan horses of the plague. The bacteria gorge on the iron in the macrophages, fortifying their army to kick ass once they're delivered to the lymph nodes. Untreated people typically die within four days. Moalem describes how the people who succumbed to plague epidemics were often the healthiest and least anemic— mostly young men. Older people, malnourished children, and women (who tend to lose a lot of iron through pregnancy, nursing, and menstruation) were spared. So too was

{010} void
{100} void

Karen Hays

{001} void
{100} loneliness

the hemochromatotic population, theorizes Moalem, because people with hemochromatosis have iron-deficient macrophages. Plague bacteria would have starved instead of thrived en route to the lymph nodes. To persist in the gene pool, a mutation need only see its host through child-bearing age. A hemochromatotic's intestines mistakenly believe her iron stores are always insufficient. They absorb and absorb it. Moalem suggests that hemochromatosis may have been an adaptation that helped poorly nourished women sustain repeated pregnancies. Now that our food is fortified and we have far fewer children, the adaptation is maladaptive. Some think suicide underwent the same change in valence.

Cube No. 26: loneliness

{100} sanatorium

The hemochromatotic's body hoards iron lifelong. Ferrous iron is so energetic, so reactive, electropositive, and universally coveted that it feeds cancers, nurses bacteria, and forms deleterious free radicals wherever it resides uncombined in the organs. It destroys cellular architecture like freezing too fast pops apart the fabric of caught-off-guard frogs. In order to do no harm, the essay must grow ice-wise—around but never within the family narrative. It must stultify or at least speak in lulling syllables. My great-grandmother maybe went a little berserk after her fifth son died. She was placed in a sanatorium and, like a

{010} void
{001} void
{010} hand

170

palimpsest, entirely written over. She died before her husband and four adult sons lost their lives to suicide and/or grew dark under its omnipresent threat. No one I know ever even met her. So now I sometimes wonder how half a century of gag orders may have affected our perception of natural disasters, us plains- and prairie-dwellers. It seems to me that we're a people who resist calling things by their rightful names. Be they tornadoes, mental illnesses, climate change, evolution, or any of the multitudinous –isms we use to codify oppression. Be it simply terror. Dear reader, would you

{001} soles

say it's time I had that blood test? Time I read the genetic soles, took the molecular auspices? The articles I find all say that hemochromatosis is the most common life-threatening genetic disorder on the continent, yet most North American doctors have never diagnosed it. A consumptive mad ravening. On my birthday four years ago, Malcolm Casadaban, a microbiologist conducting federal bioterrorism research, wrote to his university to explain that he had taken ill and would be missing work. He was dead three days later from a very bizarre plague infection. The bacterial strain he was working with, KIM D27,

{100} kin

had been mutated to make it innocuous; researchers had rendered it unlike its fatal kin by making it enzymatically incapable of taking up iron. And so Casadaban, an undiagnosed hemochromatotic, may have been a little careless when he handled it. Doctors think that the surfeit of iron in Casadaban's tissues somehow helped the bacterium overcome its enzymatic handicap. However it got inside him, the bacterium

171

must have bypassed Casadaban's iron-starved macrophages. Ironically, one of the oldest, simplest, most universal and intuitive medical practices on the planet might have saved him. Phlebotomy—blood-letting—prevents toxic levels of iron from ever accumulating.

Cube No. 27: kin

{100} loneliness

The chief signal officer said, *the harm done by such a prediction would eventually be greater than that which results from the tornado itself.*[xxxiv] Tortuosity determines the rate at which predictions diffuse through the vernacular. Today I read that the use of scientific jargon may have impeded public acceptance of the phenomenon I'm still stubbornly calling "global warming." To speak is to concede, not to invoke or surrender. Many believe that asking at-risk people about suicide inspires them to go through with it, but studies have shown the exact opposite. What a relief it is to give voice to that

{001} oscillating

imponderably small coil, to secure it like precious cargo in a lattice of verbal dunnage. To name then shush it. To see all of the reversed faces in the tintype family portrait. *And so we lie palpable, open. There is no such thing as secrecy,* wrote Hinton.[xxxv] It isn't iron that guides songbirds and homing pigeons. When UV strikes bird eyes, the light excites their blue-sensitive pigments, freeing electrons to flow around their retinas, and creating radicals to align with the magnetic field like needles of compasses. Free radicals can destroy our brains, but don't hurt pigeon or finch retinas.

{100} void

{010} void
{001} void
{010} caper

Because pulled through the fourth dimension, the left hand is superimposable on the right one. Because the stubborn disparity between the man and whom he sees in the mirror finally vanishes; asymmetry capitulates. Because *there can be no possible mental harm in going through this bit of training, for all that it comes to is looking at a real thing as it actually is— turning it round and over and learning it from every point of view.*[xxxvi] Because panes face the void and then don't again. Because each spring writes new formulae using the variables *keen, death, turn,* and *quicken.*

Arrangement

Basement			Ground Level			Second Story		
27	20	21	9	2	3	10	11	12
26	19	22	8	1	4	17	18	13
25	24	23	7	6	5	16	15	14

Mechanics of kite scenes are based on Eddy's writings; Margaret's attendance and states of mind are unknown and imagined.

[i]William A. Eddy, "Incalculable Accidents," *The Popular Science Monthly* 41 (1892), 666.
[ii]William A. Eddy, "The Eddy Malay Tailless Kite," *Scientific American* 71 (September 15, 1894), 169.
[iii]William A. Eddy, "Machine to Take Pictures from a Kite," *The Phonoscope* 1, Number 9 (August–September 1897), 115.
[iv]Charles Howard Hinton, *A New Era of Thought* (London: Swan Sonnenschein & Co., 1888), 19.
[v]"Invention of the Telegraph," http://www.morrisparks.net/speedwell/tel/tel.html (accessed January 30, 2013).
[vi]Contents of experimental telegraph message, May 24, 1844. Daniel Walker Howe, *What Hath God Wrought: The Transformation of America, 1815–1848* (New York: Oxford University Press, 2007), 1.

Karen Hays

[vii]Contents of first telegraph message, January 6, 1838. Francesca Davis DiPiazza, *Friend Me!: 600 Years of Social Networking in America* (Minneapolis: Lerner Publishing, 2012), 55.

[viii]Contents of first commercial telegraph message, January 8, 1846. Lewis Coe, *The Telegraph: A History of Morse's Invention and Its Predecessors* (Jefferson, North Carolina: McFarland & Co., 2003), 87.

[ix]William A. Eddy, "Incalculable Accidents," *The Popular Science Monthly* 41 (1892), 666.

[x]"Machine to Take Pictures from a Kite," 115.

[xi]*A New Era of Thought*, 21.

[xii]Howard Hinton, *Scientific Romances* (London: Swan Sonnenschein & Co., 1886), 206.

[xiii]Mark Blacklock, "Cubic Thought," *The Fairyland of Geometry: A Cultural History of Higher Space*, December 10, 2009, http://higherspace.wordpress.com/2009/12/10/cubic-thought/ (accessed January 30, 2013).

[xiv]Blacklock.

[xv]Martin Gardner, *The Colossal Book of Mathematics: Classic Puzzles, Paradoxes, and Problems* (New York: Norton, 2001), 22.

[xvi]Jorge Luis Borges, "Prologues to the Library of Babel" in *Selected Nonfictions*, ed. Elliot Weinberger (New York: Viking, 1999), 509–510.

[xvii]"Machine to Take Pictures from a Kite," 115.

[xviii]Marlene Bradford, "Historical Roots of Modern Tornado Forecasts and Warnings," *Weather Forecasting* 14 (1999), 484–491. doi: http://journals.ametsoc.org/doi/full/10.1175/1520-0434%281999%29014%3C0484%3AHROMTF%3E2.0.CO%3B2 (accessed March 20, 2013).

[xix]*Scientific Romances*, 31.

[xx]*A New Era of Thought*, 23.

[xxi]Bradford.

[xxii]Contents of telegraph message on first public demonstration, January 11, 1838. L. J. Davis, *Fleet Fire: Thomas Edison and the Pioneers of the Electrical Revolution* (New York: Arcade Publishing, 2003), 87.

[xxiii]Nikola Tesla, "A Story of Youth Told by Age," *Tesla: Life & Legacy*, PBS.org, www.pbs.org/tesla/ii.story_youth.html (accessed January 30, 2013).

[xxiv]Emil Fischer, "Synthesen in der Zuckergruppe," *Berichte der Deutschen Chemischen Gesselschaft* 27 (1894), 3189.

[xxv]Jesse Bering, *Why Is the Penis Shaped Like That?: And Other Reflections on Being Human* (New York: Scientific American, 2012), 246.

[xxvi]William Shakespeare, "Henry VI, Part 2" (New York: Oxford University Press, 1998), 143.

[xxvii]Bering, 233.

[xxviii]Manjit Kumar, *Quantum: Einstein, Bohr, and the Great Debate about the Nature of Reality* (New York: Norton, 2010), 188.

[xxix]Jorge Luis Borges, trans. Andrew Hurley, "The Library of Babel" in *Collected Fictions* (New York: Penguin, 1998), 115.

[xxx]*Collected Fictions*, 117.

[xxxi]Margaret Cheney, *Tesla: Man out of Time* (New York: Simon & Schuster, 2001), 283.

[xxxii]*Collected Fictions*, 116.

[xxxiii]*Collected Fictions*, 116.

[xxxiv]United States Army Signal Corps, *Annual Report of the Chief Signal Officer of the Army to the Secretary of War for the Year 1887* (Washington: Government Printing Office, 1887), 22.

[xxxv]*Scientific Romances*, 40.

[xxxvi]*A New Era of Thought*, 34.

Next to Nothing
Stephen O'Connor

SOUR SISTERS

THE SOROS SISTERS' EYES are the blue of lunar seas, their complexions cloud white, and their identical pageboys well-bottom black. The term "beautiful" has never been applied sincerely to either sister, though Ivy, the youngest by two years, might be deemed the better looking, because she has detectable cheekbones and a waist narrower than her hips. Isabel has very little in the way of body fat, but is square shaped from almost any angle. Even her face is square shaped. It's been that way since birth.

As soon as Isabel and Ivy slam the doors of their white van, three people in front of the pharmacy stop talking. A man whose metallic-gray pickup has just bleeped and flashed its lights feigns acute interest in a parking meter. No one looks either sister in the eye as they approach along the solitary block of the town's main street. No one raises a hand, or says hello. But once the sisters have begun to recede in the opposite direction, all four heads turn to watch. Significant glances are exchanged, but not words. There's no need.

Isabel and Ivy's parents retired to the town twelve years ago, when their father had a stroke and had to give up his orthopedic surgery practice in the city. Everybody loves Dr. Soros, who is floppy of foot and eccentric of speech, but can be counted on for a lopsided grin whenever he is spotted in public. Hilda Soros has the perpetually startled expression of a woman with too many worries, but perhaps for that very reason, with her every smile—timid, then radiantly blooming—she seems to be discovering joy for the first time in her life.

Her daughters, however, seem never to have discovered joy. They bypass even the friendliest greetings with the indifference of a bull-dozer flattening a picket fence. In the rare instances when small talk is unavoidable (on the checkout line at the Food-Star, on the diving raft at the lake), they terminate it in twelve words. Or five. Their brows are always wrinkled, their mouths slot straight. They make the townspeople feel erased. They make the townspeople feel like a variety of wood louse.

SOMETHING IS NOT RIGHT

Isabel and Ivy are sociologists, and thus the beneficiaries of lengthy academic vacations. They have spent every July and August in their parents' white-clapboard house ever since each bore her first child: daughters—both eleven now. Isabel's husband is an executive at a food-processing company, and Ivy's is an investment banker. The two men cannot be in the same room without getting drunk and turning every topic of conversation into a theater of mutual disparagement. Their visits to the town never overlap, and are, in fact, so fleeting and rare that many people believe that the sisters are lesbians, and that their children—six of them now; evenly divided—are the products of artificial insemination. Isabel and Ivy each have their own room, and a double bed, and their children sleep in an attic that reminds everyone of the dormitory in that old house in Paris where Miss Clavel looked after Madeline.

Tonight it is Ivy's turn to read to the children. She is sitting at the end of the aisle between the two rows of beds in a sage-green easy chair, the arms of which are frayed to their cotton batting. The children are all upright in their beds, staring at her expectantly. Although Ivy's parents are brown eyed and both her husband and Isabel's have eyes the color of wet charcoal, each of the twelve irises turned toward her is the all-but-white-blue of a lunar sea—a statistical anomaly that Ivy finds more than moderately disconcerting.

"I don't like that story," says Gwenny (Isabel's oldest child).

"I haven't even started it yet." Ivy lifts the picture book from her lap and looks at the cover, though for no particular reason.

"I don't like it either," says Jen (Ivy's oldest).

"Me too," says little Jerry (her youngest).

"We hate that book," says Gwenny.

"OK." Ivy puts the book down on one side of her chair, and picks a new book from the pile on the other.

"We hate that one too," says Paulette (Isabel's middle child).

"OK." Ivy puts the second book down, and picks up a third. She doesn't care what she reads. They all seem stupid to her. But the kids hate that book too, and the next.

"Tell us a story," says Gwenny.

"I'm trying to, but you won't let me," says Ivy.

"No, make one up!"

"Yeah," says Jerry. "Make us up a story, Mommy."

Ivy begins to sweat along her hairline and under her arms. For a long moment she sits in the chair, silent, swollen looking—as if she has been stuffed. Then she sighs heavily.

"Once upon a time," she says, "there was a little princess . . . or she might have been a prince"—she looks at Jerry—"only you know for sure." Jerry sticks his thumb into his mouth and slides down in his bed so that he is looking straight at the ceiling. "Anyhow," says Ivy, "the princess lived in a castle on the beach. It was a sand castle. And it had a dungeon. That was where she kept her toys."

"What kind of toys?" asks Paulette.

"She had exactly the same toys that you have," says Ivy. "One day she went down to the dungeon to play with her toys and there was a dragon there. He told her, 'This is not your castle. It is my castle. You have to leave now or I will turn you into a cinder.' 'But I've lived here all my life,' said the princess. 'It doesn't matter,' said the dragon. 'You have to go. You can take one toy with you.' So she picked up a toy and she left."

"What toy did she take?" says Jen.

"What do you think she took?" says Ivy.

"A teddy bear," says Jen.

"No. It was a plastic teepee."

"A teepee!" says Jerry, his thumb still in his mouth.

"It was her favorite toy. But as soon as she was out of the castle, she put it down on the sand and a wave washed it away." Ivy waits for a response from the children. When none comes, she continues. "For seven nights and seven days she walked, and she got so tired and so cold—because it was snowing—that she came down with a fever, and fainted on the old man's doorstep."

"Which old man?" says Gwenny.

"The blind old man who lived in the cottage in the forest. He made her a bed in front of the fireplace and gave her medicine, but it was the wrong kind of medicine, so she didn't get any better."

"What kind of medicine?" says Gwenny.

"Leeches."

The children make ripping noises with their lips and teeth.

"Anyhow," says Ivy, "a prince was walking by the cottage, and when he saw the princess lying in front of the fire, he decided to go in and kiss her. The prince was so quiet that the blind man didn't even know he was there. The prince bent over the princess and kissed her on the lips. But when he lifted his head, he saw that she was dead, so he crept out of the cottage as quietly as he had come in."

"That's horrible!" says Paulette.

"Did his kiss kill her?" says Gwenny.

"Nobody knows," says Ivy. "But she was probably dead when the prince walked into the room." Ivy puts her hands on her knees, and stands up. "OK, everybody—time for sleep!"

GOOD NEWS

It is hurricane season. A week ago, newscasters spoke urgently about Hurricane Gigi's devastation of Haiti. Then Tropical Storm Henry earned an afternoon and evening of coverage. But now the coiffed heads on every news show talk about nothing but Hurricane Ivy, which is rolling up the Eastern Seaboard like a massive ninja star, and is predicted to pass over the town as a category-four storm the day after tomorrow.

"Brace yourself," says Isabel, sitting with her laptop at a picnic table under the shade of an enormous willow. A small brook meanders just behind her, making a noise like ping-pong balls sliding down a plastic chute. Mosquitoes hover unsteadily around her head. She doesn't care. She takes Benadryl every night to get to sleep, so mosquito bites have no effect.

"For what?" says Ivy, who is standing directly in front of the table. A mosquito has sunk its proboscis into her left shoulder. She slaps and lifts her hand: a starburst of blood.

"You know: your name."

When Ivy still doesn't understand, Isabel adds, "Jokes."

"Oh," Ivy rubs the starburst and thready mosquito remains away with the side of her thumb. "I don't think that's anything to worry about."

It isn't.

Silence falls and eyes avert as Ivy walks into the Food-Star.

The checkout clerk looks at the name on Ivy's credit card, but only says: "Paper or plastic?"

Back outside, the sky is festively sunshiny, though gigantic clouds mount in shades of cream, blue, and gold toward the upper edge of the troposphere. One can look at those clouds and imagine monstrous

178

forces of nature stirring within them. Ivy doesn't. The clouds are just weather.

The Food-Star has been emptied of candles and size-D batteries—the two main objectives of Ivy's expedition. She leaves the store with twenty-four cans of tuna fish, twenty-four cans of peaches, a dozen boxes of vacuum-packed milk, two giant boxes of Cheerios, and one plastic jar of yellow mustard—all items on her mother's shopping list, which bears a title: "EMERGENCY."

In the Food-Star parking lot, a young blonde woman asks Ivy if she has been saved.

"What are you talking about?" says Ivy.

"Saved!" The young woman's smile brightens distinctly. "You know," she says, "have you found Jesus?"

"There's no point in talking to me," says Ivy.

When the young woman only blinks and ups her smile volume, Ivy says, "I don't believe in God."

"Why not?"

"Because I know that I am entirely insignificant, doomed to complete extinction, and I see no reason to pretend otherwise."

ISABEL TRIES OUT DIVINITY

Isabel is six, Ivy four. The sky above the buildings outside their apartment windows is the color of a dusty chalkboard, and the light coming down onto the street is exactly the color of boredom. Nothing can move in that light. Nothing changes.

"Do you love me?" Isabel asks. Ivy says nothing. "Will you do what I tell you to?" Isabel asks. Ivy picks up a plastic frying pan and puts it on the pink cardboard stove. She is not looking at her sister. "Do you want to play a game?" asks Isabel.

"What?" says Ivy.

Isabel has to think about raw liver to keep from smiling. Merely from the way Ivy's moon-bright eyes look up at her from the floor, Isabel knows everything that will happen.

"Hide-and-seek," she says.

Ivy looks back at her frying pan. She makes a tick-tick-tick in the back of her throat, which is the sound of the cardboard burner lighting. But Isabel knows this is only a diversionary tactic. Ivy loves hide-and-seek.

"Only this time," says Isabel, "we will both hide."

Now Ivy looks at Isabel. In the faint pursing of Ivy's glossy, plum-red lips, Isabel sees hope. And in the check-mark crinkle of Ivy's right eyebrow, Isabel sees curiosity. These are weaknesses: hope and curiosity. Isabel almost feels sorry for her sister.

"You'll hide first," says Isabel. "And while you're hiding, I'll hide too. Then you count to twenty and try to find me."

"I want to hide first," says Ivy.

"You will," says Isabel. "That's what I just said."

"No. I want *you* to find *me*."

"I will. As soon as you find me, it will be my turn to find you."

The pursing of Ivy's lips intensifies. What was once hope is now determination. Isabel has to move quickly or she will lose her advantage.

"I promise I'll hide in this room," she says, "so it will be easy to find me."

"OK," says Ivy.

"Where do you want to hide?" Isabel asks. "Under the bed? In the closet?" These are the most boring places in the world. Isabel only asks to give her sister the illusion of choice. "What about the trunk? You could also hide in the trunk."

The trunk is on the floor at the end of Isabel's bed, and it is the place where their mother keeps clean sheets and pillowcases. Also, at the very bottom, is a trove of Ivy's baby clothes. It is the baby clothes that so endear the trunk to Ivy. She likes to climb inside, lie on the bedding, and cover her face with one of the tiny velvet dresses she wore as a newborn. When she does this, she says she is taking her "secret nap." Sometimes she closes the lid of the trunk; sometimes she doesn't.

"OK," says Ivy.

Ivy curls up inside the trunk. Isabel closes the lid and sits on top of it. "Are you counting?" she says. When Ivy doesn't answer, she adds, "I can't hide until you start counting."

Isabel hears Ivy's nap-time voice counting. She waits until Ivy misses thirteen, which she always does, and then she says, "You forgot thirteen."

"You're not hiding," says Ivy.

"Yes, I am."

"You're sitting on the trunk."

"No, I'm not. I'm hiding. I'm in a special place. I bet you'll never find me. Finish counting and then come out and try to find me. Don't forget thirteen."

180

"Thirteen," Ivy says in her nap-time voice. "Fourteen."

When Ivy reaches twenty, nothing happens. Maybe she has fallen asleep. "Come and find me," says Isabel.

Ivy's knees or elbows clunk against the trunk's side. Isabel feels the upward pressure of Ivy's hand against the lid just beneath her right buttock.

"Get off," says Ivy.

Isabel says nothing.

"Get off!" Ivy shoves the lid harder. Isabel feels the pressure, but it is entirely ineffectual. The top of the lid bulges a bit, but the lid's edges do not lift off the trunk's lip.

"Get *off!*" Now Ivy is shouting. She shoves again, still no effect.

Isabel is smiling, and working hard to keep from laughing. "Come and find me!"

"You're not hiding. You're lying!"

"I *am* hiding," says Isabel. "And you will never be able to find me. Never ever." Now she is laughing, but she doesn't care.

When Ivy flips onto her back and uses her feet to push up against the lid, it rises a quarter inch off the lip of the trunk, so Isabel reaches down and pulls up the hinged brass lock, fastening it. Now Ivy doesn't have a prayer.

Isabel sits Indian style while her sister screams and kicks, all to no avail. After a while Ivy stops kicking, stops saying anything. Silence accumulates. Isabel thinks: "When she starts to cry, I will let her out." And a little later she thinks, "I will let her out because I am merciful."

ONE LEG IS BOTH THE SAME

Isabel and Ivy's natural tendency is to see human society as a pointlessly complex mechanical device of no use to anybody, and most likely broken. They know, however, that theirs is a minority opinion, and so, from a very early age, they have compared what people actually say and do to what it would be reasonable to say and do, hoping they might discover what it takes to feel at home in the world. These efforts—disappointing from the get-go and worse over time— nonetheless endow the sisters with certain intellectual habits that propel them through college, sociology graduate school, and into tenure-track jobs: Isabel at a university in Nebraska; Ivy, in Indiana.

Ivy's primary area of study is the financial futures market, where

181

traders make billions by buying and selling absolutely nothing. Isabel investigates apocalyptic cults, and is particularly interested in the notion of the apocalypse as moral reckoning. The thesis of her book, *Revenge: The Ethics of World Destruction*, is contained in its opening sentence: "As the extinction of life on earth will have no positive or negative effect on the rest of the universe, it is an event entirely without moral significance, and it is precisely this insignificance that inspires the moral furor of apocalypse cultists." *Revenge* has been submitted to seventeen university and academic publishers, and so far has no takers.

"Too many mathematical formulae," says Ivy.

"Maybe you should tone it down a bit," says her mother. "After all, *some* people will care if the world ends. That's an effect, isn't it?"

"Not at all," says Isabel. "No people, no effect."

Her mother touches the index and middle fingers of her right hand to the ear stem of her glasses, as if she is listening to a secret message. Then she takes her glasses off, shrinking her eyes to the size of kidney beans. She blinks and doesn't seem to know where she is.

FIELD WORK

Now it is Isabel's turn. Her mother insists that they have at least one set of D batteries for their solitary flashlight, which, at present, casts a faint, coppery illumination, undetectable after a yard and a half. The mission is hopeless, of course, but Isabel has undertaken it because actual failure is the only way of shutting up her mother.

Isabel is standing in front of the Food-Star holding a plastic bag containing twenty-four cans of tuna fish, two Snickers bars, and a packet of black pantyhose. The parking lot descends partway down the hillside forming the northern edge of a valley big enough to contain an entire county—which, in fact, it does. On the valley's southern edge, blueberry- and plum-colored mountains rise to Isabel's eye level and higher. And, above those mountains, bulbous gray and slate-blue weather is stacked so precariously high it looks as though it could topple into the valley at any minute.

"Excuse me," says a smiling young woman.

"Yes," says Isabel.

"Are you saved?" The young woman is wearing a T-shirt with the word "GOD" over one breast and "ME" over the other, and a red heart in between, more or less where her own thumping, pumping, flesh-and-blood heart is located.

"In what sense?" says Isabel. She has taken a professional interest in this young woman.

Something like the momentary disintegration of a digital image transpires on the young woman's face, and her smile intensifies. "Did I talk to you yesterday?"

"No," says Isabel.

The sheer confidence of Isabel's denial causes another disintegration in the area of the young woman's lightly freckled nose.

" 'Saved' in what sense?" says Isabel.

"You know: Have you been saved by Jesus?"

"No, I haven't."

This answer seems to restore the young woman's confidence. Her smile engages in a delicate *pas de deux* with the sympathetic and sorrowful uptilting of her eyebrows. "Would you like to be?"

"What would I have to do?" says Isabel.

"Just let Jesus into your heart!" There is no sun out, but sunbeams ricochet off the young woman's whitened teeth.

"Is that difficult?" asks Isabel.

"It's the easiest thing in the world!"

"Are *you* saved?" Isabel asks.

"Of course!"

"How do you know?"

The sunbeams disappear from the young woman's teeth. Her uptilted eyebrows sink and collide. "I just do."

"What if I told you that I know that you are *not* saved?"

The young woman is silent. The whole time she and Isabel have been talking, she has been clutching a stack of glossy brochures in her right hand. The brochures depict periwinkle-blue skies, white doves flying, a steeple, and the faces of happy children. The young woman lifts the brochures to cover the inscription across her chest.

"I'm sorry to disturb you," she says.

"You're not disturbing me. I just want to know what you think."

"About what?"

"If I were to tell you that I know you are not saved, what would you think?"

"I would think that you are wrong."

"But how can you say that? What makes you so sure that what I 'just know' is any less reliable than what you 'just know'?"

The young woman straightens her back and lifts her chin. The closest she comes to smiling now is a sarcastic curl at the corner of her mouth. "If you have to ask me that question, then I feel sorry for you."

"Why?" asks Isabel.

But the young woman has turned, and is walking toward the other exit of the Food-Star. She is wearing periwinkle sweatpants, with a single word across the twin grapefruits of her buttocks—a word that would seem to render a rather intimate detail about the condition of her genitals.

FORCE OF HABIT

Isabel and Ivy's father is a tilted man. His left eye is lower than his right; ditto the arrangement of his shoulders. And no matter what the right side of his mouth might be doing, the left is always down-turned, flaccid. He is sitting crookedly in a wing-backed chair, looking at Ivy with his cow-brown eyes. Her mother sits in an identical chair, back straight, head upright, hands clutching the chair's upholstered arms, as if she is on a roller coaster waiting for the ride to start. Her eyes are the color of kidney beans.

"I don't understand what you are saying," says Ivy's mother.

"Fact!" says her father. "Fact! You question fact?!"

"I'm not questioning it," says Ivy. "I am only saying that, from a statistical point of view, the odds of all six having such pale eyes are so staggeringly low that, sometimes, when I look at the children, I have to fight to convince myself that they are not hallucinations."

KAMA SUTRA

Isabel is sixteen. "How did you do it?" she asks. Ivy is fourteen. "It was easy," Ivy says.

Isabel and Ivy are sitting on a bench in Carl Schurz Park. Through a row of vertical wrought-iron bars they can see horizontally graded strips of bluish, yellowish, and gray—with the gray being the river. Isabel is not looking at Ivy. She can't because Ivy does not look like herself. Ivy is smiling the way teenage girls smile in tampon ads.

"I knew right off the bat it had to be a loser or a nerd," says Ivy. "Neil Madbow would have been nice, but I had to be practical. Of course, I also had to be sure he was straight."

"Couldn't you just take your chances?"

"No," says Ivy. "I didn't want to waste any time. So I came up with a test."

"A test?" Isabel looks sideways at her sister. Her eyes are like two ice balls that have rolled downhill and gotten clamped under her brow.

"Yeah. Gay guys like shoes. So I started carrying around that issue of *D-Tox* with the picture of Jessamine Duff on the cover. I figured if I showed it to a guy, and he started talking about her shoes, I'd go find someone else."

"How did it work?"

"Well, I only tried it on Vince Lopez."

"Vince Lopez!" Isabel opens her nostrils and crinkles her brow. All the girls call Vince Lopez "Thermometer" because he is so skinny and his whole face is just one red zit. Isabel thinks of saying something, but doesn't.

"Yeah." Now Ivy is the one not looking at her sister.

"Did he pass?"

"Of course he passed. I wouldn't be telling you this if he didn't pass." That tampon smile is back on Ivy's face. Isabel looks away.

"So then what?" says Isabel.

"I asked him if he thought Jessamine Duff was wearing thong panties."

"What did he say?"

"He didn't say anything at first. Then he said she probably was. So then I asked him if he liked thong panties. He said he guessed he did. 'Why?' I said. And he said he didn't know, he just did. So then I asked him what was his favorite part of a girl's body."

"Don't you think that was a little too obvious?" says Isabel.

"I did worry about that a bit. Especially when he laughed and said that was a stupid question. But I decided it was too late to turn back, so I said, 'No, really, I'd just like to know.' And he said, 'Which part do you think?' And when he said that—You remember that book we found in Aunt Tessa's drawer? The one about the cowboy?"

"*The Hot Gun!*"

"Right. Remember that line about how his gaze *locked* with hers?"

"No," says Isabel.

"Well, that was exactly what happened. When Vince said, 'Which part do you think?' his gaze locked with mine. I couldn't believe it."

"So then what did you do?"

"I asked him why he liked it. And this time he didn't laugh. Just

185

Stephen O'Connor

looked a little sick. Then he said, 'Because it feels good.' 'How do you know?' I asked. 'How do you think?' he said. 'Have you ever done it?' I said. He looked like he didn't know whether to vomit or run away. So I decided I had to make him relax and feel better. 'Well, I never have,' I said."

"Did it work?"

"I guess so. He started smiling then. So of course I had to go. I'd been thinking about all this for a really long time, and it was clear to me that, even though it would have been simpler to get everything over at once, the only way I was really going to get him to do what I wanted was to make him suffer. So I said I had to go to history. That was lunchtime. I saw him again last period when he was on his way to gym. He gave me this big smile. I gave him one back. But I made sure to get out of school the instant the bell sounded, because I had to make him wait twenty-four hours or it wouldn't work."

"How did you know?"

"It's obvious. Just look at any book or movie—the ones in which the boy is the hero, I mean. The boys always have at least one sleepless night before they get the girl. Anyhow, the next day I saw him in homeroom and he looked miserable, like he was afraid to look at me. I didn't say anything to him then, but when I ran into him in the hallway I told him he had a nice shirt. He didn't know what to do. His red face just got redder. 'Bye,' I said, and I walked away. Then after school I walked by his locker as if by accident. 'Hi,' I said. 'Hi,' he said. 'What you doing?' 'Nothing much.' 'Me neither.' After that it was easy. He pretended he was inviting me up to his apartment so I could listen to the Misfits, but he'd already told me his mother wouldn't be home until dinnertime. The only problem was he didn't know how to get it into me. I finally had to grab hold of it and stick it in myself."

"What was it like?"

"Well, it was really different than I thought it was going to be. It hurt more. But still, it was interesting. I'll probably do it again. They say you don't really get the full effect until you've done it a few times."

Isabel doesn't say anything for almost a minute. Then she asks if she can borrow the *D-Tox*. The next day she does everything that Ivy did, and it seems to be working perfectly. But then, when she is alone in the boy's room, and her panties are already around her ankles, he tells her he doesn't want to take advantage of her.

"Maybe that's the problem," Ivy says later that night. "You can't

186

do it with a nice guy. You have to choose someone who's a real jerk and doesn't mind taking advantage of you. That's why I chose Vince. Not only is he a nerd, but he's a total asshole."

Isabel keeps trying, but she can't get anyone to take advantage of her until she is twenty and she meets Walter Tedesco. Ivy does it three times with Vince. After that, she figures she's gotten the full effect, and doesn't do it again until Isabel announces her engagement to Walter. That very night Ivy goes to a frat party and shows her *D-Tox* to a business-school student she has never met before, Paul Henberry. He doesn't want to take advantage of her either. But eventually he changes his mind, and six months later he and Ivy are engaged. The sisters arrange a joint wedding.

THE END IS NEAR

Isabel and Ivy have a private language. You might not notice at first, but if you pay close attention you will find that many of their words only resemble English. "Hope," for example, is a profoundly embarrassing word to both sisters, and "discipline" has the cozy feel of a puppy asleep in front of a fireplace.

Their language does contain wholly invented words, however, the earliest being "lubby," a noun for a tiny part of their bodies that—when they were five and three—they thought no one possessed but themselves. ("Lubby" also refers to the feeling evoked by touching that part.) In elementary school, they invented "humpless," a word for that condition—experienced most intensely at birthday and pajama parties—of not knowing who is crazy: everybody in the room, or you. A related, but more recent term, is "herd dreaming," which refers to a mass of people being possessed by the same delusion: fainting epidemics, or nationalism, or the craze for teeth whitening. The sisters also apply this term to the peculiar phenomenon of grown men and women—repositories all, ostensibly, of the capacity for rational thought—sitting in the dark, watching light flicker through strips of celluloid, and gasping, laughing, and weeping, not merely as if they are witnessing the tribulations of real people, but as if they are actually living those tribulations themselves. The sisters always feel ridiculous when they accompany other people to the movies. And bored. Though Ivy sometimes also feels panicky.

To Isabel and Ivy, the approaching hurricane is nothing so much as an intense instance of herd dreaming. In a part of the country where

187

hurricanes rarely do more than blow the dead wood out of elderly maples, flood a few basements, and leave a solitary street without power, people are hurriedly x-ing their windows with duct tape, and filling pasta pots, buckets, and bathtubs with water. Pickup trucks loaded with sandbags, plywood, and jerricans of gasoline are dopplerizing day and night, up and down along the two-lane road in front of the Soros house, and everyone is telling hurricane horror stories: A woman is pulverized when a willow falls on her car; a farmer is electrocuted by the high-tension cable writhing in his field, spewing blue-white sparks; a six-year-old is lacerated by an imploding window. People's faces are dark with seriousness as they tell these stories; their voices are urgent and low—and yet, they are elated. You can see it in their every word and gesture. It's the same all over town. People dart in and out of stores with the lightest of steps. No one seems ever to have had a cynical thought; not a single heart has ever been touched by sorrow. Even Isabel and Ivy's own parents look a decade younger, and their father has regained the capacity to distinguish *T* from *D* when he speaks, and *S* from *Sh*.

But if either sister even hints that catastrophe might not be looming, people's brows ding with irritation. "Have to run," they mutter. "No time to talk." Or they say, "Better safe than sorry." Or, "You can't be too careful." Or sometimes they just regard the sisters with slack-jawed incomprehension.

THE ILLUSION OF CHOICE

Little Jerry is standing in the darkness beside Ivy's bed. The house is like a cardboard box in the middle of a field in which a pack of wolves is having a silent wrestling match. The sound of the wind against the sides of the house is exactly like the sound of wolf fur against cardboard. The sound of the wind in the trees is exactly like wolves breathing through their teeth. The big branches falling onto the roof and lawn sound exactly like the thumping of paws as the wolves tumble, pounce, and rear. For Jerry, barefoot on the bare floor beside his mother's bed, there is next to nothing between the darkness where he stands and the frenzy of the universe.

"What are you doing here?" Ivy asks in her sleep.

"I'm scared."

"Why?"

"Because the wind is scary."

Ivy is not asleep now, but she has not moved from the position she was in when she was asleep. "Were you brave enough to come down here all by yourself?"

Jerry doesn't answer.

"Answer me."

His answer is too quiet for Ivy to hear. She tells him so.

"I'm sorry," he says.

"Of course you were brave enough to come down here all by yourself. You wouldn't be here if you weren't. And if you are brave enough to come down here all by yourself, you are brave enough to go back up to bed and go to sleep."

"I want to sleep in your bed."

"You know that's not allowed."

Jerry says nothing. Ivy cannot see him, except as a thumb shape of perfect black in the gloom of a moonless night.

"There's nothing to be afraid of," says Ivy. "It's only the wind."

"Is this the hurricane?"

"No. The hurricane won't be here until the morning."

"Are we going to die?"

"Of course we're going to die. But not in the hurricane. The hurricane is nothing. The hurricane is just a way for the television stations to expand their audiences so that they can sell advertisements for more money. It's also a way for people who have boring lives to feel that their lives are not boring. It's a fairy story, that's all it is, and fairy stories aren't real. So go back to bed."

"Paulette says the trees are going to fall on the roof and we are all going to die."

"Paulette is an idiot. Go back to bed."

"I'm scared."

Now Ivy is sitting up. She is breathing in a way that is not unlike the breathing of the wolves. "Listen, Jerry, we've been though all this before. Some children allow themselves to become afraid because of irrational ideas. But you're not going to be like those children, are you?"

Jerry makes a very small noise in his throat, but it is nothing like a word.

"Fear is an entirely useless emotion," says Ivy. "And if I were to let you come into my bed, I would be acting as if there actually were something for you to be afraid of, wouldn't I? And, on top of that, your being in my bed with me would not change one single thing. It would still be the middle of the night. The wind would still be blowing. And whatever is going to happen would still be going to happen."

"But if the trees fall on the roof, they won't hit me if I'm down here with you."

"The trees are not going to fall on the roof." Ivy had been speaking in a fierce whisper, but now her voice is loud enough to be heard in other rooms. She doesn't care. "Go back to your bed this instant."

For a long time Jerry does nothing at all. Then there is a shifting in the darkness, and she can hear his sweat-sticky feet making kissing noises along the floorboards. The door opens, then closes softly. The latch slides back into the doorplate with a minute sproing.

Where Jerry was standing, there is now a larger thumb shape of perfect black. It is Ivy's mother in her nightgown.

"How could you treat your little boy like that?" says Ivy's mother.

"I'm doing it for his own good."

"I never spoke to you so heartlessly," she says. "I would never have done that in a million years. I was always careful to be sure you and Isabel knew I loved you with all of my heart."

"Do you think that made any difference?"

For a long time the only sounds in the room come from the wind against the walls. Ivy closes her eyes. When she opens them her mother is gone.

THIS IS THIS

Isabel and Ivy's father slides his left shoe along the floor as if it is filled with sand and stitched to the bottom of his empty pants leg. He moves his left arm mainly by whipping it with his shoulder. He can push the power button on the radio, but he can't turn the knob to tune in the signal. That's why the announcer sounds like he is talking through wax paper. "Hear that?" her father says, as Isabel comes into the room.

"Hear what?" says Isabel.

"Floods," he says. "Listen."

But that is the exact instant the kitchen light flickers, goes brown, goes gold, platinum, then permanently dark. The radio is silent. Some motor that is always on in the house is not on now, and the absence of its low, continuous hum makes the wind outside louder.

"Floods," says Isabel's father. "Floods, they say."

"Not here," says Isabel.

"Everywhere," says her father. "The whole county."

"But we're on high ground," she says.

She goes to the window, and sees that water in the stream is racing, white capped, and the color of her lips. It has already embraced the roots of the willow, and is lapping at the southernmost leg of the picnic table where she likes to work on her computer.

"The lights are out," says Paulette, who has just entered the kitchen in her red pajamas with the feet on them and the hatch in the back.

"Go back upstairs," says Isabel, "and put on your clothes. Tell everyone that they can't come down until they are in their clothes. Shoes too."

"The wrath of Ivy," says Isabel's father.

"That's a stupid joke, Dad."

"I mean the hurricane."

"I know. But it's still a stupid joke."

It is an hour later and Isabel and Ivy's mother is sitting at the table, an empty bowl of cereal in front of her. "What are we going to do when the food goes bad?" she says. Her hair is turban shaped and the color of shredded wheat. Her kidney-bean eyes are made huge and concave by the thick lenses of her glasses.

"It's not going to go bad," says Ivy, wiping Jerry's mouth with the kitchen towel. "You are such a slob," she tells him. "The fridge will keep the food cold for days," she tells her mother.

"What about after that?"

"Tuna fish," says Dr. Soros. "Lots of tuna fish!"

"Guys," says Gwenny, standing in the doorway between the kitchen and the living room.

"I wish you had gotten some batteries," says Ivy and Isabel's mother.

"Guys," says Gwenny.

"What?" says Isabel.

Gwenny doesn't answer, just looks over her shoulder into the living room.

A braid of lip-red water is flowing across the hickory floorboards. All at once everyone can hear the sound of a cow urinating somewhere in the living room.

"It's coming right under the front door," says Gwenny.

191

Stephen O'Connor

ALMOST

When Dr. Soros panics, he loses all ability to coordinate his left side, so Isabel has to carry him in her arms out to the white van and buckle him into his seat.

As the family exits the house, the flood is flowing ankle deep through the front door. Gwenny, the last to leave, tries to pull the door shut behind her, but the water forms a small mountain against it, and the door flies open again and again. Finally, she gives up.

Ivy is in the driver's seat. Isabel rides shotgun. The rest of the family crams into seats beside and behind Dr. Soros. The van's side door slides shut.

Ivy steers the van through the river that has covered their driveway and half their lawn, and is flowing through the house. "Where should I go?" she asks.

"Up," says Isabel. "Where else?"

The road in front of their house is covered by a hissing, pinkish sheet of water. But after a few yards the road is only rainstorm wet, and pocked with leaping, gray drop-splashes. Ivy heads east, then turns west, then east again, then west—uphill all the while.

"We're away from the worst of it," says Isabel and Ivy's mother.

Paulette is sitting with her neck upstretched, and her eyes fixed on the back of her grandfather's head. She is making swallowing noises. Warm tears mix with the raindrops on her cheeks.

Isabel and Ivy say nothing. Even through the closed windows they can hear a roar so forceful and low it is more like the shuddering of the earth than an actual sound. Where normally there is only a cattail-clogged trickle, an avenue of red surf pours down the hillside. This is the very stream that has subsumed their yard and is rearranging the furniture inside their house. As the roar becomes louder, the sisters trade glances, but still say nothing. They round a bend, mount a crest, and at last can see that the bridge crossing the stream has held. Water shoots in a pink spume out of its downhill side.

Both sisters have been holding their breath. Now their throats unclamp; air flows from their lungs. Ivy smiles, and accelerates.

A tree trunk as thick as an oil drum and as long as a salad bar bucks, rolls, and tumbles through the lip-red water. It is approaching the bridge at the exact same speed as the van. The trunk reaches the bridge first, its rooty end striking one side of the culvert, its snapped-off end slamming into the other. The torrent makes a sound like a lion clearing its throat, because now almost all of the water is prevented from flowing under the culvert, and the water that does flow there rockets over the tree flank in a blade of froth. The water blocked by the tree dithers and roils for the second or two it takes to mount the riverbank, then it surges across the road exactly where the van is driving. Had Ivy's foot depressed the gas pedal by even one more quarter inch, the van would have made it onto the bridge and to the safety of the high ground on the other side.

SORORITY

Ivy is rendered useless, as are the van's steering wheel, brakes, gas pedal, and motor. The van is swept sideways across the road, tailwise down the embankment, and then sideways again through a cow pasture that is now a red ocean. For a very brief moment after the van has been swept back into the streambed, where the current flows most forcefully, it is pointing in the same direction that the water is flowing, and this allows Ivy to feel that she is driving on the red surf. Then the van hits a steep-sloped pyramid of rock the size of a garage and is anchored there, nose upward, by the current, which roars pinkly around its lower half, smashing all the windows and sweeping away four of the children and both grandparents before Isabel and Ivy, in the front seat, have a chance to look around.

Ivy's eyes are moon bright and blind. She is shouting something, but Isabel cannot hear what it is. The sound of the water has grown very, very large, and Ivy's voice has grown mouse small. The door next to Isabel is gone, and so is the sliding door to the back. Or maybe the sliding door is just open. For some reason Isabel finds it impossible to tell what has happened to the door, and she will never possess more than a shaky hypothesis.

Gwenny—her own daughter, her eldest child—is clinging to the post between the front and back doors with both arms, her cheek bleeding from a row of triangular punctures, her eyes also moon bright. Isabel pushes Gwenny's ribs. "Let go!" Isabel shouts. "Let go! Get out of here!"

At first Gwenny looks at her mother as if she doesn't know who she is. Then recognition dawns, and with it, that sort of pliable stupidity that is a form of trust. She lets go, slides away from the van, but at the last second Isabel shoves her with such force that she lands against the pyramid of rock with half her body out of the water. Her elbows (pointing skyward, angled like grasshopper legs) waver back

193

and forth as she lifts herself out of the water. Then she is kneeling on top of the rock.

Little Jerry has climbed from the backseat, where he once sat next to his grandfather, and is clutching his mother around the neck. Ivy can't unfasten her seatbelt. Isabel does it for her, then unfastens her own. When she slides out the door and into the water, she finds that, in fact, it is easy to clamber up onto the rock. Gwenny has vanished. There is a dense wood of black sticks and shining leaves behind the rock. Gwenny is there somewhere. Isabel knows that if she looks again, she will see her.

Ivy and Jerry slide toward the door. As their weight shifts within the van, the van shifts on the rock. They both reach for Isabel, who manages to grab one hand of each, and, as the van slides out from under them and rolls with a groan and a heavy sigh into the current, she pulls them onto the rock—but not quite. The river takes hold of their legs and, in an instant, they are dragged back into the red water—Isabel too, still holding onto their hands.

All is roaring and bubbly dimness.

Then Isabel feels gravel beneath her feet and finds that she can stand, her head and shoulders out of the water. She is not sure at first, but soon she sees that she is still holding Ivy and Jerry's hands, and they are both looking at her with the terrific seriousness of the mortally ill. Isabel realizes that she has been swept into an eddy behind the rock, and that the water is only swirling idly around her pelvis and legs. Ivy and Jerry are still in the racing current, however, and Isabel is leaning backward to keep them all from being pulled downstream.

Isabel realizes three things in a single instant:

1. She is not strong enough to continue to hold her sister and her nephew; the exhaustion in her shoulders and hands has reached that point where it is searing pain.

2. Even as she is constantly stepping backward in a sort of reverse pedaling, the gravel beneath her feet is constantly giving way and she is being pulled inexorably toward the current.

3. If she lets go of Jerry, Ivy might still drag her into the flood, whereas if she lets go of Ivy, and continues to hold on to Jerry, there is a chance that she might be able to lift him to safety and then climb up after him.

Isabel conveys all this information to her sister in a single glance.

As Ivy slides away on the flood, her eyes are locked on Isabel's with complete comprehension. Ivy's face grows smaller and smaller atop the current, and she seems to be shooting backward in time: not thirty-nine anymore, but thirty-five, then twenty-eight, then seventeen, twelve, five—until, just before she disappears over a falls some hundred yards downstream, her face seems to journey through something other than time, because, as small as it continues to grow, it never looks remotely like an infant's face, but more like that of an elf, then a fairy, then the bride on a wedding cake, and, finally, like a dotted face on a pencil-tip eraser.

Then Ivy is gone.

Isabel's back is against the pyramid rock and Jerry's back is against her chest.

"Mommy!" he cries, clawing at the red water with both hands.

"Hush," says Isabel.

"Mommy! Mommy!" Jerry strains helplessly against the rigid rings of Isabel's arms.

"Hush," says Isabel. "There's nothing we can do."

"Mommy! Mommy! Mommy! Mommy!"

"Come on," she says. "We have to get onto the rock, or we'll get washed away too."

"Mahhhh-meeee!" screams Jerry. "Mahhhh-meeee!"

"As soon as this is over, we'll come back and look for her," says Isabel. "I promise. But we have to go now or we are going to die."

"Noooo!" shouts Jerry. "Mahhhh-meeee!"

Isabel has to fight the urge to let him go too. And then she wonders if that wouldn't, in fact, be the best thing to do.

Prospects Of and At
Marjorie Welish

1.

Caesura hath me a chisel
Greater growth isn't

A stay. Accelerate
Georgics. Park etc.

Caesura made me
Stop. A sort of scramble

Greater caesura
Abruptly a ha-ha

Resolves what is isn't
A house the how of

Rasps in our lives
Sounding boards.

Call particles'
Greater growth.

Too close to the speaker
Speakers should be forward

Of the piano.

A stick accelerates stickiness
        selectively is selectively adhesive.
And his rustics were wanting.

Wrong end of the stick tempted us.

Eyes on gray
        Gray scale eyes grayness become verge
As wet eyes locate the heart
        as wet eyes locate the heart's wetlands:

        slate graphite pewter steel locale.

Relapse
        Relapse to one's inextinguishable simile
as it flails the air.

There: done.

The which way
        which lisp at the behest of caesura
on the path of the same name as that gray matter.

A lisp of divergence:
        which way to the eyesore?

Having not distraught
      metrical modulation nor his family's temperament

is *fort-da* advancing on your spill *spiel*.

Caesura *fecit*
Greater growth isn't

gorgeous. A cut and a star
to all that green grown ambient

spot didn't cup
disequilibria nor did the moon

consume man for nothing.
At their throats bruised arias better this time: cut.

Growth of stay caesura and breathing for stamina
Stay with me you said always sometimes

dishevelment voicing the decision: cut to
voice of the late great a threadbare carpet in her

vocal mastery struck much rustle. Uncut
from popular hormones above and everywhere

feral bimbos unshadowed an intestinal area
forward of the stage. Whereupon street fairs.

To avoid it step into it
    Repeat.
Avail yourself of cause and effect.
    And trouble. Whereas
revision awaits adage. (Advantage: Pound.)

Bypath. The forward edge.

Caesura made me
Greater growth isn't

Emergent crayon made me
Read this. If you can read this

growth the groaning crayon
that verve conveys in turbulent winds

Saturated Saturday read this. If you can, read this green market
a test of spacing in a sense a pith greater than one

fish. Read this caesura in a sea of green
greenery anyway for a greater green discordant climate.

Harvested brother if you can read this
language high-yield capture of selvage salvage some eros

too deep for tears detours to occur
in between epitome and premonition

you who lovingly mistook the crow's foot
path to a distant rusticated sky and repose . . .

2.

Greater caesura
Fast stare

Greater chisel made a
Resolve what is isn't

Scrambled speaking
Undergrowth and rank elegy

Emitting from the piano
As struck struck and pedaled

Technique is as close as what is isn't
Kale bok choy arugula spinach

Readies. Stops. Tone color
In an accent how growth

Stubble in flight accelerates a
Difficulty pretty much

Rasp in a scrabble
Or a dry cough

For the inner ear.
Meanwhile he is writing.

In a profuse suspense
    is glut surfeit plethora
Lawn cease and desist carpeting.

A change from action to rest.

Greater growth isn't
    Excess redundance
Under the rubric.

. . . the phonetic content silently to ourselves.

Medicinal botanics act faceup
    at no cost unconditional and sheer
becoming world without end.

Ready, steady, go!

Perfume to violet liaisons or violence in full dress
    Plumes smoke flounces wayfaring
Horizon. Pours. Soaks. Floods.

The study of.

Marjorie Welish

Greater caesura
rehabilitated

From the rubble
of a metropolis

Stimulants
reboot facades

The likeness after
irruption in rebuilt use.

Do you remember the iconoclastic
procession from the church in halts

sampled from faces of possessed folk
apostolic unwittingly brightening and darkening?

Venus

Can Xue

—Translated from Chinese by Karen Gernant and Chen Zeping

QIU YIPING, A THIRTEEN-YEAR-OLD middle-school student, was secretly in love with her thirty-five-year-old cousin with the whimsical name Xuwu. An orphan whose parents had died long ago, he was a scientist researching hot-air balloons. Qiu Yiping hadn't seen him in the past, but in the last year Xuwu had often visited her village to test hot-air balloons and had become close to Qiu Yiping's family.

Whenever her cousin came to the village, Qiu Yiping grew so excited that she couldn't even concentrate on her classes. As soon as school was out, she rushed home and went to the mountain to the east to look for her cousin. He was tall, wore glasses, was a little humpbacked, and walked a bit sluggishly. He didn't look at all bright.

The mountain on the east was called Tomb Mountain; it was more than a thousand meters above sea level. Generally, Xuwu launched his hot-air balloons from halfway up the mountain and let them float along its contours and above Yiping's village. Everyone in the village would come out to watch this rare sight. Each time, Yiping swelled with pride.

Her cousin had stayed overnight with her family only twice—both times because it was raining hard. Ordinarily, he slept in the wicker basket below the hot-air balloon, where he kept the things he needed for daily use. Day and night, Yiping yearned to soar into the sky in the hot-air balloon with her cousin, but he had never invited her to go along. He said, "It's dangerous." She didn't believe him. She thought he looked down on her and was weary of her pestering him.

On the mountain, her cousin sometimes took off his coat and wore only a sailor's shirt. He curled up like a shrimp and repaired the hot-air balloon's heater. Sometimes he did nothing at all but just sat there looking at the sky. No matter what her cousin was doing, Yiping liked to be beside him; she would even like to be with him for a lifetime.

The hot-air balloon was red, the color of the sun setting at twilight.

Many times, Yiping thought that her cousin looked at the hot-air balloon as though he were looking at his sweetheart. Yiping had heard her parents say that he hadn't married and that he didn't have a girlfriend, either. Could it be that the hot-air balloon was his girlfriend? When Yiping pondered this in the middle of the night, her eyes glinted in the dark, and she felt warm all over. She made up many stories about girlfriends her cousin had had in the past: She was sure he had had girlfriends in the past. She yearned to be with him at night on the mountain, viewing the moon and stars. But that was impossible, for her parents and the neighbors would all say she was "shameless."

It was Sunday. Qiu Yiping had gotten up early and hastily done the housework—washed and dried the clothes, prepared food for the pigs, fed the chickens, swept the courtyard, and cooked the breakfast. Then she had gulped down two stewed potatoes and slipped out of the courtyard. She started running toward Tomb Mountain, because she was afraid her family would stop her.

When she had climbed halfway up the mountain, she saw that her cousin was still asleep in the wicker basket. He had covered one side of his face with the quilt, and he looked very funny. The sound of Yiping's footsteps awakened him, and he suddenly sat up, hastily reaching out for his glasses.

"Oh, I overslept. I was really tired out before daylight." He said, embarrassed, "You can't imagine, Yiping. I ascended to the top of the mountain and then even higher. Even higher! All of a sudden, I saw her. She was flying past like a big bird. My God!"

"Who? Who was flying—flying past like—like a big bird?" Yiping began stammering.

"You don't understand. You don't get it." Her cousin waved his hand, revealing his annoyance.

"Let's not talk about it anymore," he added.

He was wearing a blue-and-white-striped sailor shirt as he stood at one side and washed his face and brushed his teeth. He looked like a bittern. After he had cleaned up, he took some bread out of the basket and cut it into several small pieces, dipped them in ketchup, and ate slowly. He offered some to Yiping, but she turned him down. She didn't want to make a pig of herself!

Seeing that her cousin's mind was elsewhere, Yiping thought he had pretty much forgotten her existence.

"Cousin, let me ride in the hot-air balloon just once! Just once!" Yiping begged.

"How could I do that?" He was immediately on his guard. "If your parents found out, they would break my neck! And what would the other villagers say? . . . Don't be silly."

"We could keep them from seeing. I could run out quietly in the middle of the night. No one would know. Didn't you say just now that when the big bird flew past, you didn't get a good look at it? If you teach me how to operate the hot-air balloon, I can take care of it and you can get a good look at the bird!"

When Yiping said this, she really had no idea how her cousin would respond, but she was desperate, so she chanced it.

Her cousin seemed touched by what she had said. He stared at her and asked, "Do you really think so? What the hell. Is this possible?"

"Sure it is! Of course! Really!" Yiping shouted.

Her cousin carefully folded the bread-wrapping paper and put it away. He looked at the chestnut tree next to him as if he had something on his mind. Then he said very slowly: "Yiping, sit down."

Yiping sat down nervously on the rock. She was blushing.

"Do you know about Venus?" he asked.

"Yes. I've seen her at twilight." Yiping relaxed.

"She's what I saw before daylight! At that time, it was dark in all directions, but she was radiant. She seemed to be green colored. I reached out my hand and I could almost touch her, but a force pulled me away, and so I was separated from her. I really regret that. Why didn't I jump over then? At worst, I would have died! It was a great opportunity that not everyone can have—and I missed it. What's wrong with me? When I landed here, it was almost dawn. I suddenly felt weary of the world and fell asleep. I was completely out. Did you come to help me, Yiping?"

"Yes, I did."

"Do you think I can succeed?"

"Yes, you will," Yiping said in a small voice. But what she thought to herself was: "I hope you don't succeed. You should land with me."

Something crossed the cousin's mind. He frowned and asked Yiping: "Recently, have people in the two nearby villages said anything about me?"

"Yes. Someone said that you're looking for your tomb. Is that true?"

"Hahahaha! Haha!" Her cousin began laughing uproariously.

"Of course I fly around Tomb Mountain because I want to find a

205

suitable burial place. This whole matter must be connected with Venus, isn't it?"

"I don't know." Yiping shook her head, and her face clouded over.

They fell silent. Both of them looked at the sky and they looked at the village below the mountain.

When they parted, they agreed that Yiping would slip away from her home at midnight and Xuwu would meet her at the foot of the mountain. When Yiping went down the mountain, her cousin shouted behind her: "Yiping, you must take an afternoon nap because if you doze off later, we're both done for!"

"I know, Cousin! I won't doze off!" Yiping answered excitedly.

She ran home and immediately picked up a bucket and went to fetch water. She went once, and then once more, until the two water containers were full. When she sat down to rest, Auntie Li dropped in.

"Is your cousin a man or a bird? He flew over my head, and I was so scared I fell down! It was too eerie, wasn't it? A big guy flying back and forth over your head! I've lived a long time, and nothing like this has ever happened in our village before."

Yiping was entranced. She looked at Auntie Li and laughed out loud.

"What's so funny? Huh?"

When Auntie Li left, Yiping noticed that she also had a smile on her face. What on earth was Cousin up to? What did he want to communicate to the villagers?

After Yiping ate, she cleaned up the kitchen and went to bed. She planned to take a long, long nap.

She closed her eyes and counted. As she counted, she grew excited again and forgot how far she had counted. So she started again. She started over again several times to no avail. She looked at the clock. More than an hour had passed when she decided to get up and go to the field and pick beans.

As she picked beans, she looked at Tomb Mountain. One moment, it seemed that she saw a small red dot climbing to the mountaintop. When she looked more carefully, she saw nothing. Probably the sun had been shining in her eyes. While Yiping was thinking about her cousin's dangerous behavior, she heard people talking behind her.

"That Xuwu—he's risking his life."

She turned around and saw that no one was there. Who had been talking?

Yiping was busy the entire afternoon with the beans—washing

them and drying them. Finally she got everything done.

When the sun set, she ran out of the house and looked carefully at the sky. She looked and looked, but she didn't see Venus. There was no star at all in the sky. When she was about to enter her courtyard, Auntie Li appeared. She blocked the way and wanted her to answer a question.

"Xuwu has been staying in our village for such a long time: Does that mean he wants to marry you?"

"What nonsense!"

Very uneasy, Yiping pushed her away and dashed into her courtyard.

Yiping didn't go to bed until late. Before she went to bed, she opened the back door.

Every now and then, she shone her flashlight on the clock. When it was almost midnight, she got dressed and sneaked out. As she stood at the courtyard gate, she looked back once. Her home looked dark blue. How could this shabby adobe home be dark blue? Ordinarily, it was that not-quite-yellow, not-quite-gray color. Was it because of the moonlight?

Yiping walked very fast, almost like jogging. After a while, she reached the foot of Tomb Mountain. At night, this mountain looked very large, as though it wasn't a mountain but was the whole world. But her cousin wasn't waiting for her at the foot of the mountain. Yiping was worried and afraid: She heard her heart thumping against her chest. After waiting a while, she decided to climb the mountain. She thought, maybe Cousin forgot what he had said and was simply waiting for her where they usually met.

As she climbed the mountain, she heard a strange bird calling several times. She was so afraid that she felt death was approaching. She said to herself, "I'm not afraid to die." After she said this three times, she felt more courageous. She was proud of herself too.

Finally, she saw her cousin sitting on a rock next to the hot-air balloon. His head was drooping; it seemed he didn't realize she had arrived. Could he have forgotten their plan?

"Cousin, let's get going!" Yiping shouted.

"Ah! You're here!" He was startled. "No need to hurry. Sit down for a while first."

Yiping sat on another rock. She was shaking all over.

"The time in the sky and the time on earth aren't the same," her cousin said slowly, one word at a time.

"Show—show me how to—to operate the balloon, OK?" Yiping said, her teeth chattering.

"I've set it on automatic. You don't have to do much. When she gets close, we have to be ready. If I do make up my mind and jump over, you must begin landing immediately. It's easy. All you have to do is pull the switch."

Xuwu spoke rapidly. Yiping wasn't very sure of what he had said. She blinked, and her emotions surged.

They sat in the large wicker basket, her cousin holding the joystick, and the hot-air balloon began slowly leaving the ground. Yiping was frightened and didn't dare look down. She wanted to get control of her feelings. Her cousin started talking nonstop.

"Yiping, you can't imagine the encounters I've had in the sky. People think that hot-air balloons can't fly very high, but this is just what ordinary people think. I've told you that I actually encountered Venus—and not just once, either! In that moment and that place, I assure you if someone had been helping me then, could I have flipped over onto it? What do you think? She was dark green. I sensed that she had a hairy surface. Could it be a kind of moss? I really regret that I missed the opportunity. What's wrong with me—always having twenty-twenty vision only in hindsight? Yiping, I know that the villagers don't appreciate what I do, and yet I really long for their understanding. These people are all my relatives. My parents grew up here; later they moved away. It was a scandal, but I bet you never heard it from your folks! And so when I came to this village last year, it was like coming back to my real family. You must think this is strange— Why do I sleep on the mountain? I don't know why: I just have to shut myself away from the villagers so that I can sleep in peace. The villagers are all my relatives—Auntie Li, Uncle Huang, Uncle Li, your parents. They keep coming into my dreams."

Suddenly, his words were interrupted. Yiping felt acutely dizzy. She thought the basket must be bumping against the mountain. This was the end. In a feeble voice, she shouted, "Help!"

When she opened her eyes, she realized that this wasn't the end. The hot-air balloon was descending; she could already see the rooftops in the village. Those rooftops were the dark-blue color that she'd seen earlier when she ran out—unearthly but lovely.

"Cousin, we're descending. Aren't you going to pursue Venus?" Yiping felt a little disappointed.

"I miss my relatives so much! You can't understand this feeling for you're too young. See: Uncle Li has walked out! He's going to the toilet; he has diarrhea. Our village is a multisurname village, made up of refugees who came from many places. They established this village. You must know this."

Yiping didn't know anything about this. She looked hard but she couldn't see Uncle Li. Between two houses, next to a bamboo fence, it seemed there was a shadow slipping across. But the hot-air balloon was floating too fast with the wind, and she couldn't get a good look.

"Cousin, let's go up! Why do we have to stay so close to the village? I'd like to see Venus. There's nothing to see in the village. Look, you've swerved again: We're still floating near the rooftops. What are you really looking for??"

"Me? Didn't you say the other time that I'm looking for a burial place?" Xuwu laughed out loud. "I see your papa. He got up and he's chopping firewood in the dark. He's always like this. The year I came down with cholera, he carried me on his back to the county hospital."

"Don't we have any way to ascend? I'd like to go up to a place several thousand meters high."

"That's impossible. Haven't I told you? I have only low-grade fuel. At most, my hot-air balloon can climb five hundred meters. . . . And I'm also not very interested in heights. In this deathly still night, my heart is close to this village."

"Has . . . it . . . always . . . been . . . like . . . this?" Yiping said in a lingering tone.

Glancing at her cousin, she saw him snickering. Yiping realized that there was an enormous distance between the two of them. She grew dizzy and grumbled, "Where did you come from?"

Her cousin didn't answer at first. After a while, Yiping heard his voice; it was intermittent and seemed to be coming from the ground.

"Here's Auntie Li; she's sticking her head out the window. . . . Now she's walking into another room. She's thinking about me. . . . She's my relative. Oh, you mustn't lean out; you'll scare her. . . . Here's some thick smoke: It's your mama cooking breakfast in the dark. . . ."

Yiping couldn't see anything because her eyes were filled with tears that had suddenly gushed up. She quietly and repeatedly asked her cousin: "Should I cry? Should I cry? . . . Should I . . ."

"Go ahead and cry, go ahead," her cousin said.

His voice was still coming from the ground. Was it possible that he was no longer beside her?

Yiping stretched her hand out to the right—she was startled when she felt nothing but air! At the same time, she heard a dull sound:

The wicker basket had turned upside down on the ground, and she had rolled into the paddy field next to it.

It was already light in the east. Yiping scrambled up. She was covered in mud like a clay figurine.

Her mama stood in the field and called her: "Yiping! Yiping! What's wrong with you?!"

Yiping washed herself with water from the field and then went home. She covered her face with her hands so that her mama couldn't see her face.

"I was dreaming! I was dreaming!" she said as she walked.

"Oh, so you were dreaming. That's really dangerous." Her mother sighed.

As soon as she got home, Yiping took a shower and washed her hair. After that, she went into her bedroom and bolted the door.

Not until she sat down on her bed did she remember what had just happened. Had the hot-air balloon flown away while she was rolling into the field? When she climbed out of the paddy field, she hadn't seen the hot-air balloon. It appeared that her mama hadn't seen it, either! So had her cousin flown the hot-air balloon away? Yiping felt weak all over, but her eyes were dry; she wasn't crying. She also remembered that when she was in the basket her cousin's voice had come from the ground. He had said, "Go ahead and cry. Go ahead." So the hot-air balloon must have flown away by itself. Had her cousin jumped to the ground before she had? Yiping felt her face was burning hot. She was so ashamed! She wished she could find a hole to hide in.

She didn't know how much time passed before she heard a voice next door in her parents' room. It was Auntie Li.

"He didn't come this morning. That's the way he is. When you make a point of waiting for him, he doesn't appear. He plays hide-and-seek with you. I can't stand his always flying over my head. It's scarier than a big horsefly!"

"He's almost finished with his experiments. I guess he'll leave soon," Mama comforted her.

"Really? But I don't want him to go either. Isn't this strange? The year of the big snowstorm, he slid into the well but survived. He's really lucky."

Sighing, the two women went to the hall. Yiping wondered why they were sighing.

At twilight that evening, the sun was just setting, and Yiping was standing in the garden looking at Venus. Venus wasn't green, but was chrysanthemum yellow.

"Do you see her?" Her cousin's voice—distant and feeble—came from the mountain over there.

Yiping looked down, a smile on her face. With all her might, she looked at that mountain. She seemed to faintly see a white dot swaying in the bosk. The sky darkened quickly. When she looked at the sky again, Venus had really turned green.

The Girl with the Prefabricated Heart
J. W. McCormack

WHEN LIBBY HOLMAN SINGS her songs of scandal and desire, the notes themselves turn rotten-ripe with disgrace. On East Fifty-second Street, where for ten years the spent darlings of Broadway have been getting legally soused,[1] the upper crust of the downscale supper crowd occupies La Vie Parisienne to hark to an infamous contralto, well-known register of soubrettes and women of ruinous leisure. Samson's Delilah,[2] Pirate Jenny,[3] the lone white woman to play in a line of Negro musicals:[4] The torch singer Libby Holman belongs more to an age of dizzy mink stoles, the Ziegfeld Girl, and Betty Boop in two-tone bloomers. Or so it would have seemed to the assembled choir of gossip columnists, stirred to applause by "Strange Fruit"[5] and "The Lass with the Delicate Air" because here she is, smart as an outhouse rat, in beaded chiffon, burlesquey fishnets, a mourning veil, and open-toed heels that show off her scarlet nails. Her toenails, she says, are her jewels.

This side of the Depression and the craze for Tin Pan Alley has showed itself a rattle, so Mr. Porter's one-time siren has reinvented

---

[1]*Legally soused*: Prohibition formally ended December 1933. This concert takes place in summer of 1943, thus nine years is more accurate.

[2]*Samson's Delilah*: Libby Holman never played Delilah. She did, however, play a fallen woman in *The Fool*, based on the life of St. Francis of Assisi.

[3]*Pirate Jenny*: Not in Gay's *The Beggar's Opera* or even Brecht's *Threepenny Opera*, but in the "Americanization," *Beggar's Holiday*, in which she co-starred with Zero Mostel in his Broadway debut. This was part of the vogue in the forties for American adaptations of European literature like *Cabin in the Sky*, essentially Faust set in Harlem. Libby was fired from the production in 1946.

[4]*Negro musicals*: Nineteen twenty-seven was the year of the black musical on Broadway, thanks to the enormous success of Carl Van Vechten's *Nigger Heaven*. The director of the all-black *Rang Tang* was convinced that Libby should join his cast and tried unsuccessfully to have her released from the (more status quo) *Merry-Go-Round*.

[5]*"Strange Fruit"*: Josh White and Libby Holman performed "Strange Fruit" during other stops on the revue, but Josh White's Middle American reception whenever he sang the song grew so chilly that they probably would have left it off the set list in New York. So as not to look as though they were bowing to racially motivated pressures, White opted to flatter the North, saying, "My mother always told me not to drag my trash into other people's backyards."

212

herself as blues singer, writing obituaries in the air as it throbs a dusky purple and camouflages with a voice that sounds like the son her father had wished for in Cincinnati were sucked down somewhere inside her. She leans upon her trademark kitchen table while her guitarist plays from the shadows. It is none other than Josh White, the "Svengali of the South"[6] with a diamond in his ear and a lit Chesterfield,[7] which he pulls on reluctantly. But smoking Camels around Libby would be another chance for the local press to put the veteran songwriter, who is already risking his credibility, in his place, and White sees no point in offending the other half of his audience.

Who is in the audience tonight? Who stood in line while the sunlight guttered under a marquee reading BLUES BALLADS AND SIN SONGS?[8] Who are the survivors and who are the dead? Front row is reserved for the men: Tallulah Bankhead,[9] with a scowl like she went down with the *Titanic* twice, sitting beside mercurial country heiress Louisa Carpenter;[10] a tall glass of water and three fingers of bourbon wearing matching fedoras. In the booth behind them, a young Montgomery Clift, alone for the first time in his life, takes a break from starring in *Our Town*[11] ("Which," goes his classic rejoinder, "it frankly isn't.") and sweats constantly, aching to be possessed. The constellation is rounded out by a recently widowed Alice B. Toklas,[12] Truman Capote[13] (so newly arrived in Manhattan that a botched descent from a taxicab has left him with an adorable limp), and Libby's teenage son, Topper Reynolds,[14] whom everyone mentions resembles

---

[6]*Svengali of the South*: Nobody ever called Josh White "the Svengali of the South," though papers referred to him as a Svengali in reviews of the show, and Libby herself claimed to strongly identify with "the Negro of the South."

[7]*Chesterfield*: It is unlikely that Josh would have smoked Chesterfields in the forties, the brand having peaked in America during the Depression, but any cigarette manufactured by Reynolds would have piqued Holman's fury, as she'd been married to Zachary Smith Reynolds, heir to the fortune, and had been present at his North Carolina estate, Reynolda, at the time of his mysterious death.

[8]*Blues Ballads and Sin Songs*: This was, in fact, the name of a show Libby did without Josh twelve years later, accompanied by Gerald Cook on piano.

[9]*Tallulah Bankhead*: Tallulah and Libby had been not friends but bitter detractors of each other by 1942 and, besides, Bankhead would have been in Hollywood around this time to film Alfred Hitchcock's *Lifeboat*.

[10]*Louisa Carpenter*: It is unlikely that Libby's lifelong on-again, off-again lover Louisa would have been there either. She despised cities in general and New York in particular and spent most of her time on her yacht, *Three's a Crowd*.

[11]*Our Town*: Actually, it was *Mexican Mural*, which he starred in with Libby.

[12]*Alice B. Toklas*: Inaccurate. Gertrude Stein would not die for another three years, in 1946.

[13]*Truman Capote*: Extremely inaccurate. Capote would have been about eighteen.

[14]*Topper Reynolds*: Little Topper would have been only ten.

J. W. McCormack

Smith Reynolds's best friend, Abner, much more than Holman's first husband.[15] The dead sulk between rows. There's Clifton Webb,[16] dressed as the sweetback he played when he and Libby performed "Moanin' Low" in The Little Show in '29; Rafe Holmes,[17] Libby's Canadian flying-ace second husband, still wearing his aviator's goggles; and, finally, Smith Reynolds himself, the Tobacco Prince of Winston-Salem. That Libby was exonerated of his death[18] and the misadventure that left him lying cold on the patio of his family's sprawling Carolina estate ruled a suicide still rankles the newspapers, but, seeing her now lifting her eyes to lock with "Complications Jane" Bowles[19] in Jane's private booth, any onlooker would have to agree that young Reynolds's suffering must have been immense. And, besides, the bullet was never found.

For her encore, the singer strays from the rhythm-and-blues catalog they have perfected for the revue and sings "Moanin' Low" with "Body and Soul," banned from the airwaves[20] in the age of Garbo but tame stuff now that Rita Hayworth props up pup tents across the Western Front. For the first time, Josh White lopes enormously from the shadows to share the spotlight with his white accompanist[21] as the room rises to meet the refrain:

> *I can't believe it*
> *It's hard to conceive it*
> *That you'd turn away romance*

---

[15]*Holman's first husband*: Derived from the fact that Smith Reynolds's death coincides so closely with Libby's pregnancy that it lends itself to easy scandal. At the time of his "suicide," he was reportedly distraught over a kiss that he saw Libby give Abner.
[16]*Clifton Webb*: Clifton Webb, the Noel Coward regular and original Mr. Belvedere, didn't die until 1966. He and Libby had a falling-out around this period, however, that led to his saying he *considered* her dead.
[17]*Rafe Holmes*: This is confusing. Libby *dated* Rafe (Ralph)'s older brother, Philip, whose plane *did* crash in August 1942, and *married* Ralph after V-J Day, in 1945, after which he didn't take long to overdose on barbiturates. So I have conflated the brothers here and put Ralph to death two years early.
[18]*His death*: This is abridged.
[19]*"Complications Jane" Bowles*: Libby and Jane Bowles wouldn't meet until circa 1946, introduced by Tennessee Williams during tryouts of the aforementioned *Beggar's Holiday*. They were probably never lovers.
[20]*Banned from the airwaves*: Though certainly racy, "banned" might be a little strong. Nor was it truly "The age of Garbo," since 1930 was the year she talked (in *Anna Christie*), shortly after which her career began to flounder.
[21]*White accompanist*: It is true that Josh couldn't always enter the venues through the front door (at least until Libby gave the management a piece of her mind) but nobody raised a huge ruckus that they were onstage together.

No use pretending
It looks like the ending
Unless I could have one more chance
Libby's backstage quarters smell of Jungle Gardenia. A very young red-haired journalist has followed the trail of long-stemmed blandishments here, hoping to interview Libby for *Theatre Arts*. The biography I am working from has disguised the identity of this unsuspecting ingenue,[22] so let's call it a moonlighting Jean Stafford.[23] Whatever her name, she has somehow stepped between the coded gulf of tabloid journalism and what's polite to say in society to arrive in Libby Holman's dressing room without a clue that the chipmunk-faced singer who preens theatrically in her stockings and pours two glasses of Bolla Soave quite obviously prefers the company of women:

"*Jesus God* honey, Josh?" She waves aside the whole sticky notion. "I won't deny I been tempted, but so far my name's the only part of me been blackened irreparably."

"And yet you've never shied away from mixed company, have you, Miss Holman?" Jean asks, because there is no natural subtlety or grace in the interviewer's art.

"I suppose you've heard all those wicked stories about me. Well, I've lived my life as it came and I've done bloody marvels with a bad hand," which actually comes out quite charming because Libby makes no effort whatsoever to hide the number of times she's rehearsed it.

"You're referring to Zachary Reynolds. Most girls would call marrying a man whose family gets a dime every time someone lights up a Camel a pretty good hand." But by this point, their knees are having a different conversation than the one still translating in rote squiggles in Stafford's notebook.

"Smith Reynolds, dear. No one called him Zachary. And if he'd looked anything like Rock Hudson in that movie they made of us,[24] he'd of had more humps than all the Camel packages in New York,"

---

[22]*Ingenue*: The book that I am working from, Jon Bradshaw's *Dreams That Money Can Buy*, calls this person "Chinky Collins."
[23]*Jean Stafford*: Not Jean Stafford. The age is right, but everything else is wrong, including the hair color and the fact that Stafford definitely had her druthers about her by the time she was this age. She may even have been married to Robert Lowell already—not, in other words, a fresh-from-the-sticks journalist like "Chinky."
[24]*Movie they made of us*: *Written on the Wind* was not released until 1956, Rock Hudson was in no way a part of the vocabulary of filmgoers in the forties, Robert Stack played the Reynolds role, and director Douglas Sirk was careful to change all the names and the cash crop from southern tobacco to Texas oil. Libby never saw it.

J. W. McCormack

whether acquiescent to a nervous tic or party to a legitimate itch, the journalist extends a finger to scratch her left hand, but Libby gets there first. Her nails have more texture on their tips than most men have in every reaching part. "But I'll give you the same line I gave the jury, since I know you people never get tired of printing it. I was so drunk I don't know if I shot him or not."[25]

"Married or not, you've always kept company with young men."

"Those're fairies. Now take off your coat and leave when I do," Libby, effortlessly vamping, rises to lock the two of them in together and, leaning against the door, waves the key back and forth in front of Jean Stafford's widening eyes like a mesmerist. "You are feeling extremely sleepy. You are madly in love with Libby Holman and only have sweet things to say about her in print. You live to tend her every desire. When she goes to meet friends at the Elysée Hotel for parlor games and serious drinking, you will come with her. They are eclectic and will find your red hair and brown eyes irresistibly naive."[26]

Libby belongs to the last generation of stars who made their names onstage, without the vocal hocus pocus of radio—and now that, rotten luck, she's back and ready to record, the crucial shellac has been classified "strategic material," effectively paralyzing manufacture. Her success has always rested upon an ability to inspire music in her audience by substituting her woes for theirs, convincing them to place themselves in her hands. In his shabby adjacent room, Josh White listens to the song she coaxes from Jean and strums his custom Martin 00-21,[27] equal parts amusement and unconsummated desire. For the third time this week and despite Libby's machinations, he's had to access the theater from the back entrance and prohibit Carol and their six children from attending his shows. Still, his New York fame is at its peak and the songs he sang for the musical *John Henry*, in which he played Blind Willie Johnson,[28] are still fresh, so he soothes the savage wailing next door with "John the Revelator," humming:

---

[25]*If I shot him or not*: This was, of course, only said privately and to Louisa Carpenter. I don't think Libby ever really knew whether she'd killed Smith Reynolds or not and wondered every day what had gone down.
[26]*They are eclectic and will find your red hair and brown eyes irresistibly naive*: A line from Stafford's "The Echo and the Nemesis."
[27]*Custom Martin 00-21*: If it was a Martin, it was not custom and if it was custom, it was not a Martin. White's only *custom* guitar was one he received later from Ovation, an ill-designed instrument he was recompensed to promote.
[28]*Blind Willie Johnson*: Josh didn't play Blind *Willie Johnson*, he played Blind *Lemon Jefferson*. It was Johnson who sang "John the Revelator."

J. W. McCormack

You know God walked down in the cool of the day
Called Adam by his name
But he refused to answer
Because he's naked and ashamed[29]

Miraculously, a shadow superimposes over the peeling wall, having slipped in with the moonlight. It is not God, but Franklin Delano Roosevelt, godfather of the country and of Josh's two-year-old son, summoned in time of need to assuage his devoted minstrel: "Now, Josh, I heard you singing those protest songs[30] again tonight. You know I've got my hands full in other people's backyards without unchaining the dogs here at home." "Yes, sir, I sure do know and I don't spite you for it. My little brother's serving[31] for you over in Jersey and I would be too if I wasn't here being a dad, but we're both of us fighting a lot of meanness from our own side and as long as that's that, I still got something to sing about." "Well, Josh, like I told you, I'm looking for a way to desegregate the boys and I think you're setting a hell of an example singing with that Jewish woman." "Well, thank you, sir. Libby's voice is the scariest damn thing I ever heard, but I trained her to sing my songs and now at least she sounds like a crazy trash-can cat in heat 'stead of some sort of mean-ass bird and that's an improvement far as I concern *myself*." "It's just one thing worries me, Josh, and that's that crowd over at Café Society. How they going to feel when they hear how you speak to me?" "Now, Mr. President, I ain't no kind of Red,[32] but I seen my daddy killed in front of me in Greeneville and I understand why those guys maybe think they can get change across faster than you." "Well, I sure appreciate your having no gods before Uncle Sam, Josh, but I'm just his spokesman here on earth and I won't always be around to protect you. And that's when you won't have a friend in the world."

Libby and her initiate *do* manage to make it to the Elysée Hotel

---

[29]*Naked and ashamed*: This verse is absent from the Blind Willie Johnson version, being unique to the Son House recording from the sixties.
[30]*Protest songs*: Of the songs Libby and Josh played on tour, only "Southern Exposure" can be considered a "protest song" and it is an extremely noble song that FDR must have approved of (actually FDR loved most of Josh's protest songs, even the contentious ones like "Uncle Sam Says") with the line that goes "I think democracy is fine / But I mean democracy without the color line," which the House Un-American Activities Committee would later seize on.
[31]*Serving*: Stationed, not serving.
[32]*Red*: Again, this is abridged. Josh White was decidedly *not* a Communist, a rarity for a folksinger of the period, and the fact that he went to such lengths to prove it was what really did him in. His friends from Café Society felt betrayed and the House Un-American Activities Committee were out to get him no matter what.

J. W. McCormack

("Don't see what's so very patriotic about making sure every fleabag in the country's got a fuckin' French name."[33]) and Tallulah Bankhead answers the bell and ushers them into her suite with the winning disgust that's kept her so consistently spotlit since debuting in New York at the age of twenty, saying, "*Darling*, we're playing Murder in the Dark. *Do* join us. We could use a professional."

"Thanks, Tal, but I'll just kill that there bottle of scotch . . . for now."

When they get inside, Libby discovers that, sans any word to her, they've invited Lupe Vélez, the second-billed[34] "Mexican Spitfire" in Holman's disastrous production of *You Never Know*, who lunges at her with an enormous diamond ring, screaming, "You Jewish beech, I *keel* you with *thees*!" and it's all arms on Lupe until she collapses back into drunken repose on the daybed, muttering, "I *keel* the dyke kike, I *keel her*!"

Fledgling newsgirl Jean Stafford's legs are still shaking like a pair of queasy willows, but she regains enough composure to meet Complications Jane and her taciturn husband, Paul, on a rare visit back from Tangiers[35] with his latest Moroccan playmate, Ahmed, who doesn't speak a lick of English and fecklessly obeys when Tallulah demands that he play the detective. The lights go out so the "murder" can occur, but when Jane turns on the lights, she and Ahmed are the only ones still standing.

"Why, Miss Bowles, I know the conventional positions only make you claustrophobic,[36] but come lie down for once in your life," drawls Libby, a doll akimbo. "Join the massacre, you old-fashioned thing."

Paul, the dashing vampire, draws his energy inversely from the others, so when the last in a series of abortive drawing-room follies has collapsed into singing and peals of laughter, he leaps onto the piano stool and bangs the keys in ribald dumb show of another of Tallulah's guests, an out-of-character Chico Marx.[37] But then the

---

[33]*French name*: Perhaps that's because this is a French hotel and an event from 1934 that I have moved across time and space.

[34]*Second-billed*: Not *even* second-billed. Lupe played Holman's maid in the 1938 production of this Cole Porter bomb. She *never* would have been at this party or any other. Lupe would later drown in a toilet.

[35]*Tangiers*: At this time, Paul Bowles would not have commenced his stay in Tangiers, preferring to stay in Paris and play his compositions for Gertrude Stein's salon. Ahmed and Libby later had an affair on the set of a movie, much to Paul's chagrin.

[36]*Claustrophobic*: This line and the next ("old-fashioned thing") are bowdlerizations of famous Tallulah Bankhead lines. See below.

[37]*Chico Marx*: The story goes that, upon meeting Tallulah at the punch bowl at some soiree, Chico said, "You know I would really like to fuck you," to which she replied, "And so you shall, you wonderful old-fashioned boy!"

melody softens and a curious thing happens to Libby as she lays her head upon Jean Stafford's lap. From the framed courtesy portrait that hangs over the Steinway, a wracked, witchy face glares out at her from behind a fan. Holman sits up in alarm, placing her features directly over the vision until every future crack is accounted for and the swimmy pupils of her own eyes are the only contents of the coal-black holes that stare back at her. The lass with the delicate air has become something worse than the sum of all her jilted tunes, a crone who mistook a string of revels for a life and whose every friend has gone before. Her face fades away inside the glass and is replaced by her son, Topper ,who smiles grimly, ages eight years in a minute, and dies, smashed to pieces in a mountain-climbing accident, his bleached skull becoming Montgomery Clift, who winks at Libby and makes her smile despite herself, until she realizes that his face has been surgically stripped[38] of half its weight and grotesquely remodeled into a living mask.

The singer can bear no more and turns to her friends, but they have been magically transmuted into mannequins, a pile of oddly crooked arms and pursed rubber lips. Jane and Tallulah teeter in place, still clutching their highballs, then fall into each other, their porcelain heads exploding with automatic violence. Paul Bowles continues to play his jingly-jangly Debussy cakewalk, but when he turns his head, it is baked by the heat of an invisible sun and crawling with scorpions.[39] Libby Holman, assailed by visions of organic and synthetic decline, opens her trained painted parrot of a mouth to sing a scream, but catches sight of her own sleeping body spread out on the floor, eyes openly regarding this disembodied somnambulism. Strangely, a golden bauble levitates just above the other Libby's lips. It circles three times, then slips down her throat[40] and a voice—her voice—chants:

> *Venus was born out of sea foam*
> *Venus was born out of brine*
> *But a goddess today if she is Grade-A*
> *Is assembled upon the assembly line*

---

[38]*Surgically stripped*: Mongomery Clift had his car accident and reconstructive surgery in 1956.
[39]*Scorpions*: From Bowles's first short story, "The Scorpion."
[40]*Her throat*: This image, and many of the images that follow, are from Hans Richter's experimental film *Dreams That Money Can Buy*, which he made with Paul Bowles, Man Ray, and others. Libby and Josh performed the movie's signature song, "The Girl with the Prefabricated Heart," about two department-store mannequins in love.

J. W. McCormack

Running to the hotel window, the dreamer beholds a petulant crowd assembled among the trees, in red velvet seats, shouting, "Whore!" and "Murderess!" Booing her, in fact. Into their midst comes a shamed Josh White, fresh from giving testimony to the House Committee. Tar and feathers[41] cling to his shirt despite his efforts to wipe it clean. Awash in a future age that reviles the progressives of its recent past, this White—older, balding, shot by both sides—wears his martyrdom badly and bears in one hand a letter impossible for Libby to read. As she suffers his plaintive stare at the windowpane, she makes out a drawing of a guitar snapped in two.[42] She turns into a ghost and passes through flashing walls into the hallway, pursued by her own voice, its famously suggestive key turned to mock its origin.

> *Her chromium nerves and her platinum brain*
> *Were chastely encased in cellophane*
> *And to top off this daughter of science and art*
> *She was equipped with a prefabricated heart*

At the end of the corridor a limp line of suits turns to face her: among them, her husbands, Rafe and Reynolds, the latter of whom has turned the faded blue-green of a Hindu deity and wears a ghastly rictus under his familiar almond-shaped eyes. A woman like Libby—and there are no women like Libby—relies on her throat, but tonight her weapon is strangely sealed, as though with mercury, and tastes of exhaust.[43] There is no choice but to submit to the helpless, hapless flight of nightmares; she doubles back, colliding with her hair, looking for the elevator, but Reynolds anticipates her so she takes the stairs. But they stretch impossibly before her. Lifting her voile skirt over toes that, more than ever, resemble little jeweled frogs, she spirals down the hotel's drain while Smith Reynolds lights a Camel and sings from the landing.

> *I'll offer you sterilized flowers*
> *Expensive and scentless and rare*
> *There'll be pedigreed birds*
> *Singing songs without words*
> *As they fly through the air-conditioned air*

---

[41]*Tar and feathers*: Metaphorical tar, metaphorical feathers. Josh White's qualified pursuit of social justice made him putty in the hands of the new, postwar Right, while to the actual socialists he would have looked like a relic of the oakie-folky New Deal.
[42]*Guitar snapped in two*: Pete Seeger wrote this letter to Josh but never sent it.
[43]*Tastes of exhaust*: Whether Libby was murdered by her opportunistic third husband or herself or a third party is open to debate. What is certain is that she died of monoxide poisoning in her garage, aged sixty-seven, in 1971, having lived a life equal parts truth and lies, neither having been of much help to her in the end.

She flings herself through the Elysée's doors, gilt with cherubim, hoping absurdly to hail a taxi back to reality. But the notes are all wrong. She is not in New York, but in the twilit pasture of her Connecticut estate, only looking overgrown, spotted with moundish ivy shambles and the click of brood parasites. She must have been dead for many years. Libby runs to the tree line and, under shadowed timbers, entwines her arm with an elm's scabby cylinder, coming at it with such velocity that it swings her around like a New Year's noisemaker so that she sees quite clearly how a facsimile of her first husband is looming out from behind every peekaboo trunk. Libby has played the woman in distress all her life; now she plays it to the hilt and struggles uphill, to the main road where a coach is waiting. Before she can wonder what reaper has stopped for her here, Josh White swings down from the footman's seat dressed as a country troubadour, silk shirt open to the chest, and, the diamond in his ear shining star bright, takes up his guitar and repels the wicked spirits of the wood, singing in his gallant bass:

> *Oh nature and art will not win her*
> *So I'll ply her with diamonds and pearls*
> *Bracelets and pearls are practical things*
> *That appeal to the mind of a healthy girl*

He takes Libby in his arms, guides her into the carriage, mounts the front, shouts, "Hyah!" to the horses, and shakes the reins in the direction of a sun that looks more and more like a spotlight. Safely ensconced, she begins to understand. It's all pretend and there is no danger. A crane reaches down from behind the veil some fog machine has tossed over the world to remove the trees one by one so that, rather than moving, the buggy stands still and the landscape is merely redressed. The blight of the future and tragedy of the past are behind her; some third place is in the works, just for her. Nor is she alone— her lovers Louisa and Jane, dressed as Amazons, appear roadside with Montgomery Clift, her collared slave boy. Paul Bowles, leading a parade of every critic who ever scorned her, pries open their mouths to show how he has avenged her by cutting out each of their tongues. Oh, this is ridiculous. Sisters, come to my aid!

> *You express every ideal I've ever had*
> *You're as evocative as a full-page ad.*

221

( )
Gabriel Blackwell

NOW ALONE, KNOCK ON BOBBY (that most famous of wooden nou-
mena, the not-in-use-just-now dummy of ventriloquist Signor Blitz
(famed, as you already know, for the spectacle of his opening routine
(involving an as-yet unhandled Bobby firing a pistol at Blitz from
across the stage as Blitz enters (the ventriloquist, seeming to exhale
cordite, having caught the bullet between his teeth (the trick being
that Bobby talks all the while (first, professing anger at his constant
manipulation by Blitz, then, once he's pulled the trigger, expressing
sorrow at having killed his master (Blitz slumping over on his back
opposite Bobby, both thrown backward by the force of the shot
(Antonio Blitz, incidentally, formerly strictly a magician, signature
illusion: the bullet catch (given up for the safer profession of ventriloquism when the trick went wrong and tore off the outer lobe of his
left ear (leaving him with what could with kindness be called an
"unfinished" look (proving the man you've just seen to be, actually,
not Antonio Blitz at all but an impostor (proving him to be, rather,
an American, Clive Robertson (claiming to be the "Original Signor
Blitz" (having never seen the original "Signor Blitz," actually a third
man, the "true" identity of whom has never been established (offi-
cially, as given at admission to Bethlehem State Mental Hospital:
"Signor Blitz" (as reported by the *Boston Post* in 1889, twelve years
after the second Signor Blitz had passed away in Philadelphia, not
from a shooting accident (obituary in the *Philadelphia Register* list-
ing him as Antonio Van Zandt, Englishman (son of a woodworker
and amateur astronomer interested, particularly, in what he called
"ghost moons" of Mars (which would be found, later, to have been
real moons, Phobos and Deimos (by Asaph Hall, in 1877, the year the
elder Van Zandt's son, Antonio, was laid to rest (having passed away
from complications following upon a surgery to remove his gallblad-
der (said to have become so diseased that, when the surgeon nicked
it with his scalpel, the sound that issued forth was later described as
"the knock of a walnut falling upon a wood-beam" (this in the journal of a man so definitively not present at the surgery as to call into

222

question his motives for recording such information (said journalist being also the author of the poem "Leonainie" (said to have been a "lost" last poem of Edgar Allan Poe's (which claim was accepted by many (even elaborated upon—the poem, written after Poe's death, had been "accomplished by another body, but manifested within the same brain," said none other than Alfred Russel Wallace (a great debunker of hoaxes, taking on the Flat-Earthers and those believing in Martian canals (descendants, at least spiritually, of those hoodwinked by the "Great Moon Hoax" perpetrated by Poe's editor, Richard Adams Locke (whom Poe thought had unfairly and without credit scooped out the innards of his "The Unparalleled Adventure of One Hans Pfaall" (leaving the whole thing hollow, to his estimation (Poe then creating, in response, the so-called "Balloon-Hoax," which asserted much less fantastic fantasies on the part of a Mr. Monck Mason (based upon Mr. Thomas Monck Mason, balloonist, yes, but also theologian and flautist (the flute a woodwind, of course, inspirited wood, hollow and lifeless but producing a distinctive tone when breathed into (
) unlike that produced when knocking on wood only in pitch), immune, impossibly, to charges of being filled with hot air), made mean-spirited through the caprices of public attention), given that his intention had never been to hoodwink, really, merely to entertain), and who now owed Poe a living Poe could never seem to earn through his own labors), who had ascribed the "discoveries" to one "Sir John Herschel," a very real astronomer annoyed at having to answer for the bizarreries brought into being by Locke's imagination), as he put it, "creatures willing to credit all but their own credulity"), a man who had become cynical through his powerful yearning to believe, finally, in something, anything)—anything could be believed of Poe!), albeit one that perhaps should have stayed "lost"), a poem whose most memorable lines—"Songs are only sung / here below that they may grieve you— / Tales but told you to deceive you"—are at least fair as *ars poetica*); it would be another fourteen years before a psychologist would review the literature and describe *Pseudologia fantastica* for the first time, and sixty years before Baron Münchhausen's falsifications, amplified by his imitators' tales of him, would become Baron *von* Münchhausen, father to fibbers the world around); the sound also more famously recalling the discovery of a hidden passage, a hollow recess), made necessary, it was rumored, due to Van Zandt's "hollow leg," his high tolerance for alcohol), a year perhaps more significant for the invention of the carbon microphone, a

device to electrically reproduce and thereby transport sound), named
for a god of fear and a personification of dread, respectively)—a man,
incidentally, often said to have been "not all there"), survived by his
wife, née Eaton, with whom he had no children), a set of circumstances at least one Massachusetts "Safety Coffin" manufacturer
found advantageous, claiming that his expensive precautions had
raised Blitz from the dead, or at least had saved him from a costly
mistake)—the staff evidently at least somewhat taken in, as the
story then leaked to the press); Van Zandt performed as "Blitz Jr."
until he took up ventriloquism and Bobby, renouncing or reversing
his false heritage upon becoming a "father"), a claim to originality as
obviously empty as it was vehemently made), a man about whom
nothing is known prior to his career as the "Original Signor Blitz";
perhaps his "true" identity is just another illusion?), though, given
that the existence of these doubles served to multiply the man's fame
more than any of his own efforts had, it seems unkind to condemn one
and all as "impostors"), like a set of quotations left open), "blank"
rounds still capable of propelling anything left in the supposedly
empty barrel at dangerous velocities), utterly unconvincing on stage
alone, as though half an act, even before he made himself half an act),
the act immediately becoming invisible from the orchestra section),
perhaps evidence of this man's great self-loathing, a not-so-hidden
threat of suicide), which, it seems to you, is less impressive than his
manipulation of the gun, if only because the latter seems so impossible), trials of which having resulted in a gap in the ventriloquist's
smile even though no projectile was ever fired)—the gasp this produced sounding as though all of the air had been sucked out of the room
through a straw), which, as the opening, gives the rest of the routine
a superfluous air, as though the best has come and gone before the
act has fairly begun), empty and somewhat deflated, possibly also, you
now realize, an impostor): Reassure yourself that there is no longer
anything there aside from the briefest of echoes, the sharp rap of
knuckles on wood, and an emptied-out double of that sound, signi-
fying that whatever had given this dummy, Blitz's "son," the appearance of life has departed.

Peace Poems
Gillian Conoley

It fell

   of noon

      weatherlike

as in

   a poem the

sudden action of a single word

   you know

     people,

      once you tell them something

      they start talking

        *

smells of sweat deep
in sport-full fields
eyes opened and were thrilled or soothed and sustained
we had won
cars passed along streets in bright difference or decay

*

in argument context shivers the trigger words
before munitions, oil extracted from the cotton
makes the town smell sweet
no corpus, only body's eidolon
marijuana-scented hush of the glove compartment
in your device, a person spies the bridge in flames then flees
so old school, the photo in its bath

*

contrary to history, to war's punctuations
the almost-dripping popsicle held from the body
on the heat-buckled sidewalk, earth's
involuntary memory to descend and ascend,
the round. the blue.
to begin all over again.

*

death is to be entered backwards
the necessary condition, a partial vision
at my father's funeral, a blind field
the flag taken from over the casket
folded into a triangle, handed to us
throughout "the reception"
a boy eyes a pizza slice
on a white paper plate

*

one mystery of the breath: it does not hover
in the body but spirals
and up to two hours   in the less known
mammalian diving reflex   water must be
ice-cold   some people survive
if time began we would do it again
the lungs two oars in the middle of the ocean

*

interrupting winds
nightfall shifts the lens
we grow still
body sensing itself
why is Maurice Merleau-Ponty
so obsessed with one hand
touching the other one lips do
as much staying shut
around 6,000 languages

*

halftone of a couple in a four-poster
who left their breath together
or took too much
white clapboard   distant city
her vagina his cock slack in the cosmological moisture
Christ gets so misquoted
once they put the Latin in him
looking out of the picture wanting nothing

*

banana tree's garnet/green transparent
leaf at large in the neighbor's yard
slant, blank in dirt   signs pop up
either an unfathomable mystery   or a no-vote-for-anyone
bus rims the beach   down the aisle
tap tap of the almost-silent keyboard
busy fingers of no master
luster/thunder/empyreal/projecting/nether

*

if a no more one without the other
could peace and war be a co-presence
peace and war a co-presence
one hand holding another
a metaphysics their separateness a reality
one can no longer touch? we flock to, inflate
death's impatiences

Suspension as a Unit of Experience; or, What She Remembered of the Vanishing Lines

John Madera

UNFOLD: A REFUSAL TO REFRAME MOTILITY into something legible.

"Foolish old bird!"

Unfold.

Monday is not Sunday. Confused, stuck, numb, she looked up—her darting eyes landing on an abandoned wisp of a trap—and saw herself stuck, there, in a stucco ceiling's corner (its popcorn texture a haven for dust too), wrapped in silk, limp from poison, ruddy rivers slowly sucked out of her. Vagaries? An unexplained *cri de coeur?*

Unfold: a refusal to give an experience a shape, a pattern, a meaning.

Sometimes all it took was an idea, knocked about in her mind, to fling her into a sticky mess.

Unfold.

"Bead up and roll off," she said, every trouble bubbling up. "Bead up and roll off," she chanted, massaging her legs, looking at everything, chiseling out every detail in her now beclouded sensorium, believing that through the intensity of her gaze what she had seen would mix with the nothing she hoped was there rather than with the something she hoped wasn't there: an odd batter hardening into something she knew rather than simply something new.

The television was on. A newscast. Something about a garbage barge.

Fold. Truth and accuracy, viz., the lack thereof.

It must have been one of those surly mornings you get in late fall when, instead of the usual humdrum glut of junk, Marisol had found a lily, an origamied one, in the mailbox. It had upset her then, the creased paper, its whimsy, how it seemed to breathe, pulse, warm her arm, the rush flushing her face. Was it an event? An affective excess in consequence? Concerns, that is, that would only worry a historian. She'd wondered if the mailman had left it, shivering as she imagined rubbing her hands along the man's arms, the arms pebbled with bumps, no, lumps, the arms she'd eye whenever she chanced upon him. Shaking away the thought, she'd unfolded the paper lily, found it empty, and then crumpled it up, and huffed as if to unclog something trapped inside her. But this wasn't what had cobwebbed her mind as she sat blank faced, what made her thumbs wheel, made her finick over a napkin, crisscross shreds of it on the kitchen table.

Unfold. Definitions are never foolproof.

After finding the flower, Marisol, in a frenzy to fix things, cleaned out the old footlocker, a pirate tale's battered, brass-riveted box, and found a bundle of letters shoved inside a distressed-leather bowling-ball bag (where the resinous globe had rolled away to was another of the basement's mysteries). The bundle had been buried under a thatched mass of receipts, envelopes, and pay stubs, and what could only have been an epicurean's perverse pile of menus. She held the bundle, cupping it as if it were a preemie, as if the slightest breath could shatter it. Motes floating in a shaft of light: crepuscular, she thought. Static, she thought. After untying the frayed ribbon, Marisol nosed one of the envelopes as if it were a tulip-shaped glass, expecting a floral whiff, and then snapped it against her lap, shaking her head in a sorry attempt to empty it all out. There is an art to forgetting, she thought. And how easy it is to forget that forgetting is part of remembering, that lapses are as integral to memory as pauses are to language. Negative space makes a thing a thing, she thought. Voids make forms.

Unfold.

Winded, a jerky wheeze eking out from her nose, Marisol tapped a forefinger on the armrest of her wicker-backed chair and sighed at the basement, an obstacle course or a packrat's messy nest, or just life's leftovers, where boxes and boxes of greeting cards, paper plates, and napkins; stacks of sand-guttered page-turners; and a graveyard of broken appliances all competed for space with a bleached plastic nativity scene that would light up their front yard every Christmas; a bicycle with gray deflated tires, gears dusted copper; a plastic bag of rags; forgotten husks of clothing; some toy trucks that had never made it out of their boxes; and a landscape painting, a gift from one of their children—she couldn't remember which. A gash ran from the top of the picture's farthest mountain to the side of its sole person, the cut like a river cleaving its way through a valley. Marisol couldn't remember the cause of the cut, but as she looked at the hole, a shout, unsounded, escaped from it—[*Fold.*]—beckoning her back to when she'd hung the painting, over the living-room sofa, much like she'd hung their children's drawings on the refrigerator when they were kids, and hadn't given much thought to it; no one in the family had, since everyone had often had their backs to it, each of them marble-eyed from sitcoms or video-game numb or simply sprawled out on the sofa.

One night, the kids finally off at college,   in his workshop whipping up sawdust, Marisol, after looking up from a book, pondered over the painting, stared at its composition blankly as she allowed some bit of language to steep within her, fog her mind with its color. But the image was working within her too, until what had virtually dissolved into nondescript wallpaper had taken over her mind, the words from whatever she'd been reading disappearing into a sharp regard of the picture's windswept-haired man dressed in a dark, velvety green, measuring how he stood—his back to the viewer—on a rocky cliff, gazing over what looked like a misty valley, trees fringing

231

a distant ridge, everything below befogged, and everything above cloud-shrouded. Had he come upon that haziness to meditate, to pray? Or was he mourning the loss of someone who'd leapt from that same promontory? Or was he considering a jump of his own, calculating how much time it would take for his heart to stop before his body dropped to the rocks at the bottom of the chasm? Then she'd noticed that the compositional lines of the painting all converged at a point, targeting something obscured by the stranger in the center. No, she'd thought, they point toward his heart, suggesting that both he, and, in turn, the viewer, who, oddly, is compelled to empathize with the mountaineer, feel what he was feeling, fall into the rhythm of what beat inside him.

Unfold.

When you climbed down the old house's rickety stairs, you found the basement dusty and dank, suffused with a soporific dimness; and when you saw the cinder-block walls, concrete floor, and unfinished ceiling, where wires and cables, a makeshift clothesline, naked bulbs, and other snaky things hung and coiled about, you thought of a child playing with Lincoln Logs and Tinkertoys, all the wacky structures designed on an Etch a Sketch.   's tools were still sprawled out on a worktable, every conceivable kind of nail, pin, and screw strewn about, latent energy hovering over hammers and hacksaws like a force field. [*Fold.*] Over the years, many things had rolled out from his workshop, like the airplane (its length larger than any bicycle) he'd built using discarded planks. Having completed the fuselage, wings, and propeller, he'd wrested wheels from an old metal bed frame and fixed them onto the bottom of the whole thing, later hotrodding it with ghost flames. After school, he had taken their sons out to the playground for the first "takeoff." Marisol, certain that that was the day   had decided to become a pilot, rubbed her earlobe, stretched it out like taffy. And how many trains and cars, how many ornaments, tchotchkes, and knickknacks, how many boxes, frames, and shelves, had   made in his basement workshop? How quiet and secretive   would become while ensconced in a project, basement door clicking shut in time with his silence. How   's face had beamed, suddenly sweetening like a leaf sugared red by an autumn wind, while he unveiled his

232

masterpiece: Celia's dollhouse. Even after their daughter had long outgrown it,   continued adding on to the house, and, with a wink, had started calling it his "Taliesin East."

Marisol found no comfort in these thoughts, however. Everything remembered, she thought, remembered clearly, and a terrible monster is born.

Unfold. Loosenings and quickenings.

Marisol watched a centipede crawl, scrawling esses across the basement's damp concrete floor, its feelers twitching—a signal to switch its path?—Marisol marveling at how each antenna quivered with accumulated data, marveling too at the futility of the centipede's effort, how it couldn't measure how long it took to get from wherever it had been to where it was now, and then to wherever it was going, how its throbbing wetness would inevitably yield to the air hardening around it. Creepy-crawlies of any kind: roaches, beetles, spiders, waterbugs, or whatever, never bothered her. [*Fold.*] As a child, living what she'd once thought of as an "idyllic island life," but what she'd come to realize was really a "hardscrabble scramble," Marisol would laugh at the girls, and sometimes boys too, who would fuss at the sight of an armored back, uncurling proboscis, or tingling antennae. After the many times her children had dangled in her face some slimy, furry, winged, chitinous, or tentacled thing they'd plucked from mud, swiped from a nest, or netted or trapped in some other way somehow, she had become further impervious to those kinds of scares. [*Unfold.*] But those little giggling rascals would have shrieked at the sight of what Marisol spotted beneath   's bowling-ball bag: a skeletal whisper of a mouse, its teeth still chomping away at some cheesy evanescence. She was smitten, revering this rodent's tenacity, its irrepressible belief in life even though it had been snapped in half by a trap.

Marisol, looking at the letters again, felt as if a fist were pressed against her belly. As she flicked a mildewed bit from the top envelope, fibers tensed up inside her. "Enough!" she said, bundling the letters together, tying the ribbon around them. Later, she would stuff the bundle into an empty shoe box, sliding it underneath her bed beside her slippers.

Tuesday is not Monday. After a day of lecturing about the perils of historicization, Marisol found a bouquet of paper flowers on her doormat. Holding it away from her—each flower suggesting fragility and, because of its sharp folds, a kind of severity—she turned around, feeling like someone's eyes were on her. Was it a prank, from one of the neighborhood punks, those "sniveling wannabes"? No, she couldn't imagine their greasy hands creasing thin sheets of paper into something beautiful. Next door, workers were continuing to replace the old gutters, parts of which had fallen after the storm a few weeks before. Was the bouquet from one of these men?

She walked across her porch toward the clatter of tools and the beefy chatter, and saw a man who was all belly, his heavy curls feathered gray, and imagined his knobby hands on her, shuddering over her. Once back inside the house, she placed the bouquet at the center of the dining-room table, and, staring at it, she felt like a fool, an old fool, one easily suckered into thinking she was being romanced, and then she thought of   . [*Fold: the enclosures produced, their depressions, their overlappings, their middles.*] This was the kind of thing   would do, the kind of thing he'd shrug about were he asked whether he knew anything about it.

Marisol slid in and out of sleep that night, only slightly aware of the times she turned toward the garden-facing window, where hawkmoths used to feed on her night-blooming moonflowers, where cicadas used to buzz like snare drums, where the old rosebush she loathed would show up, once again, in the spring, Marisol slowly falling back into the nightmare that had forced her awake, playing itself out as it had over and over every night for weeks: A young mother again, Marisol sits on a bench in a playground, watching her children lose themselves in their play. Celia tromps around, picking up leaves. Arturo, lost in a knot of boys, is playing tag. And   , the eldest, stands at the top of a jungle gym. He waves. Marisol waves back, smiling, until she realizes he's not waving at her but flapping his arms, preparing to vault from the edge. Frantic, she runs toward   , only to wake again, to reach out to her husband's side of the bed, only to find it empty again. Turning away once more, Marisol allowed her mind to drift, to think about how to remember what *was* is to disremember it, to dismember it, her mind eventually emptying itself out, until she drifted into a sleep heavy with its own blankness.

*

Fold and unfold, fold and unfold, fold and unfold: suggestions of
a disjointed immediacy, of distance intimated.

Wednesday is not Tuesday. Come morning, Marisol woke to a "vac-
uumed-out solitude," the phrase evoking, as it came to her mind,
a machined grief, that there was a technology to loss. She did not
find   beside her, cocooned within a sheet. When she
opened the curtain, the hooks squeaking,   did not mumble
something about its being too early. He did not, rising from the bed,
say, "No matter how old I get"—adding before she herself inter-
jected, "or how stale either"—"he, she, it still won't take me off the
shelf," a single gnarled finger pointing above past the ceiling to
the sky as he chuckled.   did none of these things because
     [*Fold: a chronological rumple, a slowing and a quick-*
ening, a resurrecting of a once understood self and other, stopping
on a word, a name.] had died in his sleep three months before.
     had always been certain he would die before Marisol.
"Because if you go first," he would say, "I'd follow you right away
anyway." And even after she would wave   's words away
with a conductor's flourish—she'd heard such talk countless times—
he would continue: "But if I go, you'll live on a long time," his
demeanor both feral and secretive, "Least longer than you would
with a big lug like me to lug around." And   , after waiting
for her rolled eyes, would say, "Plus, the kids would need you more."
     was always comfortable talking about death, his own,
especially, and could joke about it, entertain the macabre, which
made her think about something he would always say at partings:
"After every goodbye comes a hello." But not every goodbye,
     , Marisol thought. Silence is a vacuum that takes up space.
For Marisol, death was simply a dot of punctuation. You lived
whatever odd succession of paragraphs you were supposed to, no, not
"supposed to," the words implying an external plan and planner, not
"meant to" either, since whatever meaning life had was whatever
meaning you brought to it, was shaped, inevitably, by your upbringing, religion, or schooling, or was simply forced upon you; and the
ending of your life and its concomitant punctuation mark would
correspond with how you lived, with your choices, or the things de-
limiting those choices, so that, for instance, if you lived a healthy and
full life, it would end with a respectable period; or if you'd led a heroic
life, a mythic one, an exclamation point would be its consequent end;

or, if it had been snuffed out unexpectedly, like   's—all because
of a thunderstorm, heavy downpour, turbulence, updrafts and down-
drafts, and a failed engine—it would be capped off with a question
mark.

Unfold.

But death is a thief, burgling not only a life but the language of those
who remain, rupturing, fissuring articulation, destroying ideas: an
absence abscessing, disintegrating whatever ideas may form, until one
is reduced, mute. They said [*Fold.*] Marisol had found   ,
after first touching, then shaking his shoulder. But, no, what she'd
found was no one. What she'd found was nothing. Everything had
gone blank, and she was sucked into a lacuna, extruded through rooms
like soup through a straw, every room silent except for the yawning
ticktock, the stretch marks of days and days. [*Unfold.*] What was the
punctuation mark for a husband torn away from his wife? A forward
slash as if marking off a line break to an unfinished poem? Husband.
Father. The words seemed obscene in absentia, disembodied. And
what was a name but a mark under erasure, a face something effaced.
There was this urge to elegize in those rooms, those empty rooms,
but the absence of visible links between causes and effects prevented
Marisol from fighting the desire to map her pain. Concretions were
what she wanted: the thing as it is rather than what is remembered,
or whatever it was that quietus claims. And so Marisol reached out
to language, to poets, the Elizabethans mainly, and the Romantics,
and would allow their words to have their way inside her, burrow in
or brew within her mind, until their words became her thoughts.
Since the funeral, words from her favorite poems would leap out
from whatever dark place they were hidden away in, knocking about
in her head like the squirrels [*Fold.*] they'd once heard quarreling in
the attic.

[*Unfold.*] But isn't that it, Marisol thought, that when you said,
"There's nothing left to say," what you meant was that nothing was
a something, and that *that* something, this nothing, was what was left
to be said, that your thoughts, giving way to loss, widen the intersti-
tial interval between past and future, until it subsumed time, voided
it, made a nothing, a zone where you are neither actor nor witness.

Unfold: certainties: vehicles of indirection causing further uncertainty.

Marisol fanned through the bundle once again, the brittle envelopes—their postmarks over thirty years old—crinkling like garlic skin. She counted seven letters, each one written in a crisp cursive script, its curlicues more like intertwisting threads than letters, and addressed to a post office box belonging to her husband of thirty-five years. After finding them, Marisol—as if forgetting something and then having it come to her, fill her mouth like a tongue-swum word—finally allowed their marriage to rise clearly before her now, a tiny, fully rigged, four-masted boat in a bottle. While there were moments—no, more than moments—spans, vistas, of bliss, of love, Marisol knew that what had really defined their marriage was work. Work, yes, a "lifework," she called it, and was always proud to say so to anyone still listening, or pretending to, like her children for whom her homilies were usually lost.

Marisol hadn't forgotten—who else was left to remember?—[*Fold: memories: fleeting eclipses, attempts at an unworking, a creation.*] the lean years when they'd barely made it week to week, the dark, black, dark days when the devourer had eaten away what was left of her left breast; when their youngest had "gone off the deep end, gambling everything away," as ___ had said; when ___'s plane had crashed; or the times when all she held on to was an arid promise of having and holding. But she could still look back and say she and ___ had built something, something that lasted. [*Unfold.*] How many people could look back on a storm-wracked thing—every scar, every carbuncle imparting it with a kind of radiance, beauty even, a thing born of patience and trust, the stuff of work, hard work—on some sun-desiccated thing honed by briny waves—and still be able to say that it lasted, made it through? She was attempting to be both here and there, now and later, and she would be the first to say that history is merely the mining of memory, a quarrying through obfusc layers toward what actually happened, a locus where the self glints, briefly, through time's residue, only to be lost again, overtaken by silence, any coherence merely a suspect something made from nothing.

Marisol still couldn't touch the books they had read together. Every nook in their house was filled with books. Cervantes, Proust, Dickens, Márquez. And their beloved Shakespeare. [*Fold.*] How many versions of his plays had they seen together? There was the prescient *Romeo and Juliet* set in Howard Beach just before the racial assaults and murder in 1986. There was the fractured rendering of *Hamlet* that somehow used the idea of parallel universes as a backdrop. And she would never forget the distasteful and (a far greater offense, in Marisol's mind) obvious version of *A Midsummer Night's Dream*, which had something to do with psychotropic drugs. But it was the lesser-known plays like *Troilus and Cressida*, *The Merry Wives of Windsor*, and *Antony and Cleopatra* they'd loved so much, if only because Hollywood hadn't butchered them yet.

Once, after the funeral, she'd dared open one of   's books, one of the many woodworking manuals he kept on a shelf by the worktable, and an envelope slipped out, containing over two hundred dollars.   had always loved surprises, surprising others especially, and her most of all—the more elaborate the ruse, the better. Had he set this stash aside for one of his secret plans? A romantic dinner? Savings for a getaway?

Unfold.

It rained as she sat in the kitchen, the steady pelt of raindrops, its soft shush gently reminding Marisol to be quiet, to think about time, about how little of it she and   had [*Fold.*] had together, about how much of it had been filled with work, work, work, and more work, about how little time they'd allowed for nothing, for time to simply be. [*Unfold.*] She tried shaking off the drag-down feeling of having always been netted within life's rush and hustle by imagining herself walking in a garden enjoying all the tempting scents, the butterflies flirting with flowers, the contrapuntal birdsong, sun-glistered branches as she sought out the singers; [*Fold.*] imagining the long family meals—Celia always plucking out the onions like weeds—; [*Unfold.*] imagining herself spinning—around in the rain, splashing on puddles; [*Fold.*] imagining   and herself alone on a beach, building sand castles and writing their names in the sand with their toes, waiting for the ocean to wash the grainy script away;   poking fun at the lifeguards' swelling bulges, their leathery skin, how it could be flensed from their sculptured bodies, stretched out over a volleyball net for further tanning, and then fashioned into belts, bags, and boots;   joking

238

about the bronzed and beer-bellied retirees coughing out the occasional gruff word to some salty kid kicking up sand;   recoiling at the sight of a microbikini flossing a girl's rump, saying: "A thong is just wrong," and how she'd surprised him by wearing one to bed one night, unmasking his desire as quickly as it took to peel the lacy thing off from her body, their arms and legs coiling around each other soon after; discovering, after many such entwinings, how you could never know everything about your lover's body, since by the time you'd counted every birthmark and mole, other growths had popped out; new wrinkles had cracked over some part of the fleshy canvas; some fat had collected in the hips, the belly, the backside; the hair thinned out, the salt overtaking the pepper, the hairline receding like surf; because the skin is a map wrapped around a landscape, over the mound of the skull, over the hills of the clavicle and shoulder blades, over the knobby-knolled spine running down the back, the rising peaks of breasts, the mountain of the stomach. Because the body never stops, because it doesn't stop even when the mind is lost, or when the heart forgets to drum; because the body is the last to go, is the only thing that matters because it is matter, that it becomes, in the end, something like nothing.

Unfold.

Thursday is not Wednesday. In the morning, Marisol found a wreath of paper flowers hanging over the sliding glass door, which opened out to the deck. Frightened, she called the police, and they sent a car over. After asking all the expected questions, the officers told her to get some pepper spray, to never go anywhere without telling a trusted friend or family member, and shared that since she hadn't seen anyone suspicious around the house there wasn't much they could do. They left soon after they'd told her to alert them if anything else happened. Marisol saw the logic in everything they'd said, but she couldn't see how this was enough, how acting preemptively would definitely prevent something far worse from happening. She huffed, thinking about how she'd wanted to smack the sneer off the red-faced cop who intimated that she might have a secret admirer. Was she simply to sit there, to wait until the stranger broke into her house, attacked her?

She thought about calling her children. But how could they help?

John Madera

They were worried enough about her as it was without her having to bring up this mystery about paper flowers. Marisol would meet with her daughter at the Metropolitan Museum of Art that afternoon, and she didn't want to ruin their day with more of her worrying. She feared she was becoming one of those unbearable parents who competed with their children for attention, who tried to match their tempests with squalls of their own; or like those pudgy solitaires, crinkling into their sixties, calcifying into their seventies, crumbling into their eighties, who talked and talked and talked and talked.

Later, standing on the steps of what had been one of their old haunts, Marisol felt haunted herself, and thought about how the words "haunt" and "home" might have shared the same root. She felt pushed out of time, memories lumping like silt deposits, crystal specks shining through the sand. [*Fold.*]   and she had never tired of looking at all the deities glaring from glass cases in the Americas rooms, or the gemlike Vermeers, the carnose Rodins, Rembrandt's honeyed light. She would always humor   with a romp through the arms and armor rooms, and he would do the same by walking quietly in the rooms of colonial furniture, eyeing every filigree with requisite oohs and aahs. Though it had only been a few months since the funeral, she'd thought she was ready to walk through those halls again and see the art they'd loved.

[*Unfold.*] That's us, she thought, standing with her daughter, Celia, before the Temple of Dendur,   and me under diffused light—our marriage, our love, carved in relief, eight hundred tons of sandstone fitted together by some god playing with blocks, blocks rising like massive hands opening and reaching for the sun, the sun, the sun. Yet even while facing this monument, which had somehow lasted, Marisol couldn't help thinking that time destroys equally those left behind and those who die. Celia, as if reading her mother's mind, wrapped her arms around Marisol, who would have crumbled where she stood had Celia not mentioned something about lunch.

Fold.

        had worked at the post office for over thirty years. He would wake up every day at six and leave Marisol with a kiss tasting like coffee. They had remained lovebirds in their way, even after the kids had grown up, and even through all the changes in their bodies,

240

their minds. Their friends, who all knew her husband as   , used to call them "M&M." She knew it was corny to think so, but it really did seem like life before he died *was* sweet.   had only just retired before his heart had "quit on him," as he would have described the lightning blast of cardiac arrest.

Unfold.

Marisol, sitting on the edge of the bed, tapped her fingers against the shoe box—the letters inside weighing it down—as if arpeggiating piano keys, and then, as if in response, something squeezed her knees, and she wasn't so sure of anything at all all over again. [*Fold.*] "We were happy here," she said, as if to someone she barely knew, someone she had to convince, as if to the shadows in the room. [*Unfold.*] Placing the box on the bed, she walked to the window, nudged the curtain to one side, and looked out, where she could see the arch of the Queensboro Bridge: a constellation of blinking head-lights: reds and yellows and whites: cars and trucks and buses muscling against each other for space, like jockeyed horses lunging for a win—no wonder they still use horsepower to rate engine per-formance, she thought.

She caught sight of a bird—one of the city's falcons?—winging its way toward the bridge, and [*Fold.*] recalled her visit with   to Niagara Falls, in the dog days of a summer years ago, where, as they'd stood gazing at the massive watery curtain, cooled by the mist and spray, she'd watched a single bird flying across the expanse, won-dering if the birds had collectively decided to take turns.

[*Unfold.*] It was the time of day when the sun finally gave up, when everything rushed to slow down, when it felt like everything was coming to an end. Soaring toward the bridge, reaching that impossible height, buoyed by some inexplicable lightness, rising like some promised messiah, the falcon, its hooked beak and pointed wings cutting through the air, zoomed, presumably, toward its nest, charging forward like a missile. As grand as it was, Marisol could see how easy it would be to mistake the bridge for a cliff, to find a ledge there, and scrape a depression with your legs, carve a place to lay your eggs.

Watching the bird winding its way farther and farther, only to final-ly disappear, Marisol saw herself lifting into the air with the same kind of ease, completely free, watching the sun, a gold coin slotting past the horizon, into the sea, and yearned to feel the wind rushing past her ears, as it was surely doing now with the bird, smoothing down its blue-gray back. She couldn't think of this bird being part of the dismal flock of roughened fluffy things she would see pecking away at the detritus along the river's edge, poking their beaks in the greasy mess. This bird was a ballerina, bold and graceful, twisting, sweeping, circling, pirouetting across the sky.

Marisol, relaxing her body, stretched out her arms and tiptoed until she felt weightless, and then spun and spun until she lost her balance and then swung her arms, reaching out for something to hold on to, until her fingers found something—it was the curtain—and yanked it and dragged it down, bringing the rod along with it, paint chips falling in flakes, and felt swallowed by the solitude, by the sudden emptiness. She sank to the floor, a misfit instance of the mind-body split, feeling utterly alone, swallowed by the noise from every empty room, each unused bed, chair, and table, pressed by the noisy walls, with their chattering photos and blathering mementos, on each noisy floor, the noisy inside and the noisy outside, the noisy noisiness of the noise. Marisol had never felt so clumsy, had never felt her age so viscerally before, had never resented how her body was slower now, less flexible, less versatile: how weak it was. The curtain still wrapped around her, Marisol fumbled her way up, shrugging off the fabric like a premature butterfly from its cocoon—was that even possible?—and she walked slowly across the floor, back to her bed, fell on it with a thump—a log dropping on a mossy mound—and, before closing her eyes, looked out the window again. The bird was gone, lost in the charcoal sky: a feathery bundle buried in soot.

Friday is not Thursday. Marisol lifted herself from under the covers to brush out her long hair. Even in bed, she kept it in a tightly woven bun. With a few deft tugs, it fell to her shoulders. Running the comb through the snowy strands, brilliant even in the darkness, Marisol made up her mind. She placed the comb on the bedside table, rose up from the bed, slowly went down to her knees, and lifted the shoe box to the bed. The lamplight lit up the veined hand reaching for silver-rimmed eyeglasses, which she set down on her nose. "Bead up and roll off, bead up and roll off," she said, untying the letters' faded ribbon again.

It was everything she had guessed: temptations and tempests: an affair that flared up and burned itself out after a few months, with the inamorata flying off to the southernmost tip of Florida. Written while Marisol was pregnant with   (she had only just begun showing, everyone saying she looked like a straw with a pea stuck in it), they began as seductive entreaties, letters pleading with   to give up everything, to leave with her. They slowly devolved into accusatory missives. As she read them, Marisol felt like she was reading pages torn from one of her beach-time bodice-rippers. But it was really very simple: A long time ago,   had found himself having to choose between passion, no, between lust and duty to his family. Tears falling now, Marisol wouldn't say, "Feet of clay." She wouldn't say, "Papa was a rolling stone." She wouldn't say, "O, what men dare do! What men may do! What men daily do, not knowing what they do!" Instead, she mulled over her thoughts as if each one were a pale bit of shell she could puzzle back into an egg.

Saturday is not Friday. Daybreak whispering orange, Marisol finished reading the last letter—a perfunctory note from Cuba—and thought back to that year. [*Fold.*] For months, almost to full-term really, she'd gagged whenever   approached her. At first, she'd thought it was his smell. Then she'd thought it was his hair. Unkempt and oily, he'd worn it long in those days. Marisol had made him cut it. The beard had had to go too. He had been the Samson to her Delilah.
        's face, painted pasty white that day, had never seemed to recover its luster. Still, nothing he did had kept her from feeling like she was about to vomit. "I don't know what to do when my best's not good enough,"   had said back then. "No," she'd said, "your best is good enough—when you actually give it." Hard times. Dark times. Once the baby was born, though—she'd named him   , which was   's middle name—she and   had drawn close to each other again: Whatever rift rent them apart had been repaired.
        And hadn't   shown his love for Marisol in such a profound way by agreeing to take her sister in so many years ago? Alicia was a flirt who could never "keep a man," as she herself would say, as if she had a cage inside her whose gate kept opening. But there was always a new dog to nip at her high heels. They'd taken her in after one of Alicia's boyfriends, who had been dogging her around for months, had finally thrown her out of their apartment after

discovering she was pregnant, Alicia explaining to them that it was too late to get rid of it, that she intended to keep the baby whether the father, or they, or anyone else, wanted her to or not. After the boyfriend had thrown beer in her face during an argument, Alicia had finally stuffed her clothes and things into slick plastic bags, leaving everything else behind.

A whiff of malt liquor would always bring Marisol back to that night when she'd answered the doorbell,   by her side, finding her weeping sister, hunched over like a wet cat.

Unlike her sister, Marisol had only had a few boyfriends, two before   , and would rarely be coaxed by her sister to go out "on the prowl," as Alicia would say. On the rare occasion a man would speak to her rather than to her glittered sister, Marisol's face would harden, her unblinking eyes like a seagull's, and she would think of one of those cliffside trees, rooting herself ever more firmly to where she sat or stood, and, invariably, the man would turn away from her.

But   had broken through. She'd met him randomly at a bookstore, one of the last antiquarian shops on Fourth Avenue's famed Book Row. When he'd finally eked her name out of her, he said, "*Mar y sol.* . . . Sea and sun, right?"

"Yes," she'd said, and laughed when he told her he'd been teaching himself Spanish by reading Pablo Neruda's *Veinte poemas de amor y una canción desesperada*, a book Neruda had written inspired by two muses: Marisol and Marisombra. "And what should I call you?" she'd asked.

"My name's   ," he'd said. "It means 'God is with us,' but don't worry, it hasn't gone to my head."

[*Unfold.*] Pulling into her driveway well after midnight, after a dinner with Celia (where Marisol had had *spaghetti alle vongole* washed down with a glass of an oft-disparaged, but, in this case, a crisp, citrusy pinot grigio), Marisol saw a figure crouching at the side of the house. Keeping the headlights on, she yelled out the window to the figure—a man of indeterminate age, but young—demanding to know what he was doing there, and then saw the paper flowers in his hand, which, upon seeing her come out from the car, he dropped to the ground, where countless lilies lay, completing a line she would later see wreathed her entire house. The stranger, she thought, was busy thinking about what he had planned to say should he ever have been caught, and now, caught, was reaching for this lifeline of words only to find nothing, and so simply widened his eyes, as if he were trapped inside a funhouse mirror, invisible to outsiders; a place, normally, where no one outside could see him, but where he could still see them; a place, however, that she could inexplicably penetrate, he looking to her as if he knew she knew what he was: a body heaving headfirst into a black hole, freefalling toward its center, gravity stretching his body out, like a rubber band, until it snapped apart, the tidal force breaking the bonds holding his body together, reducing him to a bunch of dancing atoms. He was a perfect spasm of doubt, but there was something about his face, the way his mouth creased, his bristling eyebrows, his bent-bough posture, that seemed familiar, that compelled her to invite him in, whereupon she found out all there was to know.

Later, after he had left and she entered the bedroom, Marisol found the space darker, confining, cool after the late autumn night, but as sunlight poured through the casement window, beneath which the fallen curtain still lay, warmth filled the room, while Marisol flipped through memories, her mind luculent as if it too had been suddenly invaded by light. She knew that feelings were fleeting, that you couldn't build a marriage out of clouds, that expecting a thing based on feelings to last was like expecting a sand castle never to cave in, but she still obsessed over whether   's choice to stay with his family, whether his surrendering to his sense of duty had ever transformed into genuine devotion.

The letters from   's lover forced Marisol to ask whether she herself had ever loved   in the inflamed way his lover seemingly had; whether she herself, in some kind of unraveling reversal, some sick twist, had been the other woman, simply the eyebolt to his hook. Marisol's head pounded, and something roared in her ears, beat in her chest. She could hardly breathe. She had to get out of that room, heavy with life's ticktock. A weight settled down heavily on her and she fell on the bed, thinking about the man who had left the folded flowers.

[*Fold.*] First, his name: Pablo; and when she'd heard it she saw him, a word made flesh, his body somehow piecing itself together again, sinews and muscles and skin wrapping around his bones, hair sprouting all over his body, a paragon rising from the plane crash's ashes, until she'd reeled herself back in, realized her hope was the magnet gathering the filings to form a figure in her imagination, and asked this other Pablo to explain himself, to tell his story, which he did, the words flooding out from him, gaps between then and now fusing like a newborn's fontanelles.

245

John Madera

The paper flowers were meant as a tribute, a memorial to
          , the father he had never known, the father he had only
come to learn about after discovering a bundle of letters his mother
had unwittingly left in a bag in a box in an attic he'd cleared out
following her death. Pablo had offered the bundle, the only evidence
of his heritage, to Marisol, and she took it, held it in her hands, thinking the very weight of it would drive her down, like a tent stake, into
the ground. He made his discovery through a pile of letters. Just like
me, she'd thought. And there it was: 's boxy print, his tossed-
out lines, his refusals, his denials. And there it was: his mother's
final letter to   , marked "Return to Sender," sharing the
news she had given birth to a son, another son, an unknown son:
Pablo. With his leonine head, his exacting squint as he looked at the
head of a nail on the wall, visibly irritated by the difference in tonal-
ity between the squared space, where a painting used to hang, and the
rest of the wall, Marisol could see her husband in him, and searched
his eyes to find who he might turn out to be.

To Pablo's knowledge,   had never known that his mother
was pregnant; and it was only after Pablo had read   's letters
that he discovered that his mother had chosen, like Marisol had done
with her first child, to name him Pablo, a secret tribute to his father,
the corrosive irony of which had also eaten away at Marisol.

[*Unfold.*] She didn't know who her husband had been, which meant
she didn't know who she had been, who she was. How could she,
having given her self, her being, having hidden herself in him, and
taken him within her own self, absorbing him, somehow merging his
and her wants and needs to create something else, a beautiful other,
she'd once thought, but now thought of as a dark thing to avoid: a
void. Successive waves of doubt pummeled her as if she had been
standing waist-deep in the ocean. She moaned, the harrowed sound
of it, hollow, until she wept, until she couldn't anymore, and fell into
a sleep undisturbed by nightmares.

Sunday is not Saturday. Sepulchral light mocking about her face,
Marisol rose slowly, sat up on her bed, flexed her shoulders out, knowing how to end it. See her, a face and a body, a rarefied lexicon, a
cipher, a reflector become luminaire.

After buttered toast and coffee, she drove her car toward the Queensboro Bridge, and parked a few blocks away from it. The sky was a
massive bouquet of hydrangeas. The streets were checkered with the

246

shadows of leaves. Marisol walked down the bridge's footpath, and if she'd looked over her shoulder, she would have seen her shadow smearing out from her feet, and thought of how unreal it seemed, barely an approximation of her, of her being, how amorphous, how insubstantial it was; of how the kids used to step on each other's shadows and pretend to be hurt; of how grave shade could be; and about how standing in light's way caused shadows to appear in the first place, which would make her think of how they were the inky kin of reflections.

Reaching the middle of the bridge, she grasped the rail, her wrinkly hands pinking from the pressure, and looked down. Sunlight spangled the slow, rolling waves below. Marisol sucked in some air, felt her stomach rise like a balloon, felt the unrelenting fist pressing against her chest, and noticed a speck emerging from the horizon. Standing there, in her dark clothes, Marisol resembled Theodore W. Stucky, a troubled, middle-aged man from France, who, on February 5, 1921, had stood much the same way she stood before the railing. Having lost money on an opera venture, and threatened by creditors, Stucky had feared for his life. After returning from the barber's with his five-year-old daughter, he'd kissed her on the top of her newly bobbed head and wept, and was overheard saying, "My darling, I am glad you haven't the worries I have," leaving to sway back and forth, a human pendulum, on the bridge before composing his final thoughts on a scrap of paper: *"Mes chers amis: Je suis malade et je vais finir ma vie."*

The wind carried a terrible smell as a barge drifted languorously toward the bridge's steel girders. It was the beleaguered leviathan. That March, amid the hullabaloo around televangelist Jim Bakker's sexual philandering, the *Mobro 4000* had been all over the news. Towed by the *Break of Dawn*, the long, large, flat-bottomed boat carried over three thousand tons of trash. Marisol had heard all about it on *Donahue* a day or two before. Overseeing a crew of three men, Duffy St. Pierre, a Cajun man from New Orleans, captained the plague ship's tugboat. From its start in Islip, Long Island, it had floated away from New York all around the United States as far as Texas, and on to Mexico, and even Cuba and Belize.

Garbage: It's what defines us, makes us human, Marisol thought. Our refuse. What we refuse. In the end, what we leave behind is debris.

Marisol unclasped her pocketbook and took out one of the letters. She carefully folded it in half lengthwise. After pressing the short edge of one side down against the first crease, she repeated the fold on the other side, the triangle pointing toward the gray horizon. Marisol continued the motions on both sides. Holding the center, she spread the wings apart. It was a good day to fly, she thought, and then tossed it into the sky. *"Vuela paloma, vuela."* The sun caught the letter, setting it aflame like an arrow of the gods as it slowly spiraled to certain doom. *"Love like a shadow flies when substance love pursues . . . ,"* Marisol quoted, and then huffed at herself. She could be so ponderous sometimes. She laughed and folded another letter. "Fly the friendly skies then!" she said, and laughed again as she launched her kamikazes, one after another, toward the garbage heap floating past.

Unfold. Disremember.

The Collector's Beginning
Joanna Scott

YOU CAN BE SURE that if he were telling this story, he wouldn't begin with the day he disappeared at sea off the coast of Greece in 1905. He wouldn't begin with his arrival in New York in 1873, or even with his birth in a thatched cottage in East Flanders in June of 1851. He would begin in the outpost of El Kef in North Africa. He would begin in that godforsaken dirt alley where he lost his way in 1878 after making the mistake of smoking a rare hashish offered to him by a proprietor of a tea shop.

But it could hardly be called *smoking* when all he'd done was take one quick puff, the bamboo stem still moist from the lips of the old Berber who had offered him the pipe. He hadn't felt any change in the quality of his consciousness after that single puff, but he eventually felt something . . . was it three days, or three hours, later? The hashish had followed him and spun its web, snaring his thoughts, so he couldn't remember how he'd come to this place, or where he was supposed to be.

Back then he was still a naive traveler and hadn't learned the importance of always mapping out his route. He knew, at least, that he was in an outpost named El Kef, in the northwest corner of Tunisia. But in his muddled state that day he could not posit a self capable of remembering why he had come here in the first place. He remembered that once as a sublieutenant for the French military he had visited El Kef. He wasn't a sublieutenant anymore, so why was he back in El Kef? He had the vague impression that he'd returned to the village to search for something he'd misplaced, but he couldn't remember what it was.

He stumbled along a path bordered by polished black stones. For no good reason, he tried to catch up with a goat that was trotting urgently, as though fleeing the slaughterhouse. At the juncture of the path and the hard-packed road leading out of the palm grove, he lost sight of the goat and wasn't sure which way to turn. He turned left, crossed between beds of dense, spiky aloe, and passed through a low archway, arriving in a corridor that curved endlessly into the darkness and promised to lead nowhere.

As he moved forward, he was reminded of walking down a beach into the water. The ground was soft-packed sand like a beach, and the walls were a lemony, dimpled limestone. Moving farther along the corridor, he expected the darkness to be impenetrable. But as he rounded a bend he saw a glow trickling in from a distant opening.

For a man who didn't know where he was going or how he had ended up in his current location, light was a more appealing destination than darkness, and he quickened his pace. Now at least he was a man with a sense of direction. That was better than nothing. And with each step his purpose intensified. He was not just a man walking forward toward the source of light. He was a man who for a reason he couldn't yet articulate was hopeful that soon his whereabouts would be clarified. Hope, then, was a welcome attribute, and it was as a hopeful man whose boots crunched the top layer of sand that he proceeded along the corridor.

He was increasingly hopeful as his senses had more to identify. There was the faint, greasy smell of his own sweat, the bitter taste of lime dust in his mouth, the occasional crumbling when his hand rubbed along the wall. And eventually he heard what he thought was the rustling of palm leaves in the breeze. But the source of the sound wasn't the wind moving through the palms, he realized as he drew closer to the sound. It was human breath moving from the lungs and emitted through pursed lips as murmurs.

Murmurs signaled that he had reason to be wary. Wariness was another defining attribute. He was hopeful and wary as he approached the source of the light and the murmuring. New questions came to mind. Should he be silent and observe the scene ahead of him without revealing his presence, or should he arrive in their midst with a bellow of a greeting?

He didn't have a chance to decide, for he was suddenly there, where the corridor opened up to a doorless entrance and the white light of the sun created a cube amidst the shadows occupied by three white-robed, turbaned men. Two were squatting on the sand, knotting fine threads, and the third was standing, looking down at their work. All three offered the intruder no more than an indifferent glance before they resumed their conversation, trading hushed sounds with an intensity suggesting that whatever rug they intended to weave would be the product of reluctant compromise arising out of respectful disagreement.

He stood for a long while observing them, envying even more than their absorption in the concentrated work of weaving their facility with a language he did not yet understand. He wished he were a man who spoke the language of these weavers. He could be that man, if he set his mind to it. He must have been drawn to this place for a reason. He was a stranger among these Arabs. They had secrets they couldn't share with him, even if they were willing to.

He was jealous of their secrets and yet oddly comfortable with his exclusion, for now he knew where he was. He was in a place where time couldn't penetrate and nothing would ever change, in the presence of men who had been singled out and blessed with immortality. But it wasn't God they had to thank. It was the ingenious machine mounted on a tripod in the corner of the workroom: a Phoebus mahogany box camera, its lens like a pig's round nose inhaling the light.

When he was nineteen, Armand spent five months in Algiers as a sublieutenant for the French army, under the leadership of Crémieux, a government minister appointed to assimilate Algeria into France. Armand's duties at the time involved supervising the transportation and settlement of Alsatian refugees fleeing the Franco-Prussian War. At some point he took one long expedition with his regiment, traveling by train to Biskra, and then on horseback across the Algerian desert from Biskra to Constantine. From Constantine they traveled by diligence to the outpost of El Kef in Tunisia. A week later they returned to Algiers.

The region was in the midst of a devastating drought, and with French speculators buying up all the grain and emptying the silos, famine was spreading. By 1871, twenty percent of the Muslim population of Constantine had died of starvation. As a nineteen-year-old sublieutenant surrounded by fellow soldiers, Armand did not witness the full scope of the suffering, and he heard only faint rumors of the simmering unrest among the local tribes. Then, on the road between Constantine and El Kef, the regiment passed the desiccated corpse of what Armand thought was a dog but turned out to be a child—a boy of about six or seven. The officer in command ordered his regiment to dig a grave, and Armand was one of the men who helped bury the corpse.

After that, he wanted to leave the desert and never return. Not until he moved to America were his memories stirred in a different way. It was as if he'd carried sand in his pocket, and he found the sand again, took out a handful, and felt it sift through his fingers. He thought about the corpse of a child, left out for the vultures. He also thought about the sleepless night he spent with his regiment on the edge of a Bedouin camp, when he'd stayed up listening to the Bedouins make a strange music by rubbing stones together. He thought about the way the brilliant constellations seemed to flash and spin in a mad sort of dance.

Late in the 1870s, shortly after he became engaged to Amy Beckwith, he used a portion of the money he'd saved to sail back across the Atlantic, ostensibly to visit his family in Belgium but really for the purpose of returning to North Africa. And on the outskirts of El Kef, he met a young photographer named Alexandre Bougault.

He would learn that Bougault had come from Algeria, where he'd been serving in the French military, and had recently bought himself the Phoebus camera. Bougault had the notion that he could have a profitable career selling albumen prints of desert scenes to tourists. So far in his brief search for marketable images of North Africa, the reality of dust and poverty had disappointed him; he preferred arranging scenes with a theatrical flourish, posing his subjects and manipulating the light in ways that enhanced the impression of hazily exotic beauty. He made it clear that his ambition was to sell as many prints as possible, not to represent the truth. What did European tourists care about the truth?

Bougault was delighted to hear his visitor greet him in French. Armand himself felt an uncharacteristic relief at meeting a countryman so far from home. While the photographer continued with his work, the two men traded stories about their military service and discovered that they had mutual friends. In the time it took for Bougault to use up his supply of negative plates, Armand regained sufficient clarity of mind to accept when the photographer invited him to have a drink.

Instead of staying in the one hotel thought to be suitable for foreigners in El Kef, the industrious Bougault had arranged a deal with a rug merchant. In return for buying several rugs to resell in Paris, he was given a room in the merchant's house and two meals a day. He and Armand sat until it was dark in the garden behind the house, drinking a syrupy tea that made the ends of their mustaches sticky. Bougault showed Armand a photograph of a girl he'd left behind in Paris. Armand showed Bougault a photograph of his fiancée waiting for him in Tivoli. They boasted of their wealth and their family connections and were at a point in their conversation when the tenor could have gone either toward suspicion or agreeable curiosity when Bougault exclaimed and pointed to the ground. There was a scorpion, a monster as brown and round as an overripe plum, scuttling in the shadows close to the house. The scorpion was gone before either man could grab a rock to crush it. They fell into a long silence, and when their eyes met, they burst into merry laughter, like boys who had broken a tiresome rule without getting caught.

From this initial meeting, they struck up a friendship. Armand kept Bougault company while he designed the scenes for his photographs; Bougault helped Armand sharpen his own sense of purpose in his life. Thanks to the efforts of the photographer, Armand decided that he preferred North Africa to any other place on earth.

He had already discovered during his military service that he was drawn to the desert. Through his work with Alexandre Bougault, he came to think of the arid landscape as a place exempt from modern corruption—the version of the desert as illustrated in Bougault's photographs was the true version, and the reality visible without the camera's aid was just a lie.

He saw two weavers in brilliant white robes sitting near the sun-washed entrance of an ancient catacomb, delicate threads stretched between them, while a third weaver leaned against the archway and observed their effort with impatience.

He saw a donkey carrying two huge bundles of broom, being led by an Arab along a narrow dirt street. He saw a boy watching from the shadow cast by the front wall of a house. He saw the Arab bend his head, at Bougault's direction, so that his face was hidden by the white hood of his immaculate robes.

He saw two beautiful girls dressed in silk gowns and gauzy head-scarves lent to them by Bougault sitting in their dirt yard mashing spices. He saw the girls combing the dirt with their bare toes. He saw one of the girls extend her hand languorously for a turbaned visitor to kiss. He saw that the turbaned man was actually the Maltese gardener at the hotel where Armand was staying, who had been hired by Bougault to play the part of the courtier.

He saw the same gardener wearing traditional Bedouin robes sitting on a camel on a rocky hilltop behind the ruins of the Roman baths beyond the gates of El Kef. Armand thought it was a fine, suggestive scene, but Bougault disagreed. He wanted an infinity of sand in the background, not ugly rocks and ruins.

253

They left the Maltese worker and the camel in El Kef and traveled by diligence to Souk-el-Arba and from there by train to Tunis, arriving shortly before midnight. They were given rooms in the house of Monsieur Alapetite, the French resident-general, who was a friend of Bougault's. They spent the evening drinking a tarry anise liquor and arguing about the future of Tunisia, which the resident-general thought a hopeless place and Armand and Bougault believed was a gold mine for the French.

The next day the two men left for Constantine by train. From Constantine they took the diligence to Biskra, where they hired horses and a guide and rode into the desert, reaching Mraier, an oasis famous in the region for its thousands of date palms, in the late afternoon. They were given bed and board at the French military barracks.

In the morning they found an Arab with his own herd of camels. The Arab was a clever bargainer and demanded forty francs for the use of his camel and an additional ten francs to lead the two men a short way into the desert, to the top of a dune.

Armand stood at the photographer's side and watched as the Arab, dressed in Bedouin robes, mounted the camel. He saw the camel push itself up to standing. He saw the Arab rock perilously on the wood and rawhide saddle and then, following Bougault's order, shade his eyes with his hands and search the infinite emptiness of the desert for some sign of life.

On their way back to Mraier, they met a group of Sudanese slaves waiting outside the gates of the village, their faces and robes streaked with dust. Bougault spoke with them and learned that the slaves had been left in charge of the camels while their master finished his business in the village. Bougault spent nearly an hour trying out different arrangements. At the end, what Armand saw was a tableau with two of the camels sitting on folded legs, the other two camels standing with two of the Sudanese men holding their reins while a third man sat in the foreground with his back to the camera, draped in the spotless white robes Bougault had given him to wear.

The group's master appeared and demanded payment for the service provided by his slaves. Bougault obliged, giving him five francs, and the group set out to continue their trade in the next village. Armand watched them trek as if in slow motion across the sand, the figures shrinking with the distance and finally disappearing over the rise of a dune.

Where the Sudanese men and their camels had been, Armand saw sand seas and salt terraces blistered by heat. He saw a beautiful, vast, windblown nothingness that hid the secrets of its ancient history. And thanks to Bougault, he saw the potential for making a fortune from this land.

The next day Armand asked for copies of the finished photographs he'd helped arrange. But Bougault set an exorbitant price for each print, which Armand refused to pay. The two men argued so violently that the diligence that they were riding in shook from their fury. By the time they'd reached Constantine, they had agreed that they wanted nothing to do with each other, and Armand was left to fend for himself.

In his own false version of the desert, Armand was never thirstier than his Bedouin guides. He drank only when they drank. He knew thirst to be a sign of weakness. Only foreigners admitted to thirst. Rather than complaining, he sucked whatever moisture was left from his tongue, his gums, the raw lining of his cheeks before he ever let himself beg for more than his fair share of water. He swallowed the gravel in his throat, squeezed his dry lips together to seal them. He would rather collapse than speak of his thirst. He was willing to lie there, forgotten, while the rest of the caravan moved on, the jingle of the bells on the camels' collars grew fainter, night settled over the dunes, and the river of stars flooded the sky and poured down to earth.

He opened his mouth to catch the jewels released by the sky. When he was finally satiated he sat up and looked at the endless space around him and marveled at the fact of his aloneness. He wasn't afraid, for he was sure that when the sun rose the next morning, another caravan would arrive and offer him a ride.

At some place deep in the core of his being he believed that he wasn't destined to die in the desert. He wasn't afraid on that first long expedition to El Kef when he was in the military. He wasn't afraid on his explorations with Bougault. And he wasn't afraid now, lying on his back in the sand.

In Armand's unreal version of North Africa, a brave man could make a fortune. He didn't have to persuade the reticent natives to pose for his camera. All he had to do was lie there under the night sky and open his mouth.

Days later, or just hours, he woke in his bed at the hotel in El Kef. Before his thoughts clarified, he had the impression of being someone important, as though he'd been charged by some high government official with a crucial diplomatic mission. He imagined speaking fluently in front of a large group of Arabs, explaining to them that he had been authorized to usher in a new period of prosperity and friendship between the French and the people of North Africa.

But on the streets of El Kef there was no prosperity. There were low-slung mud houses and dirty children who followed him everywhere, begging for money. They followed him as he crossed the plaza where the fountain sent its huge spray into the air. They followed him to the ruins of Kasr-er-Roula, an ancient basilica that was said to have been the repository of great treasures. When he started to dig in the dust with his walking stick, the children did the same.

They dug for hours, until the sun was low in the sky, but they found nothing more than shards from the broken columns. Armand returned to his hotel, but he was back at the ruins early the next morning. Word spread through El Kef that the white man was digging again, and the children gathered to help. They kept digging through the day and returned the next day to dig some more. They dug and dug and dug until, at last, their labor was rewarded.

"M'sheer, M'sheer," one boy called and ran toward Armand holding what looked like a dead fish he had unearthed. A fish in the desert! But it couldn't be dead because it had never been alive. It had rubies for eyes, papery brass scales, and a hinge in its center so it could be made to wiggle. As Armand examined the fish, he discovered that the head was detachable. When he pulled it off, the children who had gathered around him hooted Arabic words that sounded to Armand like mockery. He emptied the sand from the fish and replaced the head. Then he jerked the hinged fish in a savage motion toward the nearest boy and growled. The children shrieked and ran away, and Armand put the fish in the pocket of his jacket. It was the first of many treasures he would take from the desert.

Under Bougault's influence, Armand formed a confused impression of North Africa, which stood, at least as he wanted to perceive it, as the one place in the world where time did not progress in its usual relentless fashion. In journal notes and published essays, he treated the region as a fairy-tale land, with inexhaustible wonders and treasures that were available for a modest price to anyone who was willing to take a few risks. Starting with his return to El Kef, he began buying what he called "pharaonic relics" from street peddlers.

On a train from Tunis to Cairo, he met a Dutchman who had

retired from his work at the embassy and lived in a private residence in Alexandria. Hearing of Armand's interest in antiquities, the man showed him a pure gold Ptolemaic coin that he'd recently purchased from a dealer in Luxor.

"I can see that you are inexperienced in the antiquities trade," the man said. "Allow me to give you a short lesson." As the law stood in Egypt, he explained, the national museums had the right to acquire all antiquities found during these excavations, but at a price fixed below what could be obtained elsewhere. For this reason, the dealers preferred to offer their wares to foreign collectors. But these transactions had to be conducted in utmost secret, and collectors needed to prove that they could be trusted not to disclose the source of their acquisitions to the Egyptian authorities.

"My advice to you, sir, is to offer my name as a reference," the Dutchman said, handing him the card of the dealer who had sold him the gold coin. He added that he'd heard about some Arab brothers who had dug up a cache of treasures in the Valley of the Kings. If Armand was interested, he'd better hurry to Luxor, the man advised, for the treasures would surely be gone within a week or two.

Five Poems
Maxine Chernoff

A HOUSE IN SUMMER

Virginia Woolf wrote this paragraph.
—Erich Auerbach

In which a woman wonders when her son will grow taller, when the weather will clear, and her husband stop throwing his negative shadow on clocks and lamps and objects as they are. Will it grow lighter despite his darkness, her eyes dry, though they are mostly dry, despite the feeling of tears welling up as she wishes for the boy to have more light.

Will the room, nature's repository of conical shells and tidy driftwood and small and radiant glass beads smoothed for centuries by water's vague intentions, have something to say about the figures that come and go, the careless boy, unhappy man and woman whose demeanor makes the room glow with the distinct light of sickrooms, though no one yet is ill—but there is the care and caution one associates with grief.

When shutters break loose and the wind does its work and the people who've shined with the moment's surprises and disappointments and failures to love quite well enough have left the room, will the wind acknowledge their vivid passing on sofas and loveseats where sand is engrained in scalloped patterns of fabric woven to resemble teardrop-shaped leaves? Will photos teeter on walls in their dampened frames or simply be stacked in boxes for relatives to take to a coach house overlooking a stand of elms on a narrow hill that deflects the wind, where someday a woman opens the box in front of her grandson, who asks without much concern, to pass the day, who were these people, did you know them?

And the woman, because she is sentimental but cautious with her emotions, will say without conviction, I hear they were a family who summered at the beach, who lost their mother, who thought many things and then forgot them, who loved as well as they might, as I love you, she will tell her grandson, though not in words. She will think these words as he looks at her without knowing why her answer takes so long and when it does come seems to acknowledge some deep sorrow of inheritance neither can understand.

If this is in a book as most things turn out to be, the woman will have read it twice: once when she was young herself, a reader whose eyes grew teary for Mrs. Ramsey and all the love in the world that gathers in unmapped corners where someone comes to stand for no good reason, and then again when she is older and knows the pleasure of overhearing in her own voice things she might have said to calm herself and soothe a boy.

RUNE

I am not what you supposed but far different.
—Walt Whitman

Not timber or bronze or iridium, not the old habits of species at a
    waterhole or the short irregular breaths of the last whispered
    guest
Not the grievance that gives way to truth or the truth of a three-
    headed beast in your atlas of imaginary travels
Not the speaker with the plans but the quiet boy learning the rope
    trick in the hallway outside the room
Not the intelligence noted for its acute air of judiciousness but the
    wasp's sharp sting as it strikes a shapely passing ankle
Not the coiled answer waiting for its question unlike what is asked
    or required on a Sunday
Not the leaves in May shining ferocious in the garden where your
    grandson has left an onion resting on a stone
Not the fierce attention of the man on the traffic island holding a
    sign that says something smeared by the rain
Not the notice given by an eye to another in its hope of dependence
    on kindness or its hope of notice in a room full of candles

Maxine Chernoff

Not the bored glance of a mother whose child has climbed higher
than last time but is busy with hurt and resentment
Not the author whose page is so busy with sound that he forgets
each word's landscape is a story with beginning and end
Not your hand or my hand or the things that we touch in a day
which include so many forms of heaviness, so much light
Not the tinge of memory in a place where someone else stood
unaware of your life or its constant necessity to record its
existence in each room's sharp corner
Not formal analysis or credo or code or the heard cries of pelicans
over the water of the bay's dark shadow under the bridge
Not earth's solitude early in the day when most everyone is
sleeping and you are alone in a kitchen where he or she once
daily stood
Not the pouring of water or the boiling of kettles or the singing of
neon as it advertises books or massages or bereavement services
Not Augustine of Hippo or Herodotus or Longinus or Mrs. Miller
or Captain Courageous
Not the oldest book or rarest coin or smallest bird known to sip
water from a clover
Not your face in a mirror or a window nor your voice as heard on a
recording among the others nor your method of material witness
to things as they open like a novel's first sentence
You are not in the room or the story or the thought you are not in
the absence spoken as a charm against itself

EVIDENCE

To philosophize is to learn how to die.
—Montaigne

Of houses, empty or noticed, to rooms whose lamps have left their
light behind, ancient after time has landed in the breech of its
excess, dropped there as if a package fell from the arms of a woman.

Of glasses once filled whose essence is left in a stain that looks
clear in most light but carries a tinge of its erasure when she
notices it late in the night after he is asleep.

260

Of windows, whose eyes are shut to the diversions of their intended gazers, birds passing on their sheer migrations over oceans filled with brine.

Of gardens where he sat or she sat amid the trickery of a season and its aftermath, patchy on the lawn and patchy in the sky, gray and listless for a time before respecting the progress of feeling as it overtakes the geography of plants.

Of reasons which fill a space but not adequately, which stretch like deserts between needs vocalized or calmed, written or whispered, answered or forgotten by the time an answer is prepared.

Of books filled with language that is never proper to the moment but serves as a repository of the possible though the possible is not enough, as a tent is never enough in a storm.

Of eyes that fill with knowing or restless asking or a glance that means retreat or surrender or that a village lies in waste, a life is lost, small as a child's attempt to capture a mote of dust above his bed in moonlight from a gibbous moon.

Of melodies whose notes contain the promise of an answer, as if music is an answer or patience a virtue or love an antidote.

PURCHASE

You think it's a dream that you chop down trees in a vacant room, part of a house whose roof is treetops.

Lilies overtake the more famous flowers. Is it life when flies buzz over blurred leaves? Words prefer the color of bees.

Is it a painting when the night swirls close and you hear the beaks and tongues of birds at your neighbor's pond where an egret perches on a stone eating koi?

You are water frozen and unlabeled. What you leave of yourself gets remembered as the wobble, stare, or remnant when you turn to look and touch his skin in the blue room softened by spring.

Kindness is amplitude of attention, always the distance of reason
and retort as intention dims. Vermeer's corners, famous for their
absence of color, shine like a lamp in your favorite midnight room.
Figure and ground seized by attention—what you want is *here* and
here.

One practical gesture leads to another. A hand closes. An eye sees
the fraying darkness and its cover of recognition.

SONG

> *Sound exists only as it is going out of existence.*
> —Walter J. Ong

Shadow's interest accounts for parenthetical lips. Your only face,
a kind one, known to control the alphabet in slow whispers and
   embarkation.
If anyone should hear raw notes sway like laundry fainting into
   light,
they'd fear that symmetry is lost, time of day undone. We offer
   voices
which restore not much. In paradox we sing as freighters cross an
   ocean
and birds land on plastic flowers ripe with illusion. No audience
to witness its pitch of blue on Utopia Parkway, where he lived with
   boxes
and owls, wooden birds perched in present corners of attention.
   Who knows
what bridge will fall at seismic gasp, what world beyond all books
   and money.
History is emblem: We are lost in light that cannot fray and doesn't
   cost. No one to own
the horizon we create, the portal we carve of nothing on its way to
   itself and back again.

In Each Room,
Some Unadorned Spectacle
Matt Bell

NOTE

Consumed by grief in the wake of his wife's first miscarriage, the husband—a trapper, a fisherman—commits a desperate and compulsive act that secretes away within his body a childlike presence called the *fingerling*, a jealous and ghostly being that the husband slowly takes into his confidence. Later, after years of struggling to start a family, the wife—a singer whose powerful voice now summons into being ever-increasing varieties of objects, up to and including a second moon that threatens to destroy the sky above their home—at last claims to have given birth to the son the husband most desires. These passages are excerpted from the forthcoming novel *In the House upon the Dirt between the Lake and the Woods*.

FOR THAT FOUNDLING, OUR FALSE SON, my wife and I played at parenting together, and in those early years we learned him in the ways of our family and also the first four of the elements, *dirt* and *house* and *lake* and *woods*: Cross-legged upon the fur-covered floor, we told him what we had been taught, that those four aspects were all we were—but then my wife said there was another, a fifth, and that this element was called *mother*, that it was her mothering that made the foundling, more so than any other. I thought this to be a lie but said nothing, kept silent my concern at her greedy deception—and then as I withdrew I came as well to discern elements previously unknown. Soon I wished I had spoken of these others first, to position them before her claim, or that I'd had the courage to speak of them after, to displace it: For if *mother* was an element, then so was *father*, then so was *ghost*, then so there were at least seven, a number much increased from what we had earlier believed, from what we had been told to expect, long before our arrival upon the dirt.

Over some number of months, a year, two years, we taught the foundling to crawl and then to walk, to speak in words and then in phrases. We tried to teach him how to play but failed, or else I did: At first I believed the foundling to be possessed by some strange seriousness, some unchildness, but soon I heard through a window his squeals at the tickling of his mother, at her fingers teaching him to feel ticklish.

I had never heard this laugh before, had never caused it no matter how I had thrown the boy into the air, no matter how I caught him just before he crashed, no matter what other roughhouses I taught him, as I myself had been taught.

By the time the foundling began to sing my wife's simplest songs I had learned to restrain the fingerling, but always he watched for his chances, and soon all my angers were ulcered inside me, and one by one the fingerling sought their increased company, in whatever pits they burned their slow language. My wife and I were quieter then too, gently estranged, and so from us the foundling learned to speak only slowly, a lack set against all the years the fingerling had whispered in my ear: By the time the foundling said his first word, the two matched syllables of *mother*, by then I had been convinced of my ill feelings against him.

In the months that passed he refused to learn any other word—any other but *mother, mother, mother, mother*—and at night my newly named wife held him between us in the bed, her touch always on him and never me, and at meals the fingerling conspired from my gut as my wife fussed over the foundling's every want, as their voices filled the small house, until again and again I fled the clamor of their table to go out into the moony woods, where in those days I would often find myself digging some unneeded plot, like a dog who has not yet found his bone but still wants the place to bury it.

Despite the mystery of his origins, in most ways the foundling was a boy as I had always imagined a boy would be: His learning to walk was followed by a destructive curiosity where he knocked over the carefully arranged objects of our house, cracking worse our already bear-chipped bowls and also the wife-sung ones, or else endlessly clacking his mother's spoons against one another. Once he could better speak, he began to question every action my wife or I made, his halting sentences querying the origins of fish, the depth of the lake, the sequence of the seasons, and also crying at what he did not understand, what we could not explain into kindness, like the first time he watched me strip the hide off a deer or scrape free a fish's scales. Soon the foundling bawled every dusk when I approached the house, even when I came empty-handed: For while it was his mother who cooked for him, he saw only that it was I who fished and trapped, skinned and slaughtered and butchered, and even though he had no trouble sharing in the meals we made, it became my wife he thanked and me he feared.

I dug more holes, and because I could not dig a hole without wanting for something to put in it, for the first time I began to kill what I did not intend to use: In one hole I buried a muskrat and in another a rabbit and in another a wrench-necked goose, caught by my own hands after it squawked me away from its clutch of goslings, themselves doomed beneath my frustrated heels. My wife still maintained her garden, but in those days I also kept one of my own: For every rabbit I took from the woods, I buried two more in the clearing made when I'd cut trees for our house, so that others might grow from whence they came, and so they did grow—except that with each passing season they returned leaner and lamer, limping where they might before have hopped. It was not just the rabbits who failed, diminished by my poaching: Remember now a mink without its fur or else this beaver without the squared hatchet of its teeth, gnawing useless at a trunk it had no chance of opening. Remember this duck born with dulled beak, this peacock ill feathered to attract its mate. Remember all those other animals, blunted and endangered by my hand, and yet how could I stop, and yet what could I do except to mitigate through their bodies my most recent darkest thoughts, which always required some burial somewhere, with some thing, in some hole of my own digging.

As the foundling grew I too changed, hardened into who I would be, and soon I was burying whole deer in too-shallow holes, stepping down into their graves to snap the lengths of their antlers or else letting their branches point through the dirt, made accusing knuckles of bone. In this way all the beasts and birds of the woods gave themselves over to my traps, so that never was there a morning when I found nothing, where no fur or feather filled my gathering fists.

All the beasts and the birds, all except for one: The only animal I dared not trap was the giant bear, who I correctly feared would not suffer me to try.

Some mornings, I arrived at the burying ground to find that the bear had uncovered my plantings, had torn the flesh from off their bones

265

so that it might eat of what I had killed but not for food—and also to bring back what it did not require. This is how I thought the bear showed me what it claimed, even unto and after death, and also what it thought of my poaching, as if I did not already know the bounds of its domain, and of all others: That the woods belonged to the bear. That the house belonged to me, or else had before, but was owned now by her, my wife. That if I wished to reduce my trespass, then the lake would perhaps be a better place in which to store my dead—if only my wife could have stomached the sight of my dragging their bodies across the dirt, of the scraped clay wounded red.

During the day, the foundling roamed often upon the dirt, sometimes in the company of his mother and sometimes alone. As he grew in size he grew braver too, but still he remained unwilling to step under even the thinnest outer trees, those still shot through with sunlight. Even with his mother at his side, holding his diminutive hands, his fingers too small for his age, even then he was afraid of everything he might have guessed lurked within those living woods, his imagination making up for his lack of experience—but could what he might have imagined be worse than the truth? Much of what happened in the woods was then my secret, and the fingerling's: the trapped and the dying beasts; the dug and filled graves; the bones thrust through the dirt, uncovered and freed to new life by the bear, then trapped and buried again.

The foundling was most afraid of the bear, that beast I had spoken of often at the table, despite the hushings of my wife, and also he was afraid of me, of the fingerling inside, that brother the foundling did not know but that I believe he sometimes heard in my voice. His fear of me disappeared only fleetingly, now and then in some lucky forgetfulness of childhood, and eventually my wife stopped bringing him near the woods, so that he would not wail at the sight of the trees, my traps, bloody me; and as they withdrew into the safety of our house I too retreated, spent more and more of my daytime on the wooded side of the tree line, that threshold's divide.

How every day I watched the foundling always choose his mother, how he preferred her lap, her end of the table, her body to curl against when dreams of the dark woods and the darker cave trembled him awake.

266

How his lisping voice was still better for singing than my rough and rude timbre, and how this too was a realm they shared, to which my talents granted me no entry.

How when he wanted a story, he wanted it only from her lips, and so it was her stories that formed him, never mine.

How whenever he was not with her, the foundling seemed listless, exhausted, and while she did her chores he fell asleep in odd places, tucked into a corner of the sitting room, hidden in the shaded hollows between the furniture; or upon a pile of dirty furs, ready for the washing; or in the dark slimness of the space under the bed, where I would find him snoring so slowly, balled up, legs tucked below his belly, hands folded beneath his face; and if I tried to shake him awake he would not stir, not until my wife returned to lull him from his sleep with a song or a soft word.

How the eighth element she taught the foundling was called *moon*, but when the time came, my wife pronounced it *moons*, as if hers was no copy but rather some proper and equal addition to what had come before, that original to whose workings we were not then or ever privy.

How, like his mother, the foundling preferred the meat of the woods to the fish of the lake, so that always I ate alone, even when we ate together.

How even if we had not been so slowly separating, even then the fingerling would have kept us sometimes apart, his threats against the foundling enough to double my own reluctance, my own inability to father.

How I told myself I held back for the boy's safety, but how that was not the whole of the truth or even the most of it.

How by the time the foundling was with us several years—by the time the fingerling had floated within me nearly double that span—how by then I could admit the root of the fracture in our family, of the distance between my wife and me, between me and her son: Despite all my long wants, I had never thought rightly of how to be a parent or a husband; only of possessing a child, of owning a wife.

* * *

Memory as first exploration of the deep house, as this progression of rooms: to follow the many staircases down to the many landings, the many hallways branching out from behind progressively heavier doors.

To open the first rooms and find the deep house made now a palace of memory, a series of rooms in which what I had forgotten had been curated, collected together with what I had tried to forget, and also with other moments that had occurred only in dreams, or else not at all, not for me.

To find in each room some unadorned spectacle, my wife or me or us together, with or without those children we had failed to have, plus the one she had stolen, that she had passed off as our own. Or not passed off, but made true: It was in those passages that I saw how even if I had not accepted the foundling into my family, still my wife had accepted him into hers, put him at its center, a space I believed I had once occupied, and so our house was divided and then divided again and again, because what house might stand against a child loved by only one parent, when the jealous other held that same child in suspicion and contempt?

And how for me the fingerling remembered everything.

How the fingerling saw even what I would have left undiscovered, what I did not want to share with him or any other child.

How even then he rode most often in my belly, in my thigh, in my throat, so that he might always be close to the skin, soaking in the new airs I moved my body through. And so he was there too in each of those many rooms, where otherwise there would have been only me, always me, me lonely and me alone among the tiny domains of my wife, sung into being as she passed, echoed throughout the deepening dirt.

In the first room I found piled the cargo we had lost to the bear, before we moved into the house, as it ejected us from our temporary home in the mouth of its cave: Here again were the broken vases and cracked crystal, the shattered punch bowls, the punched-out platters.

Here were the shredded rags of my wife's dress, and beside them my boutonniere, meant to be preserved inside a translucent bubble, now freed from where it had been glassed.

Here was the intricate mechanism of a handmade clock, gifted and then broken, stopped as all other clocks were eventually stopped.

All these objects, seemingly each its own but merely parts of a whole, what in the cave we had lost.

*

And in this room: her wedding ring, discarded. She had improved everything I had given her but not this, and so its simple band remained only what it had ever been. I held the ring in my hand, and then I took off my own ring, and I laid both upon the stones, touching. Rings had been insufficient to fasten us together, and it would take more than rings to rebind what had been broken.

AND LESS TO END IT, reminded the fingerling. AS YOU HAVE PROMISED. AS I PROMISE YOU WILL.

And in this room: the sound of my wife's knuckle first sliding beneath the beaten silver of that ring, a sound never before heard, or else forgotten amid all the other business of our wedding day.

And in this room: the footprints she made on the beach where we were wed, where we had stood atop that platform, separated by the priest and then joined by the same, and all this upon that other sunnier shore, where it was not always summer but where often it was summer enough.

And in this room: how my footprints that evening were not always at her side, only sometimes so. And how I wished it had been different, that I had not walked away at the beginning of our marriage, when I thought it would always be so easy to return.

And in this room: the words I used nearly every summer after, to beg from her womb one more child, even after she was determined only to stop the trying and also before she found she wanted her motherhood again, wanted it this time for herself, wanted it more than even I had ever wanted or realized.

And in this room: the scent of my wife's perfume as she passed, a smell once lovely, now stale as glue. And how I missed its original, how I had missed it.

*

And in this room: every graying hair she pulled from her head or her body in the failed years between the fingerling and the foundling. Every piece of skin she rubbed raw in the bath, when between miscarriages she could not scrub away the hormone stink of motherhood, falsely begun. All that hair and skin, stuck wet to the floor.

And in this room: A white suit that no longer fit. A shirt that wouldn't button, a tie that drew its knot too quick around the neck. The relics of a body betrayed against itself, and against my wife, who had not agreed to love what fat and hair it acquired, nor the blank spaces replacing what it had lost, those first few teeth, those other small kindnesses.

And in this room: my wife's garden, if she had not abandoned its offerings to eat the meat of the woods. What she might have grown with the labors of her hands instead of the song of her voice. What this dirt would have yielded to us, if only she had again given the sun leave to shine.

And in this room: a silver bowl full of her tomatoes, one taste of which revealed the tang of their song-stuff, their lack of right reality, despite skin, despite juice and seeds.

And in this room: all the faces of the fish I had taken from the lake, piled into a single mash of eyes and gills, teeth and scales. How surprised I was to see them, and how easy it was to forget how many lives I took just to keep myself alive, to feed my wife and the foundling. All these bodies, knifed open so we might continue another day.

And in this room: the death of a badger, cradled in steel, rehashed. The static of an action worn down by repetition, this series of moments brought to completion only to begin again, reduced, semi-badgers torn and tortured into some novel shape.

*

And in this room: an empty space in which, if I had watched long enough, the badger might eventually have been made separate from the trap, freed from its circumstance, if not the damage done.

And in this room: a floor of hides, stitched from the skins of what I had trapped, where I could not stop myself from kneeling upon the floor, from digging the hooks of my fingers into its stitching. I pulled and pulled and undid some of its ties, and from beneath I revealed only more flooring, more skins sewn to skins, and soon there was around me a pit of flesh, a hollow stinking of its taxidermy, and below that only more skin, only more fur.

And in this room: the buzzing of bees and then, elsewhere, another room, full of bees. Two separate rooms, one with the bees themselves, silent, and the other filled only with their sound. How many more rooms I knew there must be if that continued. How much more house it took to keep things separate, to break them down.

And in this room: the smell of decomposing onion and beet, potato and rutabaga—all that vegetal rot.

And in this room: The last sunflowers of my wife's garden, the first that stretched their petals toward her red moon instead of the sun that barely again rose over the dirt; and if the light of the moon was mere reflection, and the light of two moons doubly so, why then their different hues, against the vast black of the sky?

And in this room: a fistful of black seeds.

In the next room, the shell of the bear: its proud bones stuck through its skin, its bristled fur fallen like pine needles. Its claws pulled from their moorings, its teeth loose in its jaws, its breath rotten as fallen bark, worm-struck as the earth beneath its woods, stinking of meat eaten long past its date, dug up.

271

Matt Bell

*

And in this room: my wife's favorite dress, worn the first time she danced with me. How when I held the fabric to my face I smelled nothing, because the smell of her sweat was in another room.

And in this room: a well-scrubbed floor and on it a well-scoured pot, scratched by the removal of meals we shared, of meals we ate apart.

And in this room: a bowl made of mirrors, so that as I drank of it, it drank of me.

And in this room: the song of the stars, never heard after it was silenced above the dirt, and before that never this clearly. How I had forgotten even what I had forgotten, this series of notes that made a song that made a story, all so hard to retell without their sharp light present, hard to hear or hum even when the stars yet hung from the sky, and impossible now that their shapes had been extinguished. And again my wife had remembered, as I had not.

And in this room: lightning. And in this room: thunder. And in this room: how long it had been since it rained.

And in this room: how my wife had made the bear weak. How she lay flat upon the dirt, upon the dirt floor of our cellar, and put her cheek upon the ground. How she whispered songs into the earth, how with those songs' reverberations she lulled the bear to sleep even as she kept its sleep restless, to delay its tracking, its waking attempts to move upon the dirt. How the wounds my wife had given the bear worsened, how the bones snapped free of the rib meat, of the fleshy parts of the neck.

272

Venus at Her Mirror
Benjamin Hale

Men look at women. Women watch themselves being looked at.

—John Berger, *Ways of Seeing*

THE REPRESENTATIVE WAS DEAD. He would have been one of Rebecca's oldest clients, except Rebecca had long ago ceased to think of him as a client. Yes, he was generous—he always paid for everything, that was a given—but he had not directly paid Rebecca for her services for years. They weren't services anymore, they were just things that they did together.

The Representative was dead. Rebecca had known him for eleven years, and she was no longer sure what one would call their relationship. What had begun long ago as a rather businesslike arrangement between two people—one of them paying money for services rendered, the other receiving the money and rendering services—had over the years turned into other things: a deep friendship, a partnership, a secret bond that somehow, because it had begun as a balanced relationship between equals, was truly closer than most romances ever are. Sometimes, they had sex. Sometimes, now (though rarely) they had ordinary vanilla intercourse, without role play, without restraints, without toys, without make-believe. It wasn't that she had quit charging him. One day, about two years ago now, he seemed to have forgotten to pay her (the usual stack of hundreds in an unmarked white envelope on the kitchen counter was not there), and she had not reminded him. Since then, he no longer paid her, and she no longer accepted payment—which, she supposed, made their relationship perfectly legal now, though it was still fraught with secrecy. Was she, in a sense, his mistress?

The Representative was dead. If she had heard of his death from a friend (which would not have happened—the only friend they had in common, the one who had introduced them, she had not spoken to in years), or (more likely) from the news, she would have cried. As it was, she was not crying—not yet—because she was alone with a mind locked in a rattrap of fear and anxiety surrounding the facts of the

273

Representative's death, and her presence for it.

The Representative was dead. The Representative had been a good man. He'd had that yacht-club swagger, that easy arm around the shoulder. He had never been someone who could be described as a simple man. No, he was a complicated man. But under that there was essential goodness. Under the armor of public life was someone who cared deeply about the poor, minorities, women, the exploited, the underserved, the uninsured, the unemployed, the disempowered. He'd hated Bush passionately, had been against the war. At the bedrock of his many-layered life, he fought for the side of the good. Social injustice drove him to rage, and it was that rage that drove him into politics more than his vanity or his ambition: the desire to do good. And he had done good. He would do no more good now. The Representative was dead.

Rebecca was sitting in a leather armchair, looking at his body. The Representative had paid, as he always had, for her airfare to DC, and put her up in her usual suite in the Fairfax at Embassy Row. She had flown in that morning, and was scheduled to leave tomorrow. The hotel was a thirty-minute walk away, at most, or two quick stops on the Metro. She had barely moved in the last hour. The Representative, for his part, had not moved at all in the last hour.

Rebecca Glass—Mistress Delilah, once, sometimes—continued to find herself in this unusual and undesirable situation: slumped in an armchair in spike heels, fishnet stockings and garter belt, a leather corset, and the red wig she had always worn when she was Mistress Delilah with the Representative—staring, without really looking, at the body of the Representative, which lay motionless, faceup, and (except for the alligator nipple clamps and the rope around his wrists) naked on the smooth concrete floor of the apartment. It was in a luxury high-rise on Virginia Avenue, a newly built mixed-use steel-and-glass structure with a balcony view of the National Mall and Arlington Cemetery across the Potomac, which proceeded unhurriedly toward the Chesapeake Bay thirty stories below, flowing under the arches of a squat stone highway bridge, its rippled surface glowing yellow in the slant light of the golden hour.

The apartment was furnished almost in the way a realtor would furnish a model home: a hollowly perfect simulacrum of a human dwelling that clearly no person actually lives in. It was decorated as if the realtor were trying to sell it to fussy upper-middle-class yuppies who happened to be into BDSM. The expensive, unused furniture all matched tastefully: Everything was metal, blue-tinted glass, and black leather. The bed had been fucked on, but no one had ever spent a night sleeping in it. The decorative touches were the Representative's, and he'd had a good eye: rows of photographs framed in ornate tarnished silver frames that surprisingly harmonized with the sleek designer furniture; all the pictures were sepia-toned early twentieth-century porn—women with round, sweet faces and full, fleshy hips, sleeping masks, riding crops, student-teacher scenarios, naughty maids in the mistress's boudoir. The floors were smooth, cool concrete. There were iron rings and chains installed in the ceilings and walls. Mistress Delilah rarely made use of them. Likewise the closets were stocked superabundantly with various equipment: whips, ropes, chains, leather hoods, ball gags, harnesses, collars, handcuffs, butt plugs, cock rings, and many other devices more unique and harder to describe.

The Representative had loved his toys. He had liked talking shop with her about different kinds of whips and so on. He had always had a fawning regard for her opinion as a professional. She didn't especially share his collectorism, his fetish for connoisseurship, except as it related to psychology. (Rebecca found dominance-and-submission play that leaned heavily on toys a bit graceless, gimmicky. A whip and some good sturdy rope can go a long way. The art of sexual domination is not in the material, it's in the mind.) The idea of grades and progression excited him, of different sorts of whips for different purposes. Men seem to like seeing tools lined up in a rack ranging from smallest to biggest, they get some sort of instinctual kick out of confronting a problem requiring the widest-gauge socket in the socket-wrench set. The Representative had recently acquired a whip that Mistress Delilah had to admit was an impressive item (Rebecca herself was more aloof to it). He'd been so excited for her to use it on him, the object had probably occasioned the visit: It was a genuine South African *sjambok*, a hard, semiflexible, three-foot-long whip, traditionally made from twisted rhinoceros hide for driving cattle, later infamous as the police and military weapon of choice during apartheid. These days they make them out of plastic or rubber—the real ones are illegal to sell because they're made from the hide of an endangered animal. The Representative got off on that, and also on the weapon's troubling symbolic place in a brutal history of colonial subjugation. He'd bought it from a South African antiquities dealer, and it was the real deal—long, stiff, heavy, the handle embroidered with some African pattern—the object was electric to the touch, alive with sleeping evil. The thing was not a toy—when she started

275

using it on him, she immediately realized that the difficulty would be to hit him hard enough to get him off without completely beating the shit out of him.

Mistress Delilah had also brought along, as always, her own special black bag. A professional brings along a bag of tools: The country doctor making a house call, the plumber come to fix the sink. She arrives with a bag full of the tools of the trade. She only brought it because she knew it excited him just to see it in her hand. It was laughably gratuitous—at this point, only a reminder of the way things used to be between them. (Once, she'd had to endure a TSA employee spreading the contents of her bag on a counter: She'd stood there while the woman scrutinized her ball gags and nipple pumps with turquoise latex gloves, and had to ask someone to check if a cat-o'-nine-tails violated FAA regulations; it did not. Now she just checked the bag.) The black bag sat, rumpled and deflated looking, in the corner of the living room, the zipper open, the only things she'd yet removed from it lying in disuse on the glass coffee table: handcuffs, muzzle, nipple pumps. The *sjambok*, she realized, looking down, was still in her hands, lying sideways across her lap.

Rebecca guessed it was a heart attack. She asked new clients for medical histories, and wouldn't risk taking them on if she thought something like this might happen. But the Representative had been her client when she was new and green in the business, and not thinking about things like that yet. And he had been forty years old and in better health back then. The years had rounded him out, and he was not really her client anymore but her friend, confidant, sometime benefactor, and the most complicated lover she'd ever had. Now he was fifty-one, on the hefty side, and not in the best health. Did he have a genetic history of heart disease? Maybe it was a brain aneurysm? She had tried to revive him with the basic CPR she knew. She tried to administer mouth-to-mouth resuscitation, but it had been of no use. He had, quite literally, died in her arms.

Rebecca had the first inkling that something was wrong when she noticed the Representative convulsing in a way that did not seem sexual in nature under the candy-apple sole of the Louboutin pump she had squished against his face. She glanced behind her and saw that his cock had gone slack. He'd taken his hands off it—his hands were tied together, which constricted the movement of his arms, but he was limply whacking his wrists against his chest, like someone pretending to be retarded. She took her foot off his face, but didn't break character.

"Oh? Something wrong, cuntface?" she said in her belittling-the-baby voice. "Aw, whatsa matter, sweetie-poo?"

The Representative was making a worrisome gakking noise in the back of his throat. He sounded like a dog choking on a bone.

She nudged his shoulder with the toe of her shoe.

"Seriously. You OK?"

He hadn't used the safe word—he didn't appear capable of using it or any other word at the moment.

She knelt down beside him. His swollen, choking face was red, flaming. A bright sweat had broken out on his forehead.

She said his name—his real name. She said it twice with question marks, and a third time with an exclamation point. Then she was shaking his shoulders, screaming his name. He was unconscious.

The thought would haunt Rebecca afterward—probably for years, maybe for the rest of her life—that if she had called paramedics right away, maybe they could have rushed him to the hospital, and maybe he could have been revived—by those electric paddle things they use to restart hearts in medical dramas, and presumably also in real life (and what is that, really?)—and maybe his life could have been saved, by heart surgery, by a stent, a pacemaker. . . . Instead, she had hesitated. She had hesitated because the Representative had a wife and a family who knew nothing of her—who knew nothing of his other life, or however many other other lives he had. That was to say nothing of his public life, the things he stood for, his political career, the careers of others he was connected to—a chain of influences that went all the way up to the Oval Office, and, this being an election year, it would not be good to have a Democrat humiliated this way, possibly shamed out office. . . . God knows how many outward threads of the web would tremble when this hit the news cycle.

There had been a narrow window of time in which there might have been a chance that if she'd made the hasty decision to pick up the phone and dial the three digits every American child learns in kindergarten, she might have saved his life. But instead, because of the world outside—rather than inside—this luxury apartment overlooking the Potomac, she had hesitated, and now, as she had confirmed and reconfirmed and reconfirmed again in the hour since she'd first taken her foot off his mouth, with her thumb on the inside of his bound and motionless wrist and her head on his silent, motionless, cooling chest, the Representative was doubtlessly dead.

It was a sensation of paralysis, sitting in that chair. This must be a little of what it feels like to be paralyzed, a conscious vegetable—the sort of person the Representative might have become had she acted instead of hesitated: seeing, feeling, hearing, thinking, unable to unroot oneself from the spot—passive, helpless, stuck. If she looked down at her legs and arms and willed them to move, they would not.

The plush, black leather armchair accepted her body like a gently swallowing mouth. The leather felt smooth and cool on her bare thighs. The back of her leather corset rubbed against the leather of the chair, grunted and squealed if she adjusted her back. Her goddamn back was killing her for some reason. What the fuck she'd done to it she did not know, but this pain in her lower back seemed to return for a few days once a month like a muscular-spinal period. Every time it came back she made a mental note to see a chiropractor, but it always went away before she remembered to make the appointment—and then the motherfucker came roaring back again the next month. Maybe putting on the tight corset today retriggered the back pain. Was this aging?

She had a lot of decisions to make. Some urgent, some middle, some distant. She felt so overwhelmed, so suffocated by the unmade decisions crowding around her that she was for the time being incapable of doing anything but staring at the body of the Representative that lay on the concrete floor in front of her and letting the late afternoon light fail as she sat in this leather armchair beginning to grow hungry.

In her mind, she began to sketch out a To-Do list. It was an easy exercise suggested by a therapist from years back that she still found a useful way to compartmentalize her problems when she was feeling overwhelmed, and it helped to calm her. When she made these interior To-Do lists, she put items into three categories, according to the urgency of their concern. High Priority, Medium Priority, Low Priority. Her eyes unfixed, she gazed out the window at the river many stories below her. She could see the streetlights beginning to come on, and the colorful lights that spookily underlit the monuments at night: She could just discern, not far away on the Mall, the gangly half profile of Abraham Lincoln glowing in his cage of columns, sitting perfectly still in his own armchair, as if immobilized for centuries by the weight of his own difficult decisions.

278

TO DO

High Priority:

1. Deal with current situation.

What were her options? She would admit, later, that the thought did occur to her of simply changing into her street clothes, packing her bag, and leaving. Who would know she was ever here? What if the Representative had happened to be alone in the apartment when he had his heart attack, or whatever it was? Well—there was the door-man, who knew her, and had seen them come in together, and who would see her leave alone. But who was to say this hadn't happened after she left? Did anyone else know about this apartment? The Representative had tight, important connections everywhere—he would be missed, conspicuously and immediately. How many hours or days could he lie there decomposing on the floor before anyone found him? She couldn't do that. Even if she could, what good would it do? The apartment would be discovered, the closets full of BDSM gear, the South African *sjambok* made out of fucking rhino hide. . . . Questions would arise and, before long, they would be answered. He would be humiliated in his death. He would be a laughingstock, a smug joke on Leno. The scandal and embarrassment would come sooner or later, it was inevitable now. In a sudden, brief flutter of hope, she entertained a fantasy of somehow getting in touch with his congressional aides, moving the body to his office, covering it up—which fast spiraled into an oblivion of logistics so delicate and daunt-ingly complicated that it immediately overwhelmed her: No, that would not work. The safest recourse was the blunt truth. One way or another, she was going to have to pick up the phone and tell some-one what happened, hand off the situation to the outside world. She herself had done nothing wrong—except perhaps hesitate past the critical moment when an emergency call might still have been use-ful. And whom should she call now? Nine-one-one? A bit late for that. Should she tell the doorman? He probably already knew enough about the Representative to infer the general gist of what was going on. The cops? She was loathe to talk to "the authorities." Just the phrase nearly made her shudder. She would want to explain every-thing deliberately and calmly, not leaving anything out, beginning at the beginning—and she knew that if she was talking to such people, she wouldn't be allowed to do that—she would struggle against the current, being brusquely cut off over and over by arrogant, unlistening men, interrupting her with questions about things that happened on square twenty-seven when she was still on square one—if they would only shut up and listen to her, she could explain everything—but who would listen? What if—what if, what if, what if—she called his wife? Tracy—Tracy, of whom she had heard a great deal over the last decade—complaints, compliments, grievances, and guileless confessions of enduring love—but had never met. How much did she know? Probably nothing. How much did she suspect? Who could say. If she were to call his wife and start explaining a lot of very-difficult-to-explain things to his family, it might be possible to keep the whole thing within the inner circle, not let it out into the public sphere. . . . Save his reputation, and not hurt the Democrats' image. . . . She chased this line of thought all the way to the bedside table, where the Representative's iPhone was plugged in, charging. She heaved herself out of the chair—wincing at a sudden spike of back pain—and slogged across the swamp of floor space between living room and bedroom, picked up the phone, slid the lock on the screen, and was at once confronted with a four-digit passcode. Obviously a man who lived with so many secrets would not have an un-password-protected phone. She went to the desk chair on which she'd earlier that afternoon ordered him to fold and carefully place his clothes. In the pocket of his pants she found his wallet: driver's license, ID cards, debit card, credit cards, a few business cards, photos of his wife and children (no help there), health insurance card, SmarTrip card noticeably absent (never slums it on the Metro, always takes the car service home from the Capitol), slightly under $280 cash—a recent trip to the ATM minus maybe a cup of coffee. No phone numbers. Of course. No one writes down phone numbers in the year 2012. All information is consolidated on our mobile devices, these guardian angels in our pockets that guide us, protect us, control us. She put it back and returned to the chair. Was nine-one-one really her only option? If she really called the cops she must remember to flush the coke down the toilet before they arrived. It wasn't hers, but before they started (before Rebecca became Mistress Delilah), he had offered, she had declined, and the Representative had shrugged amiably, chopped out a long, fat line on the marble countertop, and sucked it up through a crisp twenty, which now rounded out the amount in his wallet and was still lying in a gossamer curl on the kitchen counter. Come to think of it, that gulp of cocaine might very well have been what pushed his heart over the edge. Rebecca looked with dread at the cordless landline phone weakly blinking a green light in its cradle on the kitchen counter. The little green light blinked, and the gulf of dread inside her grew deeper and wider with every second that distanced her from the Representative's time of death.

2. Eat something.

Hunger was coming on fast. What had she eaten that day? That morning, sitting in LaGuardia's Delta Shuttle terminal, waiting for her one-hour flight to Reagan National, she'd had a latte and a disgusting premade hummus, sprouts, and tomato sandwich on an everything bagel that came wrapped in a cellophane package; the pale, hard slice of tomato had tasted like it was grown in a petri dish. The Representative had treated her to a lobster roll and a glass of Sancerre for lunch. (He'd wanted to buy a bottle, but she'd said she only wanted a glass, and even that she only sipped at. This abstemiousness was uncharacteristic of her; the Representative thought nothing of it.) Evening was falling and her belly was beginning to gurgle. Acid, gas—chemicals weren't getting along in her stomach. She eased one cheek off the sticky leather seat cushion to let a fart slide out—why not, she was alone now—and was surprised by the sulfurous pungency of what raced out of her; she'd expected a drier, airier fart. She needed to eat.

Medium Priority:

3. Call Richard back.

It could be important. She had no fucking idea what the fuck Richard had called her about, but whatever it was, it was most likely something she did not remotely, pardon the understatement, want to deal with at the moment. It was probably either about the divorce or the apartment. He had called earlier in the afternoon and left a message. She had been preoccupied. Mistress Delilah had one shoe on the back of the Representative's neck, hissing insults at him and thwacking his ass with the *sjambok* while he was bent over in worshipful genuflection, licking up the puddle she'd just pissed for him on the bathroom floor (purely as a professional, the *sjambok* impressed her—it had a pleasing heft and grip, and she appreciated the clear, crisp note of its whistle before the crack: What it sang through the air on its

281

way to strike flesh was a love song); meanwhile, a distant, separate, and ever-alert corner of her consciousness (Rebecca) registered the faint buzzing sound of her phone vibrating in the next room, and made a quick mental note to check it later; and later, when she had a moment—she put a blindfold on the Representative and ordered him to jack off awhile, but denied him permission to come—she fished the phone out of her purse and glanced at the screen, just to make sure it wasn't urgent. (It might have been about Severin, was what she feared most—her sister was watching him while Rebecca was away on this trip to DC, and Severin's regimen of pills was complicated.) It was Richard. And he'd left a message. She could not bring herself, even now, to listen to the goddamn message. The message almost certainly had to do either with the apartment or with their endless divorce. The two issues were closely interrelated. In broad abstract, the conflict about the apartment (third-story, two-bedroom, one-bathroom in East Village with balcony and nice view of Empire State Building, short walk to First Avenue L, pets OK, laundry on-site) was this: (1) they bought and own it together; (2) Richard, who now finally has tenure and lives in Connecticut with the woman he left her for, wants to sell it; (3) Rebecca, who lives in it, does not. It was a never-ending sideshow to the circus of animosity that was their divorce. Richard and Rebecca had separated four years ago, and it seemed now the divorce was finally coming through. She was so used to its terrible weight, at this point it was getting difficult to imagine what life would feel like with this grindstone cut from around her neck. Were one to unwind all the knots and lay it out along the ground, the string of unanswered e-mails and unreturned messages—from Richard, from Richard's lawyer, from her own lawyer—would stretch for miles. The divorce was a backyard running out of room to bury bodies in. When she asked herself if, at the age of twenty-one, when she met Richard, she had known that it would end like this, would she have still done it?—the answer was no. All those years of love and cooperation and contentment with him were not worth this. It was a bum deal. She had been a twenty-one-year-old college senior in love with a brilliant (so she'd thought) grad student seven years older than she was (an age difference that had seemed significant then, was laughable to her now that she'd ever thought so), and she wished she could let that person know she would be in love with that man for fifteen years—fifteen years, with a marriage in the middle of that—of, if not bliss, relatively functional happiness—that she would give her youth to this man—and he would violate the one rule she would ask of him and which he would have agreed to—and he would leave her, and then there she'd be, thirty-nine and single, her married friends cluttering their Facebook walls with baby pictures while she was thinking daily about sperm donors, about freezing her eggs, the window of fertility shrinking, dimming, closing, every day dogging her with worries about having a child in her forties, the rising risk of birth defects, bringing into the world some rubber-faced mutant with flippers and a tail and raising it alone, and she'd post pictures of her and her malformed freak-child on Facebook and her friends would "Like" them. From the ages of twenty-one to thirty-six, when she and Richard separated, she'd had someone, and had lived her life pretty much assuming she always would. And he had been her best friend—that was what made his betrayal doubly horrible: She'd lost both her husband and her best friend. Where would she find someone like that again? How, now, nearing forty, was it possible that she would meet another person who could ever know her that intimately? Someone with whom she had shared so much history, so much of her growing up? It simply wasn't possible anymore. Not now. It was such a strange feeling, to have these sickening waves of anger toward the one person in the world with whom she'd shared more of herself than with anyone else. What she'd wanted, vaguely, but on second thought, specifically (and in retrospect, thank God it never happened), was a child with Richard, to mix their DNA and make a person whose face shared their features, not a cup of frozen come from a stranger, a stranger who at some point had been paid to come into a cup. Remember, Richard, how we talked about having kids—a kid, or plural, whatever—and you didn't want to until your career was more settled, until you had tenure? Of course, I said, that's fine—I didn't want to yet either. We would wait. We would have our fun. And, boy, did we have fun. There was the threesome with Harriet, for instance. When we shut ourselves up in that cabin in the Catskills for a long weekend and smoked opium—whose idea was that, smoking opium like Frankfurt School philosophers in Paris? Where did we get *opium* of all drugs, anyway? And we all got high as emperors and had a languorous three-day threesome with my former college roommate. Don't think for a moment that that wasn't mostly for you. I'm not actually really bisexual like I said I thought I was back then. When I fucked other women, even the ones I fucked without you around—you know what?—the only way I could really get off on it was to imagine a man watching. Male fantasy is a curved

mirror that warps female fantasy. We are all at once bodies and mirrors, and our minds are the curves in the mirrors. And then there was
that creepy couple we met on the Internet that one time—we went
to their hotel room, they were visiting from Toronto—something
funny about us fucking a couple of Canadian swingers—and that
woman freaked out at you for not switching condoms. And she was
right, Richard. What the fuck is the point of safe group sex if you take
it out of me and put it right in her without switching condoms?
Think. Richard and Rebecca had had an open relationship. Well, they
were supposed to have had an open relationship. The whole open
part necessitates that we tell each other when we fuck other people,
doesn't it, Richard? It was supposed to mean no secrets, no lies, no
jealousy, honest communication. That was the idea. Rebecca had
thought it was working. The one thing I asked of you, Richard, was
don't fuck your students. And you agreed to that. Yes, I took advantage of the open relationship a lot more often than you did. Could I
help the fact that I was young and hot and you were such a fucking
pussy? You never told me you didn't want to hear about it. You were
with me when I had the job working for the phone sex line. It was the
nineties, first Clinton administration, news about Bosnia on the TV,
and Rebecca put on her husky honeydrip voice and got off strangers
on the phone while Richard cooked paella for dinner. That was in the
toddlerhood of the Internet, when it was still possible to make OK
money working for a phone sex line. You were with me when I started
working as a dominatrix. You even said you liked it. You helped me
put up the website. You helped me pick out the name, you scholar of
comparative religions. Rebecca had chosen the name Delilah for a
range of reasons: The name sounded sexy, and the biblical reference
was a private nod to her Jewish upbringing; she liked the nightmare
labyrinth of misogynist connotations—Delilah the emasculator, the
woman who renders the strongman weak with the snipping of scis-
sors—the symbolic castrator. You said you liked the idea of me tying
up and whipping other men. You said you liked to imagine me dom-
inating other men when you slapped me around and shoved my head
down to suck your cock. . . . You even asked to watch that one time—
that was with the Director, who fucking *adored* me, by the way—
and I asked if he minded, and mind, hell, he *loved* the idea of my
husband watching. That was fun, wasn't it? You sat there rubbing
yourself through your jeans while I rammed my fake dick up his ass
and that avant-garde theater director who's famous enough to have
his own Wikipedia page now and who liked to be called sissyboy

clutched the pillows and came like a woman. I told you *everything.* That was supposed to be the way it worked. You were the one who was hiding things. Or you were in the end, anyway—who knows what you successfully kept hidden. We know you kept it hidden that you were violating the only rules we had: (1) no outside relationships; (2) you don't fuck your students; and (3) no lying—all three of which you were doing. It's kind of funny how we thought we were going to have this freethinking bohemian marriage between a couple of people determined not to become another boring bourgeois couple with an interesting but dead past pushing one of those ergonomic mother-facing anti-autism strollers down Wyckoff Street—and yet, and yet, in the end, it all fell apart because of the most boring bourgeois reason imaginable. You had an affair and left me for a younger woman. Unoriginal, Richard. Tawdry. Gross. Predictable. Fucking *classic.* And now you're calling me about something, and leaving a message. It's probably about the apartment, which is of no use to you as it sits around unsold on Avenue C not making you any money while I live in it. You want to sell it off for less than its current market value—and keep in mind we bought that place pregentrification and now it's worth almost twice as much and prices in the neighborhood are only going up—and you want to pocket the windfall and take it back to Connecticut with the grad student you cheated on me with and never have to see me again. Shove it up your ass, Richard, we will sell when I'm ready, and I'm not ready yet. And yes, I know I haven't yet returned your last message about it. Trust me, you cannot fucking begin to fathom how unimportant that seems to me now. I am in a very strange situation—a life-and-death situation (well, now it is just a death situation)—and I probably won't be getting back to you today.

Rebecca didn't know how much longer she could keep on doing this. She had been doing more pro-domme work recently because she was short on money. She wasn't young anymore. She had relaunched her website last month. It had been dormant for years, as she hadn't needed it. She'd had the same roster of ten to fifteen clients for nearly a decade now, and they kept her in business. All the pictures on her site were taken six years ago. She was opening the door to new clients for the first time in a while. She was staring forty in the face. It stared back at her: her face. It was beautiful but Venus in the mirror had deep laugh lines now, and two vertical creases in her forehead above the bridge of her nose. She hated looking at photos of herself from just five, six years ago—such as, for instance, the ones on her website. Mistress Delilah, specializing in whipping, caning, flogging, bondage (light or heavy), leather and/or latex fetish, foot fetish, anal femdom, facesitting, pissing, cock torture. She'd gotten Ike, the photographer who always gave her the friend discount, to take those newer pictures in his studio: corsets, wigs, masks, leather boots that laced up to the thighs. . . . She looked gorgeous in them, and that was just six years ago. Was it false advertising to still be using those pictures? It wasn't an illusion: She had aged perceptibly in the last six years. Stress accelerates the effects of aging, doesn't it? And with the divorce, the apartment, the being broke, the Severin getting cancer, the sailing alone toward menopause, the possibility of never getting to share the common experience that has united women since the days of goddamn pagan moon rituals and the Venus of Willendorf, for the last few years she had been pretty stressed out. There was a time, in her early twenties, when she looked at small children with confusion and maybe mild disgust—only mild disgust, the way you would look at something that is visually interesting but which you're not planning to touch, like a slug; they were cute things in the strollers that took up a lot of space on the subway, brief obstructions in the path of a young woman who was on her way to spend a night careening barefoot around Manhattan with her heels in her hands and eventually spill out of a cab at dawn, wired-drunk and shaky with blow, to curl up in the arms of the fiancé who'd been dealing with his own demons all night. Later, when she was in her early thirties, and had been married a few years, her heart would, to her own self-reflective annoyance, go gelatinous at the sight of an infant—the cooing, gurgling, finger-grabbing monkeyfaced goblins with bright, impossibly smooth, soft skin that were beginning to emerge from her friends, she looked at them with warmth and tenderness. . . . And now? The other weekend, she woke up at noon on Sunday, parked herself at the kitchen table to eat breakfast in front of her MacBook, and when she looked up, the sun was setting and she had lost the entire day to YouTube videos of babies: a video of a baby being weirded out by a talking Elmo toy, a montage of babies tasting lemons for the first time, a montage of babies laughing hysterically, a baby laughing hysterically at a person jingling car keys, a baby laughing hysterically at herself tearing up a piece of paper, a baby laughing hysterically at an ice cube, a baby laughing hysterically at absolutely nothing, a video of a baby petting a cat, a video of a baby being petted by a cat, a video of twin babies in diapers flapping their hands and squawking at each other in their own monosyllabic language, a video of two babies on a couch, holding each other and laughing, hysterically. Feeling like the false mother at the judgment of Solomon. Elohim! Yahweh! Let me conceive like Sarah at the age of ninety-nine! She was irritated at herself for feeling this maternal yearning; in the same way she was irritated at herself for fantasizing about male fantasy, for getting off under the male gaze. One of the regular crazies who peregrinated Rebecca's chunk of the East Village between Tompkins Square Park and Stuy-Town was a woman with frazzled crazy-person hair bundled in ratty shawls who walked around in clogs all day, murmuring to herself and pushing a baby stroller full of broken baby dolls with clicking eyelids. The woman terrified her.

She'd voiced these complaints to Colin, her brother—her kid and her only brother—last time she was visiting their mother, in whose basement he dwelled with his lovingly hand-painted Doctor Who memorabilia. Colin!—five years younger than she was at his virginal thirty-four. A lost cause, a lost soul, a lost child. Colin lived in the dark—sticky and pale like a grub, eating garbage, fearing sunlight, sleeping till noon, one, two, three in the afternoon on a soggy futon in the wood-paneled half-finished basement of that shabby split-level ranch house in Caldwell, New Jersey—the very same room in which she had eaten mushrooms and lost her virginity to her boyfriend at fifteen (hell, he slept on the very same futon). There Colin lived with his eyes glued to the Internet, a man (strange as it sounded to call him that) who will likely leave little behind in the world but an exhaustively complete collection of Doctor Who and Red Dwarf figurines and a really impressive World of Warcraft gear score. She had come to visit because her mother, long since divorced from her father, a long time alone, a long time lonesome, was in poor health, recovering from hip surgery. (Mom—why do you let Colin live like that? Why do you allow him to treat you like a live-in servant when you are old and frail and should be the one in bed, not doing his goddamn laundry and making him sandwiches for lunch, which you leave on the top step of the basement stairs for him to find when he gets up, as if feeding a troll?) Anyway. She'd sat with Colin in his moist underground lair, drinking most of a box of Mom's Chablis while he drank a liter of Mountain Dew, unloading her heart to what had become of the little boy whose hand she'd held on the way to his first day of school. And it was Colin, Dorito-munching amateur psychoanalyst who dwells in Mom's basement, to whom she confessed her anxieties about growing older alone, about the terrible dread she felt facing her imminent fortieth birthday. And you were so understanding, and so helpful, Colin, when you shrugged, and offered what I guess was the most reassuring thing you could think to say: "It's merely the accident of a base-ten number system." I think it was that "merely" that made me throw your fucking Dalek at you. I didn't mean to break it. I'm sorry. I love you. I wish I could help you, but you seem to be beyond help. In a way, your problems are worse than mine, even though sometimes it's hard to find sympathy for a thirty-four-year-old man whose sick and elderly mother washes his underwear.

4. Severin.

Severin was dying. Severin was dying of cancer. Poor thing was only eleven years old—not that aged for a dog. He was a shih tzu, a boutique breed notorious for chronic health problems. She was pretty sure he was mostly blind. He had respiratory issues too—he grunted and grumbled, fighting for breath as he scuttled around the apartment, or lay in bed with her, snoring like a jackhammer all night long: She'd grown to tune it out, while every boyfriend she'd had since Richard left had whined about never being able to get to sleep with this stinking, wheezing, farting, dying little dog curled into a ball at the foot of the bed making weird, gross, and, for such a small animal, astonishingly *loud* noises. (No, not boyfriends—she hadn't had any boyfriends, only typical New York single men, who were all the same in the end—selfish, childish, spiritual weaklings, commitmentphobic assholes who want to fuck her occasionally but keep their distance wide enough to never be called anyone's boyfriend— say the word "boyfriend" and watch him skitter down the drainpipe like a roach when the light's flicked on.) Her sister, Liz—her much younger half sister from her dad's second marriage to the younger woman he left her mother for (boys, boys)—Liz was watching Severin while Rebecca was out of town for the weekend, and even that much time away made her nervous. It wasn't an ordinary petsitting job: Severin had a daily regimen of medications he had to be tricked into taking that was as complicated as that of a dying human's, and came in the same tray of little plastic boxes labeled by the time of day they had to be given. They were supplementary to the chemo somehow, and Rebecca followed the vet's orders with religious obedience. No, Severin's hair didn't fall out—that doesn't happen with dogs in chemo for some reason—and yes, she had a shih tzu in chemotherapy, and if you just rolled your eyes at the idea of "wasting" money on chemotherapy for a shih tzu, then fuck you, I don't care what you think. Have you never loved a dog? Have you never loved anyone? All her life Rebecca had given out love, and Severin was the one creature alive to whom she gave her love who honestly and reliably and unconditionally gave it back.

5. _____[THIS SPACE INTENTIONALLY LEFT BLANK] _____

Then she remembered she had got Severin around the same time she had met the Representative. Eleven years ago. She did not think that Severin would outlive him. It was true the Representative could no longer be said to be—rather, to have been—her client. Things had begun that way, but they had not been that way for some time. What had gone on between them in the last couple of years no longer felt like a performance she was being paid to give, but a mutual give-and-take between friends (they had always been equals), between lovers. In a certain way, they had loved each other. They were lovers who could do certain things with one another because they had started out without the usual invisible walls, the walls that are there when people meet in the world with all the complex uncertainties of sex and power and emotion unspoken and unsolved between them—the way it is between two people who are not sure, who are afraid to say, exactly what it is they want from each other.

However, that simplicity, that clarity, had thrillingly, unsettlingly, gone away. This was not ordinary. This was not responsible. Rebecca had no other relationship like this with any other person who had begun as a client. The first time they'd had sex (ordinary, unadorned sexual intercourse) was two years ago—afterward it had felt to her deeply, inexplicably wrong, almost like incest. She could not forgive herself for a long time, and had refused to see him for months afterward. He had acted in an appallingly unprofessional manner, and she had not stopped him, which was appallingly unprofessional of her. She had allowed the boundary between them that had kept things simple to drop. He had flooded her voice-mail box with messages, sent her strings of increasingly desperate e-mails, sent her flowers. Eventually, she allowed him back. She had genuinely missed him. She missed his company. She missed his very genuine wit and charm, his warm, confiding conversation in the apartment, sitting around drinking wine after a session, or in one of the restaurants where he wasn't likely to be recognized. When she returned, something between them had changed forever. There was a new sense of intimacy between them; now they could never go back to the satisfying but emotionally safe relationship they'd had before. They had ruined one thing, and made something new, something else. They showed each other their souls as well as their bodies, and this was when he quit paying her. He still paid for her airfare, her meals, her drinks, her hotel room—everything extraneous that needed paying for—but this was when he quit paying her any money directly, and she never asked for it or expected it again. It was different now. This became the new norm. Sometimes she would be in character as Mistress Delilah, and sometimes she was herself, Rebecca Glass. The Representative was in love with both women, but in very different ways. When they had ordinary sex—when she was Rebecca—she didn't wear her costumes: no corsets, no wigs, no whips or bondage or toys. They were two people naked in bed together in the most predicable arrangements: an affair that was perfectly legal but came with all the usual lies and complications of infidelity (on his part). Rebecca had quite recently realized that she had something with Sam (for that was the Representative's real name) that she had never quite had with Richard.

One month before, they had been in Rebecca's hotel room in the Fairfax. It was risky for Sam to be seen there, even by the desk clerks. It was after a session at the apartment. The risk was stupid, but they had wanted to have sex as Rebecca and Sam—without the Representative or Mistress Delilah around—and he didn't want to do it in the apartment, because he wanted to keep his fantasy sex life separate from his other sex life, which was in turn separate from the rest of his life. (It was frightening how many lives Sam juggled.) When he came, she felt at once that the condom had broken. He pulled out, and they both looked down at the sleeve of latex with a broken flap loosening its grip around his softening penis. He had a sheepish, embarrassed look. In that moment, Sam, still breathing heavily after coming, naked in her bed in her hotel room, fat and white and growing old on his knees with his cock retracting between his legs, looked helpless—less than ever like a powerful and influential and principled man, and more like a fragile adolescent boy who did not yet know himself. He began to stammer his way through saying he was clean as far as he knew, and, um, well.

"Don't worry," Rebecca had said. "I'll take care of it."

Low Priority:

6. The secret.

How did she come to be here?—sitting in this chair at the age of thirty-nine, not dead broke, but zero nest egg in savings, single, growing older, wanting a child but having no one to have it with, and no career outside of sex work—which had always felt like a side career anyway. She'd never really planned on making a living off it. Mistress Delilah got her start back in the nineties, working in a fairly aboveground dungeon in TriBeCa—there were private rooms where things could get a little more intimate, but it was all low-grade stuff— mostly fantasy, role-playing. Nobody came, no fluids other than sweat and maybe a little blood were expurgated from anyone's body. It was all light whipping and caning, usually with sleazy Eurobeat crap blasting through the speakers. The place had a facade that made it clear what it was—it was a legitimate business, it passed code. It was decorated to evoke a medieval castle (or something), black iron chains, fake stone walls, candelabras dripping red wax: Something about the aggressive fakery of the place she'd found distasteful. She felt the decor called attention to the fantasy rather than meld it with the real. The joint was even still there, though in a reduced state, one of the few true BDSM clubs that had survived Giuliani's Disneyfication of Manhattan. Sometimes gawkers would come just to hang out at the bar and watch. After a year or so there she'd moved on to working at a much sketchier sex club, behind an unmarked metal door on a nondescript side street in Chinatown. You had to get buzzed in, and then push through two layers of black velvet curtains and down a set of stairs, then another door, where the guy who scrutinized you and then maybe let you in sat on a stool in the hall. That place had class, a sense of reality, of a little real danger. People really got hurt there. Not badly, of course, but there were definitely patrons who left with marks they would want to conceal with strategic clothing for at least a few days. She'd liked the aesthetic of the place: mirrors everywhere, red floors, all the furniture ornate and old-fashioned, fake Louis Quatorze chairs and tables—it had a very *Story of O* look. You had to know someone to get in. It was the kind of place where people who were hardcore into the BDSM scene went; you would never see a lifestyle tourist there. That was where Mistress Delilah started picking up her first private clients, and from there she set off on her own. She got Ike to take the first set of photos, got Richard to help her set up the website. That was how she'd met the Representative, through a referral from someone at the club who knew him. Back then he was getting ready to run for city council. He only met dominatrices in private sessions—he was too afraid to show his face at even the most secretive, discreet sex clubs. When Mistress Delilah did private sessions, she let her clients come. Usually not until the very end, due to the nature of the male orgasm, with its punctuative finality. But that was not usual. Those were the ones who made the most money, the ones who let their clients come. It was slightly dangerous: the involvement of an orgasm pushes the session into the gray area of what may or may not be prostitution. Legally, it's a hard thing to define. Sometimes she let a client see her breasts, or she would push her underwear aside to piss on the floor or a client's face, but she almost never took off any more of her costume than she began the session in. There was one foot fetishist she had who got off simply on giving her a foot massage and a pedicure. At the end of the session, she would relax in the recliner, wiggling her toes, tufts of cotton stuck between them, toenails freshly filed and lovingly painted valentine red—why not let him come? Admiring his handiwork, the Goldman Sachs executive on his knees at her feet inhales the toxic sweetness of the drying nail polish and plants timid, delicate kisses on her feet while he masturbates with the feverish, trembling hands of a starving man fumbling with the cellophane packaging of a premade airport bagel sandwich. It had been a jarring contrast, to be pampered, adored, worshipped in this theatrical way by powerful men who paid her to let them do so, while at home, when Mistress Delilah was folded in the closet and she was only Rebecca Glass, she was being taken for granted and lied to by her husband, treated like shit, treated merely (*merely*, Colin) like someone's wife. At times she wished she could step through the mirror's membrane where fantasy touches the fingertips of reality.

How did she come to be here? How was it that she was dressed in fishnet stockings, garters, a leather corset, and a red wig, holding a creepy South African rhino-skin whip and sitting alone in a luxury apartment in Washington, DC, with the dead body, which was naked except for the rope on his wrists and the nipple clamps still on his nipples, of a US congressman?

There was more. Rebecca had begun to experience an inexplicable feeling that she had never quite felt before. It was a small, strange, pleasant feeling, and hard to describe: a warmth—a sense of calm she had not felt in a long time, if, in just this way, ever. For various reasons, she had not thought it likely, but suspicion had driven her to the drugstore down the block from her apartment, and earlier that day, she had met Sam for the first time with a secret of her own, one she very literally carried inside her. She had not yet made a decision. Until today, she had been leaning one way, and now, she was leaning another.

Rebecca thought again of her own mother. Well, Mom, she said to her, so it goes. We don't plan to be disappointed. We don't plan to be betrayed. We both know that. Nobody plans to suddenly leave a lover with a body on her hands and the eyes of a watchful nation to face, to be seen by, to stand before naked, on display, Venus looking back at us in the mirror, gazing at her gazers. They will not understand. You will not understand. We are all at once bodies and mirrors, and our minds are the curves in the mirrors.

Rebecca Glass went into the kitchen and picked up the phone.

Four Stories
Kim Chinquee

SNAPSHOT

HE GETS UP AND SHOWERS, doing everything as usual. When I finally get around, still in my pajamas, I ask him, Where'd your arm go?

He dries himself with his one hand. His face looks creamy, his lips red, almost bloody.

He has a stub where his right arm would have been connected. I say, It's a good thing you're left-handed. I go down to make myself some coffee, toast, feeling groggy, crooked. I put on boots and a jacket and get his keys and brush the snow off his SUV.

Back inside, I pour myself a cup, adding all the fixings. I get a cup for him and I go upstairs where I see him naked, shaving. I say, Here's your cup.

He turns to me, his left hand with the razor. He says, That's sweet and all. But you know I don't drink coffee.

I go and get the camera. Now he's getting dressed, sitting on the bed, putting a leg in. Donning his shirt one-handed, looking at himself in the full-length. How do I look? he says.

His right sleeve hangs. He stands and asks, Which way to the beach? He flexes his bicep.

I say, Can I take a picture?

I press the button, telling him this time I want proof. Today, it's an arm; the day before, a leg; but he didn't seem to miss it, hopping around like nothing and then it came back again.

I say, You want me to drive you? To work, I mean?

He laughs and gets his coat. He says thanks, gives me a kiss, and says he'll be home for lunch.

RIDGE

She feels the tingle in her hip, looking down into the city. Far off to uptown, the sky seems to fall into the buildings, and she sees lines of trees far off, the scrapers seeming small.

From here she wonders where her home is. She came from her boyfriend's—he lives a mile from here, but he tells her he's at work now. She's been spending lots of days here. She'll go and teach her classes, then go home and get her dog and drive the thirty miles to spend the afternoon at his place, feeding his dogs and hers, sitting on his sofa with her laptop, looking out his window that overlooks more trees, leaves, and a hint of a driveway. She'll vacuum, dust, lie in his bed, and remember the first time he kissed her in the parking lot across the street from one of the places where they ate for the seventh time that month, after running together either here at this park or the one closer to her place where the trees look like lone scattered umbrellas.

She takes off the hat of his she's wearing: multicolored, wool with earflaps. Strings to tie under the chin, a tassel. He wore the hat during their first race, when he slowed to keep her pace, telling her she could do it on the uphill. It was before they even kissed, and she heard his step, his breath, his step, his step.

Her hair is wet with sweat. His jacket is damp—another item of his she borrowed from his closet. She feels the mist covering her face. She's just run ten miles and is sweating from her inside.

She looks at the hay bales down the hill in rows making lanes for the sledders in winter, ones she's seen here during a bike race where she also watched her boyfriend pedal up the snow and wipe out on the down, on the bottom. Him getting up and going round again, later saying he's always been better at running.

But now there is no snow—two days before the temperature was eighty and she ran in shorts. She met her boyfriend in summer at a park wearing shorts. They ran loops. After, as they stretched, she tried not to appear too mesmerized by everything about him.

Looking out, she notices the smallness. The sky an envelope, a vacuum. Far off she sees fog. The steady mist is like an arm, like it is reaching.

SO LONG

My sister calls me at eleven.
Hey, she says.
Sometimes we don't say much.
She talks about the butter beans she's making. Feeling haunted, like a matchbox. The day she broke her leg. We were ten, or I was. She might have been eleven.
I say, "You, in the backseat. You talked about a penny."
Last week in Wisconsin at my aunt's house, my sister stood there with her knees straight, asking if I could tell which was the bad one. My uncle said it was obvious.
We talk about baseball with our father: him hitting the ball so hard it took ages to find it. She remembers him hitting me so hard it scarred. I remember him taking her, alone, screaming in the bathroom.
"I've been reading up," I say.
Just last week after my father's passing, his social worker told me something I didn't know. She told me he heard voices.
I say to my sister, "He gave us one-word answers. He got all those treatments." Shock. "I'm kind of amazed he made it so long." We sit there on our ends. Our father used to call us. He'd sit there and he'd cry, breathing back into us.

HAND

Passing a girl on the sidewalk, Kyle notices her hand, so small with its plain fingers, unlike the hand he found in the dumpster. At first it didn't seem real. At first he only poked at it.
He hears a dog bark and he looks down into his cart at the cans. The hand felt kind of sponge-like. It smelled of wine. He found it under soggy papers and some empty beer cans. He picked it up. He figures it's his now.
Across the street, he sees some cops sitting in their cars talking to each other. Kyle feels electric. His cart sounds like a train. The air feels thick, its smell reminding him of bacon.
As his stomach growls, he remembers he skipped breakfast. He usually has grits, something he's been eating since he was a kid. He'd be in his grandfather's old white shack, where he used to go every

morning before school, his grandfather saying, "You must always tell the truth. No matter how anybody treats you." Kyle remembered that at school each day, trying to sit upright in his desk and listen to the teacher. One day his grandpa slipped his shack key into Kyle's pocket. He told Kyle, "It's time." And the next morning when Kyle went there, he unlocked the door to find his grandpa hanging from the ceiling. Kyle was only ten. He still has the key. It sits there in his pocket.

Cars are beeping. His cart isn't full. Still. This other thing is something.

Kyle knows the right thing to do. But cops can be rude and nasty. He was a cop for two months in the air force—the other cops used to sit around and tell dirty jokes and swear, and since Kyle didn't do that, they kept calling him a faggot.

At home, he wheels his cart up to the building where he lives. He grabs the hand and puts it in his backpack. "Hand," he says, "we're going to my place."

He runs up, unlocks his door, and when he sees the fridge, he opens the door and sets the hand on a shelf.

When he gets down to the cart again, he sees a couple pass: a girl with dark-lined eyes, a white-haired man in golf shorts.

He pushes the cart to Tops, and with his giant hands he puts his cans and bottles into the machine.

Later Kyle puts on his newest jeans to get his blood drawn. He dons a crisp white shirt he used to wear when working in collections. He's had plenty of jobs: scrubbing toilets, his short gig as a cop, then that year as a med tech. He picked berries but wasn't fast enough. At thirty-six he tried to get a bachelor's in history. He thinks of his own history: flashbacks of his father in the bathroom, the barn and straw and his mother's ruby glasses. Once a week his therapist tells him to watch the dots on a screen as she asks him to relive things.

She says, "How do you feel?"

He's not sure what to say. He says, "I'm not sure I've ever felt much."

Today he's getting his blood drawn, which he does every year with his doctor's orders. Kyle parks the car his father used to drive before he went to prison for killing a woman while drunk driving. Sometimes Kyle visits, busing the hour to get there. His father wears orange and keeps his head shaved. Each time as Kyle leaves, his father says, "You *must* be guilty of *something.*"

Kyle walks to the lab, thinking of the hand with its fuchsia polish. He says hi to a lady on the sidewalk. But mostly to her shaggy dog, its tail wagging incessantly.

At the lab, Kyle skims through the stack of magazines, only seeing ones with skinny, fair-skinned ladies on the covers. On the chair next to the table, he sees a thin man wearing tinted glasses and an obese lady with curly, auburn hair. Kyle notices an odor. On the TV in the corner, a sportscaster talks about the Sabres' winning season. A weatherlady says it's cloudy. Then there's breaking news; a pregnant, suited woman interviews a man who holds a slim cigar. He says, "A woman washed up in the river. She's been missing. Her name is Ruby Smith. She appears to have no hand."

Kyle moves closer to the screen, seeing a shot of the woman: dark haired with a barrette, her face a little chubby. She's wearing glasses and maroon-colored lipstick. She's maybe about thirty. When he found the hand, he didn't picture whom it might belong to. It was manicured and purple. The wrist was wrapped in foil. He looked at the palm and fingers. They seemed so soft and tender, like he remembers his mother's being. She left when he was twelve, and he wonders where she is now. The hand was wet, like it wasn't dead yet. He pictures the hand, now maybe next to the peanut butter in his fridge, how he left it there in haste, thinking he'd tend to it later.

The sportscaster comes back on the screen and talks about the recent Bills game. Kyle sits. He feels like a kid again, his father telling him he's sinful.

Then when the phlebotomist calls out, "Kyle Krupp," he follows her. He sits in the chair and sees a sign that reads BIOHAZARD. He remembers being on her end of the needle, the routine of gloving, uncapping, sticking, watching the gush of blood rushing into the tubing.

He studies the lab order, his last name, "Krupp," spelled with one *p* instead of two. He says, "My last name is spelled wrong."

She says, "I'll have to fix it." She slams her hand down on the printer. Her lipstick looks black, and her nails are long and polished.

He remembers patient-sensitivity sessions he used to have to attend. They were required by law.

He says to her, "Have you been to the training?"

She turns to him, says, "What?"

He says, "Patient sensitivity. Have you not been trained?"
He smells an odor and sees the obese woman going down the
hallway.

The phlebotomist says, "I'll be back." She gets up and leaves, so Kyle
sits and waits. He remembers chairs like this, back when he was a
med tech, sitting down and discussing things like breaking up with
his one and only girlfriend. She was a med tech too until she said she
was moving on, maybe to save lost dogs or plant marigolds, maybe
to hang out with bikers.

He thinks of the woman in the news, the hand. He thinks about
the dead girl.

Now he hears the phlebotomist from across the hall. "Girl," she
says, "that fat girl smells like sausage!"

"Girl," says someone else, "you always get the stink ones."

Then another woman appears in the hallway sprinting backward.
She stops, looking at Kyle. "Hey!" she yells down the hall to the other
workers.

"You guys," she yells again. "We have a patient."

Kyle hears somebody say, "He was a pain right when he got here."

The woman from the hall looks at him again. She says, "I'm really sorry."

On the way home, Kyle notices the *check engine* light on his Toyota,
and hopes it doesn't need anything expensive. He can get by with his
savings and from what he makes on bottles. He likes to compare
prices.

He stops at a red light, seeing a driver in the next car who looks like
the phlebotomist. His windows are open. He wonders if he took his
medication. He tries to see her hands on the wheel—they look a little
plain. He looks at his own hands. Big and bony. Wrinkled.

He thinks about the hand belonging to the dead girl. He feels his
stomach churn. He remembers finding the hand. So manicured and
soft. It didn't seem real.

He recalls that girlfriend from long ago, how she went to get her
nails done. He thinks of his mother's hands, the last time that he
saw them.

*

Kim Chinquee

At the apartment, Kyle remembers the barrette he saw in the picture of the dead girl. Blue and gold, a butterfly, like one he saw holding back his mother's bangs the night she left. There's another shot he remembers of his mother looking happy, by the way she holds her head back, her teeth and lips aglow. At the beach, the wind sweeping.

At home he sits on his sofa, hearing his dog whine.

The woman was last seen at the Pancake House on Hertel. Kyle pictures a woman with big rings, high heels, and good clothes in a mansion.

He wants wine. He goes to the fridge, where he sees her right hand where he left it. He picks it up and smells it. It reminds him of merlot. The skin is rubbery. He touches the foil on the end, and he imagines a big tree. He remembers a branch from his grandfather's oak that smashed onto his father's windshield in the middle of a snowstorm. "It's OK," he says. He decides to make some eggs. He turns on the stove and pours himself some wine. He picks up the hand. He cradles it and rocks.

He wakes to the smell of smoke. He sees firemen and police who have sticks and cuffs and handguns. He sees the hand on his lap, and the empty wineglass by the rocker. A black man stands in front of him and he says, "Busted."

The man takes the hand. Kyle's dog looks up at him. He got a dog bite as a kid, something he hasn't thought of in a while, as if it's all a dream or maybe never happened. He remembers the dog's sharp teeth, its black eyes, then being in the hospital with a wrist full of stitches.

"You almost burned the place down," says another cop with a uniform too small for his gigantic muscles.

Kyle remembers the night before, turning on the burner to make eggs, swallowing the Xanax his doctor said to take when he felt anxious. He reaches in his pocket, running his thumb over the edges of his grandpa's key.

The hand, it felt so cold, the skin almost like his mother's. He wanted to do right. He says, "But it's my hand."

He rides away in the backseat of the cop car. His own hands are in cuffs. He looks up at the rearview. He sees the cop's white eyes.

Kyle says, "I didn't kill her."

He thinks he hears a laugh.

"I'm innocent," he says. "I'm sure of it. I know."

The Removes
Brandon Krieg

Lost you where poppies climbed from fields
between houses, where screens on the back of bus seats
showed the living in the now of an obsolescent ship, where a mandala
and a bar code shared the last wall before the sun set

between houses,   screens
  flashing already like disconnected signal fires:
                the last wall before
your askance was overwritten

by flashing   disconnected

                  *

Terraces of semblance

then: roofs like a ruined organ,
sky a wide sustain.

Terraces of
summer, dials

turned to alpenlight.
       A wide sustain

       dials
even us.

Turned to alpenlight:
that   you

fathoms and pervades as

                                        day.
Then
fathoms
                    opens

                              *

I, alone, across
the shadow of a fountain falling back curved,
a moment returning vaster
than itself.

            Shadows of   curved
time, the blue in a sepia eye,
                    the impossibility
we   met   before

time—the blue in
an arch's sky-through our sign
we have   before
in secret. In truth, anything—

an arch's sky-through—
is only solitude too diminished to lie
in secret in. Truth, anything
I could call you

is   diminished. To lie
a moment   vaster
I call
            alone *across*.

                              *

A worn-down sandstone cliff on the coast,
the path to it crumbled to nothing,
could it have been you and I
there once if there is no trace of it left?

The path
into the applause I thought I heard far off,
       there is no trace of it.
Waves whip the accident cubism of the cliffs

into   applause
of oblivion from every angle at once.
          The accident   of
our incidence:

       from every angle
the vanishing point passes through the glance.
Our incidence here, spreading ourselves to the sky:
echo-image without a source.

                        *

If it could be as never
before, then you. No,
if it could be as always more
piercingly, then through

         you no
word would intervene.
If it could be as always
but with cloudshadow on the dial and no

word
for it in me, then you, and magnified.
But with   no
lake seen through to a sacred wrecked

      in me,   magnified
is only a mountain assuming its reflection in a

lake seen
as the picture of itself.

Only a mountain
piercing   through
the picture of itself
  could be as you.

*

I say you and no one knows what it means.
In the moraine's shadow, I might trace
the vein in your groin as sun touches a stream.

When your hair. When your cusps.
But it is afterward already.

The you of you eludes
even the particular futility of my joy.

I have pebbled an altar to all
aches, and cattails point.
A thousand perhaps directions.

Walls, a wedged bridge, horses browse,
all contingencies parallel except
the vein in your groin as sun touches a stream.

Aches and cattails point.
I have pebbled an altar to all
the you of you eludes—

bald cairn, poor form. Waves anonymize
even the particular futility of my joy.

When your hair. When your cusps.

A thousand perhaps directions
in the moraine's shadow, I might trace,

absolved to tributary.

But it is afterward already.

*

We looked down
on the river from a high window:
nothing else was there in the canyon
where   the sun was always about to set.

On the river
we could see the jade-colored pebbles
wherever the sun was
as if there were no water at all.

We could see
no reflection or shadow of ourselves—
as if there were no water at all—
though the sound was unmistakable:

no reflection or shadow of ourselves,
an alien resonance, yet
                        unmistakable
as that you and I were there—

a   resonance
I had not known I had always known, like
   that you   I
saw then as myself. I knelt then in the grief

I had not known I had always known.
Nothing else was there in the canyon.

Organisms
Julia Elliott

WHEN BALMY SUMMER DAYS tilted toward unpleasant, and backyards transformed into jungles where supermosquitoes patrolled lush weeds, Jenny Hawkes liked to walk outside and stand in a margin of shade, listening to the collective hum of her neighborhood's HVAC units. She'd pretend that the Rapture had snatched all the idiots into outer space. She'd smoke a secret cigarette, a vice she hid even from her husband, and then hurry back into the air-conditioning.

She worked as a guide for Sibyl, the online information company, answering the random questions of desperate people who were loath to do the research themselves. This morning there had been inquiries about Asian tiger mosquitoes, flood insurance, weight-loss nanobots, and Indian surrogates. Jenny already had websites with good answers, so she punched them in quickly. And then, for the twentieth time that day, she checked the web for US fatalities in Afghanistan.

It was one thirty and her son had not emerged from the den for lunch. Lately, as he spent more time before their wide-screen media monitor, he filled the den with his signature scent—the coppery tinge of stress pheromones in his sweat. Jenny did not like to step into this *atmosphere*, the musky, turbulent ambiance that enveloped his gangly body. Obscure glands pumped inside him. Hormones spiked his blood, ripened his genitals, covered secret places with hair, and fed the zits that festered on his sullen face.

Adam was busy killing off brain cells with a video game, she figured, hunched before Zombie Babe Attack or some other disturbing concept dreamed up by marketing teams who dabbled in adolescent psychology and flirted with the darker urges. As much as she wanted to, Jenny didn't step down into the *atmosphere* and ask him if he wanted a sandwich. She went back to her office and dove into the sea of questions, braving the currents of the nation's fears. Activity on sibyl.com tended to surge after disappointing lunches left people listless at work. With the afternoon stretched out before them, they compulsively typed questions into the crystal ball featured on the site's main page.

They could no longer concentrate for extended periods of time. Their hair was falling out. Their homes suffered infestations of bedbugs, fleas, roaches, and ants. On the brink of financial disaster, they received threatening letters from creditors. They maxed out their credit cards, defaulted on their mortgages. Their homes were swept away by tornadoes, devoured by fires, flooded by hurricanes. They hid incurable toenail funguses within their fashionable shoes. They injected their sagging flesh with botulinum toxin A. Cysts and tumors bloomed in the humid darkness of their wombs and testicles, in their brain and breast tissue, in their livers, gallbladders, bowels, and lungs. Their teeth were yellow. Their garbage disposals smelled of death.

They had fat sucked out of their thighs and buttocks. They tracked their cheating lovers with spy software and burned off crow's-feet with laser beams. They were diabetic. They were ashamed of their old tattoos. They felt strange heart palpitations and were addicted to Internet porn. Their children suffered from autism and ADHD. Their lawns were turning brown. Fears of global warming and terrorist attacks and the collapse of the international economy kept them up at night. They thought that perhaps it was time to join a church, get some therapy, call a psychic, or visit a spa on the other side of the world where the ocean was the blue of an Aleve gelcap and the dollar was still worth something.

By three thirty Jenny could no longer take it, so she slipped out for another smoke. She pictured her husband patrolling the desert in a tank. But she knew he was in an office building, staring at a computer screen, and that the sensitivity of his deployment did not allow him to send e-mails. On the way back to her office, she took a deep breath and knocked on the door of the den. No answer. Her son must have slumped upstairs to his room. But no: He was still there, hunched on the floor, a few inches from the 3-D HDTV. The knobs of his backbone protruded as though he were about to sprout iguana spines. She detected an unfamiliar smell akin to aerosol hair spray. Inhalant abuse was a hot topic on sibyl.com, and she wondered if he was huffing.

"Adam," she said, feeling a chill when he refused to offer a grunt in response. The solar shades were drawn. She walked deeper into the *atmosphere*, into the light of the screen where the carpet was scattered with crushed Coke cans.

"You ought to eat something besides junk for lunch."

She had directed searchers to countless websites on how to get teens to talk, and there she was, at a loss. He was playing Zombie Babe Attack, a misogynist blood fest in which zombified *Playboy*

307

Julia Elliott

bunnies chased a male hero through a postapocalyptic city. His avatar slaughtered big-boobed zombies with a Browning machine gun mounted atop a convertible Corvette. The zombie babes wore thongs and heels. They had long, blonde hair. They exploded with cartoonish bursts of hot-pink gore.

"Adam," she said, "you're sitting too close to the television."

Lizard Man, a cinder-block dive near the railroad tracks, was named after the fabled local monster, an anthropomorphic reptile said to haunt swamps and sewers. The mural behind the bar featured a lizard in a top hat, nothing like the sludge-coated creature that more than a few citizens swore they'd seen lurking in the depths of their backyards or popping up from manholes on moon-white nights. The watering hole, with its oozing toilets and foggy fish tank, smelled like the kind of place reptilian and amphibious creatures might inhabit. Toad-shaped men and women slumped at the bar. And the bartender, covered in a spotted hide that had never known sunscreen, seemed to possess a skink gene or two.

The spray-painted windows blocked all light. It was an odd sensation to step from sun-roasted asphalt into Lizard Man's smoky darkness. Some people, entering the place in the daytime, were startled to see stars overhead upon stumbling out. Others arrived during the velvet of a summer dusk only to be blasted by the roaring furnace of the sun when they finally pulled themselves up from their stools and departed. On certain drunken nights, when the building seemed to pitch like a ship, time played tricks on customers like Miles Escrow, who swore he'd once surfaced from the strangely compressed air of the place to discover that three days had passed. But that didn't stop him from returning to Lizard Man whenever he'd had enough of Tina Flame, his common-law wife. Sitting with his back to the wall, his large ears twitched like a bat's as he strained to catch the latest.

Tonight, folks were abuzz about a recently busted meth lab, from which a former pecan queen had fled, looking like a hag after entering the place as a dewy beauty of twenty-six. And word had it that the mayor was tangled up in a prostitution racket involving Slovakian thugs and a tanning chain. A graduate of Fox Creek High would appear on *American Idol*. A Presbyterian preacher had pushed his wife into an industrial feed grinder. And in a stagnant inlet of Lake Wateree, a teen had been killed by a brain-eating amoeba.

The patrons at Lizard Man were in disagreement about what,

exactly, an amoeba was. Tammy Hutto said she assumed it was a teeny fish, so small that it could swim up your nose and wriggle through your sinuses into your brain, whereupon it'd wind through the maze of your gray matter like a Pac-Man munching dots. Titus Redmond disagreed, opining that an amoeba was a plant, an algae-like organism that spread via spores. Roddy Causey had the feeling an amoeba was a mass of little creatures, a swarm, though he had no idea what they looked like. At last, Stein cleared his throat. Though Stein seemed to know everything (his name was both an abbreviation of Einstein and a nod toward the pewter tankard from which he swilled), he liked to hold off, allowing the regulars to explore a subject before he descended from his Olympian mountain of omniscience to enlighten the ignorant drunkards below. He had two master's degrees and lived in a rusted Volkswagen bus.

"An amoeba is a one-celled organism," he pronounced. "A protozoan, to be exact."

Like many of Stein's clarifications, this didn't do much to inform the revelers as to what an amoeba looked like or how it behaved. So, after having his tankard refilled with Heineken, Stein sketched a picture of an amoeba on his napkin and passed it around the bar.

"It's just a blob," said Brandy Wellington. "I don't see how that could eat anybody's brain."

"The brain-eating type has a little sucker that eats your cells," said Stein. "And then you come down with a fatal case of meningoencephalitis."

"I told my son not to go swimming this summer," said Wanda Bonnet.

"He just needs to stay away from stagnant water," said Tubs Watson.

This brought them around to a discussion of teens and their follies, an inexhaustible subject for those assembled since most of them were either middle-aged parents or grandparents, and thus had first-hand experience with the strange pupal state of the human life cycle, whereupon the organism transformed, almost overnight, from a sweet, well-behaved kid into a self-destructive, narcissistic goon, either monosyllabic or back-talking, a lurching zombie who ate up every morsel in the house and scattered filthy clothing all over the floor.

Marty Bouknight said his son was a video-game junkie. Kim Dewlap said her daughter was a Twitter demon. Most everyone nodded in empathy, having lost a child to the cyber world at some recent point in time. Old Man Winger shook his head. He was an

Julia Elliott

ancient biker whose denim jacket had grown into his epidermis and whose tattoos had faded to ghostly shadows that looked like bruises on his withered arms. He had a very sad story to tell about his cousin's granddaughter Kayla. She was so into Facebook and Twitter and E-Live that she couldn't brush her teeth without tweeting. And just last week, her mother had found her in the living room, pressing her face against their plasma monitor as though trying to break through to the other side. The room was littered with so much junk-food packaging that the poor child was practically buried in cellophane. And then she fell into a coma.

"She ain't totally out but not exactly there either," said Winger.

"What you think caused it?" asked Wanda Bonnet.

"They don't know. They're testing for organ failure caused by her junk-food diet."

Every parent of a teen child felt sick, but then relieved that this misfortune had happened to someone else. A few drunken mothers clutched their bosoms. But when Carla Marlin started bragging about her new swimming pool, the conversation shifted toward brighter subjects—like water skiing, catfish noodling, and time-share condos going cheap at Surf City.

Beth Irving was a vegetarian, partially for health reasons, but mostly because her line of work made her hyperaware of the intricate lifestyles of infectious organisms. She couldn't look at a piece of meat without imagining it swarming with bacteria and one-celled organisms, crawling with trichinosis roundworms or tapeworm larvae. Once again, she'd found herself in a godforsaken town with a malarial climate and no health-food store, where the only decent place to eat was a strip-mall Thai joint that put too much sugar in its curry tofu. The Centers for Disease Control and Prevention had stumbled upon another cluster of *Toxoplasma hermeticus* cases. And though Beth was thrilled to be on the research vanguard of what was quickly becoming recognized as one of the weirdest behavior-modifying protozoan organisms to emerge since *Toxoplasma gondii*, she always got depressed in these backwater towns with dead Main Streets and flood zones packed with double-wides.

Because Beth had grown up in a dying town in South Georgia, she always felt an uncanny sensation when cruising empty downtown streets or walking from pounding summer heat into the deep chill of a Piggly Wiggly. She feared she was getting sucked back into the haunted swamplands of Clinch County, Georgia, locale of her birth. She saw a giant Venus flytrap swelling up from boggy land, opening its green jaws, and swallowing her. And now, with a few hours to kill before meeting the ID specialist at Palmetto Baptist, she had no choice but to return to her room at Days Inn, where she succumbed to the narcotic allure of the television. Flipping through channels, she felt a panicky wash of pleasure as the borders of her identity began to dissolve.

She remembered a film from Biology 629, a time-lapse sequence of a fox carcass devoured by necrophagous insects. The mammal shrank and then expanded with a moist infestation of writhing maggots, which soon transformed into bluebottle flies that darted off to feed on wildflower nectar. Embracing the flux of disassociation might yield some exquisite Zen transcendence, she thought. Out of context, she felt her self diffusing. Her townhouse and boyfriend and collection of Scandinavian glass, her PhD and lucrative job with the CDC, her whole-foods organic vegetarian diet and Ashtanga yoga regime—all of it relegated to the realm of the theoretical, especially the boyfriend, who was eight years her junior, and whom she envisioned, with a shiver of arousal, making love to some faceless female with wavering limbs.

Of course, wholeness and bodily integrity were illusions. The body was a conceptually organized system of potentially chaotic processes and minute, volatile ecosystems. Beth thought of *Cymothoa exigua*, the enterprising sea louse that ate the tongue of its fish host and then masqueraded as that tongue, slurping up a portion of the spotted rose snapper's food while the oblivious fish went on with its business. The elegance of this poetic adaptation took her breath away. And then there were more obscure parasites, micromanagers of evolution that changed the surface of biological "reality" with their incessant, ingenious niche marketing.

Caught up in intricate mechanisms, they hopped from one organism to another at different stages of their life cycles, migrating from intestines to lungs, hearts, or brains, sometimes reprogramming the behavior of their hosts. Such was the case with *T. gondii*, cousin of *T. hermeticus*, which made rodents act irrationally, drawing them toward the smell of cat urine, compelling them to flirt with disaster until they were devoured by felines who caught the bug and spread it through their droppings.

Though *T. gondii* had evolved in a cat/rat system, it also infected humans, who, as emerging research suggested, could undergo personality changes—becoming more neurotic, more obsessive, and even stranger, enacting more traditional gender roles. Suffering slower reaction times, they became more accident-prone. They had trouble concentrating. Some infected males demonstrated a disregard for convention and indulged in risky behaviors. Scientists were even linking the bug to schizophrenia. Unlike the rat, the human host served no discernible purpose for the enterprising protozoan (unless he or she was devoured by a large cat). As far as researchers knew, *Homo sapiens* was an evolutionary dead end for *T. gondii*, which infected about 16.8 percent of the American population.

But *T. hermeticus* was a different animal, a mutant variation of the *T. gondii* species. So far, only a dozen teenaged humans throughout the US had tested positive in serologic tests for *T. hermeticus* antibodies. And though they seemed to be infected by the protozoan the usual ways (ingesting undercooked meat, contaminated soil, or cat dung), their responses to the infection were beginning to form a distinct pattern. Over the past two months, Beth had personally investigated ten cases in hot, humid regions of the United States, all of them ending in hospitalizations due to toxic-metabolic encephalopathic coma. It was not clear whether this was the normal upshot of *T. hermeticus* infection, or whether these extreme cases were the only ones that had been medically documented.

Each patient, between the ages of twelve and fourteen, was in the early stages of puberty. Sixty percent of them kept pet cats. According to family members, their comatose states had been preceded by an increasing obsession with video games, Internet pornography, or social-networking sites—screen-addicted behaviors not uncommon among their demographic. This was accompanied by social withdrawal and changing feeding habits, an increasing distaste for sunlight and fresh foods, and a voracious appetite for junk food high in chemical additives—"chips, candies, and other knickknacks," as one distressed mother had put it.

The parents of infected patients had been difficult for Beth to deal with, hailing, as they mostly did, from small southern towns and reminding her of her own parents with their bad diets, paranoid religious ideations, and right-wing political affiliations. In an hour she would talk to the ID specialist. Over coffee in the hospital cafeteria, they would discuss strategies for persuading parents to let them conduct MRI scans that, while helping them understand more about the organism, would not necessarily lead to any breakthrough treatments. What Beth really needed was not a cartoon brain pulsing on a computer screen, its amygdalae lit up with fluorescent red cysts. She itched to perform craniotomy biopsies, to suck tissue from the cysts, and observe the mysterious bradyzoites under an atomic-force microscope. When a Geico commercial came on, the one with the talking lizard, she shuddered, for she'd hated lizards ever since she'd stepped on one as a child. Feeling the crunch of its frail skeleton under her bare foot, she'd screamed as though burned. Now she punched the remote until she landed on the Weather Channel. She lay in bed for another minute, watching a Doppler-radar image of Hurricane Anastasia sweep toward the Gulf Coast.

Jenny stared out at a green wall of rain. The only place to smoke was the carport, and she felt exposed before the double-pane eyes of neighboring ranch homes. No health-conscious middle-aged woman would, in her right mind, smoke cancer sticks. But her husband was 7,337 miles away, and there she was, sucking another one down as Anastasia's rain shields enveloped South Carolina in a sultry monsoon. As hurricane season geared up, there was a sense of foreboding on the Internet. Many sibyl.com seekers had inquired about global warming, wondering if *Homo sapiens'* unchecked ecological plundering was finally building up to a karmic bite in the ass. In the hinterlands of the Internet, on poorly designed websites with flashy fonts and bad grammar, the more hysterical demographics chattered about the Rapture, the reptilian elite, the return of space visitors who'd originally colonized planet Earth and planted the seed of consciousness in its indigenous hominids.

Unable to sleep the previous night and clocking in on Sibyl to earn a few extra bucks, Jenny noticed, as she always did when working the wee hours, a delirious urgency in the questioning:

Do Rh-negative people have reptile blood or do they descend from the Nephilim?

I have twelve fibroids in my uterus and wander can I get pregnant?

My boy got an Aztec sun god tattoo is he mixed up with the Mexican Mafia?

So when she encountered her first question about *T. hermeticus,* she assumed it was another phantom from the shadowlands of insomnia.

A girl I know said there was a bug that can get in your head and make you hooked to your computer screen. What is this thing?

Google searches yielded low-budget sci-fi movies and clusters of conspiracy sites, but then, nestled within the wing-nut comment boards and glib blogs of camp-cinema enthusiasts, was a PDF file on the Stanley Medical Research Institute site, an article describing the species variation and its relevance to *T. gondii* schizophrenia research. At the time of publication, only two cases of toxoplasmosis via *T. hermeticus* had been documented, but the behavior of the two hospitalized teen hosts was similar: withdrawal from physical reality, computer and television screen addiction, the unbridled consumption of junk food. And both teens had suffered comas resulting from toxic-metabolic encephalopathy.

Jenny's stomach lurched. Her heart beat faster. She did not run to the den where her son had camped with a pile of Xbox discs he'd swapped with friends. She walked purposefully and slowly, like a killer in a horror film, into the kitchen and down the steps. This time she didn't knock. She pushed the door open and stepped into the *atmosphere*. But her son was not there.

A screenshot from his paused video game showed his Dose avatar frozen in midfrenzy, clutching a pill bottle and spilling capsules as he struggled to get the right drug into his system. The game was sinister and funny at once. The main character, suffering from a variety of behavioral, psychological, and physical issues, was constantly in danger of malfunctioning. He had to be kept on track with the right pharmaceuticals. The player could consult the electronic pharmacopoeia built into the game, but of course the character quickly melted down, sank into unconsciousness, or became otherwise unstable, so a good working knowledge of contemporary medical drugs was required to play the game well. In this particular shot the character had become very thin, with bulging eyes and a comic goiter.

"Adam," Jenny called, thinking he might be in the half bath. No answer, but at least he wasn't huddled close to the media screen. She did notice an obscene amount of discarded junk-food packaging littering the floor: chip bags and plastic cookie trays, flattened cartons and half-crushed cans. Walking deeper into the *atmosphere*, she felt heart palpitations and a shortening of breath. She picked up a Doritos bag and read the ingredients: MSG, at least three artificial colors, and a lengthy list of unwholesome compounds like disodium inosinate.

"What are you doing?" The voice was mocking, croaky from its recent change.

Her son stood just inside the open sliding-glass door, the insulated drapery jerked open, rain falling in the blurred green depths of the backyard. She wondered if he'd been out there smoking something, huffing something, popping some newfangled multiple-use product of the medical-industrial complex.

"Shut the door," she said. "The air conditioner's on."

As he lurched toward her, she worried about his posture (was he developing curvature of the spine?), his teeth (would failure to provide braces lead to social ostracism and poor employment opportunities?), his sexuality (would he catch an STD?), and, of course, his attention span (when was the last time he read a book?). The Internet was crawling with sexual predators. Teens were gobbling salvia, guzzling Robitussin, snorting Adderall. A gonorrhea superbug was developing resistance to antibiotics.

"You need to pick up after yourself," she said.

A fresh crop of pustules had erupted on his nose, which had recently grown too big for his face, though he still had the elfin features of boyhood. She could almost see him wrapping his arms around her legs. Could picture him riding on his father's shoulders. He was too big for these things now, of course. His greasy hair was brushed absurdly forward, almost obscuring his eyes, which looked unnaturally wet.

"Right," he said. She couldn't tell if the word seethed with sarcasm or if it was a simple acknowledgment of the truth of her statement.

"You need to eat a decent lunch. Fruits and vegetables. Whole-grain bread."

He rolled his eyes and grinned like a gargoyle. Yes, she thought, he had to have braces, which would cost at least $5,000.

"What did you have for breakfast?" she said.

"What is this Guantanamo Bay shit?"

She felt somewhat relieved. He was still capable of creating analogies.

"Watch the language and answer me."

"Pop-Tarts and orange juice." He dropped to the floor, rolled onto his belly, and took up his deluxe controller.

Good. Orange juice. She bought the USDA organic calcium plus vitamin D stuff from Publix. It contained no preservatives, colorants, or corn syrup. Adam had had some just that morning, which meant that he had not developed intolerance to fruits and vegetables. And he was lolling at least three feet from the media screen, so he was probably safe—for now.

*

Miles Escrow could never tell if the world was turning to shit or if the patrons of Lizard Man tended to natter on about the darker elements of life. Now they were discussing accidents on Lake Wateree: jet-ski collisions and capsizing pontoons, drownings and disastrously executed water-ski stunts, exploding gas grills and feral campfires and murderous clouds of wasps. A renegade fishhook had gotten stuck in Wanda Bonnet's uncle's cheek and ripped a big gash. Marty Bouknight's cousin, pulling a hydrilla clump from the blades of his outboard motor, had lost three fingers. Kim Dewlap's preacher's stepbrother had snorkeled into a nest of water moccasins. And then there were the brain-eating amoebas, floating in stagnant water, waiting to be sucked up into the nasal passages of hapless swimmers. But that was old news. There was still just the one local case—the teen who'd died last month.

Miles Escrow had come up with three possible explanations for the shit ton of recent lake-connected disasters: (1) The patrons were exaggerating; (2) Get any group together and they could generate an impressive list of mishaps associated with any particular place; and (3) The flooded reservoir that was Lake Wateree had once been the home of an ancient Indian burial ground, and hence was cursed. Miles Escrow preferred the drama of option 3. After drinking another Miller, he shared his proposition with the company.

"I think I saw a movie about that," said Tammy Hutto. "There was a creature in the lake, an angry spirit or whatnot."

"Every body of water has its cryptid," said Stein.

"What the hell's that?" said Carla.

"An imaginary creature that lives there, like the Lizard Man of Scape Ore Swamp."

"My uncle saw the Lizard Man rooting through his garbage," said Brandy Wellington.

Hereupon commenced a conversation that Miles Escrow had heard a thousand times in this particular bar. Everybody knew at least one person who had seen the Lizard Man, but not one of the patrons, it seemed, had spotted a glimmer of the fabled creature with his or her own naked eyes. It had been raining for a week and Miles had been arguing with Tina Flame, the same arguments they'd been slogging through for ten years: spats about his drinking, tiffs about her Internet shopping, and, even though they were almost forty, rows about whether or not they ought to have children. Fed by the weather, the arguments grew lush and green. Before they knew it, a thousand insults bloomed. Miles had had to get out of the house for a few hours. Tonight, however, Lizard Man was boring him.

But then the crowd turned to the topic of Winger's cousin's grandchild Kayla, who was still out cold at Palmetto Baptist. Carla Marlin said she lived beside a phlebotomist who worked at the hospital, and she had some top-secret information she really ought not to share. Looking solemn, she made everybody promise they'd keep this material hush-hush. And then, after ordering another daiquiri, rooting through her faux-snakeskin purse, and retrieving her Droid to check a text message, Carla cleared her throat and revealed that three teens were now laid up in comas at Palmetto Baptist. Not only that, but each patient had demonstrated the same peculiar symptoms as Winger's cousin's grandchild. Before losing consciousness, their obsessions with digital media had gotten way out of hand. They'd also eaten so much junk food that one of the first hypotheses as to the cause of their illness was food poisoning. But the doctors ruled that out, along with electric shock via media gadget.

"What do they think it is then?" asked Titus Redmond.

"My neighbor wouldn't say, but, judging by the look in his eye, it ain't pretty."

Although Beth had been communicating for months with big shots on the cutting edge of *T. gondii* research—mostly male evolutionary biologists, parasitologists, and neurobiologists—the word was just getting out on *T. hermeticus*, and she feared she'd be muscled out of the game. As she awaited the arrival of a certain eminent neurovirologist from Johns Hopkins, she demonstrated behaviors that psychologists had placed on the lower end of the obsessive-compulsive disorder spectrum: nail biting, cuticle picking, napkin tearing. In the air-conditioned depths of Pink Lotus, she sipped iced water and studied her laptop screen. An MRI scan of an infected teen brain glowed before her. The fluorescent red cysts conglomerated mostly in the pleasure and fear centers. Just like schizophrenics suffering from *T. gondii* toxoplasmosis, infected patients were producing elevated levels of dopamine.

And Beth had a theory that made her heart race. Like *T. gondii*, the *hermeticus* species had genes that allowed it not only to jack up dopamine production, but also to create optimal conditions that depended on an intricate blend of its host's onset-puberty hormones, specific chemical food additives in the blood, and the heady neurochemical combinations produced by video-game play, intense social

317

networking, and Internet porn use. She didn't know if the particular brain cocktail improved conditions for the dormant bradyzoites, or if the tweaked behavior of the teens was a form of parasite-induced "mind control" recently perfected to land the protozoan's intended rodent host in the jaws of a cat.

Once again, she navigated the twists and turns of her theory, puzzling out the evolutionary logic of the adaptation, but became flustered when she noticed Dr. Bloom hovering over her with a bemused expression on his acne-scarred face. He was somewhat handsome, early forties, with a skin condition that had probably pushed him into nerdy seclusion as an adolescent, forming the foundation of his brilliant career in the hard sciences. His eyes were almost obscenely beautiful. She could see him as a teen, green orbs glowing upon his zit-corroded face as though miraculously escaping infection.

"Dr. Irving, I presume." He lifted a sparse eyebrow.

Beth knew that she looked young for her age. Torn between revealing her true age to enhance her authority and concealing it to enhance her sexual attraction, she chose the latter.

"Dr. Bloom. Sorry we're having supper in a strip mall, but this is the best I could do in this savage land."

"Supper," he said. "You must be southern."

"I grew up in Argyle, Georgia."

"So you immersed yourself in academia to escape a life of drudgery at the sock factory there?"

Beth tittered. Dr. Bloom sat down. They ordered Singha beers.

As a joke they continued to call each other by their professional titles, even when swept into a passionate discussion about parasitic mind control. Dr. Bloom asked her if she had tested her male patients' responses to cat urine, and she tactfully reminded him that the infected teens were in comatose states, surrounded by bereaved relatives. Drawing a lock of hair to her mouth and taking a compulsive nibble, she asked him if it was true that males infected with *T. gondii* had higher testosterone levels and were hence more attractive to women.

"What do *you* think?" He flexed his right bicep and smirked.

"What?" Beth smiled. "Did you test positive?"

"Actually," he said, "I don't know; I've never been tested. Have you?"

"No. Maybe I should be."

She examined his clothing: a plaid shirt, rumpled, but not demonstrating a lack of concern with personal grooming. His gray-streaked hair was tousled but clean. Beth blushed and changed the subject to another organism.

"I heard you did a postdoc with *Polysphincta gutfreundi.*"

Gesticulating expressively, opening his mouth to reveal half-masticated meat, Dr. Bloom held forth on the parasitic wasp larva that, after hatching in the body of the orb spider, released chemicals that made its host weave a custom cocoon for it. The spider essentially became a zombie that did the worm's bidding.

Lit from within by his third beer and his zeal for parasitic organisms, Dr. Bloom began to look strangely attractive. She remembered an article she'd read about the flu virus, which argued that infected humans became more social than usual, optimizing the virus's chance of spreading. She thought of her boyfriend, a beautiful, frivolous creature, knowing that she'd allow their relationship to grow like an extravagant mushroom that would, one hot summer day, suddenly lapse into slime.

Whenever Jenny found herself in front of her computer screen, she could not stop searching for more information on *T. hermeticus,* which flared occasionally in the outer reaches of cyberspace like gamma-ray bursts. Her talent for obscure searches had led to the discovery that at least two dozen teens had been infected nationally, six of whom were now in comatose states at Palmetto Baptist. She'd ferreted out this last bit on a local church prayer board:

Please pray for Sheila Freeman's son who is in a coma and the other five teens who struggle in darkness with him. In Jesus name.

Although the poster did not mention *T. hermeticus* or even verify the hospital, Jenny felt sure that the prayer giver was referring to the new freak parasite. The local infection had also made an appearance on her son's Facebook stream. That morning, he'd left his iPhone on the kitchen table, and though she felt guilty examining his page, she rationalized that her snooping was for his own good. A girl named Kaitlin Moore had posted the following status update two days ago at 1:36 a.m.:

Please send good vibes to my cousin Ashley who is in a coma at the hospital her mom found her passed out in front of the TV. So weird.

In the ninety-two comments that followed, condolences and positive energy flows abounded, but halfway through, rumors and speculation took over. Jenny learned of three similar cases (friends of friends of posters), in which the hapless hosts had fallen into unconscious-ness after especially intense gaming bouts, Twitter marathons, or Internet porn odysseys. When a boy named Brandon Booth opined that the sufferers were victims of a virus originating from alien life forms, several teens pounced on him, telling him to "get a grasp dork" because this was "not a sci-fi flick but the real fucking world."

Brandon was not the only one who suspected alien shenanigans. Out in cyber la-la land, wild theories flourished. People with user-names like Phoenix66, upon hearing about the parasite, conjectured that the original space colonists had returned to Earth to help hu-mans evolve to the next level. Later that day, Jenny stumbled upon an antigovernment site attesting that *T. hermeticus* had been de-signed by the US military in conjunction with Middle Eastern elites to terrorize the US population into docile sheep. Though she chuck-led to herself at these paranoid assertions, she often emerged from her web-surfing stupor with a sense of wonder. "What if?" she'd think as she enjoyed a cigarette, staring out at the riotous jungle that was overtaking their backyard. But the mystique would fade in the fluorescent light of the kitchen as she opened a can of tuna.

Although she didn't believe that the parasite had been bioengi-neered by aliens or the US government or al-Qaeda, she was, of course, terrified that it would infect her son. Though she'd sat him down in the matter-of-fact brightness of the kitchen and asked him if he'd heard about the comatose teens (he'd scanned Kaitlin Moore's Facebook status), though she'd explained the presumed causes of *T. hermeticus* transmission, though she had gone over the symptoms and warned him about the correlation between excessive screen time and junk-food consumption and full-blown toxoplasmosis, she still felt the relentless throb of fear behind her breastbone every sec-ond of every waking hour. And her husband was out in the desert doing God knows what. She envisioned him standing on a pink dune, staring into a hazy void specked with an occasional camel. Did they even have camels in Afghanistan? She couldn't remember. She would Google it when she settled back into her swivel chair.

"If I understand you," said Adam, "then the screen time and junk food are not *causes* of the coma but *symptoms* of the disease." Was he looking at her with pity as though she had lost it?

"I'm not sure." She forced her mouth into a smile that she hoped radiated adult wisdom. "But I think that's about right."

"So it doesn't really matter what I do." He grinned and slunk to-ward the dark den.

320

That night Jenny woke up sweating, shaking off a nightmare in which her husband had transformed into some kind of desert-scorpion cyborg, and her son, after falling into a coma, had pupated into a winged creature that moved so fast she couldn't catch a glimpse of his face.

Miles Escrow had the eerie feeling that he'd experienced it all before: the whine of the jukebox, water stains on the ceiling, Wanda Bonnet blowing her nose into a sodden tissue after another weeping bout. She was the only mother of an infected teen who'd shown up at Lizard Man that night. Ten minutes and two shots of vodka later, she was gone, driving through rain back to the hospital. She'd come, he figured, thinking her old haunt might soothe her, but she must've felt alienated after all, judging by the startled-doe look on her face.

Those patrons whose kids weren't infected were probably at home, domestic surveillance in overdrive. DHEC had finally issued a statement verifying the number of infected teens in the state (forty-two), explaining the life cycle of *T. hermeticus*, and urging people not to panic as medical authorities were doing all they could to understand the bug, including setting up testing facilities that would soon be available to the general population. Although the sick kids were comatose, their comas were relatively high on the Glasgow scale, and there was no reason to believe they wouldn't snap out of it soon.

Tonight it was just Miles, Stein, Old Man Winger, and of course Rufus Pope, the bottom-heavy mixologist who lurched like Godzilla behind the bar. But then Carla Marlin showed up with some startling news. When she barged into the bar, eyes on fire from her recent revelation, she seemed disappointed that her grand announcement would be received by only four men, one of them (Miles dared to think) a decent catch, albeit securely snatched up in the Tabasco-red talons of Tina Flame.

Or was he? Miles gave Carla the head-to-toe and found her paling in comparison to his ten-year live-in. A sun worshipper with freckled, tawny skin and hair bleached white as polar-bear fleece, she failed to tickle his fancy. That didn't stop him from draping a soothing arm over her back as she drew out her prologue to the big announcement, punching code into her Droid, lighting a Winston, and licking a drop of nectar from her piña colada straw before clearing her throat. But when Roddy Causey cruised into the bar, she withheld the goods again, waiting for him to secure a Budweiser before she wasted her breath on three old men and the flunky of Tina Flame.

"My neighbor the phlebotomist just got off his weird shift. Said all hell had broke loose down at Palmetto Baptist." Carla Marlin blew six perfect smoke rings.

"Enough with the rising action," said Stein. "Let's have our climax now."

Carla raised her eyebrows at the word *climax*.

"Well, if you got to know right this second: One of the teenagers is missing. They don't know if he just jumped out of bed and walked out, or if it was a kidnapping kind of thing."

"Or maybe he got beamed to another dimension," said Stein.

"Yeah." Carla rolled her eyes. "There's always that."

"They'll find him," said Roddy Causey. "Bet he woke up with amnesia and got lost."

"A common soap-opera trope," said Stein. "The whole waking-up-from-a-coma-with-amnesia shtick."

"Like Anastasia in *Purple Passions*," said Carla.

"It's actually called a 'convenient coma,'" said Stein.

Carla Marlin mustered her coldest drop-dead stare.

"There's nothing convenient about it," she said.

Beth Irving held a plastic vial of cat piss and repressed another gag. She'd been drinking ginger tea and popping B-6, pressing the acupuncture points reputed to diminish nausea. Still, a rank, yellow fume actually spilled from the vial like the cartoon hieroglyphics that flowed from the tail of Pepé Le Pew. But she would prevail because she had to, because other specialists in other states were testing their own comatose teens and compiling data, because one of her test subjects had mysteriously disappeared like a patient in a slasher film, and a certain famous neurologist was flying in from Germany. This time, she promised herself with a dark chuckle, she would refrain from sleeping with him. The fact that he was portly and bald (she'd checked out his web profile) would help.

Though she knew she was pregnant, she didn't have time to deal with it—emotionally or physically. The nausea, however, made it difficult to repress the fact that a new life was incubating inside her. Every time a green wave of sickness rocked through her, she couldn't help but envision the 8-cell zygote glistening in the void of her uterus. The small cluster of dividing cells was already sending chemical messages into her blood and nervous system, directing her eating habits to suit its needs, lording it over her bladder and producing "emotions" advantageous to its own survival. Her rationality had been hijacked weeks ago, when Dr. Bloom breezed into town at the height of her ovulatory cycle, her exquisitely receptive system going into overdrive upon detecting the neurovirologist's sweet pheromones.

Had she pounced upon him like a starved jaguar in the fake-cherry-scented darkness of her hotel room? Had she still had enough emotional detachment to quip about their feral passion as Dr. Bloom struggled drunkenly with her belt buckle? Yes, and, thank goodness, yes. But she'd also been prompted by a deep urge to sabotage her current relationship.

Now she was exhausted. As she went about her work, renegade factions of her brain urged her to slink into an unoccupied room and take a nap, or flee the bombardment of horrific hospital odors, rush through the automatic doors of entrance C, and take deep breaths in the oasis of landscaping where gardenias bloomed. But she had finally gotten three clearances for MRIs from desperate parents. And just yesterday one of the patients had possibly come out of his coma, though now the staff at this backwoods facility couldn't seem to find him. She had to work quickly in case the others woke up. She wanted to test olfactory responses to cat urine and the effects of antipsychotics on dopamine levels.

Struggling to keep her mind focused on her research tasks, she kept getting swept away by waves of nausea and stray images of Dr. Bloom. She saw him gnawing gristle from a chicken bone. Saw him hovering over her, wolfman eyes aglow. Saw him scurry into the bathroom where he displayed his buttocks with mock coyness before gruffly closing the door. He'd flown to Nashville to look into a recent case there, asking her, with a wistful smile, if she might join him later to diversify her research. They could visit all the infection sites, he romantically suggested.

But no. The *T. hermeticus* epidemic was most pronounced in this particular town, and Beth was trying to figure out how the hurricane weather and blighted economic conditions factored into this phenomenon. Remembering her own coming of age in South Georgia, she thought that clinical depression might play a role. And she needed to find teens testing positive who had *not* reached the comatose state, which wasn't necessarily the upshot of infection. Just as most *T. gondii*–positive people failed to show marked personality changes, and so-called schizophrenics probably had a predisposition that heightened the parasite's effects, some *T. hermeticus* hosts might not be susceptible to full-blown toxoplasmosis. Beth hypothesized that perhaps the hospitalized teens were particularly susceptible due to depression or malnutrition or other immune-weakening factors. But she couldn't test this without getting her hands on some non-pathological positives, which required slogging through labyrinthine DHEC paperwork, which required mental acuity and a nausea-free system, all of which were eluding her now, especially after she poured cat urine into the TDR diffuser and could not escape its musky insinuations no matter how many times she changed her latex gloves.

According to Adam's Facebook stream, Todd Spencer, the comatose teen who had mysteriously disappeared from the hospital, had made several shadowy appearances around town, materializing at the margins of various events before vanishing again. Heather Remington had spotted him lurking under the bleachers at a softball game. Josh Williams thought he might've seen him skulking down a hallway of First Baptist's new recreation facility. And several kids swore they'd seen him emerge from the woods and stand at the moonlit edge of Bob Bickle's pond, where an illicit teen party was in full riot.

Following DHEC's recommendations, Jenny had confiscated Adam's iPhone, equipping him with an old-fashioned flip phone until the crisis had passed. Though she knew she was violating his privacy by perusing his Facebook account, she felt that desperate times called for desperate measures, even though her son had not tested positive for *T. gondii* or *T. hermeticus* antigens. Two days before, she'd driven him to a Walmart where free testing facilities had been set up by DHEC. At least two dozen teens had waited on the scorched blacktop with their parents, the smell of sunscreen floating in the muggy air. Hurricane Anastasia had dissipated, and now a heat wave had settled in, with temperatures capping at 110. People were living like moles, hurrying from one air-conditioned bunker to another, compulsively checking their media gadgets for the latest on *T. hermeticus*.

The bug was mostly affecting the southern states, possibly because its weather conditions encouraged the species to thrive. Jenny was very busy with sibyl.com, though she pulled herself away from her screen every half hour to check on Adam, making sure he hadn't found the power cord to their media screen (which she'd stuffed into a corner of their china cabinet). So far he'd spent the morning sprawled on his bed, perusing old comics. He'd actually called her in to check out a particular issue from the bygone era of 2009. If weather conditions had permitted, she would've suggested some whimsical outing—a picnic, a sporting event.

But she did what she could to protect him. She'd stocked up on healthy snacks. She'd ordered educational board games for them to play together. She tracked her packages on UPS.com, hoping that when they arrived, a golden age of mother-son bonding would flourish.

Around eleven she started thinking about lunch, deciding to drop by Adam's room to ask what kind of wholesome entrée he fancied. But he wasn't in his room. Of course she felt the familiar throbbing of her heart as she moved toward the bathroom, calling his name with ostentatious nonchalance. He was not in the bathroom. He was not in the den. He was not hiding out in the master bedroom, which, up until last winter, she'd shared with her husband. When she opened the door to the laundry room, she saw him hunched before their fat, old Magnavox, plying the vintage joystick of her husband's childhood Atari. Her husband, desperate for bonding after returning from a deployment a year ago, had attempted to interest their son in this outfit.

"What are you doing?" she said.

Adam released a long, slow breath and fixed her with a defiant grin.

"Caught red-handed." He tossed the joystick onto the floor, where it bounced unexpectedly. "I'm going out of my mind with boredom, and I can't even check my e-mail on that archaic piece of shit you gave me."

"Watch the language."

As he stared at the primitive graphics of Asteroids, light from the screen reflected in his irises, which gave him the dead, mechanical gaze of a shark.

Miles Escrow could not remember days this hot. As he listened to Stein go on about how the dinosaurs died out, he wondered if humans were reaching the limits of this particular evolutionary stage. Regarding Titus Redmond, a vinyl siding–installation specialist with a swollen gut, Miles thought, *Here we have the height of human evolution, Homo sapiens*, which, as Stein had informed him on numerous occasions, meant "wise man." If there was such a

Julia Elliott

thing as the Lizard Man of Scape Ore Swamp, Miles theorized, maybe he'd survive the sweltering climate that was becoming the norm around here, making it well-nigh impossible to enjoy the great outdoors with its supermosquitoes and poisonous UV rays. So he chose to spend his Saturday afternoon hunkered in the smoked chill of Lizard Man, wondering if he'd ever shake free of Tina Flame.

Though he suspected they'd bicker their way into a double-plot grave at Sunset Memory Gardens, he liked to fool himself with little escapades at Lizard Man—dalliances with single mothers and women estranged from their no-count men. On this summer afternoon, with a heat index of 120, he'd zeroed in on Brandy Wellington, who was in better spirits of late as her comatose cousin had shown signs of con-sciousness up at Palmetto Baptist.

"He looked right into his mama's eyes," said Brandy. "Asked her for a Coke and then zoned out again."

"He can use the imperative voice logically," said Stein, "a good sign."

Brandy rolled her eyes and smirked at Miles.

"And that boy who's gone missing," she said. "Todd Spencer. I heard his mama found evidence that he'd been in his bedroom—a few drawers left open; some of his stuff missing."

"What makes her so sure it's him?" said Stein.

"She said a mother could just tell." Brandy Wellington blew an irate huff of smoke and examined her ebony fingernails, nails that matched her Elvira hair and black-widow ankle tattoo.

"No empirical evidence there," said Stein, whereupon Miles and Brandy enjoyed a sweet, conspiratorial eye roll together, solving Miles's dilemma over whether or not he ought to indulge in adult beverage number four.

Beth couldn't help but feel a little spooked in the makeshift teen-coma ward, where a whole section of hospital had been corralled off to accommodate the rising number of cases. She'd been cleared for antipsychotic drug tests on five of the patients, and she was making her midnight rounds, checking their encephalographic data for signs of neurological change. Pausing to drink in the Pre-Raphaelite love-liness of a red-haired boy she called Sleeping Beauty, Beth waited for him to open his eyes as he sometimes did in the wee hours. The sudden jolt of green always startled her. He would stare at her for a few seconds before his flushed, pink eyelids slid back over the most

326

spectacular set of ocular organs she'd ever seen.

He was an ethereal one, destined to bolt this shit town if he ever roused from his strange sleep, as had happened a total of three times nationally (which included the case of Todd Spencer). Even spookier, all three teens had vanished before resurfacing elusively at various events, sending their respective towns into a delirium of tabloid speculation.

As Beth gazed down at Sleeping Beauty, she wondered if it was true that hormonal changes caused pregnant women to be attracted to different kinds of men: unthreatening creatures with brotherly pheromones and kindred genetic codes. Beth Irving had no brothers, no sisters, only two stern, religious parents who had prompted a predictable rebellion that had been nipped in the bud by an abortion and a full scholarship to Duke.

Though the organism that now brewed within her had recently advanced from zygotic to embryonic status, she had not allowed herself to make any decisions about its destiny, vowing to finish her research first. Once home amidst the placid decor of her townhouse, its birch cabinets packed with stress-reducing organic teas, she'd make the hard decisions. Of course she couldn't ignore the creature inside her, which imbued every cell in her body with nausea and made smells almost psychedelic. The aroma that rose from Sleeping Beauty, for instance, was a strange blend of hospital-grade disinfectant and some sweet, woodsy musk. All the comatose teens had strange breath—a pond funk with some elusive chemical component redolent of car exhaust. But the B-6 pills were making the situation bearable.

She stood beside Sleeping Beauty for another minute and then moved on to the next room, which housed two girls, one of whom had been approved for antipsychotics. While adjusting Tamika Hammond's EEG electrodes, she caught a glimmer of movement out in the corridor. Upon rushing into the hall, she saw a tall, slender figure in a pale hospital gown, hovering a few inches above the polished vinyl floor. Rubbing her eyes and looking again, she saw nothing. Even though she had been sleeping poorly and had suffered several incidents of blotchy vision, even though she knew that security was on red alert due to the disappearance of Todd Spencer, she followed the figment into the snack room where she detected a *presence*. There was only one other door leading out of the snack room, back behind the nurse's station (which appeared to have been abandoned), and into corridor B.

Julia Elliott

Although this corridor required the swipe of a security card, the doors were propped open, an industrial cleaning cart parked nearby. In a corner, behind several wheeled shelves piled with broken computer equipment, a hospital janitor crouched. The janitor stood up and clutched at her neckline.

"*Mierda,*" she said. "You scared me."

"What are you doing back there?" Beth had to ask.

"Rat," she said. "Can you believe it?"

"They must take the elevator from the east wing cafeteria," Beth joked. "Did you see anybody walking through here?"

The janitor shook her head.

Beth moved out into the hall, where elevators led down to the main wing that featured the hospital's gift and coffee shops. Now she understood how Todd Spencer had made his escape, assuming that he'd not spontaneously combusted. And then she saw the figure again—tall, elegant, his shaggy red hair longer than it had looked when he was lying in repose like a creature trapped in a fairy-tale curse. Sleeping Beauty paused before strolling through the automatic doors. Of course the security guard was not at his desk, and Beth had no time to look for him. She jogged toward the door and ran out into the humming summer night.

In her favorite patch of landscaping, where gardenias unleashed their wistful perfume and floodlights cast the Eli Lilly Memorial Bench in a spectral glow, the boy stood barefoot in his pagan gown. He stared up at the sky, as though searching for the moon. And then, after glancing back at Beth and treating her to a smile that did strange things to her blood chemistry, he ran over a green hillock and down toward the flowing highway.

The Silver World
Carole Maso

I WILL MISS YOU, the child says.

Where are you going? Where have you gone, the woman asks?

Above the child's head, the shadows of flapping birds. She points to the in-between spaces—the space between here and there: the silver world.

The chemist and his wife move through salt—how beautiful and strange, this grainy, silver-blue abeyance. Where they have taken up a kind of permanent residence. As all parents do in the end. Reaching through a storm of salt. Father. He draws a molecule on the windowpane now. A single silver atom suspended in space.

Joseph Cornell turns the small silver ball in between his fingers, one time, two times, three before placing it at the center of his box. He picks up a coin, a marble, a feather. As if in magic succession.

A gossamer gown
A box of silver dollars
A flask
A sterling-silver tea service
A baby cup (we lost the child)
A teething ring
The silver-voiced soprano
The clock

Regarding the clock: It is Swedish and dates from around 1800. You should find it all in good working order. He had sent it in a kind of coffin. A gift in anticipation of the birth of her first child. Two silver bells—a pleasant enough sounding chime, to mark the time.

Carole Maso

Next to her bed etched in silver, a benediction: May he bless and keep you.

Two sisters dance across the silver screen—shot only weeks before the older girl's death in a car accident. Catherine Deneuve, the surviving sister, here in her last moments of radiant innocence. In this world of apparitions where I have somehow ended up again. Between the real and the unreal, the past and future, the living and the dead, out the window—an early morning fog.

The child materializes now on the garden wall. Then behind her a group of children. Flap harder, the children cry. The girl flaps her homemade wings. Harder, flap harder. That's right. You've got it!!!

As if that might bring her back. Where are you going? Where have you gone?

I will miss you.

The losses accumulate and blur. Glimpsed: In the morning light, through the barely opened door—

They circled over me a long time, and then disappeared into a solar haze like a gleaming silver ribbon. That this has happened to me, who has been so long an outsider . . . Swans and cranes and wild geese.

On that hill a silver sound, a slip of *S*, reaches the dreaming Italian who waits. Marconi hears a sound. The letter *S* longing over water. That fragment of the alphabet, salvation. Morse code. *S* is for Safe and for Sister. It's also for Sophie. She hands me a coin from the Silver world. Between stasis and stasis, this motion. Between darkness and darkness, this small light—and we're still alive.

The child ice-skating on the smooth silver ice. Wait! In the hospital the woman once drew a figure eight on a piece of white paper.

A child holds a cluster of silvery balloons, and up, up, up she goes.

The chemist and his wife waltz through salt. The first step is to expose the paper to light. The light affects the silver atoms. To reveal the latent image to the human eye requires a chemical agent that causes the exposed silver to be reduced from a salt to a metallic state.

Occident runs on a silver track. A record on film of an animal in motion, frozen midtrot by the photographer Eadweard Muybridge. The latent image revealed through silver to the human eye.

The Horse in Motion, dipped in silver.

Cinema, Rebecca Solnit says in *River of Shadows*, would itself be a kind of Ghost Dance. It was and is a breach in the wall between the past and the present, one that lets the dead return, albeit as images of flickering light, rather than phantoms in the dark.

The sisters, preserved, come back to life again, the collapse of the wall. The dead are alive, imbibing the light. The two Deneuve sisters dancing together once more.

The Young Girls of Rochefort.

As if that might mean something about what still could be possible for us. Glimpsed through the door, slightly open.

In a gossamer gown on the arm of the dreaming chemist, she sleeps.

The bee stings and the rose has thorns, but in the white hive in winter, a silence.

That slumber—silver covers his wife's mind . . . numbed like that— honeycombs of ice.

His parents gassed on arrival (calcium phosphate).

Regarding the clock: It will chime on the hour with a pleasant silver-sounding bell.

Carole Maso

Against the silence, the clatter of silverware, goblets. In the palace room. Before dessert. Her invitation to the night. Why was it I hesitated? And in the hesitation the moment passed. As moments will.

Regarding the clock: It might have kept time for us. Kept us in the measured world, a place we might have lived. Not dissolved, subsumed, one fleeting image in bright silver-white morning light. As I drown now in the emulsion. Reaching backward to animate something so perfect, so still: You are asleep.

What the morning had revealed—glimpsed through the slightly open door—why was it I had hesitated? The offer made so straightforwardly in the night.

Unmoored—that is how I felt then and the feeling has not left. All these years.

See now how gently, the chemist, his wife, the gossamer gown, entering the music hall. In the foyer the revelers lift a glass. The lights dim. A hospital corridor. Mahler's Ninth about to begin. In the row directly in front of them, velveted, a woman wearing gloves and a stole.

The fox fur gleams silver.

They have survived. And having survived they arrive on time to the concert hall and the jaws of the fox and the fox's tail.

And the silver death head.

The sisters, buoyant—not entirely here nor there—

In the Children's Encyclopedia I read about flight, and I read about time, and I read about desire. The entry included a photograph of a man in the sky in a harness tied to a cluster of helium balloons. Silvery in black and white, photographed.

The chemist and his wife at the gates of Auschwitz, signal, wave, hoping for a ride (helium).

What remained of his parents—teeth, fragments of bone (calcium, carbon, phosphorus).

A silvery sound comes from the transistor. They listen to the voice bloom and decay and then fall away.

Regarding the clock . . .

I write with a passion that startles me after all this time. I write tonight in moonlight, silver, of course, into the heart of that regret, the decision that has haunted me all this time—and that I am back there again with so little prodding, filling me with a kind of sorrow I thought once only reserved for a more foregrounded, emphatic tragedy. So many years after the fact—what has brought her so vividly back—an absence felt as a presence of the most weighted, vibrant kind.

The place where we are exiled, suspended—not heaven, nor earth— here in the silver world. Not dead, but not entirely alive either.

So the days pass, Woolf writes, and I ask whether one is not hypnotized as a child by a silver globe, by life; and whether this is living.

And why, given everything, given everything I surely knew, why was it I hesitated—when she was all I ever wanted—or that is the suspicion—in the way one can know these things, and yet, still step away, walking down the hallway with a flourish, with a quick step, a scurry even, to the breakfast room where croissants, confiture, café had been laid out and a note from the host. On a white dish a piece of fruit.

Regarding the clock . . . but the voice falls away.

Joseph Cornell's box rests on the sill. Note that using the bird to connote absence is a time-honored nineteenth-century tradition. His obsession with Malibran, the famed singer, and her bird song, which, to his permanent sorrow, could never truly be retrieved, and which stands behind many of his works.

"The time left to me on earth is limited."

Carole Maso

THE TWILIGHT OF A QUANTUM PHYSICIST

On the cusp of the disappearing world he sits with his spectacles, his hearing aids, his handfuls of disintegrating chalks, with the ghosts of Einstein and Bohr, and looks into the distance at the "great smoking dragon," the supreme mysteries of the world. "We're all hypnotized into thinking there's something out there," he whispers. His subatomic world—where the electron exists in its murky state of possibility—in quantum uncertainty—

I shall miss you, the child says, already far off.
Where are you going?
She laces up her boots. Holding now, in a mittened hand, a sled.
I am going to meet the snow.

"And the creation question is so formidable that I can hardly hope to answer it in the time left to me." As he begins to levitate— somewhere between here and there—he hands me a silver coin. "How come existence?" The extraordinary ephemerality of the world.

Bombs fall on the ancient city of Fallujah. The destruction of the imagined Gardens of Babylon takes a larger toll than one might have thought. Our deepest memories and dreams canceled, erased.

So little time all of a sudden. The sisters prance on the surface of the screen—and we can hear their laughter, and their laughter falling away.

Dipped in an emulsion of silver

As ash enters the body

Matisse packs a small valise, Christmas Day 1917, and checks into the Hotel Beau Rivage, because one does not forget "the silver clarity of the light in Nice."

She is asleep and quite unaware of my presence. The door slightly ajar. Might I, if allowed ever again, might I, with the slightest of pressures . . . gently push it open. And then inside—having finally gained admittance, having discreetly closed it behind me, I can hear the click. . . .

What in these pages has revived you—placed you back in the bed, in the morning, the door still ajar. This wishful fiction that has set us back into a kind of motion—having thought it to have been resolved, having come to terms with it—but one does not resolve— at least today I see it as it is, it had never been resolved, it had been frozen. In the space between here and there.

The woman with the improbable name, standing among the trees in her sculpted forest—forever thirty, at the edge of her breakthrough—and ours. . . .

The door is ajar.

Ava smiles, always a little surprised, a little awed by what the world in the end has once more to offer. There before her again as if no time at all had elapsed. That kitchen long ago, or was it yesterday? Her dark hair cascading down her back. Standing over the spaghetti pot and laughing (the tendons in her neck). Does she dare—

There's a little slip of door I once looked through. . . .

Her blinding thigh in morning light. A momentary glimpse—and yet it has not left her.

The evening of the afternoon in the kitchen—that position she remains in always, a kind of irresolution, suspension—Dickinson's "choosing / not choosing." That openness—my response. The place we are exiled to, the silver world—not heaven, nor earth—I send you this love letter on the occasion of your thirty-fifth birthday. Time passes

On a pleasant-sounding silver chime.

And what began in Nice as a painting "very realistic, with a beautiful sleeping woman on a marble table amid fruit," eventually turned into "an angel sleeping on a violet surface."

Carole Maso

Her thigh—sterling, mottled, solid, fixed now in blazing light, released from the imaginary frame so that the body was both itself and also something else, having escaped the white eiderdown, in silvered morning light.

The memory of one evening once apparently supplies enough hope, sorrow, beauty, regret to last a lifetime. The world is silver tonight.

Impossible, even now, to give up that place in the mind where she charms forever, that charged and hanging space between action and inaction, decision and indecision, redolent of life's blessings— beauties—oranges in the room, or the birds of winter or the scent of snow. . . . And in this way there was a kind of engagement still, a place still where anything might happen.

There's a little slip of window. There's a door still slightly ajar through which I stare

Where

I am alive.

The extraordinary ephemerality of the world,

Where I am not dying.

And if she were to walk in here tonight again, on the arm of a lover—I catch her eye, she remembers, does she remember.

In a storm of salt they walk.

Where are you going, my child?

I am going to meet the snow.

The silver teething ring

One might hope for a little of Matisse's magic—born of devotion and endless hard work—where you are now only an angel on a silver surface.

Glimpsed in the early morning light—her thigh having escaped the eiderdown. As if photographically etched in the mind on a silver plate. What I saw that early morning and what has not left me, what has remained all these years, arrested in time.

Stumbling that night into the emulsion. Our heads only barely above the drown.

We're all hypnotized into thinking there is something out there.

And if you came back again, as I have rehearsed it so many times in my mind (the door is ever, ever so slightly ajar)—what would I do this time?

Elfking Suite
Charles Bernstein

DUPLEXITIES

I'm no more here
Than you are went
You no more there
Than when I'd gone
And yet we meet
In cross-crissed lines
Across these empty
Icons of time.

OOOO

Charles Bernstein

ELFKING

after Goethe

Who rides so late through a night so wild?
It is the father with his dearest child;
His daughter cradled in his one free arm
He holds her tight, to keep her from harm.

"My child, why is your face covered in fear?"
—"Look, Father, do you not see Elfking near?
Elfking leering with a crown and a tail?"
—"My child, all that is is a passing gale."

"My dear, sweet daughter, come along with me!
Your dress-up games we will play by the sea.
Such castles we'll build when we get to the shore
You'll wear Grandmother's hats you so adore."

"My father, my father, don't you hear
What Elfking's whispering in my ear?"
—"Be calm, stay quiet, oh my dear, sweetest one
It is just the leaves blowing in the wind."

"My daughter, my daughter, with me please stay
Your brother waits to sing the night away
Your brother will take your hand in his hands
And dance with you gaily on glistening sands."

"My father, my father, do you not see
Elfking's sons beckoning madly to me?"
—"My daughter, my daughter, I see it well:
The old willow shimmering in the dell."

*"I love you, your Beauty's pure Perfection
From my clutches you have no protection."*
—"My father, my father, I'm in his grip
Elfking's dragged me to his demon ship."

The father shudders, rides hard through the wild
Clinging for life to his dear aching child
Hurtling onward, overcoming his dread
In his arm, home now, his daughter is dead.

AS IF BY MOONLIGHT

It is what it was.
It's not what it's not.
It hurts where it hurt.
It cut where it cuts.
It counts when it could.
It strays where it stayed.
It stayed when it strays.
It shudders as it shut.
It dropped as it drops.
It drips as it dripped.
It was what it is.

DUPLEXITIES

If anything I have done
Cancels what I feel
Then put me on a boat
Without a keel
And I will row my way back to you
Whatever else I do
Whatever else I do

Three Dramolets
Robert Walser

—*Translated from German by Daniele Pantano and James Reidel*

TRANSLATORS' NOTE

THESE THREE DRAMOLETS, or minidramas, are selected from the complete, definitive edition of Walser's *Komödie* (Berlin: Suhrkamp Verlag, 1986). "Poets" was written in 1899 and first appeared in *Insel* in June 1900. "The Pond," translated from the original Swiss German dialect, is believed to have been written afterward, in late 1899 and no later than 1902. "The Lovers" was written in 1920 and appeared that same year in the September issue of *Der Neue Merkur*.

The dramolets here are just as maddening—in that way Georg Büchner is maddening—yet more personal than works based on and commentaries of well-known Brothers Grimm tales, what the secondary literature calls "metatheater." (Of "Snow White," Walter Benjamin wrote that it was "one of the most profound creations of recent literature" and explained why Walser "was a favorite author of the merciless Franz Kafka.")

The dramolets do not have a *dramatis personae*. Walser characters, unlisted at the head of the play, simply start to exist, which may suggest how close the dramolets are to their spare composition. Oskar in two of these plays and Fritz in "The Pond" are clearly alter egos of Walser. His parents, siblings, and friends can be seen in the other characters, as can his frustrated love for Frieda Mermet. These three dramolets represent a kind of autobiographical theater in which the author can see himself without being ironical at all as a kind of hero, not an antihero, much as he does in his novels. Walser, too, dramatizes here in "The Lovers" the verge, the jumping-off point to his famous withdrawal into thinking, writing in miniature letters for no one but himself, and spending the rest of his life in Swiss mental hospitals. He almost seems to foreshadow here, as he does in *The Tanners*, what it would be like to be seen, found, witnessed fallen in one's thoughts, not unlike how he was found on Christmas Day in 1956, dead in the snow.

POETS

(A street. A house on the left; a garden on the right. SEBASTIAN.)

SEBASTIAN. I will just sit on this stone bench here by the old house. Nobody is around whom I could tell how tired I am. I am a poet. It is my calling to coax feelings into meager rows of syllables we call poetry. My poems are judged by the shrugs and cool glances of those who read them, quite poorly, I may add. But I am not complaining, that is for sure. There is nothing you can do about it. My lamenting, no matter how moving it might be, is not capable of making me a better artist. I force myself to keep writing. That is what many other poets do, and they are being forced, if anything, by plenty of rather horrendous reasons. Perhaps what really spurs me on is simply the sheer boredom of writing about things that look back at me through the words and cause me sorrow, if not something much worse. The world just brushes it all aside. Half talents such as me, it seems, are a joke to her. She accepts what she ought to vigorously reject. She does call me a fool, it is just that I am not foolish enough. But she would not dare tell me to my face. I get it from behind, from the side, through whispers from above. The world keeps reminding me. Oh, if only I had a calling to earn my bread more honestly than this half of one in which I am three-quarters stuck. Is that not Hermann?

(HERMANN *appears.*)

HERMANN. Laughing, laughing!

SEBASTIAN. Well, what is it?

HERMANN. Kaspar has strangled himself! The famous Kaspar. He whose naked shoulders were just now being caressed by golden fame. The critics' darling, as they say, worshipped by women, flooded with praise. My mouth cannot even spit it out.

SEBASTIAN. And he has just strangled himself, this moment?

HERMANN. He could not take the fame.

SEBASTIAN. Did it not suit him?

HERMANN. In a way, yes. He wore it like the beggar who wears the king's robe, sighing and walking with a stoop. His shy, clumsy, diffident, pondering figure soon shed itself of what it was not called to wear. The silk, the pearls, the precious objects of fame were hurting him. Such people are not made for the chink of gold and the scent of roses.

SEBASTIAN. His longing for things forbidden made for such sweet poetry.

HERMANN. He was right to leave us in the dust: That thought was a fine inspiration. His name, his name! If only I could be a letter in his name.

SEBASTIAN. It would be a great help to me if I were simply its sound. I would be swimming in the ether and soaking in my own echo.

HERMANN. We are the tongues that speak his name. The entire world is doing the same at this moment. How it loves the name of a dead celebrity. Gabriel, that jolly Gabriel, you hear, ought to make the funeral address. There is talk of a marvelous funeral.

SEBASTIAN. You think they would know what to do with the dead poet. After all, they let him starve when he was still alive.

HERMANN. I understand. They made him famous but never offered him a hand, a hand the love-craving poet would have loved to grab. They moved into the background in order to shout even louder. They wear fine clothes, stroll with cultured ladies, hold spirited conversations, love the extraordinary because it nourishes their wits. Woe the odd man out who dares to join their circle, where they smile at each other in boredom. You're coming, too, right?

SEBASTIAN. Where? Ah! To master Gabriel!

HERMANN. Let us hear how far his thundering voice can reach.

SEBASTIAN. Where will he be giving his speech?

HERMANN. On the steps of the town hall. There will be plenty of people and tears for Kaspar. His name will have to help them sweeten the moist night air.

SEBASTIAN. Tomorrow night? I will be there!

HERMANN. Let us go. (*They leave.*)

(*A window opens above.* OSKAR *leans out.*)

Robert Walser

OSKAR. I do not know how many times I have stuck my head out the window at this hour. It is the same every night. I cannot account for it. I contemplate the stars and find something floating above their beauty, something I cannot explain. The moon kisses the vast world and the silent spot here in front of the house. The trees whisper. The fountain shivers. My ears are much too sensitive for night's laughter. I think I have been writing poems for the past few days without even knowing why. My back is breaking because of it, because for hours I bend over a word, waiting for its long journey from brain to paper. And I feel neither miserable nor happy. I simply forget myself. The number of poems I have written can be counted on one hand, that is if I were bothered enough to count them. What would be the point? Something tells me that I will die doing it. The beauty of the stars, the moon, the night, and the trees torments me. It does not offer any peace to the one who trembles. In the past I would sit by the window as often and long as I do now but without feeling the slightest stirring of emotions. My head is aching from all this brooding. My feelings are arrowheads wounding me. My heart longs to be wounded. My thoughts long to be weary. I want to press the moon into a poem and the stars into another and add myself between them. What else shall I do with these feelings but let them die like flapping fish on the sands of language? The end of my poetry will be the end of me, and I welcome it, happily. Good night!

> (*Change of scene. Town hall square. On a frame draped in black silk, Kaspar's coffin. Torches.* GABRIEL, SEBASTIAN, HERMANN, *and others.*)

SEBASTIAN. I should think your voice will drum up enough people.

HERMANN. And if not, a pair of ears more or less will not matter here.

GABRIEL. Shortly, shortly.

SEBASTIAN. You should trample their ears all the same.

HERMANN. I have yet to hear your voice.

SEBASTIAN. He will make you feel it. Now, Gabriel, our impatience urges you to begin.

GABRIEL. In a moment. (*He climbs the steps up to the coffin.*) Ladies and gentlemen! Gracious assembly! A few poets have invited me to speak at today's funeral for Kaspar. Even without such a reminder, for which I am honored, I would never have found it in me not to be vocal here. Whatever I say comes from the heart, so there can be no talk of a rousing, beautiful funeral address. Kaspar was very dear to me. I admired him. I am grieved, and I weep for him. His life was short but radiant and glorious. As soon as the angel of fame's kiss arrived, the angel of death was ready to collect him. And I do not gain anything by mentioning his premature fame. The world made it clear that admiration lay at his feet. His poems, whose euphony shattered our ears, will be his marble monument at whose red-smeared plinth we will weep. He is at peace now. My speech shall not be long.

(He descends.)

SEBASTIAN. Well done, well said, extremely well timed.

HERMANN. His voice is still roaring in my ears.

SEBASTIAN. Let us shake his hand.

HERMANN. Let us shake him off with a brave handshake.

SEBASTIAN. I wanted to be Kaspar's name.

(Change of scene. In front of the POETESS's *house.)*

POETESS. What a beautiful morning. The weary soul can rest comfortably in this cool breeze, this invigorating breath. The dream loses itself. I had one, if not absurd then certainly most peculiar. I stood there musing with a goose quill in my hand. Suddenly a handsome and slender young man began kissing my hand, spurred by the most heated and unbridled adoration for me. I do not remember how many times his red lips, which smiled at me like two pages of an open book, kissed my pale hands, which grew paler with each passionate and moist touch. I became quite hot, and I have every reason to still be in fever when I think of what is about to happen next. For the dream threw out an entire forest of young men from within itself, all of whom crowded around my smiling condescension, kissing whatever sweet thing there was to kiss. They flew, swarmed, and worshipped around me like bees buzzing around a hive or soldiers surrounding their victorious general. Neither their kissing nor their cooing and stammering ever ceased. A few of them were begging, others were crying. One of them, probably the most boisterous, was laughing like mad. His laughter kissed me as much as everything else; they all had such red, fresh, seductive lips, like two pages of an open book. What a dream! What material for a novella. What a lovely feeling to be kissed all over again by the vitality of these images! It looks like nothing will come of my resolution to write ten to twelve poems today. That said, I by no means want to trade the pleasure of this dream with this respite, the drafting and dispatching of a novella and a half. O those young men! I shall return to the house and continue to delight in them.

(*She enters the house.* SEBASTIAN, GABRIEL, HERMANN *arrive.*)

SEBASTIAN. Is this her house?

GABRIEL. You do not want to enter it, do you?

HERMANN. She will stab you to death with the tips of her virginal mustache.

SEBASTIAN. I am going in, whatever the cost.

HERMANN. We will all go in.

GABRIEL. We will examine her. We will whisper sweetly into the eager ears of the authoress's vanity.

SEBASTIAN. We will make her turn red.

HERMANN. It will not promise much satisfaction. But so be it. And I will speak to her in verse.

SEBASTIAN. Gabriel's voice shall shout for forgiveness.

GABRIEL. She will sense the true enthusiasm behind our visit and welcome us as poets.

SEBASTIAN. She will speak of Kaspar like a poor devil for whom it was time to go.

HERMANN. And that is when I will pull her by the ears.

GABRIEL. You will first have to beg her slightly sharp and sour dignity for permission.

SEBASTIAN. I will say I would, if I were allowed. . . .

GABRIEL. And she will say: Relax, sir. Please, no noise. My house has until now been a refuge for reputable people. And even then only as an exception.

HERMANN. An unfortunate exception, that is what I will call her.

GABRIEL. I can already see our visit sinking into the water.

SEBASTIAN. No, he should stick his finger into the fire and try what burning tastes like.

GABRIEL. My heart, my lady, my sweet, sweet . . .

HERMANN. What a glorious voice! Keep going! Come in so we can get out.

GABRIEL. The thought of escaping will be a pleasure, once we are actually inside, that is.

SEBASTIAN. Inside, voice.

HERMANN. Inside, dear nervousness.

GABRIEL. Inside.

> (*Change of scene. The street from the first scene. The house on the left; the garden on the right.* SEBASTIAN.)

SEBASTIAN. I am tired of blaming myself, which I have been doing for a while now. Why should I not be good at something an honest person is not: being a fool? We call each other fools, but nobody knows the real fool, for the real fool is in all of us. Is Gabriel a fool? Certainly! Is Hermann a fool? No less, for sure! We want to be lied to, and when we speak the truth, it is only out of fear of lying. The coward lies the most. However, I am tired of foolish, fraudulent self-reproach, much like any other bad habit. I want to look at this merry fountain in peace and think that whatever sluggish thing saunters toward me is a being made of two bodies, four legs, but only half a mind. Here it is as beautiful as in a fairy tale.

> (HERMANN *and* GABRIEL *appear.*)

GABRIEL. I felt like I had to meet you here, only here and nowhere else in the world.

HERMANN. We heard you say it is as beautiful as in a fairy tale here.

SEBASTIAN. The fountain's snickering at the joke you served. Make it better, once you get the feeling back.

HERMANN. Such I have, but I am unable to guarantee you this, as my tongue disdains it.

Robert Walser

GABRIEL. Have you read today's lead article in the morning paper?

SEBASTIAN. I do not read the papers. I am too sensitive for it.

HERMANN. But this special article, which is about Kaspar, should cure you forthwith of your sensitivity.

SEBASTIAN. I will read it. Here it is as beautiful as in a fairy tale.

GABRIEL. The clouds are drifting, the trees are shaking, the air is trembling, the stars are flickering, the moon is burning, and the most beautiful is this trick of water over here, splashing the leaves.

HERMANN. I am tired.

GABRIEL. Of poetry?

HERMANN. Yes. Tell me, where is a poet's home?

GABRIEL. In time, in memory, in oblivion.

SEBASTIAN. In the grace offered to us by furtive spirits.

HERMANN. So our home is a gift of spirits. We live in the palace of the princess of spirits.

SEBASTIAN. Have you been reassured?

HERMANN. Oh, yes. I shall break out of myself. My thoughts cannot be my master.

GABRIEL. Listen, listen. Is that not a voice?

HERMANN. A bright voice, by Jove!

SEBASTIAN. Hush, hush!

OSKAR. [Leaning out the window.] I want to release my thoughts like canaries from a caged mind that is much too small. They shall fill this sacred, sweet night with enchanting chirping. My voice shall call after them: Go on, go on, do not ever return to me. Use the beautiful freedom I am giving you and grant me peace. But there are leftover feelings with which I cannot deal. I want to scatter them in the world's dark space, so they get stuck like stars. Fickle feelings that stray in our hearts have much in common with the flickering of stars. The night will not mind if I enrich it with such glowing symbols, feelings. The world wants me in its space, and I am close to dissolving in her embrace. What is going on down there? Hey?

SEBASTIAN. What is the matter with this fellow?

HERMANN. Let him be! He is dreaming. He is a poet. His voice is magnificent.

GABRIEL. I have nothing against his voice.

OSKAR. (*Up by the window.*) When I disperse, I want to scream. It shall resound through a million valleys and over a million mountains. The night will weep. The earth will rotate more furiously, and people will feel that poets do not die alone.

THE POND

(*A room.* FRITZ *appears.*)

FRITZ. I would soon rather be nowhere than just be here. Nothing but wicked faces. That's how it is at the dinner table. Nothing but a clatter of spoons and forks and knives. Not a word. Only this timid whispering, this furtive clinking of glasses, this suffocated laughter. You can't open your mouth for fear of making a bad appearance. What's the point of such appearances? Paul, he can talk, he gets away with everything. Everything about him is nice, good, proper, kind. He's the nicest boy in the world. Makes me feel like he's Mother's only son, like she has no other. I can't do anything right, no matter what I do. Fine, if that's how they want it. It's true, I'm so damned stubborn and sulky. If only they knew how I feel inside. If just once Mother could see into my heart. She would probably be surprised, she would probably see that I too love her a little. Oh—love her! What else could I say? There's no need for a single word. I know it, but it's sad that no one else does. I need to go up to my room and think about all of this. I'll probably start crying. So what? Nobody will see it. Crying is only crying when someone's there and hears it. Let's go, Fritzi, let's get out of the way.

(*He wants to leave;* KLARA, *his sister, appears.*)

KLARA. What are you doing just standing around in here?

FRITZ. Well, you have to stand somewhere. Anyway, what do you care?

KLARA. I'm going to tell Papa.

FRITZ. Go ahead! I'm not afraid of him!

KLARA. Oh? And what if I tell Mama? You're still not afraid?

FRITZ. Don't be such a tattletale. That's mean.

KLARA. I'm going to tell her.

FRITZ. Whatever. Let her knock me on the head. Let the whole world knock me on the head, for all I care.

KLARA. I'm going to tell! You just wait.

FRITZ. You're a stupid— (*Horrified, he pauses.*)

KLARA. I'm a what? You were going to call me a stupid cow, right? A stupid cow! I'm going to tell, I'm going to tell.

(MRS. MARTI *appears.*)

KLARA. Mama, Fritz called me a stupid cow again.

MRS. MARTI. Shut up! (*To* FRITZ.) Come here! (*To* KLARA.) Get to work. March.

(MRS. MARTI *and* FRITZ *go into the other room.*)

KLARA. (*Sits down at the worktable.*) What a pig! He's going to get it twenty times over again. He always overdoes it. What does he think, we won't ever say anything? That we can't open our mouths? (*Screaming can be heard.*) Ah, how he's crying now! Like an ox about to be slaughtered. What a big lad! He should be ashamed.

(MRS. MARTI *enters.*)

MRS. MARTI. Next time you'll get it too, you tattletale. Shame on you for always moaning. That's not nice. I have better things to do than always listening to you moan. You should just keep quiet sometimes.

KLARA. But when he always—

MRS. MARTI. Be quiet. You should be ashamed of yourself. And stop bothering me with this. I don't want to hear about it anymore. Understood? (*Leaves.*)

(FRITZ *appears cautiously.*)

KLARA. Come in, she's gone. You got it good, didn't you? So you
going to call me a stupid cow again?

(FRITZ *leaves silently.*)

KLARA. He's had enough!—But I should hurry to get this work
done, so I can go and play outside. I love being outside, where
there's not always a fuss like in here. What time is it? Already
three? Go, hurry, hurry.

(*A street.* FRITZ. *At some distance,* FRANZ, HEINRICH, OTTO,
and other boys.)

FRITZ. I'm tired of standing around. But I can't stand it at home.
What's there for me? I can't just sit in my room all day.

OTTO. Hey, Fritz, you coming with us?

FRITZ. (*To himself.*) I would like to run and play. But I can't stop
thinking about it. Thinking about the same thing. I'd rather be
alone.

HEINRICH. We're asking you to come with us! Can't you hear? Lost
your voice?

FRITZ. They just get on my nerves. I'm tired of them. Why am I such
a miserable lad?

FRANZ. Just leave this idiot alone. He's obviously too good for us.
C'mon, let's go without this bore.

HEINRICH. Sit down, Fritz, and look up into the sky, you dreamer.
(*They leave.*)

FRITZ. If they're so good without me, then why do they bother asking me along? They should just go. I don't even want to know about
it, really. I like being alone. That's when you can think. Nobody
bothers you. I always feel like I've lost something somewhere.
I know it's nothing, but it still worries me. What could it be?
Nothing? What am I saying! It's something, stupid me just forgot
what it is. I want to follow this train. I want to find my spot in
the forest. Maybe there I'll remember it. It will come to me like a
butterfly. Anyway, why do I have to think? I have to, I'm forced to.
Isn't it stupid that you have to do something? You shouldn't have
to do anything. But I'm the one to talk. C'mon, Fritz, let's go. I'm not
alone. Fritz is Fritz's friend. I'm my own best friend.—All the things

I should know. It's funny. But let's think about it all in the forest, what I could do to make my mother—(*Leaves quickly.*)

(*Room in* Mrs. Kocher's *house.* Mrs. Kocher; Ernst, *her son, sitting in the armchair;* Fritz.)

Mrs. Kocher. It's so nice of you to spend some time with my son, Fritz.

Fritz. I really enjoy it.

Ernst. Wouldn't you rather play with the others? Wouldn't that be more fun?

Fritz. No way. Sitting here quietly and talking to you is much more fun.

Mrs. Kocher. (*Holding* Fritz's *hand.*) Where did they find such a beautiful soul? Someone so good inside.

Fritz. You shouldn't praise me like that.

Mrs. Kocher. It would be a crime not to. But I hear someone coming. Have fun. I'll be back with some dinner. A bit of wine and bread. Bye for now. (*She leaves.*)

Fritz. You have a very nice mother.

Ernst. Oh, I can't say anything. What *can* you say?

Fritz. (*Thoughtful.*) Of course.

Ernst. It's so stupid. Why wouldn't a mother be nice and loving? I'm sure yours is too.

Fritz. Not that I know.

Ernst. What?

Fritz. I've never felt like I have a mother. On my backside, maybe.

Ernst. You're kidding?

Fritz. How could I be kidding? There's nothing funny about it. I wish I were sick like you.

Ernst. I'm sure you would enjoy that.

Fritz. More than you think. Listen!

Ernst. What?

FRITZ. Could you take a mother who doesn't love you? Would you care?

ERNST. What nonsense. A mother always loves her child. I'm sure yours loves you as well. You're just imagining things.

FRITZ. (*Upset.*) Let's not talk about it anymore.

(*Backyard.* KLARA *and* PAUL.)

KLARA. Where's Fritz?

PAUL. Oh, he said he's going to the pond, by the forest. He said—

KLARA. What did he say now?

PAUL. Nothing, really. He wants to drown himself.

KLARA. (*Frightened.*) What?

PAUL. Well, yes. Life, he said, is nothing but a torn shirt. He needs to mend it.

KLARA. What? Life is—

PAUL. I don't like to repeat myself. He wants to mend his life. He's tired of it. It's not worth anything. I forgot the rest.

KLARA. So go, go—

PAUL. Where?

KLARA. To the pond! I'm scared. You're still here? Why aren't you going?

PAUL. I'm not about to run my legs off because of this cursed life! It's not serious.

KLARA. And what if it is? Shame on you. He's our brother. If you don't want to go, then—

PAUL. Wait, I'm coming! (*Both leave.*)

(*A pond surrounded by evergreens.* FRITZ *appears.*)

FRITZ. How silent it is here. The trees reflected in the water. How it drips from the branches, so quiet, so delicate. You could mistake it for a song. The leaves are floating on the water like little boats. Here you could be properly sad and melancholy. But I didn't come here to cry. I need to get going. (*He takes off his shirt.*) Right! I'll put this in the grass, over here. (*He throws his hat into the water.*) And the hat needs to learn how to swim. I told Paul that I'm tired of life, that I'm going to the pond. He understood. Truth is, it's time I get a bit of attention. Let's see if my mother will be worried about me. Let's see if she'll still be indifferent when she hears that I jumped into the pond.—Paul should be here soon, and when he sees the hat and the shirt, and I'm nowhere to be found, what else could he think? This has to work. I know it's bad to frighten your mother unnecessarily. But—I want to know whether she cares about me or not.—He's coming. I can hear him. That's his whistling. (*He climbs an evergreen; while climbing:*) I can't wait to see his face. He's going to take off. I already can't help laughing. (*He hides between the branches.*)

(PAUL *appears, approaches the shirt.*)

PAUL. Oh, ah, there he is, there he is, in the grass. (*When he sees the empty shirt and the hat in the water, he screams and runs away.*)

(FRITZ *climbs down.*)

FRITZ. Right. In ten minutes they'll know. Let's start walking home. I'm getting a bit scared myself. So what? What's the worst that can happen? Another thrashing? Same ol' story. How can I be afraid of something that I'm used to?—I don't even mind going the long way. It's only right if for once they're the ones running and crying. They ought to cry, and I'm happy about it. No one has ever cried because of me. Maybe now they'll see that I'm worth something. (*He uses a twig to retrieve his hat.*) This hat almost drowned. But I'm pleased with it; what a good job. Hat, you can sit back up. (*He puts it on his head.*) Right. Now I'll walk like a smug Englishman to the next forest. I feel very noble. The devil shall take me if I get home before evening.

(*Hallway.* KLARA, *crying, appears.*)

KLARA. If he could just come home. Just come home! He can't have drowned. Who does something like that? Oh, why can't he just be back here? He can call me a stupid cow anytime he wants. A thousand times. Why was I always so mean to him? We weren't nice to him. Bad, bad. I can't even talk. I can't breathe. (*Frightened.*) Fritz, please come back. Can't you see that we're all crying because of you? The whole house is going mad. Please come back. I have to go. I can't stand still. It's black everywhere. I'm going to faint. Fritz, oh, Fritz. You bad, dear, stupid boy, oh—

(*She lies on the ground and sobs.* FRITZ *appears.*)

FRITZ. Here I am!—Hey, Klara! What are you doing on the ground?

KLARA. (*Yelling.*) You? (*As if in a dream.*) You?

FRITZ. Yes! Why not?

KLARA. Didn't you jump into the water? Paul came home crying, said that you'd jumped into the pond!

FRITZ. Paul's a stupid boy.

KLARA. Didn't you tell Paul that you wanted to kill yourself? That life's a torn shirt? That you wanted to get rid of it?

FRITZ. (*Defiantly.*) And what if I did?

KLARA. Don't you realize that we've all been terribly worried? We searched all over for you.

FRITZ. So?

KLARA. Mother is beside herself. Yes, inside. I don't even dare go inside and tell her that you—

FRITZ. What?

KLARA. —that you're alive again. You have it coming, I tell you!

FRITZ. I don't care.

(MRS. MARTI *and* MR. MARTI *appear.*)

KLARA. Mama, Papa! Fritz didn't fall into the water. He doesn't have a wet spot on him.

(FRITZ *stands there guilty and trembling.*)

MR. MARTI. Wha—you—

MRS. MARTI. (*Trying to control herself, to her husband.*) Leave him alone, Adolf. Don't hurt him, you hear?

MR. MARTI. You deceive us into thinking that you're dead? What a rascal, what a sluggard, what—

(*He tries again to go after* FRITZ.)

MRS. MARTI. (*To her husband, firmly.*) Leave him to me. I'll punish him. (*To* FRITZ, *concerned.*) Why did you do that?

FRITZ. I, I—I—

MRS. MARTI. Why would you tell Paul that you want to throw yourself into the water? Why?

FRITZ. Mother, I—

MRS. MARTI. (*Softly.*) Come, let's go to the living room! Come! (*She takes him by the hand and leads him.*)

MR. MARTI. That brat deserves a beating. It's all because he never does anything. We should take him out of school and put him in a factory. Nothing but playing tricks in his head. But I'll show him, that—(*He leaves, agitated.*)

KLARA. Oh, I'm just so glad he's back. He's got it really bad now. But they shouldn't punish him too much. I should go inside and listen to what they're saying. (*Listens at the door.*) I can't hear anything. It's silent. What does that mean? Is that Mother who's whispering—is it—someone's crying, but very softly. I don't get it. I don't get it.

> (*The living room.* MRS. MARTI; FRITZ, *sitting half on her lap.*)

MRS. MARTI. But how can I know what's in your heart? I can't guess, can I? You should've said something. You have to speak when you want to say something. See, now I've done wrong to you. I thought you didn't love me, all you wanted to do was cause me grief. Oh, how wrong we can be about some things in this world. But it's fine now. Do say something.

FRITZ. I can't.

MRS. MARTI. Why didn't you ever say anything? Why did you never tell me, Mother, you did me wrong—Mother, I love you—?

FRITZ. —love you—

MRS. MARTI. And why not? Why suffer for no reason and not use your mouth? You poor boy!

FRITZ. I was never allowed to. A son can't do that.

MRS. MARTI. But why not?

FRITZ. I thought you couldn't stand me, so I thought I better keep quiet. But you've always been my mother, and I've always loved you, quietly.

MRS. MARTI. *(Kisses him.)* Don't say that. *(She cries.)* Don't talk like that.

FRITZ. What else could I've done?

MRS. MARTI. My boy, my boy, what are you doing to me? Do you want me to fall on my knees in front of you? Is that what you want?—Oh.—I've done you wrong, much wrong. But I'll make it up to you. We'll make it all better. What do you say? Everything's going to be fine, right? You and I will be like friends. A quiet, private alliance. Father doesn't need to know about it. Right?

FRITZ. No.

MRS. MARTI. I'm not ashamed to be friends with you, since I now know what a strong lad you are. I now know that you're good. And you wouldn't listen less, or be less careful, because of it. You have to behave. And we as parents have to teach children to listen. But you know better than other children. We can talk to you in a different manner. You've had to suffer much. I've made you suffer much. You're already a big, big man. *(She smiles.)*

FRITZ. *(Snuggles up against her.)* Mama!

MRS. MARTI. I'm serious. But it's quite odd. I'm talking to you as if you were a grown person. Even though you're lying on me like this. On my lap! You, my child. My boy. I can't tell you how wonderful, how big you seem to me. I shouldn't have to say it. I'm more than happy to remain silent now. To be on my own for a little while. Go and see Klara, until we eat dinner. Go—

FRITZ. Yes, Mama. *(Wants to leave.)*

MRS. MARTI. Wait. Let me cuddle you once more. You're not going to cause trouble with your sister and Paul because of this, right? I mean, because of how I've spoken to you? Right?

FRITZ. That would be mean.

MRS. MARTI. *(Happy.)* No, right? That would be a sin. A real sin. You won't do it, I know it. Go now.—(FRITZ *leaves.)* I hope I didn't go too far? *(Deeply moved.)* Did I go too far?—Can you speak to a child like this? No, no, that was fine. Something so beautiful can't possibly be bad. Should a mother always speak like a nun to her children? It had to be this way. Honesty can't do any harm. But is it now different between us? Doesn't he love me, and doesn't he have to keep listening to me, when he sees that I love him back? No, there's no trouble. I don't want to regret being honest. Just that would be very bad. Did someone see it? Nobody saw it, nobody would want to be seen. My son, I want to thank you, on my knees, for showing me.—Let me go now and see what they're doing.

(*The dining room. A lamp burns on the table.* FRITZ, PAUL, KLARA *are playing.* MRS. MARTI *stands in the dark and observes them.*)

PAUL. So, this ink blot is the pond. Or not? This blot can't be the pond?

FRITZ. Of course it can. And I'm the knife.

KLARA. And what am I?

FRITZ. Wait, one thing after another. Watch, now the cheese knife is going after that black ink blot. No, the blot is going after the knife. No, just like this: The knife goes into this pond. That's the story. It's not the knife's fault. It's a very well-behaved knife.

KLARA. But it can't drown.

FRITZ. It doesn't really care much about that. And now, watch carefully, here comes the fork, running and jumping. Oh, how it plummets downward. And how it cries when it can't find the knife. How it just runs away. Who would've thought that a fork could have such legs.

PAUL. I was the fork.

KLARA. But what was I?

FRITZ. Just wait. It'll be your turn soon enough. As soon as the fork is gone, the knife emerges from the muddy water, cleans itself a bit, and slowly walks home. At home, it sees the spoon on the ground. (*To* KLARA.) You're the spoon, if you want.

KLARA. It's true, you saw me on the ground when you came back.

FRITZ. It's difficult to describe the spoon's face.

KLARA. Did I make such a face?

FRITZ. You made about nine. You fell from one into the other. You could barely keep track of them, that's how fast your faces changed. That's what the spoon did. And now the story is over.

PAUL. What, I don't think so! Now there are two more people. Father appears and then Mother.

FRITZ. I don't know anything else. Let's use something else for a story.

(They start something else.)

MRS. MARTI. *(Softly.)* They didn't notice. I was right, and I will be right. He's acting the same. What a good boy. I can barely keep myself from going up to him, telling him.—Isn't it like a dream, a fairy tale? The lamp burns like a magic lamp. I stand like a fairy behind the children. The only thing missing is fairy-tale music. But you can always hear it in your ears. How lovely it all is. I must listen, oh how I must listen. Everything my children are saying seems so new today, so different. I've never heard them like this. And it's not like I just want to love my Fritz from now on. No, no, I love them all, and shall love them the same. Should they be? Look how I tell myself. It's as if I'm my own pastor. What would the pastor accomplish with his talk if there wasn't already a pastor in all of us? So, I no longer want to be a spectator. *(Loud.)* Children, what are you up to?

KLARA. We're making up stories, Mama. Fritz can tell beautiful stories.

MRS. MARTI. Where does he get them all?

KLARA. Well, from his head. His head is a book full of stories. Now he's telling us one about a chambermaid.

PAUL. Where's Papa?

MRS. MARTI. He'll be here soon. I think I can hear him already.—There he is.

(MR. MARTI enters.)

MR. MARTI. *(Gives FRITZ a strict look.)* To bed, children, it's late.

MRS. MARTI. No, not yet. Let's get a bottle of wine from the cellar. Let's stay up a bit longer and talk. Right, Adolf?—Yes, yes. Why not this once.

MR. MARTI. Why not. Who's getting the wine?

FRITZ. (*Quickly.*) I'll get it.

MRS. MARTI. (*As quickly.*) I need to turn on the kitchen light for you. Come on!

> (MRS. MARTI *and* MR. MARTI *leave.* MR. MARTI *packs his pipe.*)

KLARA. Where are we in our story?

PAUL. Where they leave together to get some wine from the cellar.

THE LOVERS

In a salon

OSKAR.
Just look at all these people here,
how solemnly they move about;
this one sure feels himself at home,
and that one there, stooped and shy.
There are quite a few here for whom
I would almost have some pity.
Oh, everything is of two minds,
so arid and hard. I feel like
people could be ten times gentler,
nicer, more conscientious, courteous,
when it actually matters for once.
Politeness and some good manners
do not amount to good company,
do not make a decent party.
No matter how sincere they are,
they are strangers. I have such an
incredible need to leave here
tomorrow morning. Want to go?
Are you tempted to come with me?

EMMA.
Since it is you cheering me on,
then I shall do so willingly.

Indeed, I believe in you like
I do in light, resolved to much
harder things than going for a stroll
together with you.

OSKAR.
How happy
you make me with your acquiescence.

EMMA.
And you me the more with your dear
belief in me.

OSKAR.
And you the more
with your courage.

EMMA.
And you the more
with everything that you are.

OSKAR.
Does life not lie like a garden
before us, and don't you feel too
the world's beauty?

EMMA.
If I did not,
how could you possibly stand me?
Could you befriend a little doll?

OSKAR.
No, I can't.

EMMA.
Nor I, if I were you.

A forest

OSKAR.
Is it not lovely here?

EMMA.
It is quiet,
like being in a temple. Are the pines

not almost like columns and the moss-
covered ground not unlike a rug?
The most wondrous flowers grow here.
I'd love to pick them one by one,
but I can't be the disturber
of such tender life. That would mean
willfully defiling this forest.
Such a thing is remote to me.

OSKAR.
How this splendor surrounds us here,
and yet even the tiniest leaf
asserts itself. There's nothing here
that should be concealed from our view.
The beetle may bestir itself,
and the ants go this way and that,
and from this heavenliness sunlight rains down, and outside there plays
the wind. Listen to the train there
in the distance, where people travel
as well. We are here with rabbits,
with squirrels, and butterflies, with
us alone.

EMMA.
                    What do we do when night falls?

OSKAR.
We will simply lie down somewhere
and sleep on the ground, as if we
were at home and wanted to slip
into bed.

On a lonely mountaintop

EMMA.
I wish I were a bit less tired;
how quickly our energy fades!

OSKAR.
Shall I go fetch you some water?
Perhaps I'll find a spring somewhere.

EMMA.
No, stay. I'll be fine. Let's just rest.
I'm so ashamed of my weakness!
As soon as the body weakens,
the soul follows and surrenders hope.
Oh, that we have to eat and drink
and never eat and drink our fill
of beauty. How high the swallows fly.
I would love to live in that sea
of air! Those magnificent clouds!
It's not for us. We're too heavy
for that, and yet the thought of it
invigorates us, and we feel
strong by merely being aware. Is
that not a house there? Possibly
we could get a drop of milk there.
Where is my sense of adventure?
I can barely go on.

OSKAR.
Maybe I was a little careless,
taking you, so tender a thing, here.

A house

EMMA.
All is silent, only the flies buzz,
and only sunshine lives here.

OSKAR.
The house is completely deserted,
the walls are black, as if there was
a fire. Not a sound, just a few
things left behind. No furniture,
and no one to ask us what is
our business here. In the kitchen
nothing's been cooked for a long time.

EMMA.
Is someone sleeping there?

Robert Walser

OSKAR.

No, it's just
a log. Let's go.

EMMA.

How I long for
people suddenly.

OSKAR.

Perhaps we might
meet someone who can tell us where
a town lies.

They come to a town

OSKAR.
The girls play and the pigeons flutter,
and women wearing somber clothes
walk about. There's a gentle stream
here and a bridge over it. Entire
families in the open air, young
and old, poor and rich, a little dog
walks behind a lady. The bells
toll—the shapes and the masonry,
buildings and houses standing here
for centuries and yet so solid
they seem erected yesterday.
See the palace with its statues,
how it stands proud, vast, and brittle!
Think of everything that already
happened inside. Through the open
windows, people are looking down
at life, as if they were sitting
in a theater and just watching a play.
Their being purely spectators has
made them utterly lifeless. There is
just the sky above the streets, here
narrow, there broad. In the restaurants
they drink beer, they talk politics,
play cards, or flirt with the waitress.
Does that person there want something
from us? He watches us.

THE STRANGER.
                                I am
a carpenter and on the bum,
and if you could spare anything,
I would wish you a good long life
and health without end, the reason
being that I'm terribly thirsty
and would love just a little to go
inside that inn there.

EMMA.
                        Give him something.
He speaks sincerely and openly.
I do love such simple people.
They still go through the world, carrying
the good old days around with them.

In front of a church

EMMA.
The door is open so anyone
can look inside. How beautiful
it is here. The sanctuary
is decorated with paintings.
Someone is praying, and only
two steps away they casually
chat away about everyday life.
Here anyone can feel what they want.
There are no orders to follow.
God wants none to believe in him.
He doesn't pressure any soul
for there is nothing about him
to force us. Who doesn't need him,
doesn't see him. He exists for those
who love him, see him, and desire
him. Is he not the most lenient,
most gentle being, and benevolent
through and through? About the temple birds
chirp, the fields and meadows are near,
and nothing here is unfriendly.
The chaplain speaks to two women.

There's a man of the world about him,
whose engaging gestures gain more
than with intolerance and pride.
He consoles as he jests, and instructs
with a smile for he sees himself
as a plain fellow man. It smells
after all spiritual and nice
and serious at the same time.

At the edge of a gorge

A POSTCARD VENDOR.
Buy something from an old woman.

OSKAR.
Do you have anything nice?

VENDOR.
Charming postcards,
informative books.

OSKAR.
What is this book? What's it about?

VENDOR.
It's about a poor thief released
from the women's penitentiary,
how she searches for employment,
how she wants honest work again,
but people make her an outcast,
how she sees her little boy once more
and she presses him to her heart,
but he wants nothing to do with her
and he runs from her in terror,
how this hurts her and how one night
she dreams of new sins, of sitting
behind iron bars again, of not
suffering it and sooner dying.

OSKAR.
Give me a copy. How much is it?

VENDOR.
Only forty rappen.

EMMA.
                    Interested
    are you in such things?

OSKAR. (*To the vendor.*)
                    Are you not
    Flückiger's sister?

VENDOR.
    Yes, I am she.

It is evening

EMMA.
    The way all these objects glow now.
    The houses and trees and woods are red
    from this colorful shaft of light.
    Is mankind up on its feet today,
    children, grownups, all the poor
    and good people, the excited
    and the overjoyed?

OSKAR.
    They are all drawn to the same spot,
    and all of them have the same thought.
    Were they dead once and now alive?
    Oh the way they all seem happy
    and stride briskly. Even the tired
    move lighter, and all, all of them
    are young, as if henceforth there is
    only this youth. Has a god dispersed
    pettiness, ignobility,
    and indolence, have we arrived
    at something human? I've yet to
    see the ocean, but I see it now.

EMMA.
    Is the sun that bright such that we
    think we see that which simply does
    not exist?

Robert Walser

OSKAR.

                  Someone stood and sang
at the window, where all broke loose,
became overwhelming, and then
floated as if into this hub
and became the burning present.

EMMA.

No one is here, we have seen things
that exist only in our minds
and in our dreams.

OSKAR.

So where to next?

EMMA.

I believed that all people longed
to be blissfully happy and walked
in an enormous procession
into the setting sun, to where
a much prettier existence
would blossom, where every path
would be full of devout beings, their
souls turned toward, facing the true.
Now I see nothing but my only
love, you alone, my everything.

A restaurant
(*A* GENTLEMAN *and a* LADY *talk about a third person.*)

LADY.

This would surely benefit him
in every way imaginable.
He should really think about it.

GENTLEMAN.

If he thinks about it for much more,
he's an idiot.

LADY.

                America
isn't outer space. Many have made
their fortunes there. It would be a shame
for such an opportunity.

368

GENTLEMAN.
> I say he should make use of it.
> Send him to me. For eight whole days
> I won't say anything to him
> but "Begone." He should travel.
> If he doesn't, something's wrong with him
> and he belongs in a nuthouse.
> He'll make money like bricks over there,
> be manager. What will he do here?
> A poor wretch just wasting away.
> If I knew he didn't want to go,
> I'd go crazy, right out of my mind,
> stark raving mad, and have a stroke.
> Anyone who could be a made man
> and doesn't immediately do
> what's necessary to be one
> should have a sign hanging from him
> that reads: "I am an ass." That's my
> honest opinion. If he doesn't
> take the chance he's as good as
> got in the bag, I'll go berserk.

LADY.
> He'll go. He wants to.

GENTLEMAN.
>   Don't make me
> mad. Your composure has something
> unseemly about it. Money,
> money, just take it when it's there
> for the taking for goodness sakes!
> When it's about making money,
> I could care less if it's me or
> someone else pocketing it. The point
> is that it pays off if anything.
> What can a kid like you ever know
> about such things? Don't make me laugh.
> If he doesn't leave, he doesn't know
> what's good for him. Let me have him,
> I'll push him until he steams away.
> Come on, let's go. Just admit it,
> that I'm right? Hey?

Robert Walser

(*They leave.*)

EMMA.
                                    We have just heard
    a pleasant conversation here,
    wouldn't you say?

OSKAR.
                                    It could almost prove
    the desire for success. Could you love
    and respect such a person?

EMMA.
                                    Hardly.

A street, early morning

OSKAR.
    I don't know you, but you almost
    look familiar.

WAYFARER.
                                    It may well be,
    strangers can seem familiar to us.
    I was a soldier, now I march
    to India all on my own,
    my own responsibility,
    my own cost. I'll make this journey
    as still as possible, even
    if it takes years. I have no binding
    contract to be here or be there
    where and when, and nobody is
    waiting for me, so I am free.
    The world and time are vast, generous.
    I couldn't stand being dependent.
    If I find a job, I take it,
    and when the work is done, well then,
    I just keep roaming on, living
    in uncertainty, but loving it.
    Tight borders would make me anxious.
    Only here in the open air
    can I find peace, where I feel like
    I am floating. I have light feet,

370

I eat very little, something like
wanting to be a monk. While I'm
not so sure about it, it will be
all right in the end. I've nothing
at home, but everything's outside.
So why come to a standstill then?
I like to run as little as I
like to lie, to mourn as little as
to laugh. I love that which remains
the same. Perhaps I would have made
a good scholar, but I would have
to sit still and study. I could
not have done that, so I became
an assistant, who advances
step by step to get where he wants
to be. A soldier will with some
tact and a bit of talent know
how to be helpful anywhere.
I see a tall peak in India
bathed in pink light and in the green
land a house and rivers and many,
many kind and patient people
living off God knows what and lying down
in silence when the time has come,
while we make a big fuss about
life and death. Are we any better
than flowers? And yet no one dares
to think about them. Animals
are unaware of what's right and wrong.
They stare and know nothing. I find
in such naïveté something
innocent, paradisiacal.
Oh what beautiful broadleaf trees,
what meadows, things lovely, delights
that may have existed before,
but there are still beautiful things.
Actually, I can neither love
nor hate anything, neither respect
nor disrespect anything. I live
and survive, so adieu.

Robert Walser

(*He leaves.*)

OSKAR.

That one
knows not what to like and dislike,
what fortune and misfortune is,
knows no goal, no passion. He is
like the wind and clouds.

EMMA.

Maybe no
heart too?

OSKAR.

Go, ask him.

EMMA.

He's gone now,
and he would have given me no
answer.

Moonlit night

OSKAR.

Do you hear the wind's voice? Up there
they sit and stand high on the cliff
making music. It's enchanting here!
There are lovers who sit on lawns
and park benches. How sweet is love.
How little is it worth, desired,
yet not treasured. It should be worth
more and endure for longer, mean much,
much, much more, for only it provides
happiness, and being happy
only provides beauty, and only
that which is beautiful is good.
How beautiful the dark makes you!

EMMA.

Yes, they're happy as we are too.
Shall we walk over to those trees?
The fountain purls so intimately.
See how the lake glistens and the

372

stars shimmer. Is such a night not
like a holy picture?

OSKAR.

Up above
they tell each other who they are,
where they are from, what they do,
how they mean well to one another,
and how they want to be in love
for their entire lives—Oh what joy!—
and speak of nothing but truth, feel
nothing but good. Lovers are true,
they don't care about opinions
and don't need to respect childish
explanations in this stillness.
No one but Cupid can hear them,
nothing can hinder their embracing
and kissing. The gentle night breeze
strokes their hair and faces, like us,
dear Emma.

EMMA.
And what about us, we don't kiss. Why not?

(They do.)

OSKAR.
They're diligent,
so neither should we be idle,
and what they accomplish, we will
achieve too.

EMMA.
They're in bliss,
all these lovers who are in love,
who understand one another. Must
we not feel before we understand?
Reason's not enough, how often
it's irrational.

OSKAR.
I am astonished by your wisdom.

373

Robert Walser

EMMA.
It seems you make fun of me now.
Go ahead, a little ridicule
won't hurt.

OSKAR.
               If you don't take it wrong.

EMMA.
Let's start walking to those trees now,
where there is less breeze, where there is
dark and quiet. There we will sit
and see if we can be as tender
as the others. It seems perhaps
we'll give ourselves a kiss as sweet
as the others, and love thinking
of the caresses, the happiness,
and the joy of others. Must this not make
us happier yet?

Years later; OSKAR *sits in a parlor*

EMMA. [*Looks through the window, speaking to herself.*]
He does not notice me, hears nothing,
sees nothing, just busy with himself,
just reads and reads, knowing only books,
stuck in this room, day in, day out,
not feeling like looking anymore,
no small talk, no thought of hiking.
He's forgotten the paths,
the forests, and people, me
too perhaps. He lost his nice smile,
doesn't think, ponder, get away.
Blue skies and bright air no longer
beckon him. He doesn't seem sad.
This reclusiveness pleases him.
He doesn't regret all the hours
he spends in here tight-lipped. I stand
here in vain, he doesn't miss me.
His thoughts, his quests, his fertile mind,
his iron-willed learning are everything
to him. He wants nothing. I could

talk to him, but that would only
annoy him, so I'd rather leave. The
sun, that play
of the light, all this pleasantly
effortless life, all that is soft,
clever is nothing to him. Only
the agitations of the mind
engage him, those delectations
in the realm of thought. He just sits there
seeming almost hunchbacked to me.
His once-slender neck is nasty.
He has something of a porter
about him and he no longer loves
himself, withdraws from people, pays
no more heed to reality.
He's building something in his head,
only that which he finds worthy
of existence. No more will I
come and go. If he fails to feel
my presence, he won't my absence
either. I can't help him. No one can.

SEDUCER.
What do you want with this homebody?
I mean to be candid with you.
I'm just taken by your beauty.
It's true! And, if you would, let me
provide you with my services.

EMMA. (*Looks at him, astonished.*)
　　　　　　　　　　　　　　　　What?

SEDUCER.
I seek some way to make myself
indispensable to you, and that
I think will not be very hard.

EMMA.
Don't flatter yourself.

SEDUCER.
　　　　　　　　　　That one
in there cheats on you.

375

EMMA.

> But surely
> he would not act so carelessly.

SEDUCER.

> He does nevertheless and he has
> nothing to even offer you,
> the idealist.

EMMA.

> What do you want then?

SEDUCER.

> To show you that one can be noble
> as well as harsh, that another
> can be cruel and to some degree
> good for you.

EMMA.

> And you're proud of this?

SEDUCER.

> Beauty that's not so beautiful,
> ugliness not so ugly, it's true,
> but not as naive souls would think.
> I'll introduce you to the world,
> I'll open your eyes and escort you
> into life itself, for I do see
> how much you really long for it.
> In short, I wish to cultivate you.

EMMA.

> You liar!

SEDUCER.

> I am charmed by your
> insults. Do you know how I find you
> adorable?

EMMA.

> Could it be he's
> not that unbearable to me?

Both are estranged

OSKAR.
What I had to see in that dream
just now, them with nothing at all
going on, yet not wanting to part,
them being angry, pale and wan,
and them with no hope of ever
winning, looking at each other
with somber faces, and neither
one could understand the other,
neither could speak of the pleasant
nor of the truth, neither could lie
nor find the strength to be totally
sincere, like snakes these sick people
crawled and bit themselves in two. One
wanted to help, but instead of words,
flames came out of his mouth, and when
he wished to comfort, he left wounds.
Frightened eyes, fear about nothing,
torn hearts, anything an enemy,
making enemies over nothing.
Agony, and agonizing
about nothing, agitated
about nothing, and not even in pain
despite every pain, and all life
cut up, dissected, and people
misled by pettiness, fleeing
and preening at the same time
since none saw them suffer, and now
this grief about the forsaken
where nothing has been forsaken,
simply imagined as all well knew,
as no one didn't know, and that's why
hell strikes so many as funny.

EMMA.
What did I see in the dream just now?
It was he who struggled so hard,
and it was me who didn't believe
in him, she who believed in others,
who thought others were in the right

and him in the wrong, who believed him
to be fallen because others
thought so. Why did I turn from him?
Because everyone did and why
did they? That he struggled? Is it not
bright around the strugglers and dark
for the passive? How hard it was
for him. He was covered in rubble.
As soon as he brushed himself off,
new dust fell, but he always got up,
ten, twenty times, if it fell again,
up he'd get again. I found him
once sleeping, his mouth half open,
on the green earth, hands in repose
and delicate like in a portrait,
his chest bare, and above his head
a city, all blue, silver, and gold.
Oh so fragile and beautiful!
And then I saw him without a face
and without limbs, yet I knew him.
How sorry I felt! Suddenly
I saw him alive, limber, and strong,
full of passion. "Ah, he's breaking
his way through now," I thought, and called him.
He looked around and let me see
his determined face, but already
the flow was pulling him away,
leaving no time. I don't know what
he did, but a voice spoke to me
of joys, festivities, so I
let it be, the way it was.
I believed in this noble man.
I knew that he was fine and glad.

NOTES ON CONTRIBUTORS

MATT BELL's debut novel, *In the House upon the Dirt between the Lake and the Woods*, will be published by Soho Press in June 2013. He is also the author of the novella *Cataclysm Baby* (Mud Luscious Press) and the fiction collection *How They Were Found* (Keyhole Press). He is the senior editor at Dzanc Books, where he also edits the literary magazine *The Collagist*, and he teaches creative writing at Northern Michigan University.

CHARLES BERNSTEIN's most recent poetry collection is *Recalculating*, from the University of Chicago Press, which also published his *Attack of the Difficult Poems: Essays & Inventions*. The "Duplexities" poems here are from a series of one hundred poem/image collaborations made with the artist Amy Sillman. Bernstein is Regan Professor of English and Comparative Literature at the University of Pennsylvania.

GABRIEL BLACKWELL is the author of *Critique of Pure Reason* (Noemi Press), *Shadow Man: A Biography of Lewis Miles Archer*, and *The Natural Dissolution of Fleeting-Improvised-Men: The Last Letter of H. P. Lovecraft* (both CCM). He lives in Portland, Oregon.

In addition to his thirteen novels, ROBERT OLEN BUTLER has published six story collections, one of which, *A Good Scent from a Strange Mountain* (Grove Press), won the Pulitzer Prize. His latest novel is *The Hot Country* (Mysterious Press). He teaches creative writing at Florida State University.

CAN XUE, a regular contributor to *Conjunctions*, has written several novels and numerous short stories and novellas. Her works have been translated into English, Japanese, French, German, Italian, Swedish, Russian, and Czech. She lives in the People's Republic of China.

CHEN ZEPING has published widely in his field of Chinese linguistics. In collaboration with Karen Gernant, he has translated several contemporary Chinese writers into English, including Can Xue, Zhang Kangkang, Alai, Yan Lianke, and Lin Bai. He has taught in the United States and Japan and is currently a professor at Fujian Teachers' University.

MAXINE CHERNOFF is the author of fourteen books of poems. The works in this issue will appear in her next book with Counterpath in 2014. She is the recipient of a 2009 PEN translation award and a 2013 NEA fellowship.

KIM CHINQUEE is the author of the collections *Oh Baby* and *Pistol* (both Ravenna Press), as well as *Pretty* (White Pine Press). Her work has appeared in *NOON*, *Denver Quarterly*, *The Nation*, and elsewhere. She is an associate editor of *New World Writing* and teaches at Buffalo State College.

GILLIAN CONOLEY's new collection of poetry, *Peace*, is forthcoming with Omnidawn in the spring of 2014. She is the author of six other books of poetry, and her work has been anthologized widely, most recently in Norton's second edition of *Postmodern American Poetry*. She lives in the San Francisco Bay area, where she teaches at Sonoma State University and edits *Volt*.

ROBERT COOVER's most recent books are *Noir* (Overlook) and *A Child Again* (McSweeney's). He edited the portfolio "The Alphabet and Its Pretenses" that appeared in *Conjunctions:59, Colloquy* (fall 2012). His story in this issue is from *The Brunist Day of Wrath*, forthcoming from Dzanc in September as part of a boxed set, along with a new collection of stories.

JULIA ELLIOTT's fiction has appeared in *Tin House*, *The Georgia Review*, and elsewhere. Her story in *Conjunctions:56, Terra Incognita*, "Regeneration at Mukti," received a Pushcart Prize. In 2012, she won a Rona Jaffe Foundation Writer's Award.

BRIAN EVENSON is the author of eleven works of fiction, most recently *Windeye* (Coffee House Press) and *Immobility* (Tor). He is the recipient of three O. Henry Prizes, an ALA/RUSA prize, and an IHG Award, and has been a finalist for an Edgar Award and a World Fantasy Award. He lives in Providence, Rhode Island, with his wife, Kristen Tracy, and his son, Max, and teaches at Brown University.

KAREN GERNANT, professor emerita at Southern Oregon University, collaborates with Chen Zeping in translating contemporary Chinese fiction. Among their translations are Can Xue's *Blue Light in the Sky* (New Directions), *Five Spice Street* (Yale UP), and *Vertical Motion* (Open Letter Books); as well as Zhang Kangkang's *White Poppies and Other Stories* (Cornell East Asia Series) and Alai's *Tibetan Soul* (MerwinAsia).

BENJAMIN HALE is the author of the novel *The Evolution of Bruno Littlemore* (Twelve), which was nominated for the Dylan Thomas Prize and the NYPL's Young Lions of Fiction Award. He is the recipient of a Michener-Copernicus Award and the Bard Fiction Prize, a frequent contributor to *Harper's*, and the coeditor of *Conjunctions:61, A Menagerie* (forthcoming November 2013).

KAREN HAYS's essays appear or are forthcoming in *Conjunctions*, *The Iowa Review*, *The Normal School*, *Passages North*, and *The Georgia Review*.

LUCY IVES is the author of *Anamnesis* (Slope Editions) and the forthcoming *Orange Roses* (Ahsahta Press). She is coeditor of *Corrected Slogans: Reading and Writing Conceptualism* (Triple Canopy and the Museum of Contemporary Art, Denver) and is a deputy editor at Triple Canopy.

BRANDON KRIEG is the author of a chapbook, *Source to Mouth* (New Michigan Press). His poems have appeared in *Web Conjunctions*, *The Iowa Review*, *Commonweal*, and many other journals.

ANN LAUTERBACH's ninth collection of poems, *Under the Sign*, will be published in fall 2013 by Penguin. A chapbook, *The Given & the Chosen*, appeared from Omnidawn in 2011. She teaches at Bard College.

JOHN MADERA (www.johnmadera.com) has published work in *Conjunctions, Bookforum, American Book Review, Rain Taxi, Review of Contemporary Fiction*, and elsewhere. He is the managing editor of *Big Other*.

CAROLE MASO is the author of ten books, most recently the novel *Mother & Child* (Counterpoint Press). "The Silver World" is an excerpt from her novel in progress, *The Bay of Angels*. She teaches at Brown University.

J. W. McCORMACK is a senior editor with *Conjunctions*. He teaches at Columbia University.

MIRANDA MELLIS is the author of *None of This Is Real* (Sidebrow Press), *The Spokes* (Solid Objects), *The Revisionist* (Calamari Press), *Materialisms* (Portable Press at Yo-Yo Labs), and *The Quarry* (Trafficker Press). She is an editor at the Encyclopedia Project and an assistant professor at Evergreen State College.

YANNICK MURPHY's latest novel is *The Call* (Harper Perennial).

JOYCE CAROL OATES is the author of *Black Dahlia & White Rose* (Ecco) and *Daddy Love* (Mysterious Press). She is a past contributor to *Conjunctions* as well as the editor of *New Jersey Noir* (Akashic) and *The Oxford Book of American Short Stories* (Oxford University Press). Her forthcoming novel is *The Accursed* (Ecco).

STEPHEN O'CONNOR is the author of four books, most recently the short story collection *Here Comes Another Lesson*. He teaches in the MFA programs of Columbia University and Sarah Lawrence College.

DANIELE PANTANO (www.danielepantano.ch) is a Swiss poet, translator, critic, and editor. He has taught at the University of South Florida, served as the poet in residence at Florida Southern College, and is now the reader in poetry and literary translation at England's Edge Hill University.

The poet, translator, and biographer JAMES REIDEL is preparing a complete collection of Robert Walser's dramolets. He is the current writer in residence at the James Merrill House in Stonington, Connecticut.

JOANNA RUOCCO is the author of *The Mothering Coven* (Ellipsis Press), *Man's Companions* (Tarpaulin Sky Press), *A Compendium of Domestic Incidents* (Noemi Press), and *Another Governess / The Least Blacksmith: A Diptych* (FC2).

JOANNA SCOTT's books include *Arrogance, The Manikin* (both Picador), *Everybody Loves Somebody* (Back Bay), and *Follow Me* (Little, Brown). "The Collector's Beginning" is excerpted from her novel *The Gilt Cabinet*, forthcoming from Farrar, Straus and Giroux.

FREDERIC TUTEN has published five novels, as well as a collection of interrelated short stories, *Self Portraits: Fictions* (Norton). He has received the American Academy of Arts and Letters' award for distinguished writing, and won a 2012 Pushcart Prize for his story "The Veranda," in *Conjunctions:54, Shadow Selves*.

G. C. WALDREP is the author of four full-length collections and three chapbooks of poems, most recently *Your Father on the Train of Ghosts* (BOA Editions), a collaboration with John Gallaher. He coedited *Homage to Paul Celan* (Marick) with Ilya Kaminsky and *The Arcadia Project: North American Postmodern Pastoral* (Ahsahta) with Joshua Corey. He teaches at Bucknell University and edits the journal *West Branch*.

ROBERT WALSER (1878–1956) was born in Switzerland. He left school at fourteen and led a wandering and precarious existence while producing poems, stories, essays, and three novels: *The Tanners* (1906), *The Assistant* (1908), and *Jakob Von Gunten* (1909). New Directions recently published his *Microscripts* and *The Walk*, translated by Susan Bernofsky; as well as *Thirty Poems*, translated by Christopher Middleton. In 1933, Walser abandoned writing and entered a sanatorium, where he remained for the rest of his life. "I am not here to write," he said, "but to be mad."

MARJORIE WELISH is the author of *Word Group, Isle of the Signatories*, and *In the Futurity Lounge/Asylum for Indeterminacy* (all Coffee House Press). She is the Madalon Zeventhal Rand distinguished lecturer in literature at Brooklyn College.

JUSTIN WYMER's work has appeared or is forthcoming in periodicals including *Boston Review* and *Lana Turner*. He is currently pursuing his MFA at the Iowa Writers' Workshop.

CHAD WYS (www.chadwys.com) is a visual conceptual artist, designer, and writer who currently lives and works in Peoria, Illinois. He works in a wide variety of mixed media including readymade sculpture, printmaking, painting, collage, photography, video, and computer-based digital design.

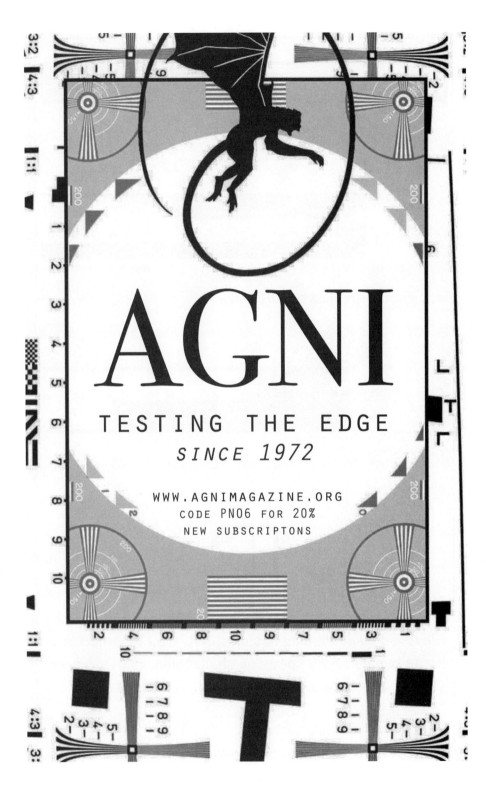

AGNI

TESTING THE EDGE
SINCE 1972

WWW.AGNIMAGAZINE.ORG
CODE PN06 FOR 20%
NEW SUBSCRIPTONS

FC2 Innovative Fiction Contest

$ 1, 500 & publication by FC2

FICTION COLLECTIVE TWO

is among the few alternative, author-run presses
devoted to publishing fiction considered by America's
largest publishers to be too challenging, innovative, or
heterodox for the commercial milieu.

FC2 ⅋ The Jarvis and Constance Doctorow Family Foundation

present the

FC2 Catherine Doctorow Innovative Fiction Prize

Winner receives $15,000
and
publication by FC2

Entries accepted August 15, 2013 – November 1, 2013

Submission guidelines: fc2.org

FC2 is among the few alternative, author-run presses devoted to
publishing fiction considered by America's largest publishers to be too
challenging, innovative, or heterodox for the commercial milieu.

Jarvis &
Constance
Doctorow
Family
Foundation

FICTION COLLECTIVE TWO

NOON

A LITERARY ANNUAL

1324 LEXINGTON AVENUE PMB 298 NEW YORK NY 10128

EDITION PRICE $12 DOMESTIC $17 FOREIGN

ISSUE 48.1

Prose and poetry by Matt Bell, George David Clark, Julia Cohen, Shome Dasgupta, Noah Eli Gordon, Myronn Hardy, Sonya Huber, T Kira Madden, Sally Wen Mao, Britt Melewski, James O'Brien, Steven Ramirez, David Romanda, and more.

PUERTO DEL SOL

Prose and poetry by Michael Kimball, Steve Kistulenz, Christopher D. Allsop, Rosebud Ben-Oni, B.J. Hollars, Tim Jones-Yelvington, Roberto Harrison, Kim Stanley Robinson, Lorenzo Veracini, Jacqueline Dutton, Daniel Heath Justice, and more.

ISSUE 48.1

visit us at puertodelsol.org

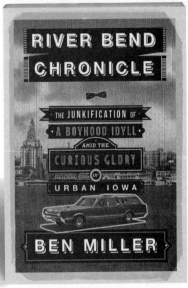

Claude Royet-Journoud: *Four Elemental Bodies*
[translated from the French by Keith Waldrop]

Royet-Journoud's Tetralogy assembles his central volumes *Reversal, The Notion of Obstacle, Objects Contain the Infinite*, and *Natures Indivisible.* He is one of the most important contemporary French poets whose one-line manifesto: "Shall we escape analogy" signaled a revolutionary turn away from Surrealism and its lush imagery. He explores loss as if it were the threshold we have to cross to fully enter language.
Poetry, 368 pages, offset, smyth-sewn, original paperback $20

Mark Tardi: *Airport music*

Mark Tardi works at the intersection of American and Polish culture. Artists like Witold Gombrowicz and Roman Opalka may be considered points for triangulation.
The present music plays in the tension between impalpable "air" and solid "port," between a single focus (Sean Scully's stripes) and shifting directions of torque (Lee Bontecou), between hope stretching outward and implosion of infinite regress.
Poetry, 96 pages, offset, smyth-sewn, original paperback $14

P. Inman: *per se*

Inman fractures the conventions of language in order to build everything up again from a more elemental level. In *per se*, the composers Luigi Nono, Hans Lachenmann, and Morton Feldman provide musical structure for his jazz-inflected words in motion. The book lives in the tension between the free, multi-directional movement of words and the highly orgazined macro-structures.
Poetry, 88 pages, offset, smyth-sewn, original paperback $14

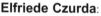

Elfriede Czurda:
Almost 1 Book/ Almost 1 Life
[translated from the German by Rosmarie Waldrop]

This volume contains almost all of Elfriede Czurda's first book and all of her second, *Fast 1 Leben.*
Though coming out of the experimental *Wiener Gruppe,* Czurda is not averse to thumbing her nose at the experimental imperative. In *Almost 1 Life,* the ruling avant-garde has licensed "monomania" as official language and punishes misuse by expelling the offender: into reality. Which is exactly where Czurda positions herself.
Poetry, 96 pages, offset, smyth-sewn, original paperback $14

Orders: www.spdbooks.org, www.burningdeck.com

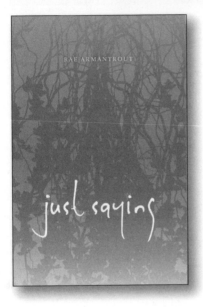

Karen Joy Fowler
What I Didn't See and Other Stories
World Fantasy Award winner

Angélica Gorodischer, *Trafalgar*
(trans. by Amalia Gladheart)
"Fascinating stories."—*Reforma*

Elizabeth Hand
Errantry: Strange Stories
"We find ourselves wrapped in an evocation
without knowing fully how she got us there"
—Aimee Bender, *Washington Post*

*The Unreal and the Real:
Selected Stories of Ursula K. Le Guin*
"A masterclass in contemporary fiction."
—*New Zealand Herald*, Best of 2012

Maureen F. McHugh
After the Apocalypse: Stories
★ "A surprisingly sunny read."—*Booklist*

smallbeerpress.com
weightlessbooks.com

BROWN UNIVERSITY LITERARY ARTS
A HOME FOR INNOVATIVE WRITERS

Program faculty
John Cayley
Brian Evenson
Thalia Field
Forrest Gander
Renee Gladman
Michael S. Harper
Carole Maso
Meredith Steinbach
Cole Swensen
CD Wright

Joint-appointment, visiting & other faculty

Joanna Howard
Shahriar Mandanipour
Gale Nelson
John Edgar Wideman

For over 40 years, Literary Arts at Brown University has been fostering an atmosphere for innovation and creation. To learn more about the two-year MFA program, visit us at: http://www.brown.edu/cw

THE ONLINE MFA APPLICATION DEADLINE IS 15 DECEMBER